DAVID DICKINSON graduated from Cambridge with a first-class honours degree in Classics. He joined the BBC where he became editor of *Newsnight* and *Panorama* as well as series editor on *Monarchy*. His novel *Death of a Chancellor* was longlisted in 2007 for Theakston's Old Peculiar Crime Novel of the Year.

Praise for the Lord Francis Powerscourt series

'A leisurely period whodunit with Dickinson's customary historical tidbits and patches of local colour, swathed in an appealing Victorian narrative.'

Kirkus Reviews

'A cracking yarn, beguilingly real from start to finish.'

Peter Snow

'Fine prose, high society and complex plot recommend this series.'

Library Journal

'Lovers of British mysteries will enjoy Powerscourt's latest adventure.'

Booklist

D0104592

Titles in the series
(listed in order)

DEATH
OF A
Wine
Merchant

DAVID DICKINSON

ROBINSON

Constable & Robinson Ltd
3 The Lanchesters
162 Fulham Palace Road
London W6 9ER
www.constablerobinson.com

First published in the UK by Constable,
an imprint of Constable & Robinson, 2010

This paperback edition published in the UK by Robinson,
an imprint of Constable & Robinson, 2011

A copy of the British Library Cataloguing in Publication
Data is available from the British Library

ISBN 978-1-84901-592-9

Printed and bound in the EU

1 3 5 7 9 10 8 6 4 2

For Chantal

1

The living walked past the dead on their way to the wedding on a bright Saturday in October. The path to the church of St Peter, Brympton, was flanked by the tombs of the faithful, laid out in random fashion in the dark Norfolk earth, the words and the letters on the tombs faded with the centuries. St Peter's was very old and very simple. Shaped like a cross, it had a large choir, an organ in a gallery at the back where there were pegs for the local farmers to hang their hats, and a series of box pews on either side of the nave. The great Hall of Brympton was a couple of hundred yards away.

In the second pew from the front Hermione Colville, mother of the groom, checked the angle of her hat and took a discreet look behind her. Solid phalanxes of relatives stretched back to the rear of the church, all ready for active service. Strange discordant noises were coming from the organ. The young man, believed to hold advanced musical views, was not delivering the Bach he had promised, but horrid sounds that might, in Hermione's view, have been composed by a gang of monkeys hanging off their trees in some damp and humid forest on the banks of the Amazon.

There were still ten minutes or more before the arrival of the bride. Hermione reviewed her forces. In the pew in front of her, the son and heir who was about to become a husband, Montague Colville, flanked by his rather dubious best man Algy Price, a young gentleman who found little favour with the more discerning mamas of the district. Marriage, her husband Randolph had often proclaimed, helped a man settle down. In Hermione's slightly cynical view, her son's marriage would have a great deal of work to do.

Behind them, the grandfather of the groom Walter Colville and his brother Nathaniel, the two men who had raised the Colvilles out of Hampshire obscurity into a position of power and prominence.

The Colvilles were wine merchants. The little firm that began in humble offices off Chancery Lane had risen to become one of the most successful in the country. One of their account-ants had calculated recently that one bottle in every twelve of champagne, wine, port and Madeira drunk in Britain was sold under the Colville label. And that was without taking account of the whisky from Scotland or the whiskey from Ireland or the gin from Hammersmith, produced in a vast factory near the Thames and shipped round the world. Next year the firm would reach its fiftieth anniversary and plans were already being drawn up for a monstrous party of celebration. Secretly Walter, now aged seventy-eight, hoped that his life's work and the fifty-year stretch might run to a knighthood or, in his wilder moments, a seat in the House of Lords. He had been contributing generously to Liberal Party funds ever since they won the election the previous year.

Behind the veterans a wide collection of Colville outriders and auxiliaries, cousins, nephews and nieces, filled the pews. There was even an overspill of some of the more outlying members of the family into the gallery near the organ.

Colville was to be united with Nash here at three o'clock this afternoon. The organist averted the wrath of Hermione Colville by switching to a more decorous Bach. The bride this day, Emily Nash, was the eldest daughter of Willoughby and Georgina Nash, of Brympton Hall in the county of Norfolk. The Colvilles might have been in trade for almost fifty years but the Nashes had been in business in their native county for three hundred years. Nashes had spread out around Norfolk

2

like the tentacles of some enormous squid, washed up perhaps on the North Sea coast nearby after a terrible storm. They began as bankers in Norwich and part of that bank had transferred to London in the eighteenth century. From time immemorial they had owned great swathes of land near Brympton Hall. You could still find Nash bankers in Fakenham, Nash landowners at Holt and Melton Constable, even a Nash headmaster at Blakeney. But it was the law that seemed to run in the blood. Willoughby Nash, father of the bride, was senior partner in the family firm in Norwich with offices near the cathedral. Upstart solicitors sought to dignify their position with multiple names by the door outside their place of work. Nash, solicitors, was all the advertising needed for the owner of Brympton Hall and his colleagues. There were other Nash solicitors at Cromer and King's Lynn and Little Snoring. The local newspaper editor swore vehemently that the Nash brainpower declined the further away they went from Norwich Cathedral, but that was only his fancy. They had one tradition, the family, that went back as far as they could read the names on their tombstones. The eldest son was always called Willoughby, the eldest daughter Emily.

It was now close to three o'clock. The less important Colvilles and Nashes at the very back of the church peered eagerly out of the door for a sight of the bride. Three o'clock passed, then three minutes past. The nervous members in the congregation wondered if there had been some terrible accident, a twisted ankle from a fall on the path, a thunderbolt sent from God perhaps. Five minutes past three. Randolph Colville was wondering if he had settled too much money on the son being married today. He had two other children to support after all. His banker, Mr Horatio Finch of Finch's, a man renowned in the City of London for his pessimism, was forever telling his clients that the good times would not last for ever. And there were new competitors springing up in the wine business all the time. Maybe Horatio Finch was right. Hermione Colville had never been quite certain about Emily

Nash. She was pretty, of course, she was clever, she seemed competent, but, in Hermione's eyes, there was something you couldn't quite put your finger on. Mrs Randolph Colville didn't think Emily was reliable, she wasn't sound.

Emily's mother Georgina had more prosaic concerns. She, after all, was in charge of the catering, the wedding lunch and all the rest. Would the caterers be as good as everybody said they were? Would it keep dry for the rest of the day? Eight minutes past. The organist seemed to be torn between the classical and the modern. One minute his instrument sounded like Haydn, the next it sounded like no music that had ever been heard before at a wedding in a Norfolk church. Then the organist saw somebody dressed in white approaching the church. 'Here Comes the Bride' thundered forth. Emily stepped shyly into the church, holding very firmly on to her father's arm. She was of medium height, with green eyes and a great shock of bright red hair. It was not Flaming June in Norfolk this day, it was Flaming October. Willoughby Nash was feeling as sad he had ever felt in his life. After this day he would never have his daughter as his own again. Of course she would visit them, but as the wife of another. He had complained to his wife about how unfair it was that he had to bring his precious Emily up the aisle on her wedding day when he would have preferred to postpone the ceremony indefinitely. Georgina had spoken to him softly about concepts like duty and responsibility and his daughter's happiness, and the possibility of grandchildren playing in the garden. So here he was, walking as slowly as he dared, hoping that this journey up the aisle would never end.

'Dearly beloved, we are gathered together here in the sight of God, and in the face of this congregation, to join together this man and this woman in holy Matrimony. . .' The vicar was a very Low Church evangelical sort of vicar with a beautiful speaking voice. High Church members of the congregation, wistful for the smells and bells of his predecessor, said it was his only redeeming feature. They sang 'All People that on

4

Earth do Dwell'. The vicar took the young couple through their marriage vows very slowly as if he'd never done it before. Then he took them through their duties as man and wife, as laid out in the Book of Common Prayer.

'Ye husbands, dwell with your wives according to knowledge; giving honour to the wife as unto the weaker vessel and as being heirs together of the grace of life, that your prayers be not hindered.' One or two of the younger children were growing restless.

'Wives,' the vicar continued, 'submit yourselves unto your own husbands, as unto the Lord. For the husband is the head of the wife even as Christ is Head of the Church and he is the Saviour of the body. Therefore as the Church is subject unto Christ, so let the wives be to their own husband in every thing.'

There was a loud snort from the middle of the congregation as if a Pankhurst disciple had made a missionary voyage to Norfolk. As the newly married pair went off to sign the register, Georgina Nash wondered if she and her husband were the only people in the church that day to know why Emily Nash looked so faint on her wedding day, and why there was something very curious about her choice of husband.

Shortly after a quarter to four, the marriage service was over. The party drifted back to Brympton Hall on the path that led past the gravestones and across a field. As they turned on to the road beyond the church the south front of Brympton Hall confronted them, a dramatic Jacobean pile of red brick and limestone, guarded by massive yew hedges on sentry duty on either side, adorned by gables and turrets and service wings at the front. It looked as though it had been dropped down from a different world.

Champagne was served in the garden at the back of the house with battalions of late roses and a fountain in the centre sending forth an irregular and intermittent spout of water. Georgina Nash had asked for it to be repaired more times than

5

she could think of in the days leading up to the ceremony. At this stage of the proceedings Nash still spoke unto Nash, Colville still spoke unto Colville. The ice was not yet broken between the two families though Mrs Nash believed her seating plan and the finest Colville burgundy should do the trick.

Sometimes on these grand social occasions the conversation seems to die away for a moment and a single, occasionally inappropriate voice breaks in to fill the silence.

'At sixty it was like going up a great wide road and coming to a very small signpost on the left, pointing at a narrow track to Death.' The speaker was the groom's uncle, Nathaniel Colville, a man well into his seventies. Nathaniel was explaining to a pretty young niece called Charlotte how he tried to write his autobiography, and how his views on the coming of death had changed over the decades. His publishers, he told his niece, expected him to spill the beans on all the manifold sins of the wine trade, fake burgundies, phoney ports, champagne made in factories, table wine that was virtually industrial waste. He had refused. It was not the behaviour of a gentleman to slander his competitors, he told the head publisher, who promptly decided to halve the print run for Nathaniel's memoir. The metaphor of the road changed over time, he assured Charlotte, pausing only to help himself to a refill of his Krug. By your seventies, the path you were walking grew ever narrower, while the side roads leading towards death became wider and wider. He did wonder, Nathaniel told his niece, what the travelling dispositions would be like when the time finally arrived for the last journey of them all.

Nobody at the wedding feast knew it but the number of guests had been determined not by ties of blood or friendship but by the number of people Georgina Nash could seat in her Long Gallery on the first floor of Brympton Hall. After half an hour of champagne and celebration the wedding guests were led up to this spectacular chamber. This room was one of the finest of its kind in England, over a hundred and fifty feet long with dramatic plasterwork on the ceiling and views out into the garden with the malfunctioning fountain. Here Georgina Nash had mixed the party up completely, Nashes sitting next to Colvilles at all the tables, bottles of champagne and Meursault waiting on the white tablecloths to lubricate friendship and fellowship on this special day. By the fireplace was a larger table for the bride and groom and senior members of the families.

The guests were circulating round the room looking for their names and their positions. Champagne corks were popping loudly as the footmen did their work. Then there was a different noise that might have been the cork being drawn from some enormous bottle of champagne, a double magnum perhaps. Or it could have been a shot from a gun. The noise came from the north end of the room, at the opposite end from the staircase used by the guests. Charlie Healey, butler to the Nash establishment, was a man well used to emergency and crisis. He had served as a sergeant in some of the bloodiest engagements of the Boer War. Beckoning a junior footman to accompany him he flitted through one ornate bedroom to the side of the Long Gallery. It was empty. The second ornate bedroom was not empty. Lying on the floor, with blood pouring forth on to the exquisite carpet, was Randolph Colville, father of the groom. And sitting on a chair some six feet away with a pistol in his hand was his younger brother Cosmo. One glance was enough to tell Charlie that the man on the floor was dead.

'Don't move,' he said to Cosmo Colville, who had turned deathly pale. 'William,' he turned to the junior footman, 'bring the doctor in here. And the man of God. And Mr Nash. And a tray. And when you've done that, go and telephone the police. Tell them there's been a murder and they're to come as fast as they can. Don't say a word to that new parlourmaid or she'll make a mess of everything.'

The doctor shook his head sadly as he inspected the remains of Randolph Colville. The vicar muttered a few unconvincing prayers. Charlie Healey motioned to Cosmo Colville that he should place his gun on the tray. Cosmo could, after all, have

7

decided to embark on a killing spree as long as he had it. Charlie gave instructions that nobody was to touch the gun, which he sent to a secret place in the pantry until the police came. The dead man did not move from his position on the floor. If you bent down to floor level and looked at his face you could see that he had a look of pained surprise on his face. Cosmo without his gun maintained the demeanour of Cosmo with the gun, a withdrawal into some recess of his mind, a reluctance to lift his eyes from the floor, a refusal to speak whatever anybody said to him. Willoughby Nash felt this was one of the most awkward moments of his entire career. His Long Gallery full of a hundred wedding guests. Vast quantities of food waiting in his kitchens on the floor below. The police about to arrive. And death, the most unwelcome wedding guest of all, staining the priceless carpet in his state bedroom. His beloved daughter Emily's special day ruined beyond repair. He conferred briefly with the vicar and returned slowly to his seat at the top table. He held a whispered conference with his wife. Then he tapped loudly on the table and appealed for silence. Willoughby made a brief address to the wedding guests. He told them of a dead man but did not mention that it was probably murder. Nor did he give a name to the corpse, reasoning that the police would not wish him to do that yet. He explained that they would all have to wait for the officers of the law to arrive. He suggested that they should proceed with the wedding lunch, however difficult the circumstances. They needed to keep their strength up. The vicar was going to offer up a few short prayers now. They would congregate back in the church when they could for a brief service of prayers for the dead. Emily Nash, now Emily Colville, held very tightly to her new husband. Neither of them knew that a father was dead and an uncle who had held a gun in his hand was under guard a few feet away.

The police brought trouble with them when they arrived. Or rather, it wasn't the police that brought the trouble, but the attitude of the guests to the police. For in apparent charge of the investigation was the Norfolk Constabulary's youngest Detective Inspector, Albert Cooper, aged thirty-two years, and still in the first week of his new promotion. Cooper's problem was that he looked much younger still, possibly in his mid to late twenties. Only a couple of years past people often asked him if he had started shaving yet, or if he had stopped growing. Detective Inspector Cooper took it all in his stride. He was almost certainly the cleverest policeman in Norfolk. His father had died when he was in his teens and it became important for him to start earning money to support his mother and the younger brothers. The teachers at his school thought he was very intelligent and wished he could continue with his education but bowed to the inevitable as they had with so many like Albert in the past. Accountancy, they suggested to him, the maths teacher was sure he could secure him a post at a firm in Aylsham. Newspapers, his English teacher suggested, the school could find him a position on the staff of the local paper in Norwich. From there all things might be possible. It was the headmaster who suggested the police force, one of the few institutions that was not totally in thrall to the class system and tried to promote on merit rather than by birth.

As he rose to address the wedding guests, flanked by a sergeant and a constable, he realized that this was the most distinguished company he had ever been part of, and that he was attending on the first blue-blooded murder of his career. He knew what they were thinking, most of these guests. And while Willoughby Nash had been politeness itself, Inspector Albert Cooper did not expect all the rest to be as well behaved. He had scarcely finished his opening sentence when he was interrupted by a choleric-looking gentleman in military uniform.

'Nash,' spluttered the man with the medals, 'this is preposterous. Can't you get us a proper policeman, for God's sake? We can't have an incident like this looked into by some babe in arms in uniform, it's absurd.'

Nash was about to rise to his feet when the Inspector waved him down. 'I can't help looking whatever age you think I am, any more than you can help looking whatever age I think you are, sir,' he said, before he was interrupted.

'Impertinent young pup!' roared the red jacket. 'Nash, can't you do something? I have some influence with the Lord Lieutenant. We need a proper policeman here, for heaven's sake. I for one am not going to co-operate until we do. I suggest we take a vote.'

Inspector Cooper had already sent for reinforcements but he was not going to tell his audience here that. Not yet at any rate. Once more he made a gesture to Willoughby Nash to remain in his chair. He motioned to his sergeant and his constable to take up their positions on either side of the military gentleman.

'General,' he said firmly, 'we have had enough of your comments. For everybody here this has been a terrible day, for many, no doubt, the worst day of their lives. You are now making things worse. If you utter one more word, you will be arrested. You are obstructing the police in their inquiries, a most serious offence. The County Jail in Norwich has accommodated all sorts of distinguished prisoners over the years. What a tragedy it would be if such a distinguished career were to end in those circumstances. ' Cooper realized that it might be time for an olive branch. Sending distinguished former generals off for a spell in the cells might not look good on his record. 'I understand, of course, General,' he went on, 'that you, like everybody else, must be very upset by what has gone on here. And I have already sent a request for reinforcements. My superior officer, Detective Chief Inspector Weir, should be with us later this afternoon. You will be pleased to hear, General, that he is a lot older than me.'

Inspector Cooper waited for any reaction and then pressed on with his plans. Two tables at the front would be taken over by the constabulary and one at the back. After people were interviewed they would be free to go provided they left an address where they could be contacted. The police would be maintaining a presence at Brympton Hall for some days, if people remembered something that slipped their mind during the first interview.

Who sat next to you in the church? Who else was in your pew? Who was in front of you? Who was behind you? Who was sitting in the pew across the nave? Did you see anybody acting suspiciously?

Some of the wedding guests whispered quietly among themselves. Some closed their eyes and prayed or tried to fall asleep. Outside the sun still shone on the Brympton gardens. Water spouted erratically from the Brympton fountain and a peacock in full glory took possession of the gravel walk nearest to the house.

Who were you talking to during the champagne session in the garden? How far along the east front of the house were you standing? Who was standing close to you?

The hosts, Willoughby and Georgina Nash, could not believe what was happening. Surely this must all be a dream. Their daughter's new father-in-law couldn't be lying on their grand carpet with blood dripping from his head. Surely his brother wasn't sitting in what appeared to be a catatonic trance, refusing to speak, the gun but recently removed from his hand. These weren't real policemen licking their pens and writing everything down in their notebooks. Were they?

Going into the Long Gallery, who was in front of you? Who was behind you? Who else was sitting at your table? How far up the room was your table? Do you remember seeing anybody or anything suspicious?

The shadows were lying across the gardens when the last guest departed. Randolph Colville had been removed to the morgue for a post-mortem report. Cosmo Colville still refused to speak to anybody and was taken away to spend the night in the local jail. The bride and groom had to change their plans and booked themselves into a local hotel where they partook of an indifferent supper and slept on a lumpy bed. Inspector

Albert Cooper looked forward to collating all the interviews about people's whereabouts into a single document which would virtually be a seating plan for the church and the Long Gallery. His superior officer still had not appeared. Chief Inspector Weir was not known for speed of movement either mental or physical. Maybe he wouldn't appear at all on this day.

'I tell you one thing, Tom,' Cooper said to his sergeant as they set off for the nearest town of Aylsham.

'What's that, sir?' said Tom.

'I hope that bloke with the gun starts talking soon.'

'Why is that, sir?'

'Well, I don't think he did it, if you see what I mean. Nobody who's just killed somebody is going to sit there holding on to the bloody weapon, even if it is his brother, are they?'

'You could have a point there, sir. But why do you hope he starts talking?'

'Think about it, Tom. You know what the Chief is like. Here's a corpse. Here's a man with a gun in his hand. The man with the gun won't speak. Man must be guilty. Nearly certain to get a conviction with those attendant circumstances. "The sentence of this court upon you is that you be taken from hence to the place from which you came,"' Albert Cooper had heard these words over half a dozen times in court and they still chilled him to the bone, '"and thence to a place of execution, and you be there hanged by the neck until you be dead and your body shall be buried in the precincts of the prison in which you shall have last been confined, and may the Lord have mercy upon your soul." Our silent friend, Tom, could be pushing up the daisies within a month.'

Georgina Nash slept badly in her enormous bedroom at Brympton Hall that night. Beside her, husband Willoughby was snoring with the same metronomic regularity that had measured out his nights for the past twenty years. Something was nagging at the back of Georgina's mind. When she thought about the day's events they all bundled themselves into a couple of moments of horror. It was something some-body had said to her that she thought must be important. But who? And when? And where? She began running through in her mind the guests who had come to the wedding on this fateful day. Nothing worked. Shortly before dawn Georgina Nash fell asleep.

2

The office was hidden away in a corner of an enormous warehouse on the banks of the Thames at Shadwell Basin in the East End of London. It was about twenty feet square with shelves covering virtually every wall. The man who worked here didn't like cleaners coming in, so there were spiders' webs hanging off the walls, dust lying thickly on the shelves and mice scampering about the floor, feasting occasionally on the rich liquids that fell there. To his left, on the far side of the wall of his office, the high warehouse was filled with barrels of every description. Above him were six floors devoted to Bordeaux, burgundy, champagne, port, Madeira and *vin ordinaire*. Stretching out a few feet above his head was a bizarre collection of wine bottles: magnums and Marie Jeannes and double magnums of four bottles from Bordeaux; Jeroboams worth six bottles and Imperiales worth eight; from Burgundy and Champagne came even larger versions, a Salmanazar equivalent to twelve bottles, a Balthazar worth sixteen and a Nebuchadnezzar worth twenty bottles. For some unaccountable reason, the man knew that people would almost always believe that wine contained in these monstrous vessels was the real thing. He did not intend to disabuse them. Other shelves were filled with nameless barrels and a surprising variety of other ingredients ranging from dried gooseberries to turnip juice.

This was the domain of the man they called the Alchemist. Jesus Christ, he used to mutter to himself, could turn water into wine. Well, he could turn rough Algerian into pass-able claret, consignments of white grapes from more or less anywhere into credible champagne, strange combinations of raisins and sugar into respectable *vin ordinaire*. He was quite short, the Alchemist, with a stoop and a thin goatee beard. He wore thick glasses to read the labels on the wine bottles and the equations that carried the secrets of his forgeries. Two or three times a year he crossed to France where he and a couple of selected collaborators visited the freight trains carrying wine from the south to the palates of the north. These trains stopped overnight at Dijon station, where they switched the labels over during the hours of darkness. He currently had an order for a consignment of pre-phylloxera wines from a very grand hotel in Mayfair which held pre-phylloxera dinners once a month, elaborate and very expensive occasions where all the wine came from before 1863, the year the phylloxera bug began to devastate the vineyards of France, spreading slowly northwards from its first infestation in the Languedoc. Hardly anybody, the Alchemist reasoned, could remember what these wines tasted of before that date. It was all so long ago, and the few genuine bottles left were locked away in the cellars of the grandest châteaux in the Médoc. He had an enormous order from a British railway company. And then there was the regular order from those damned Americans in London. The Alchemist set to work, draining off some red substance from one of his barrels. He had only one rule and he never broke it. He told nobody his real name.

Three days after the wedding and the murder Inspector Albert Cooper had completed his interviews with the wedding guests. One or two had reappeared at Brympton Hall the day after the incident with information they had forgotten in the confusion of the day. The Sergeant had been sent to make inquiries at Randolph Colville's house on the Thames about the gun. By now the Inspector could tell you who was sitting against the wall in the church three rows from the front, and who was up there next to the organ on the first floor. He could show you the dispositions of the guests as they drank champagne on the lawn. He could show you how far they had advanced towards their tables when the corpse was discovered. He had obtained from Georgina Nash the details of the final seating plan when Colvilles and Nashes were mixed up together. There were, he thought, two or three guests he could not identify because people could describe them, but didn't know their names. The Colvilles thought they were Nashes, and the Nashes thought they were Colvilles. His informants spoke of a tall thickset man with dark hair, a middle-aged lady with a slight limp, and a nondescript-looking man nobody could describe in any detail. They troubled Inspector Cooper's tidy mind, these three unknowns wandering about in the October sunshine at Brympton Hall. He was wondering if he should interview everybody all over again when the summons came to see his superior officer, Chief Inspector Weir.

The Chief Inspector was sitting at a very large desk strewn with papers. Cynics at the station said that Weir had suborned the desk from the office of the Chief Constable when the previous holder of that office had just left and before his successor arrived. A table had been substituted in its place. Weir was well over six feet tall, heavily built and with receding hair. Now in his sixties, even he would have admitted that he thought more about his retirement than about his cases. He and Mrs Chief Inspector Weir, a former primary school teacher, had bought a cottage on the coast near Blakeney where the policeman intended to devote his time to bird watching and the wife was planning an enormous piece of embroidery. Weir's colleagues would never have said that the Detective Chief Inspector was quick like Inspector Cooper. Nor did he have the sudden flights of intuition that solved a case in a moment like one or two of his younger colleagues. But all agreed on one thing. He may have been ponderous in body and spirit, his mind may have worked incredibly slowly, but he had judgement. In all his years in the force Detective Chief Inspector Weir had scarcely made a mistake in an important case. Defence counsel who looked forward to dancing round his portly person found that he carried on unperturbed and made a very good impression on the jury. Juries liked the big man from Norfolk and seldom caused him to lose a case in court. This afternoon he knew that his young Inspector, whose promotion he had personally recommended, was not going to agree with him.

'Come in, Cooper, come in, do sit down.' Weir pointed to a neat little armchair with cushions boasting some of the finest of Mrs Weir's embroidery. 'The Sergeant's back. I have his report on the Colville gun here. There's little doubt about it. The gun, or one virtually identical to it, came from a drawer in Randolph Colville's gun room on the first floor of his house. Certainly the gun's not there now. He must have brought it with him. I'm sure the brother's guilty, Albert. There must have been a struggle and Cosmo grabbed the gun from his brother. I'm going to see the Chief Constable after our conversation here. Then I'm going to charge him.'

Inspector Albert Cooper looked very unhappy. His eyes pleaded with his superior officer. He knew how difficult it was to change Weir's mind. He resolved to approach the matter sideways, like a crab on the coast near the Weir cottage at Blakeney.

'It's entirely possible, sir, that Cosmo Colville killed his brother, but aren't we being a bit hasty? You don't think we should wait a while before committing ourselves?'

Detective Chief Inspector Weir smiled at his young protégé, like a grandfather with a favourite grandchild. 'Why should we wait, Albert? Surely we've got all the evidence we need.'

Cooper knew that what was, for him, the most compelling argument for innocence was, for his superior officer, the most compelling argument for guilt. All the same, he had to try.

17

'Suppose you're a killer, sir. Suppose you despatch your victim in a quiet room on the first floor of a great house in Norfolk. Then what do we think the killer would do? Why, he'd dispose of the weapon and get himself away from the scene as fast as he could. The last thing he would want to do is to sit there with the gun in his hand waiting to be discovered. Then there's the business of his silence. Who is he trying to protect? Some other member of the family? Some woman?'

'That's mere speculation and you know it,' said Weir. Twenty-five years before in Norwich Crown Court he had heard a distinguished counsel dismiss the elegant arguments of the defence barrister as mere speculation and he had been using the phrase ever since. 'If the man wants to tell us what he was doing all he has to do is to open his mouth. But he won't. Let's stick to the facts, Albert. The gun is Randolph Colville's. It was used to kill him. His brother Cosmo was in and out of that house all the time before the wedding. He was sitting in the chair opposite with the gun in his hand. That's good enough for me. I'm sure it will be good enough for the Chief Constable. That's good enough for a jury.'

'There are still questions we can't answer, sir. The three unidentified guests at the wedding reception for a start. We haven't had time to trace them yet. And there's the whole question of the wine business, whether there was anything unusual going on there. We don't have to make the arrest so soon.'

Even as he looked at his superior officer he knew it was no good. Weir's mind was made up. It would take an earthquake to change it. Before he went home that evening, Inspector Cooper learnt that Archibald Beauchamp Cosmo Colville had indeed been charged with murder.

Five days later Lord Francis Powerscourt was crossing the well-manicured lawns of London's Gray's Inn, answering a summons from a barrister friend, Charles Augustus Pugh.

The two men had worked on a murder trial together some years before. Pugh's office was lined with even more files than it had contained previously. His feet, clad today in elegant black boots, rested as usual on his desk. His suit was pale grey, his starched white collar was immaculate. He waved Powerscourt to a chair.

'How are you keeping, my friend? Still packing the murderers off to jail?'

'I can't complain,' said Powerscourt. 'And yourself, Pugh? The clerks here still keeping the wolf from your door?'

'They certainly are,' said Pugh with a smile. 'I've got the devil of a case on now. I'm for the prosecution for a change, Powerscourt. Three high-class con men, Granville, Trevelyan and Lawrence, Financial Consultants. With names like that and their proper cut glass vowel sounds, you'd think they'd been to Eton and Oxford. Not so, my friend, not so.' Pugh shook his head sadly. 'Old ladies, that was their thing. Rich old ladies, two of the rogues offering their services round Mayfair and South Kensington, one in the Home Counties. Old ladies especially susceptible to the con man in Epsom for some reason. They offered better investment returns than anyone else, you see, not by huge amounts, that might have made people think twice about them, but by enough to make a difference. They were only caught because a solicitor became suspicious. When they got their hands on the old ladies' money, ten or fifteen or twenty thousand pounds, sometimes more, they worked out how long she was likely to live. They paid her the slightly better dividends they'd promised every year out of her own money, and kept most of the rest themselves. They created bogus accounts using real investments quoted in the financial pages that showed how much she was losing every year so that by the time the old lady died the investments had virtually all gone. These were real shares and real share prices they pretended to deal in, only they weren't actually buying and selling, just taking notes of the different prices at different times so they could show how the old ladies might have lost most of their money. When the time came to send in the paperwork after the death, they just put in the figures they already had. Nobody asked to see the actual share certificates or the records of the stockbrokers' dealings, though I suspect they could have finessed those all right.'

'How were they caught?' asked Powerscourt.

'Ah,' said Pugh, 'if you were feeling generous, you could say they were unlucky. You might not be so charitable if you were one of the old ladies or the people meant to inherit their money. Three of their victims in six months all had the same solicitors on Kensington High Street. All their clients invested with Granville, Trevelyan and Lawrence. All ended up without a penny. One might have been possible, two might just have been feasible, but three was too much. This solicitor went into every possible detail of the paperwork and found that they didn't have it. Then he called in the police. Can you believe it, the three rogues have even found a couple of old ladies who testified in court in their favour. I'm not sure they believed me when I told them they were being cheated out of their money. Anyway,' Pugh slid his feet off his desk and back on to the ground and began riffling through some papers, eventually holding up a brief tied in pink tape, 'this is why you're here, Powerscourt. Just been instructed yesterday,' he went on. 'Hopeless business, hardly worth turning up in court apart from the fact the fee is rather substantial. Wondered if you'd like to lend a hand. Solicitors keen for everybody they can find to help get our client off, particularly keen to get you on board. Heaps of money.'

'What sort of case?' said Powerscourt.

'Murder,' replied Pugh. 'I'm for the defence, you under-stand. Some defence! Here's the story.' There was a brief pause while Charles Augustus Pugh restored his boots to their rightful place on his desk and wrapped his hands behind his neck. 'Grand wedding, wine merchant family hook up with Norfolk grandees who have huge house. Hundred guests, maybe more, all dressed up as if they're going to

Royal Ascot. Groom's father found shot in room near the Long Gallery where they were all about to put the nosebags on after the service. Then there's the dead man's brother six feet away, sitting on a chair with a gun in his hand. Blood all over the priceless carpet. Same gun, or almost certainly the same gun, police discover, used to shoot the brother. Think Cain and Abel in modern dress in the bloody Fens, for Christ's sake. Brother Cain charged with murder. Bloody fool won't speak. All he will say to the authorities is his name and that he didn't do it. What, my friend, what on earth am I supposed to do with this lot? The committal hearing is next week, the Old Bailey in five or six weeks if everything goes according to plan. It could be less. Can you help me? Can you work a miracle? The loaves and fishes would have nothing on this.'

Powerscourt agreed to take the case on. His only thought at the beginning was that the silence probably meant a woman was involved who was not Cosmo Colville's wife. Pugh gave him all the details of the families and the wedding party and took him down the street to the solicitors to take up his formal employment in the matter.

Lady Lucy Powerscourt was looking at an auction catalogue when her husband returned to Markham Square from Gray's Inn. She turned slightly pale when Powerscourt told her the details of his latest case. 'I've got a second cousin, Francis, who's married to some minor member of the Colville family. I can't for the moment remember if she's on the Randolph side or the Cosmo side. How very terrible.'

'What sort of a fellow was he, the chap your cousin married, I mean?'

'I'm afraid he was rather a bad lot. He was called Barrington White, Timothy Barrington White, I think, and he embarked on a series of business ventures that seemed to go wrong all the time. The last I heard he had taken a position in the

21

Colville wine business but he didn't care for it, he never liked being told off by his in-laws. You don't think he has anything to do with it, do you, Francis? And how do you think you can help that nice Mr Pugh get the Colville person off?'

'I have absolutely no idea if your relation has anything to do with it, Lucy. I was thinking about possible lines of inquiry on my way back here.'

Powerscourt began pacing up and down his drawing room, hands behind his back, like some thoughtful admiral on his quarterdeck in the Napoleonic Wars. Lady Lucy smiled. The pacing up and down always meant that her husband's brain was moving towards top speed.

'There aren't really all that many motives for murder when you think of it, Lucy. Revenge, that's always a runner. Jealousy, especially when the opposite sex is concerned, very powerful. Money, securing an inheritance ahead of time or killing off the siblings who might be ahead of you in the queue to inherit grandfather's millions, another strong contender. Sudden blinding rage, when the murderer goes half insane for the split second it takes to plunge the knife in or pull the trigger, that's taken a lot of people to the other side. There must be more, lots more.'

'And which of these deadly sins do you think might apply in this case, Francis?' Lady Lucy began her question to her husband's back as he reached the end of his pacing and finished it to his face as he turned round to head back towards the fireplace.

'I think the silence is important, Lucy, I really do. I think it implies he was protecting somebody, that if he had to answer questions he would end up incriminating somebody, his mistress perhaps. The thing about silence is that there are no two ways about it. Even if he offered to tell just some of what he knows, once he started talking Cosmo Colville would probably find that he had to reveal everything.'

'You don't think it might have something to do with his brother, that he was protecting him in some way?'

'Even after the brother was dead, do you mean? That would have to be some secret, Lucy, don't you think? Maybe it all has to do with the business.'

'I find it hard to believe that the wine business could be the reason for murder, Francis. Surely people don't go round shooting each other in the heart because the claret's gone off or the Nuits St Georges is corked again.'

'Maybe there was a scandal waiting to come out. When you refer to the wine business in that way of course it's hard to see it as a motive for murder. But the Colville business is huge. Think of it as money or as a disgrace that might finish the firm off and it could well be time for pistols in the afternoon. Johnny Fitzgerald is the only wine expert we know and he's not back from Wales until tomorrow. And even Johnny would be happy to admit that his expertise is more in the consumption end of the trade than in the business side. Lucy, I think it's time I extended my knowledge of burgundy and Bordeaux. I'm just going to pop into Berry Bros. & Rudd. After all, I have been buying wine from them for nearly twenty years.'

The man they called the Alchemist had moved a little table to sit underneath the window. He brought over an electric lamp to increase the visibility further still. On his table he placed three plain bottles with red wine in them and rather unusual labels. The left-hand bottle's inscription read BX LG68 AG15. The second one said BX LG74 AG12, and the one on the right BX LG78 AG10. Very reverently, as if he was pouring the host at the communion rails in some place of alchemical worship, the man poured a small amount of the liquid from the first bottle into a glass. The Alchemist was humming to himself as he worked. Today it was the Drinking Song from *La Traviata*. He was very fond of the opera. He went as often as he could. He swirled the liquid round for a moment or two and then tasted it before spitting it out into a small bucket on the floor. He looked thoughtful for a moment and then made some notes in his large notebook. Each legend with the BX heading had a page to itself. When he had finished his tasting the Alchemist smiled a slow smile and replaced the corks in the bottles before placing them on a shelf. 'They're coming along well,' he said out loud, addressing nobody in particular. Blending, the man often reminded himself, was the essence of wine making, as vital to its success as the grapes or the *terroir* of the vineyard. Was not Haut Brion itself, one of the finest clarets in the world, the result of careful blending? Only the Alchemist knew the secrets of the labels. LG68 meant that sixty-eight per cent of the liquid was composed of standard red *vin ordinaire* from the Languedoc, AG15 meant that fifteen per cent of it was red from Algeria, a red often referred to as the Infuriator. In the other bottles the mixtures were slightly different, the remaining percentages being composed of good quality claret. The BX at the beginning meant that a claret was being created here, far from the southwest of France and the elegant city of Bordeaux, in a dusty warehouse on London's river. The wine would be bastard from birth.

Lord Francis Powerscourt was shown into a small library on the first floor of Berry Bros. & Rudd at 3 St James's Street, opposite St James's Palace and the London home of the Prince of Wales at Marlborough House. Powerscourt was fascinated by the contents of the glass-fronted bookshelves, most of them containing ancient bottles of wine rather than books.

'Good day to you, Powerscourt,' said a tall white-haired man of about fifty years, marching across the carpet like the guardsman he had once been to shake Powerscourt by the hand. George Berry had been Powerscourt's principal point of contact here for all his years with the company, advising more on broad strategies of wine purchase rather than recommending particular bottles. 'I trust Lady Lucy and the family are well?'

'Splendid, thanks,' said Powerscourt with a smile. He had always thought that George Berry with his military bearing, those clear blue eyes and a general impression of tidy competence would have made a perfect con man.

'What can we do for you today, Lord Powerscourt? Some white burgundies perhaps? We have some splendid wines from Montrachet and Chablis this year.'

'I want your advice, Berry, and I'm in rather a hurry. Please keep this to yourself but I've been asked to look into the Colville murder, the one up in Norfolk. Cosmo's lawyers have asked me to see if I can come up with anything to help his case.'

'You're trying to get him off might be another way of putting it,' said Berry. 'What a terrible business. We knew the Colvilles, all of them. We were meant to go to that wedding, but family commitments put a stop to it. Pity, I've always wanted to see that house, Brympton Hall. How can I help you?'

'I'm not quite sure how to put this,' said Powerscourt. 'There are all sorts of motives for murder, greed, jealousy, revenge, hatred. Some of those may have been swirling round the Colville business. I need somebody to advise me on the wine trade in general and the Colville companies in particular. Was there anything suspicious going on? Was a scandal about to break? Had they treated anybody or any other company particularly badly?'

George Berry walked over to his window and stared out into the street where a horse-drawn carriage seemed to be overtaking a wheezing motor car, smoke pouring from its bonnet. Powerscourt remembered that Berry's favourite activity was playing golf at fashionable courses like Huntercombe or Royal St George's, Sandwich. Men said that George Berry seldom lost. Powerscourt had always wondered what he drank in the bar at the end of a round. Did he have beer? Or did Berry Bros. & Rudd supply some of these golf courses with their finest wines for George Berry and his friends to sample after their eighteen holes?

'I wish I felt able to help you myself,' Berry said finally, turning back from his vigil at the window overlooking the dark grey palace with its red soldiers like toys in their sentry boxes, 'but I don't think my expertise, for what it's worth, is what you are looking for. You see, we deal with what we like to think of as the more expensive end of the market, the leading hotels in the capital, ten or twelve Oxbridge colleges, most of the top London clubs, a large number of restaurants, and a considerable number of private clients who are interested in their wine and are happy to be advised by us. People like yourself, Lord Powerscourt. But we're not dealing with the same sort of people as the Colvilles. The new middle class, as they're often referred to these days, would not buy their wine from us, they would buy it from Colvilles or one of their rivals. I think I know the man you want, he's got enormous experience in the wine trade. At the moment he is the chief wine buyer for the White Star Line. They sell all kinds of different wine from all kinds of different countries at all kinds of different prices in their ships. He could tell you straight off, I should think, what was a proper claret and what was made in a factory or a warehouse. I'll give you a letter of introduction.'

George Berry sat down at one of the desks and scribbled a quick note.

'His name, Berry, you haven't told me his name.'

'His name?' Berry laughed. 'When he's happy he says his name has been a great help in his career. When he's miserable he claims his name has been the ruin of him and he wishes he'd changed it years ago.'

'For God's sake, man, what's he called?'

'He's a hereditary baronet. He's called. . .' George Berry paused for a moment for maximum impact. 'He's called Sir Pericles Freme.'

'God bless my soul! ' said Lord Francis Powerscourt.

3

Randolph Colville's funeral was finally held a week and a half after his murder. Powerscourt was travelling to the Church of St James the Less at Pangbourne on the Thames where the last melancholy rites were to be performed. He had arranged to travel with one Christopher Fuller, partner in the City law firm of Moorehead, Fuller and Fox who looked after the Colvilles' affairs. The solicitor, a slim man in his late thirties with brown eyes and dark curly hair, was carrying a particularly large briefcase which he kept beside him on the seat rather than place it in the storage area above.

'I don't suppose you've had time to make any progress yet, Lord Powerscourt. Innings only just beginning, what?'

Powerscourt smiled. 'Has your client said anything to you yet? Has he uttered a word?'

'Not a word, not a single word,' said Fuller. 'And I've seen him twice now, once in Norwich and once in Pentonville.'

'Have you any idea what causes the silence? Is he hiding something?'

'We're rather hoping you'll be able to tell us the answers to those questions, Lord Powerscourt.'

'Look here.' Powerscourt leaned forward to stress the importance of what he was about to say. 'I know you're not meant to say anything about your client's affairs and all that, but you're not in the office now and your first duty is surely to keep your man alive, however you do it. Is there anything you know about the Colvilles that throws light on the murder? You don't have to be specific, if that's a problem, just some general guidance.'

'I wish I could help you, Lord Powerscourt, but I don't see how I can.'

'Forgive me, but do you mean that you could if you felt so inclined because you have some information, or do you mean that you can't because you don't have any information to give me?'

'The latter, I'm afraid.'

The train had left London now and was racing along through open countryside. Some two hundred yards away the Thames was meandering peacefully towards the great city and the sea.

'What about Randolph's will? Is that will in your briefcase?'

'It is, as a matter of fact.'

'Are there any surprises in there? All the money left to charity, or to mistresses tucked away somewhere, that sort of thing?'

Christopher Fuller smiled. 'You'll find out in due course, if you come back to the house after the service. There is one surprising thing about Randolph's will and I don't understand it at all.'

'What's that?' asked Powerscourt.

'Well, I don't think I'm speaking out of turn here, but there's a lot less money than I would have thought. Hundred thousand less, maybe a couple of hundred thousand less. You see, I would have thought Randolph and Cosmo took about the same amount of money out of the business over the years and Cosmo is worth over twice as much as Randolph.'

'How do you know that, Mr Fuller?'

Christopher Fuller grimaced. 'I had to draw up a new will for Cosmo in Pentonville the other day. He wasn't happy with the previous one that had been drawn up by one of my colleagues. He must be the only Colville in history to have his last will and testament witnessed by a couple of prison warders.'

'What is Cosmo like, Mr Fuller? What sort of man is he?'

The solicitor took his time before he spoke. 'In some ways they were similar, the brothers Randolph and Cosmo Colville. From their earliest years it had been drummed into them that the business came first. Nothing else really mattered. Old man Walter may have sent them off to Harrow to learn the manners of their betters, rather like Tom Brown going to Rugby, but he wasn't going to turn them into gentlemen of leisure living comfortably off their dividends. Work was the thing. Always work. Randolph spent a lot of time in France, in Burgundy. He looked after the firm's interests there and his children used to joke that he was becoming half French himself. But it was their attitudes outside the business that were so different. Randolph was a man of great enthusiasms, fly fishing one minute, French cathedrals the next. Cosmo was more steady, more circumspect. He looked after the firm's interests in Bordeaux. They actually own a château there, you know. He never lost his passion for cricket, Cosmo, and the Test Matches at Lord's. I've always thought that was where he was happiest.'

Powerscourt could sympathize with that. He would work even harder for a man whose grand passion was for Test Matches at Lord's. 'What will happen to the succession at Colvilles if both brothers are gone?'

'They say the old man, Walter, has wanted to give up the chairmanship for years and pass it on to the younger generation. But he's never been able to make up his mind which one of the younger generation, his boys or his brother Nathaniel's boys, to give it to. Maybe he'll have to hang on a little longer.'

The train was slowing down for Pangbourne now. The river was speckled with houseboats and a couple of elderly gentlemen were seated optimistically on the bank with fishing rods in their hands. Powerscourt thought he had time for one last question.

'Mr Fuller, can I ask you one final question. Do you think Cosmo Colville killed his brother?'

'I do not,' replied Fuller.

'Who do you think did it then?'

'I'm sorry, Powerscourt, I don't know. I really haven't a clue. I wish I did.'

As they walked to the church of St James the Less Powerscourt wondered if Fuller had been telling the truth in his very last answer. Had he protested too much? Was there, somewhere in the well-ordered files of Moorehead, Fuller and Fox of Bishopsgate, a clue about one of the Colvilles, a clue so dangerous it could not be divulged, even to the man employed to save a client from the gallows and the rope?

Powerscourt and the solicitor sat discreetly at the back of the church. Randolph Colville had a large turn-out come to see him off. More than half the congregation had been present at a very different service less than a fortnight before when Colville had married Nash at the church of St Peter at Brympton. Willoughby and Georgina Nash had turned up out of sympathy with their daughter's new family. Walter Colville, father of the dead man, seemed to those who knew him to have aged about five years in the past ten days. His face before the wedding and the murder looked like the face of a man who still entertains hope for the future, who even at the age of seventy-nine can still make plans for himself and his family. Now that face looked as if it had collapsed inwards. His eyes were dead and his cheeks were almost hollow. To bury one son was bad enough; to have to face the prospect of burying the other for murdering the first one, too terrible to contemplate. No parent could think of their child being hung, the rope round the neck, the drop into the dark, the last desperate fluttering of the legs and then oblivion, without shuddering. The only thing Walter had resolved to do was to change his will but he wondered if he should wait till after the trial in case he had to change it again.

At the very back of the church was an elderly porter from Colvilles' gin manufactory in Hammersmith, who had been with the firm for over forty years. He looked out for this investigator man people said the family had employed to secure the acquittal of Mr Cosmo. He identified Powerscourt fairly quickly. The elderly porter, whose name was Howard, wondered if he should tell Powerscourt about some of the strange things he had seen at Colvilles in the last six months.

It began to rain heavily when they took the body out of the church for its interment in the Colville grave. The vicar spoke the last words of the service at great speed. Some of the mourners had had the foresight to bring umbrellas. Others stood stoically as the earth was thrown in over Randolph Colville's coffin and let the water run off their heads and down their faces. One of the Colville children was crying inconsolably by the graveside. Grooms and chauffeurs huddled inside their capes or kept the doors firmly closed in the long queue of vehicles lined up outside the church. Powerscourt suddenly felt that he should not be there, that he was unwelcome.

That feeling was reinforced when he went back to the Colville house for drinks and the reading of the will. Randolph's house was a very large Victorian villa on the far side of the road that ran beside the Thames. There were handsome reception rooms at the front with views over the river and two floors above, with balconies, devoted to bedrooms and bathrooms. There was a large garden at the back with a tennis court. Powerscourt discovered that the Colvilles seemed to be divided into two hostile camps. One believed, with the police, that the only explanation for the bizarre circumstances surrounding Randolph's death was indeed that Cosmo had shot him. To this faction he, Powerscourt, was trying to pervert the course of justice. And the other faction, the one that believed in Cosmo's innocence, which you might have thought would be sympathetic to Powerscourt, was not sympathetic at all. They did not see why it was necessary to employ anybody to establish Cosmo's innocence. Any fool could see that he was not guilty and there was no need for meddling aristocrats.

31

There were just two things that Powerscourt learnt in that house of mourning by the Thames. The first came from a man, obviously a neighbour, who had taken one glass too many of Colvilles' Finest Champagne. 'Let me tell you something,' he began, trying to put a friendly arm round Powerscourt's shoulder, 'strangest thing I ever saw,' he shook his head at the memory, 'took me three or four games to work out what was going on. I was watching Randolph play tennis with a friend of his one weekend a couple of years ago. It was bizarre. Randolph never hit a backhand, not once. The fellow was ambidextrous, left-handed forehand followed right-handed forehand. Bloody effective it was too.' The other piece of intelligence, delivered with due solemnity by Christopher Fuller, was that Randolph left just over two hundred thousand pounds in his will. Everything was left in trust for his widow in her lifetime and then passed on to the children.

As Powerscourt made his way back to the station to return to London he thought about what the solicitor had said on the train earlier that day. He did some calculations about Randolph Colville's missing money. If Fuller was right, Colville should have left not two hundred thousand pounds but three hundred, maybe even four hundred thousand pounds. Where had it gone, all this money? Was he being blackmailed? Had the missing money led to his death?

In a small office north of Oxford Street the day after the funeral the newest competitors to the Colvilles were holding their regular morning meeting. Piccadilly Wine consisted of a number of shops in the suburbs of London. The locations, Bromley, Twickenham, Camden Town, were carefully chosen. These were not places where the rich would go to order cases of Château Latour or Château d'Yquem, but in these humble streets were a great many people who would buy cheaper wines regularly. Septimus Parry and Vicary Dodds, both graduates of Westminster and Oxford, were hoping to make a great fortune for themselves. They might not sell the best champagne to Mr Soames Forsyte in his beautiful house in Chelsea, but they could sell claret and burgundy in enormous volumes to Mr Charles Pooter and his fellow nobodies increasing and multiplying across the suburbs of England. In a way they were following the trail of the Colvilles themselves who had deliberately sought a different clientele from the more ancient and more fashionable wine merchants clustered round St James's.

There was only one topic of conversation this morning, the fate of the Colvilles.

'Cosmo is still locked up in some ghastly prison,' said Vicary Dodds cheerfully.

'Not much to drink in there, I shouldn't think. I met a man at the club last night,' Septimus picked up the baton, 'who said that Cosmo hasn't uttered a word in his defence. My man said that if he didn't start talking soon he'd end up on the gallows.'

Neither of the young men actually said so, but the discomfiture of the Colvilles meant a great business opportunity for Piccadilly Wine.

'Do you think we should send a card of condolence, or something like that?' said Vicary.

Septimus laughed. 'Don't think that would be in very good taste, Vicary. They say old man Walter is very knocked up about the whole thing. They've turned into a ship with almost no officers, Randolph dead, Cosmo in clink, Walter pulling his hair out. What do we do about it?'

Vicary Dodds looked at a great chart on the wall which showed the available stocks the firm had in hand of the various wines they sold. 'If we're going to steal some of their customers, we'd better get a special offer into the shops as soon as possible. We'll have to place some advertisements in the local papers too. We can't do it with champagne, we haven't enough of it and it would take too long to get some more here in time. We can't do it with port as the Colville port is so cheap we couldn't undercut them. I've always wondered where they get their port from, I wouldn't be at all surprised if it had never seen the day break over Portugal at all. Never mind, claret, that's the thing we do have lots of at the moment.'

Septimus pulled a newspaper from a drawer in his desk. 'They're offering claret – a pure Bordeaux luncheon wine at ten shillings a case,' he said. 'Pretty good offer that, if you ask me. Mind you, I've never heard of pure Bordeaux luncheon wine and I bet you the good drinkers of Bordeaux haven't either. Probably all grown in somebody's back garden and diluted with watered-down Algerian. Anyway, what do you think we could manage, Vicary?'

The young man ran his hand through a great mop of straw-coloured hair and did a few quick doodles on the pad in front of him. Vicary was the expert in money and accounting, Septimus the master in the acquisition of the wines and spirits. 'What do you say to nine shillings a dozen, Septimus? A shilling a case cheaper than Colvilles. That should send the customers flocking in to Piccadilly Wine, don't you think?'

'Will we still make a profit on that?'

'I should think so. But if it goes well we may need some more of Burgundy's finest. Could you rustle up another hundred cases or so, do you think?'

Septimus Parry smiled. 'I shall see to it now, partner,' he said and set off at once for a warehouse by the Thames.

Sir Pericles Freme lived in a small but perfect Georgian house not far from the Powerscourts in Chelsea. An immaculately dressed footman showed Powerscourt into a drawing room on the first floor. Sir Pericles still had the bearing of a man who had spent many years in the military. He was in his late fifties with neatly combed white hair and a small white moustache. He read the note from George Berry and ushered Powerscourt into a chair.

'Can't say I envy you this job, Powerscourt. Never easy getting a man off a murder charge, still harder if the fellow won't speak at all. You want to know about the Colville wine business, as I understand it from Berry, you want to know if there was anything going on there that could have led to his death. Am I right?'

'Absolutely,' said Powerscourt.

'How much do you know about wine? Forgive me for asking such an elementary question but it has a bearing on what my response is going to be.'

'Well,' said Powerscourt, 'I buy, on the whole, what the good people at Berry Bros. tell me to buy. And then I drink it. Or rather my close friend Johnny Fitzgerald drinks it. I've always thought he consumes more of my wine than I do myself.'

'I think most people have friends like that,' said Freme, 'but you wouldn't call yourself an expert?'

'No, I wouldn't,' said Powerscourt.

'I see.' Sir Pericles paused for a moment, flicking a speck of dust from his trousers. 'It's a very strange thing, wine. I often think the business is like diamonds, it has such a fascination for some people. It's totally irrational. I know some of my distinguished colleagues in the trade who will tell you how elated they become at the prospect of tasting some of those very superior Bordeaux or burgundies. They're in a state of high excitement for days or even weeks beforehand. And when they come back, if they've been lucky, they will tell you about the taste of the stuff with a faraway look in their eyes as if they've been to paradise. But there are a number of problems with the trade, always have been.

'The first is that the wine isn't the same from year to year. It never is. Some years the weather is good, some years the weather is bad. If you're growing Château Powerscourt it just isn't going to taste the same in 1908 as it did in 1906. So what do you do? Some people try to mix the bad years up with the good ones, nothing wrong with that, but it doesn't always work. At the top end of the market the merchants will tell their favoured clients not to buy any of the 1906 at all, to wait for another good year and then buy more than you need for a single year. The problem is more acute at the bottom end of the market. Colvilles and their rivals aren't going to tell their customers not to buy any of their own-label claret in 1911 because it's been a bad year. Somehow they have to try to make it taste the same, or nearly the same as in a good year. The people who can tell them how to do that are the blenders, and good blenders earn themselves enormous sums of money. Some of them indeed retire early.'

'Who decides what is good and what is not so good?' said Powerscourt.

'Very good question that,' replied Sir Pericles. 'There's a sort of Stock Exchange of views at work. The word goes out from the merchants and *négociants* and the shippers that such and such is a good year. It's a bit like the Stock Exchange deciding that such and such a share is a good investment and everybody piles in. It's not like a weighing machine where you can say this crate is exactly one ton and a quarter and everybody will agree. It's more diffuse than that.'

'Do the experts always agree with each other?'

'Usually they do. Somebody may take a contrary view but that's quite rare.'

'And how easy is it to cheat, to forge wines in the same way people forge banknotes or pictures?'

'It's easier than you might think. It's difficult at the very top end of the scale but not impossible. But in the middle range it's quite tempting. Suppose you have some land near Montrachet or Chablis. The ground is the same, the grapes are the same, the weather is the same as it is for the great vineyards in those parts. What is to stop you putting Montrachet or Chablis labels on your produce and selling it for two or three times the price you would get for it with the correct label? Labels are changed all the time and the ignorance of the public is the biggest reason the crooks get away with it.

Let's take champagne. Vast amounts of it are consumed at weddings and parties where most of the customers haven't tasted champagne since the last wedding they went to. How are they to know if it is the real thing or not? The best sparkling Saumur used to get passed off as champagne until some bright fellow – it might even have been a Colville, now I come to think of it – realized that you could sell the Saumur for much less than the champagne and still make a tidy profit because you could sell much more of it.'

'How easy is it to forge the wine altogether, so that it's never been near the Douro Valley or the Côte d'Or?'

'Powerscourt,' said Freme sadly, 'I could take you to Sète on the south coast of France or Hamburg or, I suspect, to places in London where you can walk in and order thousands of bottles of selected wines for collection within forty-eight hours. Sète is particularly famous for forgery because it's so close to Algeria and all that red they produce. This is aimed at what you might call the bottom end of the market, Colvilles' house claret if you like. I'm not saying there's anything wrong with it, but that's the end where forgery becomes very tempting.'

'Some years ago,' said Powerscourt, 'I carried out an investigation into a death that involved forged paintings. Much of that revolved round the question of attribution, whose voice would be believed when he said that the Titian was a Titian or was not a Titian. Is it the same with the wine business?'

'In a sense it is. It's a sort of con trick in a way. At the top end when the posh merchants on the Quai des Chartrons in Bordeaux say this Latour is very good, everybody believes it. At the bottom end people believe they are drinking claret when the label says it is Colvilles' own. Let me read you something. I've been collecting these recipes for years now.'

Sir Pericles Freme rummaged around in his desk and produced a large sheet of paper. He fixed a pair of pince-nez on his face and began:

'"An admirable wine, very like claret, and even surpassing claret in strength, may be prepared by the following process. Take any quantity of Malaga raisins, chop them very small, put to every pound of them a quart of water, and let them stand in an open vessel having a cloth thrown over it for a week or nine days, stirring them well daily. Then, drawing off as much of the liquid as will run, and straining out the rest from the raisins by pressure, turn up the whole in a seasoned barrel; and, to every gallon of the liquid, add a pint of the cold juice of ripe elder berries, which had previously been boiled or scummed. Let it stand, closely stopped, about six weeks; then draw it off, as far as is tolerably fine, into another vessel; add half a pound of moist sugar to every gallon of liqueur; and when it gets perfectly fine, draw it into bottles." Less than a century old, that recipe, Powerscourt. Maybe we should try to make it some day.'

'Doubtless somebody already has,' said Powerscourt. 'Sir Pericles, could I ask you a favour? Could I ask you to cast your eye or perhaps your palate over the Colville products and let me know if any of them are suspect?'

'With pleasure,' replied Freme. 'I presume time is not on your side, Powerscourt. How soon would you like to come back for my report?'

'Could I say in three days? All that tasting must be a time-consuming business. And could I beg you one further favour on my return?'

'Of course,' said Freme.

'Could we have another of your splendid recipes on my return visit?'

Sir Pericles laughed. 'Oh, yes, we can. I've got plenty more of those.'

4

Powerscourt found Lady Lucy in a very troubled state when he returned home from Freme and his recipes. Even the arrival of Johnny Fitzgerald did not appear to be enough to calm her spirits. Fitzgerald was Powerscourt's oldest friend and companion in arms. They had served together in the Army in India and Johnny had worked on almost all of Powerscourt's investigations since. Johnny was just under six feet tall with bright blue eyes that often danced with mischief or merriment.

'Oh, Francis, it's all too terrible,' Lady Lucy began, 'that poor family. And those poor children. I don't know what we're going to do!'

'Hold on a moment, my love,' said her husband, 'take it slowly. Which family? Whose children? What might we have to do?' He smiled a smile of welcome at his friend.

Lady Lucy felt that she might fall victim to one of those male conspiracies where the men look knowingly at each other and you can hear them say 'Women!' without actually opening their lips.

'Sorry,' she said, and stared firmly at the painting of one of her ancestors on the wall above the fireplace for a moment. 'You remember I said I had a cousin who was married into some part of the Colvilles? And that she had a rather disagreeable husband called Timothy Barrington White?'

'I do recall that. I remember now. I've been hearing horror

stories about this Barrington White every now and again for most of our married life.'

'Well,' said Lady Lucy, 'he's really done it this time. You know how he fell in and out of jobs all the time. Eventually my cousin Millicent, Milly we always call her, persuaded one of the Colvilles to give him a job in the wine business. I think he had to look after that enormous gin distillery they have near Hammersmith. I don't know what exactly went on but something really bad must have happened. You see, the Colvilles fired him.'

'I can't think it's a very strenuous job, looking after a gin distillery these days,' said Johnny Fitzgerald with a knowing air. 'You put the stuff in, mix it all about, wait a bit and put it into those funny bottles.'

Lady Lucy was not sure that it was as easy as all that. 'What's more, there was a terrible row with Randolph and Cosmo Colville when they fired him.'

'I always thought they looked after their people,' said Powerscourt, 'those Colvilles and the other wine merchants. Loyalty a great premium, take care of the staff, *noblesse oblige*, all that sort of thing.'

'The point is this,' said Lady Lucy, feeling that the conversation was beginning to drift away from her, 'there was this tremendous row. The Colvilles told Terrible Timothy that he'd never work in the wine trade in England ever again. They even refused to pay his last month's wages. And they've got no money, no money of their own, that family. I mean, Milly did have some money, but I think Timothy got through that fairly quickly at the start of their marriage. And they've got three children under five. What's poor Milly going to do? I must go and see her, Francis, they only live in West Kensington, it won't take long to get there.'

As Lady Lucy hurried off to fetch her coat and hat Johnny Fitzgerald opened one of the Powerscourt cupboards and pulled out a bottle of Fleurie. 'I was talking to a man this very day and he asked me about my habits with wine, Johnny.

I said that I bought it and my best friend drank it. Things don't seem to have changed.'

Johnny settled himself into the deepest armchair and suggested that Powerscourt fill him in on the details of the case. Two glasses later he knew as much as his friend.

'This silence business, Francis,' he said, 'do you think there's a woman behind it? Or maybe it's a scandal. If there was some catastrophe about to fall on the house of Colville maybe the only way to put a stop to it is to say nothing at all. If you keep it up long enough, of course, there won't be any question of you speaking out because you won't be here. Maybe you could take the scandal with you to the grave and keep it there.'

'I plan to go up to Norfolk to see the place where it all happened, Johnny. Maybe I'll get a better sense of it all up there.'

'And what would you like me to do, Francis? The latest bird book can wait a while. I've finished the text and it's with the publishers now.' In recent years Johnny had found a profitable and enjoyable occupation as an author and expert on the birds of England and Europe. He had even held conversations recently with his publishers about the possibility of the Birds of India.

Powerscourt grinned at his friend. 'Do you remember that earlier case we had years ago about the forgers and the art world? On that occasion you managed to infiltrate what you might call the underworld of the art business, the porters, the drivers, the men who carry the stuff round at auctions. I think you should do the same with the Colvilles and the wine business. Make friends with these fellows. See what they have to say about their employers. If there are any scandals at Colvilles, these people will know more about it than the people in the boardroom.'

'It will be a pleasure, Francis. Mind you, I hope these fellows don't have the head for drink some of those art people did. Prolonged exposure to them and their drinking haunts could be very bad for the health. I'll get on to it straight away.'

While he waited for Lady Lucy to return later that evening, Powerscourt wondered if reticence had stopped her drawing the obvious conclusion to the travails of Milly Barrington White. For while the husband's loss of job and loss of income was very serious, there was one other point that he felt sure Lucy must have seen. Timothy Barrington White, present at the wedding, had a very real motive for wanting to kill Randolph Colville. The undesirable husband was more than a wedding guest, he was also a murder suspect.

Shortly before lunch the next day Georgina Nash was waiting for Powerscourt in the church of St Peter's, Brympton. She was tall, with light brown hair rather than the flaming red of her daughter and pale blue eyes that looked as if they had been weeping a lot.

'Mrs Nash,' said Powerscourt, 'how very kind of you to meet me here and guide me round where it all happened. It must be very painful for you.'

She just managed a smile. 'If there's anything we can do to help, Lord Powerscourt, we're more than willing. Now, let me show you the church.'

She led the way into the empty building. The door creaked slightly on its hinges. The ropes of the bell ringers were tethered neatly at one end. All the box pews but one had their doors carefully closed. There were fresh flowers around the altar. On Powerscourt's left as they advanced up the nave was a stone effigy covered with some dark substance. Georgina Nash noticed Powerscourt's look.

'Willoughby and the vicar think it's bats up above doing the damage,' she said, 'but we sent one of the stable boys up before the wedding and he couldn't see any bats at all. Maybe they've left by this time of year. Anyway, Lord Powerscourt,' she stopped at the steps before the altar, 'it's a perfectly ordinary church. At this point it was still a perfectly ordinary wedding. The groom's side were on the right, we were on the left. The organist behaved himself up there in his organ most of the time, though he did slip in one or two awful modern pieces before Emily arrived. She was a little late, Emily, but she looked so beautiful. I'm not going to desecrate the church by saying what I think about our evangelical vicar, I'll leave you to work it out on your own. The service took about half an hour.'

'Did you notice anything unusual, any strange people you'd never seen before, that sort of thing?'

Georgina Nash was leading them out of the church now and towards the great house. 'Well,' she said, 'I hadn't seen most of those Colvilles before, if that's what you mean. There wasn't anybody looking out of place or anything. They were all properly dressed and so on. Mind you, Lord Powerscourt, if you were a murderer, now I come to think about it, a wedding would be a good place to choose. One half of the people would assume you belonged to the other side, and the other half would think the opposite. A Nash would think you must be a Colville and a Colville would think you must be a Nash.'

They were past the yew trees now, advancing towards the great Jacobean façade. Powerscourt found himself counting the tall pepper pot chimneys and stopped when he reached fifteen.

'There was the usual jostling around just outside the church,' Georgina Nash went on, 'lots of kisses and embraces and congratulations.' She stopped suddenly and Powerscourt saw the tears in her eyes. Georgina Nash took two very deep breaths and continued. 'It must have taken about ten or fifteen minutes for everybody to make their way to the garden at the back of the house. You know how it is at weddings, Lord Powerscourt, people are always stopping to chat to their friends and generally milling about.'

By this time she had ushered them both into the garden with the broken fountain that had played its part in the wedding days before.

'Did you have a time planned for the guests to stay out here chatting, an hour perhaps, something like that?' Powerscourt was counting yet more chimneys.

'Oh yes,' said Georgina Nash, bending down to pick up a pigeon's wing from the immaculate grass. 'Really, why the gardeners can't be bothered to bend down and pick up this rubbish I don't know. It was the same with the fountain. Three times before Emily's big day I asked them to mend it. They never did. It's too bad. Sorry, Lord Powerscourt, I've diverted myself. Where was I? Ah yes, timetable, that's what we were talking about. Willoughby and I reckoned half an hour should be enough for a couple of glasses of champagne and for people to loosen up a little. It seemed to be about right.'

'Did you have a seating plan for the Long Gallery?' asked Powerscourt.

'How very curious that you too should ask about seating plans, Lord Powerscourt. That young policeman, Inspector Cooper I think he was called, he looked about fifteen years old, he was obsessed with seating plans. Anyway, we did have one. We had a couple of discreet blackboards set up out here with the plans pinned to them and more on the way to the Gallery itself.'

Powerscourt resolved to leave the question of the fifteen-year-old Detective Inspector till later. He felt Georgina Nash could be sidetracked very easily from the question in hand.

She was leading them back to the gravel drive in front of the house and the main entrance. 'Forgive me, Mrs Nash, before we go into the house, was there anything unusual going on while the guests were drinking their champagne on the lawn? Any strangers moving about, that sort of thing?'

Georgina Nash stopped in front of a great timber door that opened into the interior of Brympton Hall. 'Not that I know of,' she said. 'Up till this point and a little longer, there was absolutely nothing unusual about Emily's wedding. Nothing. The horrors came later.'

She led them into the Great Hall, once the heart of the house, now dominated by an enormous double staircase leading to

the first floor. A series of eighteenth-century Norfolk gentlemen, famed perhaps in their own county rather more than in
the country at large, lined the walls. Carved wooden figures
adorned the stairs, a soldier with musket and powder flasks,
a gentleman in hose, a bearded soldier with slashed breeches
and a two-handed sword, a kilted Highlander and a Cossack.

'It's absolutely splendid,' said Powerscourt, inspecting one
of the Norfolk grandees in a scarlet coat.

'I suppose it is,' said Georgina Nash. 'If you actually live
here, of course, you get used to it and you begin to wonder
after a while how so much dust manages to settle on and
around this staircase.

'Now then, back to business, Lord Powerscourt. We had
two more seating plans on display on either side of the stairs
so people could have a check before they reached the Long
Gallery.'

She led the way up to the first floor. 'It's all quite simple
from here on,' she said. 'Once they were up here we took them
through this little spot we call the anteroom and into the Long
Gallery itself.' Powerscourt was enchanted by the room, over
a hundred and fifty feet long, great windows looking out over
the grass, a rich and elaborate ceiling. It must, he thought, be
one of the finest Long Galleries in the kingdom.

'Mrs Nash,' he said, 'I have had an account from the lawyers of what happened here that day. All I would ask is that
you tell me everything you can remember about the time
immediately before and immediately after the murder.'

'And then I could go? I could meet you down in the gardens
perhaps? That would be very kind, Lord Powerscourt.' She
paused and stared down the room. 'All the tables were laid
out up here, of course. They looked lovely. Every place had a
name on the table in front of it. I was trying to mix them up,
the Colvilles and the Nashes and their friends.' She stopped
again and fiddled with her hair. 'I remember feeling irritated
that the people weren't moving away from this entrance here
and up to the far end of the Long Gallery. There was a great

crush in this area until one of the footmen began ushering people up the room. I think the sun went in briefly. I remember thinking how improbably blonde Augusta Nash's hair was and how improbably handsome her brother Percy was. He'd just become a lieutenant in the Norfolk Regiment and he was wearing his scarlet jacket and black trousers. Who am I, Lord Powerscourt,' Georgina Nash managed a bright smile, 'to fall for a soldier at my age! After that, it all becomes rather a blur, I'm afraid. Willoughby telling me what had happened, the terrible silence while people played with their food. They felt, I think, that it would be rude to eat it, in those circumstances, and that it would be rude not to eat it. So, most of them fiddled about with this rather splendid fare. Nobody wanted to talk much, they were all too shocked, and every now and then somebody would launch a conversational boat out on to the pond, as it were, only for it to be engulfed in the surrounding quiet. Then the policemen came and we all had to wait until they had questioned everybody before we could leave. Willoughby is saying he'll never set foot in the Long Gallery again. He's even talking of selling the Hall.'

Powerscourt felt that Georgina Nash would be better away from this place with its awful memories. 'You have been most kind, Mrs Nash, and most helpful. If you'd like to take a turn about the garden I'll join you very shortly. By the way, you wouldn't by any chance have one of those seating plans left, would you? It might be helpful.'

She smiled. 'I put one aside for you, Lord Powerscourt. I shall have it with me when we meet in the garden.'

Powerscourt strolled slowly up the room. He noticed that you could see very clearly what was happening in the garden, and wondered if the same was true the other way round. He stared regretfully at the splendid ceiling, knowing that under normal circumstances he would have spent far longer examining it. One thing in particular interested him. Was the route he had just taken via the Grand Staircase the only way in? At the far end of the Long Gallery, the opposite end to the Great Hall and the double staircase, was a door which opened out on to a set of steps that led down into the garden. An enterprising murderer might have come in this way and hidden himself away until he could be lost in the crowds. And as he followed what must have been the last journey of Randolph Colville through the Peter the Great room and into the state bedroom on the corner of the Hall, he found another set of stairs leading out on to the gardens on the other side of the house from the fountain. Here was another way in or out for any wedding guest who happened to be a murderer.

Two things had worried Powerscourt about this case from the start. He found that his brain seemed to come up with new answers when he least expected it. The first related to the silence of Cosmo Colville. The second, and the one that assailed him now, had to do with the gun. The prosecution, Charles Augustus Pugh had been adamant on this point, were sure that they could prove that it was Randolph Colville's own gun. Powerscourt's initial reaction was that they might be putting two and two and two together and making six. Pugh himself was moderately hopeful that he could open some doubts in the jury's mind in cross-examination, but he couldn't be sure. Suppose, Powerscourt's brain suggested to him, as he stood on the bottom steps of the staircase leading from the state bedroom with a couple of pigeons waddling across the grass in front of him, suppose it really was Randolph's gun. Why had he brought it? Did he intend to murder somebody at the wedding? Was he bringing it in self-defence? Defence of whose self, of his own, or of some member of his family's?

He made some detailed drawings in a small black notebook and headed round the house for a final chat with Mrs Colville. She handed him a seating plan, with the writing carried out in one of the most beautiful hands Powerscourt had ever seen.

'It's Ursula, Emily's sister, who does the handwriting, she's very artistic. Willougby thinks she could be famous one day.' Mrs Nash looked much more comfortable in her garden than she had in her house. 'I tell you one thing that might be helpful, Lord Powerscourt,' she said. 'I think that young policeman had a seating plan, or maybe it should be a standing plan, for where everybody was when the gun went off. He and his men took very careful statements from everybody here about exactly where they were at the time.'

'The policeman's name, I think you said, was Inspector Cooper. You don't know where I could find him?'

'He told us he could be found at Fakenham, but that he moved about a lot. Let me tell you something about Inspector Cooper, Lord Powerscourt. This is only female intuition, if you like. I have no evidence for it whatsoever. Willoughby told me some horrid barrister would rip me to shreds if I ever said it in a court of law.'

Mrs Nash paused once more, collecting her thoughts. Powerscourt waited.

'I don't believe he thought Cosmo did it, the murder, I mean. He came back here a couple of times after the wedding and I overheard him once telling his sergeant that they'd never persuade the boss that Cosmo hadn't done it. "Cosmo's going to hang," he said, "for something he didn't do." Those were his exact words.'

'How very interesting,' said Powerscourt, fascinated to hear of dissent in the ranks of the constabulary. 'That's very helpful. Thank you so much for everything, Mrs Nash. If there is anything else you remember, please let me know. I'm so grateful for your help this morning.'

Georgina Nash watched him go. She knew there was something she should have told him, something that had been niggling at the edge of her brain for days. When it came back she would send a telegram to Markham Square.

Alfred Davis was a very worried man. Ever since he became general manager of Colville and Sons five years before, he had been worried. And this morning, as he leaned over the balcony on the first floor of the Colville Headquarters, north of Oxford Street, and watched his clerks settle down for another day's work, he was even more worried than usual. The clerks' days, he told himself, were often difficult. Alfred had, after all, begun his life with Colvilles as one of them. The accounts might not balance at the end of the day. Some minor arithmetical slip could plunge some mighty calculation involving port revenue into a spin from which it might never recover. But when these clerks put on their coats and hats at the end of the day and went home, they left their troubles at their desks. Alfred's often pursued him into the night. As he lay beside his wife of twenty-eight years, her best nightcap wrapped tightly round her head, his worries would rise up from the dark and pursue him through the night hours. Continuity of supply, that was always a problem. If the Madeira ran out, there simply wouldn't be any more customers for it. Reliable shipping. Almost daily in the newspapers Alfred read stories of strikes and lockouts and industrial disputes running through the world's shipping lines like some contagious disease. Fraudsters and con men. Alfred had been in the business too long not be aware of the dangers of some plausible rogue turning up with an offer of Bordeaux or sherry at unrepeatable prices. Rarely did the samples match up to the deliveries once the contract had been signed. What tasted clean and fruity in the trial bottles had turned into sour vinegar by the time the deliveries rolled into the Colvilles' warehouses.

And now, as he turned from the balcony and walked back the few paces to his office, there were new worries. Opinion at Colvilles' Headquarters was divided on the likely impact on business of the murder of one senior member of the family and the arrest of another on the charge of murdering his brother. The younger, jollier employees thought the publicity would be good for trade. One of these cheerful souls had even heard a man in a public house the day before ordering two glasses of murderer's claret and being served immediately without a question being asked. But the older members of the firm were pessimistic. They reasoned that people associated a glass of champagne or Madeira or sherry with fellowship and good cheer, with companionship and shared pleasure. The drinking public, they maintained, did not wish to be reminded of murder every time they opened a bottle of something.

And what Alfred realized, far more acutely than his fellows, was that the strange events at the Colville Nash wedding had ripped the heart out of the firm's management. Old Walter, still the chairman, had virtually lost his senses, Alfred had heard, and had now taken to his bed. Certainly he hadn't been seen north of Oxford Street since the disaster. Nathaniel hadn't had anything to do with the firm for years. Randolph Colville could issue no instructions from beyond the grave and Cosmo, confined to Pentonville, could do no better. The younger Colvilles had neither the experience nor the training to make a valuable contribution to the business yet. So who was left? Who would have to carry the burden in the heat of the day? There was only one candidate, Alfred Davis told himself. He looked sadly into the mirror on his wall and found the lucky man.

Powerscourt found Inspector Cooper in Fakenham and took him for tea in the town's best hotel. The Inspector was working on a more orthodox case now, a burglary and break-in at one of Norfolk's finest Georgian houses. There was, he told Powerscourt, little chance of finding either the villains or the stolen goods, which he believed had disappeared into the welcoming embrace of London's antique dealers the day after the crime. The Inspector had never met a private investigator before. He had, he told his new acquaintance, followed one or two of his earlier cases, particularly the one in the West Country cathedral which had featured heavily in the local press. But he was not prepared for Powerscourt's opening question.

'I gather, Inspector, that you don't think Cosmo Colville killed his brother.'

The Inspector blushed. 'What gave you that idea?' he stammered after a second or two.

'I can't tell you that, I'm afraid. I can't, as the newspapermen are so fond of telling us, I can't reveal my sources. But it's true, isn't it?'

Albert Cooper thought about what might happen to him if his superiors in the force thought he was giving comfort and indeed assistance to the other side. He thought about his mother and his sisters, dependent on his salary. He thought of his girl, Charlotte, so pretty and so quick when they took their walks together on Sunday afternoons. He thought of the proposal of marriage he was hoping to make on Christmas Eve. Could he throw all that away? For one thing stood out about the young man. It came from his mother and the teachers at his school who had liked him so much. He was a good boy, a regular attender at church on Sundays. Every fibre in his being wanted to tell the truth. He had never expected to be put to the test here over English breakfast tea and scones in the front room of the George Hotel.

Powerscourt waited. He watched the various emotions flicker over the Inspector's face. 'Let me try another question. I have the seating plan from Brympton Hall showing where everybody was to sit down at the wedding feast. I believe you have one or two more diagrams, seating or standing diagrams showing where people were in the garden and just before the shot was fired. Let me put it another way, if I may. Is it your opinion that Cosmo didn't kill his brother, or do you know it? Do you have some hard evidence to his guilt or innocence?'

Only two days before, after Cosmo had been charged, the young man had taken out his plans once again, not the one indicating where everybody sat down, but the two before, one showing where the guests had been in the garden, and the other showing where they were just before the shot was fired. Taken together they were, he thought, the finest work

51

of detection he had managed since he joined the force. He had looked at them again rather sadly and put them back in his drawer. He looked up at Powerscourt now with a look of appeal in his eyes.

'It's opinion, it's a hunch,' he said quietly. Surely he couldn't get into trouble for saying that. Chief Inspector Weir might tell him off but he wouldn't fire him for saying such a thing.

'Very well,' said Powerscourt, taking pity on the young man, 'let us leave it at that for now. My investigation is still in its early stages. Maybe I shall find some other evidence. But let me ask you one final question, Inspector.'

Cooper nodded miserably.

'Have you watched a man hang? Have you watched that dismal procession early in the morning, the hangman, the criminal, the reluctant vicar, the governor of the prison taking what will be, for one of them, the last walk of his life?'

Inspector Cooper shook his head.

'Pity that,' said Powerscourt. 'I've always thought that all policemen involved in murder cases should be taken to witness it at first hand. Now then, Inspector. If I find, close to this trial, that I am no further forward than I am today, may I come back and speak to you again? I wouldn't want you to have the death of an innocent man on your conscience. There are loyalties higher than those to the police service, I can assure you.'

Albert Cooper looked at him desperately. Was there to be no peace? It seemed easier to agree for now. 'Of course you can come and see me again if you wish. I can't stop you. But I can't guarantee that I will say anything other than I have said today.'

'That's fine,' said Powerscourt. 'Now then, enough of this serious business. More tea? Scone with jam and cream? A slice of this excellent chocolate cake?'

5

Questions about legal procedure were racing through Powerscourt's mind as his train took him back to London. Suppose he made no progress in this investigation before the matter came to trial. He thought they could demand access to police documents as part of the defence case. His memory of court procedures told him they could cross-examine Inspector Cooper if he was called as witness for the prosecution. Could they subpoena his various seating plans, for Powerscourt was sure the young man had at least three of them? That would cause a sensation in court. He could hear Pugh's voice now, echoing round the Old Bailey. 'I put it to you, Inspector Cooper, that you do not believe the man in the dock, Cosmo Colville, is guilty of this murder. Look at him before you speak. Is that not the case?' 'Tell me, Inspector, for I find this scarcely credible, that you, the principal investigating officer, are not sure my client the defendant murdered his brother?' Powerscourt felt sure that Pugh would not suggest that Inspector Cooper believed Cosmo was innocent. It would be enough to suggest that he was uncertain. Surely that would be enough to sow a doubt so grave that it would lead the jury to an acquittal. He heard Pugh again: 'Call Inspector Cooper's superior officer!'

And what, he said to himself, as they reached the outskirts of the capital, would happen to Inspector Cooper? Would he be dismissed from the service? Would his superiors forbid him from giving evidence? Could they save him from disgrace by leaking the story to the newspapers? 'Shame on you, Norfolk police!' the headline might scream. 'Brave policeman defies superiors to see justice done and is fired by Chief Constable!' Powerscourt suspected that the police were as closed a society as the regiments in the British Army. They would close ranks behind their inferiors and their superiors alike. Inspector Cooper would be ruined. He prayed he would never have to go back to Fakenham to speak to the young man again. He wondered if he would try to bring him to court and to the end of his career if he had to. At least Cooper would still be alive. In the meantime, he, Powerscourt, must write to Charles Augustus Pugh.

Powerscourt found a note from Sir Pericles Freme awaiting him on the hall table in Markham Square. 'Definitely something odd going on with Colville wine,' he read, 'need earlier years' supply before being able to come to a definite conclusion. Have found splendid recipe involving dried lemon peel for you next time you come. Regards, Freme.'

What in heaven's name were people doing making wine with lemon peel, Powerscourt asked himself as he went up the stairs to the first-floor drawing room. He found Lady Lucy hard at work writing letters at the little table by the windows. A pile of envelopes, all carefully addressed in her immaculate hand, were awaiting the attentions of the postman.

'Francis!' She smiled with pleasure and kissed her husband. 'How nice to see you. How was Norfolk and that poor Mrs Nash of Brympton Hall?'

'I think Mrs Nash will pull through in the end,' said Powerscourt, 'but they're all terribly upset. The husband is even thinking of selling up and moving away apparently.'

'Good Lord,' said Lady Lucy, for whom moving house was one of life's most serious enterprises, never to be undertaken lightly, 'how truly terrible for them.'

'But tell me, my love,' said Powerscourt, 'what of your cousin Milly and the villainous husband?'

Lady Lucy looked grave. 'It's even worse that we thought, Francis. It's frightful. Husband Timothy rejoiced that Randolph Colville was dead. "I'm absolutely delighted," he said to Milly, "and with any luck that other bugger Cosmo won't be far behind him. Best news I've heard in ages. One shot through the heart, the other about to feel the noose round his neck. Excellent!"'

'How did he know Randolph was shot through the heart? I thought the wedding guests were only told he was dead.'

'I expect it will have leaked out,' said Lady Lucy sadly, 'and then the husband of the year went off to celebrate in some drinking club he belongs to near Paddington station. He said he was going to drink to the end of the Colvilles.'

'And what about money, Lucy? Do they have any?'

'Not as far as Milly can find out, they haven't. That's why I'm writing all these letters, Francis. I want to see what the family feeling is about lending them some money while times are bad. We may have to call a family meeting.'

'Really,' said Powerscourt, who had never actually seen one of these mass gatherings of Lucy's tribe in action. He wondered if they would have to hire Lord's Cricket Ground or the Royal Albert Hall to accommodate all the relations. 'How will you stop the husband making off with all the money you raise?'

'I've asked them all about that too,' said Lady Lucy. 'Somebody must have an answer. There's one other thing, I nearly forgot. Milly claims she's sure she saw a man at the wedding reception who wasn't English. She didn't think he could be a Nash or a Colville.'

'Well, the wine business extends all over Europe. There are bound to have been some foreigners there on the Colville side.'

'I told Milly I'd pass it on, that's all, Francis. I don't suppose there's anything in it.'

Powerscourt did not reply. But as the hours went by that evening he found himself thinking about it more and more.

This was the first indication so far that an alien body, a person not a Colville and not a Nash, had been at the scene and could have been the murderer. He wondered if the young Inspector Colville had discovered the same thing, if somewhere on his seating plans there was a guest marked as X or Y because nobody knew their name. Was that why the detective had decided that Cosmo Colville was not the killer?

Powerscourt gasped the following morning as he read the Obituary columns of *The Times*. Lady Lucy looked at him sharply. This wasn't normal behaviour for her Francis. 'Is there anything wrong, my love? Something in the paper that's upset you?'

Powerscourt held up his hand. 'Just give me a minute, Lucy, till I've finished this.' When he had finished reading the obituary he folded the newspaper carefully and put it at the back of the table.

'There's been another death, Lucy, another Colville gone to meet his maker.'

'How sad, that's two in less than a month. Who is it this time?'

'It's Walter, the old boy, grandfather of the groom at the wedding, father of Randolph, one of the patriarchs of the Colville wine business.'

'You don't think there's anything suspicious, do you, Francis?'

'God knows. They do say he was terribly cut up about the wedding and all that followed. A fellow told me the other day he'd aged ten years since the murder.'

'Poor old man,' said Lady Lucy. 'If Randolph hadn't been killed his father would still be alive today. The Brympton Hall murderer has claimed another victim.'

The walls of Pentonville seemed virtually impregnable to Powerscourt as he made his way there that afternoon for a meeting with Cosmo Colville. Built in the middle of the last century, the prison had not been notorious until it took over from Newgate the role of Hangman's Prison in 1902. And when they knocked Newgate down, Powerscourt remembered, they replaced it with the Old Bailey, thus ensuring that the courtrooms and the wigs of the lawyers replaced the noose and the drop of the gallows. Indeed the very gallows that had despatched the condemned at Newgate were dismantled and recreated plank by awful plank at Pentonville. As Powerscourt waited in a little office looking out over the exercise yard he wondered if the prisoners still had to do duty all day on the tread wheel, turning a great wheel with their feet time after time after time for no purpose whatsoever. He remembered that some unlucky prisoners had to turn the wheel two thousand times before they were allowed to eat their breakfast. Sadistic warders were known to enforce a daily regimen of twenty thousand turns on their victims.

A middle-aged guard brought Cosmo Colville into the room and sat him down opposite Powerscourt at a mean prison table with mean prison chairs. The guard retreated to stand just outside the door. Prison clothes did little for Cosmo. It was hard to imagine that this prisoner who now looked like all the other prisoners had in earlier times eaten at London's most fashionable restaurants and danced at the grandest hotels on Park Lane and Piccadilly. He made no acknowledgement of Powerscourt's presence, not a look, not a nod, not a smile. It was as if he had completed the long retreat into his own head. Cosmo Colville had fair hair and pale brown eyes and a wide forehead. His expression, all through the interview, was one of resolute obstinacy. Powerscourt had talked to one of Colville's best friends the day before the interview. 'I was very gentle with him,' the friend had said. 'His wife and his children and his other friends are all being gentle with him. Maybe it's time somebody took a hard line with Cosmo, reminded him of what may happen. What probably will happen if he doesn't start talking.'

'Thank you so much for seeing me,' Powerscourt began, ignoring the fact that Colville had little choice about being brought before him. 'I thought I would talk to you about what happens here, if you don't want to talk.'

There was no movement of any kind from Cosmo. 'The first man to be hanged here was killed in October six years ago,' Powerscourt went on. 'John Macdonald he was, a twenty-four-year-old Scotsman. He was a costermonger and petty thief, this Macdonald. He and his partner in crime had a falling-out over the proceeds of a robbery. His victim had his head almost cut off from his body by Macdonald's knife. Then the trapdoor opened here early one morning and John Macdonald entered the history books as the first man to be hanged in Pentonville. Do you want to end up like that, Mr Colville? If you don't speak soon, you will enter the same history books as the man who swung because he wouldn't talk. Is that what you want?'

Cosmo Colville didn't even look at him. He spoke not a word.

'Then there was a man called Henry Williams,' Powerscourt continued his catalogue of murder and retribution. 'He thought his wife had been unfaithful to him while he was away fighting with his regiment in the Boer War. When he came back he took their little daughter up to London with him. That evening he put her in bed with her favourite doll beside her. When she was asleep he cut her throat and wrapped her little body in the Union flag. To the end he protested that he had done it because he loved her and could not bear his daughter living with her mother and a man who was not her father. Henry Pierrepoint, the executioner, said Williams was the bravest man he ever hanged. But courage didn't do him any good, did it, Mr Colville? Williams was still left dancing on the air. So will you be if you don't say something soon. I don't think that bit lasts very long, the legs flailing about, the neck about to break, everything about to go dark, perhaps a scream or two. What do you say, Mr Colville?'

The only sound in the little room was the distant clanging of some prison bars. The prisoner kept his counsel.

'Then there was a man called Charles Stowe. He became infatuated with a barmaid. When the girl refused to have anything to do with him he went to the Lord Nelson public house where she worked late one night and grabbed her. Then he stabbed her a number of times. The interesting thing about Stowe is that we know how the hangmen did it. They were brothers called Billington from Lancashire, these hangmen. They always took details of the height and the weight of the prisoners in the condemned cell and used them to work out how big the drop should be. Stowe was five foot four and eleven stone so they gave him a drop of seven feet two inches. I suspect they'd left themselves quite a margin of error, Mr Colville, I expect six feet six would have been more than enough but they weren't taking any chances. If you don't speak before your trial I expect the hangman will be along to have you weighed and measured in your turn. Let me see, I'd say you're about five feet ten and around twelve stone or so. Seven feet drop be all right for you?'

Silence reigned in the little room. Powerscourt could hear the guard hopping from foot to foot outside the door. He wondered how much longer he had left.

'Some of those hanged in Pentonville have killed more than one person,' Powerscourt tried once more. 'Let's take chemist's assistant Arthur Devereux. He and his wife Beatrice had a little boy and not long after that they had twins. Money was very tight. He wasn't paid very much, our Arthur, so he decided on drastic measures. He bought a large tin trunk and a bottle of chloroform and morphine, which he persuaded Beatrice to give to the twins and then take herself. He told her it was cough medicine. When they were dead he put them in the trunk and sealed the lid with glue to keep it airtight. He had the trunk sent off to a warehouse in Harrow and moved away with his son to a new address. But he'd reckoned without the mother-in-law. She didn't believe his story that they'd all gone on holiday. She learnt that a removal company van from Harrow had called at the house. She set off for Harrow where she found the warehouse and the trunk and the three bodies. Devereux was traced to Coventry and tried to persuade the jury at his trial that Beatrice had killed the twins and then committed suicide. He had found them all and panicked, sending them all to the warehouse. He was not believed. His hangman, Henry Pierrepoint, recorded that Devereux stood five feet eleven and weighed eleven stone four. Pierrepoint gave him a drop of six feet six inches.'

Powerscourt wondered if Colville had lost his voice. There was no reply, no response, nothing at all. Cosmo might as well have been a statue. Powerscourt pulled a book out of his pocket and began to read:

> '"He did not wear his scarlet coat,
> For blood and wine are red,
> And blood and wine were on his hands
> When they found him with the dead,
> The poor dead woman whom he loved,
> And murdered in her bed."'

'This is an account of the last days and hours of a man called Charles Thomas Wooldridge, sometime Trooper of the Royal Horse Guards, executed HM Prison, Reading, Berkshire, 7th July 1896.'

Not a muscle moved in Cosmo's face. Powerscourt read on until he came to the morning of the execution. In the corridor outside a group of prisoners were being escorted to some unknown destination.

> '"At six o'clock we cleaned our cells,
> At seven all was still,
> But the sough and swing of a mighty wing
> The prison seemed to fill,

For the Lord of Death with icy breath
Had entered in to kill."'

Even the Lord of Death drew no reaction from Cosmo
Colville. Powerscourt saw that the prison warder had tiptoed right up to the door and seemed to be listening to the
words.

'"And as one sees most fearful things
In the crystal of a dream,
We saw the greasy hempen rope
Hooked to the blackened beam,
And heard the prayer the hangman's snare
Strangled into a scream."'

Still there was no reaction from Cosmo. The man must have
a heart like a stone. There was one last passage Powerscourt
hoped might draw out some reaction.

'"The Warders strutted up and down,
And kept their herd of brutes,
Their uniforms were spick and span,
And they wore their Sunday suits,
But we knew the work they had been at,
By the quicklime on their boots."'

The warder had opened the door a fraction to catch the end
of the poem. Powerscourt carried on reading. Far off, deep
inside the prison, a man was screaming.

'"For where a grave had opened wide,
There was no grave at all:
Only a stretch of mud and sand
By the hideous prison-wall,
And a little heap of burning lime,
That the man should have his pall."'

Powerscourt looked up again into the face of Cosmo Colville. There was nothing there, only a flicker in the eyes that might have been contempt. Cosmo moved his chair back from the table.

> '"For he has a pall, this wretched man,
> Such as few men can claim:
> Deep down below a prison-yard,
> Naked for greater shame, He lies, with
>   fetters on each foot,
> Wrapt in a sheet of flame!"'

Still there was no reaction from Cosmo. Powerscourt could have been reading from the Book of Job for all the impact he was having.

> '"And all the while the burning lime
> Eats flesh and bone away,
> It eats the brittle bone by night,
> And the soft flesh by day,
> It eats the flesh and bones by turns,
> But it eats the heart alway."'

'Do you fancy that, Cosmo?' Powerscourt asked suddenly. 'The burning lime? Your soft flesh? Fetters on each foot?'

At last Cosmo Colville spoke for the first and last time between his arrest and his appearance in the Old Bailey. 'That's *The Ballad of Reading Gaol*,' he said, 'by Oscar Wilde. I never liked the bugger when he was alive. I like the bugger even less now he's dead.' He rose from his chair and opened the door. The last words Powerscourt heard him say were: 'Can I go back to my cell now, please?'

In his warehouse by the Thames the Alchemist was having a further wine tasting. He slid his special corkscrew down the side of three bottles of red with strange labels. He poured a small amount of liquid into three separate glasses on his table by the window. He tried each one carefully, leaving an interval of a couple of minutes between each tasting. He was humming the Overture from *Così Fan Tutte* as he worked. The Alchemist had tickets for Mozart's opera in a couple of days' time. It had always been one of his favourites. He made notes in his black book. BX LG68 AG15 was the winner of this particular session. Now the Alchemist would have to go to France to supervise the blending of this particular bastard and see that the barrels and the labels were properly French. He would also organize the shipping of the final consignment of phoney claret to its ultimate destination in London. The Alchemist had done this many times before. He still had some more pre-phylloxera wines to create. He hoped he could be back in time for the opera. And, as he contemplated his own cut from this consignment, he thought he might be able to buy a better seat. Maybe he would watch Fiordiligi and Dorabella and their lovers from the luxury of his very own box.

Emily Nash, daughter of Georgina and Willoughby Nash of Brympton Hall, was not a bad person. Certainly in the months leading up to her wedding she had behaved very well. Perhaps it would have been fairer to say she had behaved well most of the time. She may have been too romantic for her own good, Emily. She may have dreamed more often about glittering futures than was good for her. Her imagination may have run on champagne when it would have run better on old-fashioned Indian tea. But her impulses didn't often win her over completely. Consider the case of her sick grandfather. This elderly gentleman had come to stay in his son's house and fallen ill. After a couple of days his condition deteriorated and his relatives wondered if he would ever leave Brympton alive. A full-time nurse was hired to help look after him. When she disappeared Emily volunteered to take her place until a replacement could be found. The grandfather's mind was going. His memory might be sharp in the morning and disappear after lunch. He was losing control of his limbs and his faculties. For a while Emily told herself how brave, how considerate she was being, a junior version of Florence Nightingale in the Fens. Her parents were proud of her when they could drag their attention away from the old man who had come to their house to die. They found little time to praise their daughter who was helping him live through the last days.

The replacement nurse was slow to arrive. Days passed. Emily's mother helped out when she could but she had other duties to fulfil. Anyway, Georgina Nash reckoned, Emily was doing such a good job she hardly needed any help at all. For some people the mantle of heroine and martyr sits happiest when they are being praised and thanked by all around them. The praise and the thanks seemed to Emily to decrease as time went by. Sometimes her parents didn't bother to thank her at all. She began to grow resentful, not towards her grandfather but towards her parents. She longed for her nursing days to finish so she could do something dramatic to celebrate her freedom.

The replacement nurse finally arrived. Almost at the same time her friend Tristram called, fresh from his duties as Colville representative in East Anglia. Tristram happened to have brought a number of samples of the firm's finest with him. Emily longed for her freedom, for a gesture of independence. It came as the sun was setting over the North Sea, lying in a grassy hollow behind the beach, the second bottle of champagne wedged in Tristram's boot.

Some weeks later she told her mother the results of her gesture of independence. She showed little remorse. If that first nurse hadn't walked out, and if they hadn't taken so long to find a replacement, Emily reasoned, then nothing like this would have happened. Georgina Nash thought about the girl's options. She was deeply shocked but found it hard to be very cross with her daughter. Looking back, they should have taken more trouble to find a replacement nurse for her father-in-law. Secretly she was thrilled at the prospect of a grandchild. It would roll away the years, having a little one in the Hall again, playing hide and seek as the child grew older, Willoughby and the grooms teaching him or her to ride, floating on the lake in a boat in high summer with the dragonflies dancing on the water.

'I don't suppose Tristram has offered to marry you,' Georgina said to her daughter, thinking how very unpleasant it might be to have that young man as an intimate member of her family.

'He said he wouldn't,' said Emily. 'I mean, I like Tristram well enough, but I'm not sure I'd want to spend the rest of my life with him.'

'Indeed,' said her mother firmly. 'Now, this is what we must do. I am going to put in train a great deal of social organization, dinner parties, dances, balls, everything I can think of. And you, my child, are going to have a whirlwind romance. You have to be bowled over as you have never been bowled over before. Remember always, you need to be at the altar in about six weeks' time. The young man must have the normal number of arms and legs, that sort of thing. Brains would be an advantage but are not essential. We do not have the time to indulge ourselves with good looks, but don't turn them down if they come your way. You must do anything, and I mean anything, Emily, to persuade a young man to marry you. And you must do it quickly.'

6

Sir Pericles Freme was clanking as he walked across the Powerscourt hall towards the Powerscourt dining room. Powerscourt himself, speeding down the stairs to meet his guest, thought he sounded rather like the milkman nearing the end of his round. The dining room was on the ground floor, looking out over Markham Square. There was a long Georgian table with elegant candles. The highlight of the room was a full-length portrait of one of Lady Lucy's ancestors, a general who had served in the American War of Independence. Lady Lucy's family always maintained that the work was by the hand of Sir Joshua Reynolds and certainly the painting did have something of the swagger and panache of another Reynolds soldier, Colonel Banastre Tarleton, in the National Gallery. Powerscourt had never been sure. Rhys, the Powerscourt butler, was waiting for instructions by the far side of the fireplace.

'Sir Pericles, how good of you to come,' said Powerscourt, directing his guest to a chair at the far end of the table. Freme carried out a brief inspection of the general on the wall, nodded as if in posthumous salute, and drew four bottles out of his bag.

'I changed my modus operandi halfway through this inquiry,' he began, in the manner of a man telling a friend he has changed his golf swing. 'That is to say, I decided it might be more illuminating to compare some Colville wines with

66

those of their fellow wine merchants rather than my earlier policy of comparing Colville bottles of today with Colville bottles of earlier years.'

'Now then,' Sir Pericles began fiddling about in his bag for a corkscrew, 'you might think that there is a risk attached to this new policy. How do we know that our other man is a man of probity, that what he calls claret actually is claret? What do you say to that, Powerscourt, eh?' The old soldier looked sternly at his host.

'I can only suppose that you are certain that your other claret is the real thing, if you can be certain? Forgive me, Sir Pericles, how many glasses do you think we need? Rhys here can bring them in directly.'

'Let's be on the safe side and say a dozen. And could we have some cold water? Now then, this house claret here,' he pointed to the bottle closest to him, 'comes from Berry Bros. & Rudd. It is the cheapest blend they sell. I have compared it with the same sort of wine from other reputable and rather expensive merchants and they all taste, more or less, the same.'

There was a loud plop as Sir Pericles opened his two bottles of claret in quick succession. Right on cue, Rhys slipped back into the room with the glasses and the water. Sir Pericles poured a small measure from each bottle into a couple of glasses.

'Now then,' he swirled the wine around in his glasses, 'people talk an awful lot of rot about wine, always have. *Imbibo, ergo sum.* Shouldn't be surprised if the bloody Romans hadn't warbled away in their best Latin about heads and bouquets and such nonsense. Probably picked it up from the Greeks. Dodgy morals, those Greeks, always thought so. But I digress. The thing to do, Powerscourt, is to remember what it tastes like. That's all. Then have a go at the other chap and see if you think they're from the same family. That's all we have to do. For God's sake don't talk about fruit.'

Raising his glass to the general on the wall, Sir Pericles took a slug of the Berry Bros. & Rudd glass and swallowed it. Powerscourt was relieved to see he hadn't spat it out on to the floor. He didn't think Lucy would have approved. There might not be many domestic implements not present in the Markham Square household, but spittoons, unfortunately on this occasion, were among them. Powerscourt followed suit. The second glass with the Colville wine followed fairly quickly afterwards.

'Now then, I'm not going to put words into your mouth, Powerscourt, but tell me what you think.' Sir Pericles began clearing his palate with a glass of water. Powerscourt paused for a moment.

'Well,' he said at last, feeling rather nervous, as if his history essay was being marked by the headmaster in person, 'there's definitely a difference. The Berry claret is smoother and maybe richer than the other one. The Colville wine tastes a bit rougher, in my opinion. Maybe the grapes were on the wrong side of the hill.'

'Well done, Powerscourt, I couldn't have put it better myself. The question we now have to ask ourselves is whether the Colville offering is a claret at all.' Sir Pericles took another quick glass of water and rummaged again in his bag. 'Just one more. On the assumption that the Berry claret is the real thing, we can, I think, safely hazard a guess that this other bottle which says it is a claret will also be a claret. Justerini & Brooks, round the corner from Berry's in St James's. Let me just pour a couple of glasses of that for us.'

Freme poured two more glasses. Powerscourt suddenly wondered if Johnny Fitzgerald, with his greater experience of quaffing wine in vast quantities, might not have been the better man for this particular job. Sir Pericles and Powerscourt took substantial sips of the latest offering from London's finest and put their glasses down at virtually the same time.

'Well?' said the little man.

'The same as the Berry one, I should say,' said Powerscourt, wiping his lips with his handkerchief. 'I don't mean it's exactly the same, but I should say it's as if they both went to the same school or were taught to sing by the same master.'

'Capital, we'll make a connoisseur out of you yet.' Sir Pericles peered briefly into his bag as if another half-dozen bottles were waiting inside. 'But you see our difficulty, the general difficulty in the authentication of wines. You and I both think that two of these bottles are claret and the other one probably isn't. Two other people might take a contrary view. We could pay to have some wine supremos from Bordeaux to give their view on the problem, but they might not agree either. Some of these so-called experts are always reluctant to taste wines blind because they will often get it wrong.'

'Tell me, Sir Pericles, what do you think the Colville wine actually is? Does it have any claret in there at all?'

'It's certainly a blend of something,' said Sir Pericles, 'maybe there's a bit of claret in there somewhere to give it a base. Then there's probably a whole lot of cheap red from Languedoc and may be a dash of Algerian if it lacks body. The blender will have to change his proportions every year to keep each year's taste as close as he can to the taste of the year before– even cheap Languedoc isn't going to be the same in 1908 as it was in 1907. They don't have a problem with the labels, they put their own on. The stuff is probably cooked up somewhere in the Médoc and shipped from there. It'll add to the authentic look if the wine has been parcelled up and sent over here by some dodgy shippers or merchants in or near Bordeaux.'

'Can we prove it? That it's not proper claret, I mean?' asked Powerscourt, thinking of Charles Augustus Pugh grilling some unfortunate wine merchant in the Old Bailey.

'Very difficult. Almost impossible,' said Sir Pericles, rubbing his hands together cheerfully. 'For every witness the defence calls to pronounce it a fake, the prosecution will counter with one who says that it is the real thing, maybe the real thing in a bad year, but still the real thing.'

'What about the money?' said Powerscourt as another train of thought struck him.

'What do you mean about the money?'

'Sorry, I was thinking. If we could show that Colvilles bought their supplies for a lot less than everybody else in the same year, mightn't that show that they weren't buying genuine claret?'

Sir Pericles stared at the three open bottles on the table. 'On the face of it, it would. But they would come back then with a different sort of argument. They buy in great bulk so they usually get a discount. Or they have just begun trading with a new firm in Bordeaux who offered an enormous discount on the first year's supply to win the contract. Or their suppliers were able to buy a lot of wine cheaply by waiting for the end of the season when prices always go down if it's not a good year. Always remember, most years are not good years. And,' Sir Pericles rummaged about in his bag once more, 'if you can persuade any of the money men who work for the wine merchants like the Colvilles, or even Berry Bros. & Rudd, to let you inspect their account books, I'll buy you your very own vineyard in the Médoc.'

'We don't seem to have made much progress, Sir Pericles,' said Powerscourt sadly. 'Nothing that would help us in court at any rate.'

'I wouldn't say that,' said Freme. 'You asked me to find out if there was anything suspicious about the Colville wines. I am happy to say there is, certainly about the claret. I shall continue my researches with various other Colville offerings. I shall ask around in the wine trade generally. Discreetly, of course. And now, before I take my leave, I promised you another recipe. This one,' he pulled a slim volume out of the side pocket of his bag, 'is the one with the lemon peel. It comes from *The Art and Mystery of Vintners and Wine Coopers*, 1692. "How to make Rhenish Wine: Take one handful of dried limon peels and put them into ten or twelve gallons of white wine, and put in one pint of damask rose water; then rowl it up and down, and lay it upright, and open the bung of it, and take a little branch of clary and let it steep twenty-four hours; and take it out and it will taste very well."'

'I cannot imagine what that would have tasted like, Sir Pericles, I shudder to think.'

'Let me leave you with something better, Lord Powerscourt. We were travelling earlier on the lower slopes of the claret mountain. This comes from the very summit and I commend it to you and your wife.' One last dip into the bag and Sir Pericles pulled out another bottle. 'Some people think that Lafite here is supreme among clarets, the crème de la crème.'

Powerscourt told Lady Lucy after Sir Pericles had left that he expected Johnny Fitzgerald to materialize in a couple of hours at most. He had always possessed an uncanny knack of knowing when his friend had some special sort of liquid in the house, as if he could smell it from the other side of London. Shortly before six o'clock there he was in the Powerscourt drawing room, his eye drawn like a magnet to the Lafite, recently promoted from the dining room downstairs to a small table by the window in the drawing room on the first floor.

'I'm delighted to see, Francis, that you're moving up in the wine world at last. Your stuff has never been bad in the past, I grant you that, but now you're up there on Mount Olympus.'

He inspected the label with great reverence, as if he were looking at a Shakespeare First Folio. 'Did you know there's been a great increase in burglary in these parts in the last few weeks, Francis? Fortnum and Mason burglaries the police are calling them, only the luxury items get taken. The other thing they say about this Lafite stuff is that the bottles have a habit of falling over and breaking of their own accord. They're famous for it. Happens more often than you might think.'

'Perhaps you'd better open it, Johnny,' said his friend with a smile. 'It would be such a shame if the burglars got it first.'

Johnny Fitzgerald held the bottle up to the light. It glowed a deep red. He inspected the label closely. He ran his hand very slowly down the side of the bottle. 'I haven't tasted this Château Lafite since my uncle introduced me to it on my sixteenth birthday, Francis. He said it would tell me what real wine should taste like. I was only allowed two glasses of the stuff. Bloody uncle knocked off the rest of the bottle on his own.'

Johnny inserted the corkscrew very slowly. He peered into the depths of the bottle when it was open. 'We'd better have three glasses, Francis. We couldn't leave Lady Lucy out of this.'

Shortly the three all had a glass in their hand, Johnny sniffing delicately at the liquid like a bloodhound that might have just found a new scent, a new trail for the elusive fox.

'By God,' said Johnny, 'I don't think they have much of this stuff down there in the Colville warehouses, it's superb. Now then, Francis, let me tell you what little I have discovered so far.'

Johnny Fitzgerald cast a quick glance over his shoulder to check the bottle was still present and correct. 'There are two very different sorts of people who work for the Colvilles at the lower end of the trade. You could call them the workers by hand and the workers by brain as that bearded old man up in Highgate Cemetery put in one of his pamphlets long ago. The workers by hand are essentially moving the stuff around in one way or another. The wine arrives at the docks in barrels or *tonneaux* or *barriques* or *feuillettes* or pipes. The Colville men unload it, take it to the warehouses, store it or bottle it in their own bottling plant with their own label production and finally it's despatched to the Colville shops or their regional headquarters in Edinburgh or Dublin. The same thing happens with the gin over in Hammersmith. That's a very crude description. It's an enormous operation and the men are, on the whole, satisfied with what they do, though there were the usual undercurrents about low wages and the need for strike action. Are you with me so far, Francis, Lady Lucy?'

The Powerscourts nodded. Johnny paused to take another draught of his wine, his face breaking into a smile as the taste sank in. 'You learn some funny things in this line of work,' he went on. 'Did you ever realize what the most important factor is in what a country drinks? You didn't? Well, let me tell you, it's politics and it's taxes. During the Napoleonic Wars precious little French wine ever made it here. They say the Garrick Club was down to its last couple of cases of Château Latour when peace broke out. Even if it had managed to get here, the wine, that is, the government would have slapped a great bolt of duty on it. So what were Englishmen drinking for most of last century? Port, that's what went down, port from those English merchants and growers in the Douro Valley. Portugal, as the Portugese reminded the English every time they even thought of increasing the duty, was England's oldest ally. All the way back to Henry the bloody Navigator, whoever he was.'

There was a sudden outbreak of motor horns hooting outside, coming from the King's Road a couple of hundred yards away. Voices could be heard, most of them raised in anger.

'Later on,' Johnny continued after a glance out into the square, 'South African wines began to get a look in as the politicians wanted to encourage the wine industry in the colonies. Now here's a strange thing, Francis. Even those porters and warehousemen who work for the Colvilles can sing Gladstone's praises. You might think that he was somewhat odd, an austere old bugger, if you ask me, forever trying to save Ireland by day and the prostitutes of London by night, but he did one thing they've never forgotten. Somewhere in the 1860s, I think, when he was Chancellor of the Exchequer and taking five hours to deliver his Budget, he cut the duty on French wine. He wanted to encourage trade with the French, you see. That was the making of the Colvilles. Unlike the rest of the industry they cut their prices by almost the same as the cut in duty and prospered mightily. The other wine merchants hung on to most of the cut for themselves.'

'Did I hear you right, Johnny?' Powerscourt was refilling the glasses. 'Did you say they have their own label production? Does that mean you can make up any number of phoney vineyards with posh names and stick the label on the bottles? Or indeed real vineyards with posh names and stick them on the bottle, whatever might be inside?'

'It does, my friend,' Johnny replied, swirling the fresh wine around in his glass, 'and there's worse. Much worse. If you could find the right artist and the right expert in typefaces, you could make, in your Colville labelling manufactory, a label like this one here for Château Latour. You don't, of course, put Château Latour in the bottles. You find some good claret from a good year and then, if you're really clever, you say it's a Latour from a bad year. That way expectations wouldn't be so high. But your good Bordeaux in a good year would still cost about half what a Latour would cost you in a bad one. You could make a fortune.'

Powerscourt realized that the possibilities for fraud in the wine industry were virtually limitless, far wider than he had suspected at the beginning of his investigation. But he was still as far away as ever from solving the murder. 'So tell us, Johnny, what did you learn from these workers by hand down in the docks?'

'Precious little so far. They're all East Enders, most of these Colville men, Lady Lucy, and they stick together like the planks of wood on their wine cases. The younger ones were so suspicious they hardly told me anything at all. I think they thought I was an agent from the Customs and Excise, come to learn their secrets. They don't like Customs and Excise much in those parts. Some of the older ones, nearing retirement, were slightly more forthcoming but usually more about the past than the present. There are a couple of old boys who've worked for Colvilles, man and boy since about 1860. For them those early days were like a golden age. Old Walter Colville and his brother Nathaniel were the driving forces back then. They were young, everything was a great adventure and they were happy to take risks that the firm wouldn't take today.'

A high-pitched scream rose from the bottom of the stairs, followed by the noise of small feet charging up them. The twins were on the warpath once again. The parents smiled to each other.

'And they were good to their workers back then,' Johnny went on, 'far fewer of them then, of course, than there are now. I was told heart-warming tales of all employees being presented with half a dozen bottles every Christmas, and, in one memorable year, a goose for every worker. Now they fear the only present they will get on Christmas Day is the sack. Spirits are very low. I couldn't work out why. I don't think it was the murder and the arrest of Cosmo. People are always grumbling about their work, not what it was, new-fangled systems and new-fangled people coming in to replace the old ways, but these warehouse people are just miserable.'

'And what about the other lot, the clerks and the junior accountants, Johnny. Were they any more forthcoming?'

'The workers by brain? Well, they were and they weren't, Francis. They're all holed up at the back of Oxford Street with a detachment of auxiliaries at Hammersmith to make sure the gin isn't watered down or whatever you'd do to gin. The ones I managed to pour drink down were all quite junior. Once they reach a certain position, senior clerks or whoever they might be, they don't go to the pub any more, they take on airs, they're off to some little villa in north London and Mrs Senior Clerk and maybe Master Senior Clerk and Miss Senior Clerk. The odd thing about these youngsters I talked to, Francis, is they're all frightened. I think, but I don't know, that some terrible financial catastrophe is about to hit them. One over-imaginative young man told me he was sure the Colvilles were being buffeted by those winds you get before a hurricane strikes. And it's not the murder. It's as if there's something rotten that is about to come to light and maybe blow them all away. Sorry if that sounds melodramatic, I'm just the messenger for the moment. There are two or three lads I'm seeing tonight who may be able to tell me more.'

'Well, that's all fascinating, Johnny,' said Lady Lucy. 'Did you get the impression they were frightened of a person or persons, or some financial calamity?'

'The calamity, Lady Lucy, definitely the calamity.'

As Johnny Fitzgerald made his way off for an early evening's drinking session with the young men of Colvilles, Powerscourt decided to open another line of attack. He had Johnny Fitzgerald at the lower end of the enterprise, Sir Pericles with his tastings of the Colville product in the middle. Now it was time to try for the top. He made his way downstairs to the telephone in his little study on the ground floor. The telephone had only recently been installed. Powerscourt had expected to be the principal user of the instrument, but found that this was not so. Lady Lucy had fallen in love with the possibilities of morning chat, afternoon chat, evening chat with her friends and relations. These, in her turn, she persuaded to subscribe to the new service as soon as possible. Lady Lucy assured them that they didn't want to be behind the times, to be out of step with fashion. Powerscourt thought his wife should be given some large reward by the telephone companies for swelling their lists of subscribers.

He sat down at his desk and asked the operator for the number of his brother-in-law William Burke. Burke was a great power in the City of London, director of a number of banks and mighty insurance companies, a man widely respected across the City for good advice and sound judgement. At first Powerscourt thought the Burkes must be out, but just when he was on the point of putting down the instrument there was a huge bellow down the line: 'Burke!'

Powerscourt remembered that William Burke did not believe that his words would be transmitted if he spoke in his normal tone of voice. The magic concealed in those little wires would not work. So he shouted. He yelled. He spoke at the top of his voice. His brother-in-law had often wondered what happened in the Burke offices in Bishopsgate. Had his people built him some special soundproof box where he could holler away to his heart's content? If not, Powerscourt thought his conversations would have been audible all the way from London Wall to the Bank of England.

'Powerscourt!' said Powerscourt, holding the great black receiver a foot or so away from his ear. 'I need some advice, William.'

'Fire ahead,' boomed Burke.

'I'm investigating the death of that Colville, the man shot at the wedding. You remember?'

'I do indeed,' bawled Burke, 'terrible business, terrible. And the brother locked up in Pentonville. Some fellow told me the other day that you were trying to get him off.'

'I am, William,' said Powerscourt, resisting the temptation to hold the instrument even further away. 'This is where I hope you can help. There is something terribly wrong at Colvilles and I can't find out what it is. There's very little time. The clerks think some financial disaster is about to overcome them. I've got Johnny Fitzgerald talking to the porters and the junior staff and a chap called Freme trying to find out if the wines are genuine.'

'Sir Pericles Freme?' asked Burke. 'Smallish chap, rather like a gnome, ex-military, white hair?'

'That's him,' said Powerscourt. 'What of it?'

'He used to advise my parents about what wines to buy years ago, Francis. Sorry, I've interrupted you.'

'Never mind. The point is this, William. Could you ask around, discreetly, of course? Has anybody heard anything strange about the Colvilles? Is there a scandal waiting to break? Would it be a big enough scandal that it might lead to murder?'

'Even in this cut-throat world around me,' boomed Burke, 'it would have to be a sizeable sort of scandal for pistols at a wedding. Not impossible, mind you. Family honour might be involved, Francis. Now then. I don't think the Colvilles are with any of my banks,' Powerscourt at the other end of the line grinned with delight at the mention of 'my banks', 'but I think I know who they are with. And the chap that runs that bank owes me a favour, a bloody great favour. Leave it with me, Francis. I'll try to call you tomorrow.'

After a final yell of regard to Lucy and the family, Burke was gone – gone, Powerscourt thought, to the mysterious world of money he inhabited, where rumour swirled round the courts and the alleys of the City, where a man might become rich one day and lose it all the next. But were all these transactions a recipe for murder and sudden death?

7

There was a letter from Charles Augustus Pugh waiting for Powerscourt the following morning. As he slit it open in his upstairs drawing room he suddenly wondered what Pugh's telephone manner would be like. Would each sentence be a question? A suggestion perhaps? I put it to you, Lord Powerscourt, that you have been less than truthful with this court? The news inside was grim.

'Committal hearing yesterday. Bow Street Magistrates Court. Magistrate virtually asleep throughout the proceedings. Sir Jasper Bentinck on parade for the prosecution. The man is said to be very good with police witnesses for some reason. Only bright note from our side is that both policemen were called to give evidence, so I shall be able to cross-examine them when the time comes. Case looks pretty watertight to me. There is Randolph, dead on the floor. There is Cosmo, gun in hand. There is Cosmo, refusing to speak. Juries always think a man is guilty if he refuses to speak, however much you try to persuade them to the contrary. No sign of any of the wedding guests to be called as witnesses. Can you read anything significant into that? I said nothing, of course. I pretended to be holding my fire for another day. They looked at me with great sadness. As things stand, my friend, it's as if I'm the last man in to bat for England against Australia in the Lord's Test. England need over five hundred to win. The last man is a hopeless batsman. The last rites are but a few minutes away. Do you have any hope? I don't mind being beaten in court but I'm damned if I'm going to be pitied. I reckon we have three weeks at most before the Old Bailey. Regards, Pugh.'

Powerscourt swore violently under his breath. Time was running out. Somewhere at the back of his brain there was a question hovering just below the surface. He began to write his letters. He wrote to Nathaniel Colville, requesting an interview. Nathaniel in a way was the last Colville left standing, his brother dead, one nephew murdered, another enclosed in the unforgiving brick of Pentonville. Powerscourt assured him that he had no intention of upsetting him, but hoped the old gentleman might remember something that would help his nephew become a free man once again. He wrote to the Norfolk police requesting another interview. He wrote to Mrs Georgina Nash asking if he might call on her once more. The trial was very close now. And then, just before he left his house, the thought surfaced. He began pacing up and down the drawing room, ignoring the traffic outside in the square, ignoring the paintings on his walls, ignoring the coals spitting in his fire.

Why hadn't he thought about it before? Fingerprints. Fingerprints, first used by the British in India to make accurate records of people who spoke no English. Fingerprints, coming into use by police forces in Europe and in Britain. Fingerprint evidence had already been accepted in British courts of law. He didn't know if the Norfolk police used fingerprint techniques. He rather thought not. Cosmo's fingerprints must be on the gun. But were there fingerprints of another as well, another person who might be the murderer? Even if not, the idea could certainly be used, in Charles Augustus Pugh's immortal phrase, to throw mud in their eye. Powerscourt knew that no serving police fingerprint expert would give evidence against another police force. Could he bring one in from America? Somehow he suspected the twelve good men and true on Cosmo's jury might not be too impressed with foreign evidence from a faraway country which had kicked the British out a hundred and fifty years before. Maybe there was an alternative. With a look of determination about his person, Lord Francis Powerscourt set off for New Scotland Yard to find a British fingerprint expert who might yet save the life of Cosmo Colville.

Two questions were swirling round Powerscourt's brain as he made his way to the Metropolitan Police Headquarters on the Embankment. The first concerned the motive for murder. Powerscourt did not believe, as he had told himself so many times already during this inquiry, that wine could lead to murder. People did not kill for bottles of Krug. They did not murder for Meursault. So what was left? Money? So far there was precious little evidence of that apart from the solicitor's rather Delphic reference to Randolph being worth one or two hundred thousand pounds less than he should have been. Affairs of the heart? Of that there was, as yet, no sign at all. Then there was the question of the gun. It seemed scarcely credible that a man would go to a family wedding with a gun in his hand or his pocket unless he was going to some marriage in the American Wild West years before, when guns were as necessary an item of clothing as socks and shoes and those big hats they all had to wear. And, if Randolph had taken the gun with him, who was he defending? Himself? His brother? His family? Round and round they floated, these questions, like children's ducks on an aimless progress round a bath.

Sir Edward Henry was the third Commissioner of the Metropolitan Police known to Powerscourt. He was a tall man with a military moustache that looked as if it might have been more at home on a Prussian grenadier. The walls of his office were still lined with the four great maps of London with the more recent crimes marked out in red. Powerscourt observed that the greatest concentration of red dots was where it had been every time he had been in this room, over the East End of London.

Powerscourt explained that he was investigating the Colville murder in Norfolk.

'Terrible business that,' said the Commissioner. 'I've been buying our wine at home from those Colvilles for years. How can we assist you, Lord Powerscourt? I gather that our colleagues in East Anglia are fairly certain they have the right man.'

Powerscourt did not think it prudent to mention that the junior detective himself, an Inspector, no less, harboured doubts about the case. The police forces would close ranks like a cavalry squadron on drill duty.

'In my position, Commissioner, I am merely a hired hand. I have to do the best for my client, the unfortunate Cosmo Colville, currently, as you know, a guest of His Majesty in Pentonville prison. I wanted to ask your advice on the question of fingerprints. After all, you are one of the great experts on the subject – you were a leading member of the committee which recommended their introduction in London back at the turn of the century.'

'Fingerprints, Lord Powerscourt. . .' said the Commissioner with a dreamy look in his eye. 'Back then I could have talked for days about the things, origin in India, advantages in the solving of crime, the fact that no two fingerprints are the same. I am pleased, if that is the right word, when a man is hanged at the end of the trial, that his fingerprints have been the decisive proof of guilt, as they were in a murder trial here in London a couple of years back. Some of the officers who work in the Fingerprint Bureau see a great future in the science. Two of my brightest young men tried to persuade me the other day that every citizen in the land should have their fingerprints recorded and placed on file. Crime, they said would be eradicated in five years. I could hear our elected representatives in the House of Commons braying on forever about the ancient rights of freeborn Englishmen so I turned them down. But I have gone off the subject. How can our expertise be useful to you, Lord Powerscourt?'

Powerscourt explained about the gun in Cosmo's hand, the strongest piece of evidence against him. 'If, Commissioner, and it is a very big if, I grant you, fingerprint evidence could show that another hand had held the gun, that might help his case, might it not? And am I right in thinking that the expertise of fingerprinting in such cases has not yet reached Norfolk?'

'You are, and they have made no request for our assistance in this case.'

'Would it be possible for the defence to request that the gun should be sent for examination here by one of your officers?'

'Theoretically, it would be,' said the Commissioner. 'But each police force in this country is master in its own house. The Norfolk police could refuse. The prosecuting barrister would almost certainly raise a host of objections – how are the jury to know that the gun has not been tampered with, so the evidence is corrupt and should be thrown out and so on and so forth. Do you happen to know who the lead barrister for the Crown is?'

'I believe it is Sir Jasper Bentinck, Commissioner.'

'Sir Jasper?' Sir Edward Henry permitted himself a slight laugh. 'Have no doubt of it, I tell you, Lord Powerscourt, the objections would stretch out like a string of milestones all the way from the Old Bailey to Wells next the Sea.'

'What would happen if the defence were to consult an expert in fingerprinting who is not attached to any police force? An independent man?' Powerscourt had finally arrived at the question that had brought him here.

'There aren't many of those around, I'm afraid. Some of our men are lured off to America where the pay is better.'

'A retired officer? One who had to leave the force for ill health or personal reasons?'

The Commissioner stroked his moustache for some time. 'Apologies, Lord Powerscourt, I believe we could help you there. But I have something of a moral dilemma. If I give you a few names, am I undermining the cause of my colleagues up there in East Anglia? Am I giving comfort and succour to the enemy?'

'The life of an innocent man may be at stake here, Commissioner.'

'I know, I know, Lord Powerscourt. That weighs very heavily with me. And you yourself have always been a great friend to our force. Very well. I think we have two retired fingerprint men on the books. We did have a third but I went to his funeral only last month. I shall send the relevant addresses round to your house in a couple of hours. It'll take some time to dig them out. But I would give you a word of warning about all this.'

'Please do. I am most grateful for your assistance. It is beyond the call of duty.'

'On the face of it,' Sir Edward rose from his desk and went to his window, looking out over a grey sky and a sluggish Thames, the seagulls swirling round the shore, 'nothing could be simpler. You find the fingerprint expert. He examines the gun. He finds that there are other fingerprints on it. Whose are those? Surely, says the defence, those are the fingerprints of the killer. The Pentonville Colville merely happened to pick the gun up. I do not know if that would carry as much weight with the jury as the physical presence of your man sitting opposite his dead brother. And the legal complications and obfuscations and arguments would be tiresome. Sir Jasper might well try to wrap the jury up in so much legal undergrowth, case of Rex versus Butterworth 1904, Rex versus Turner 1906, and so on, that they are left with only one fact they can cling on to, one safe port in the legal storm raging round their heads in the Old Bailey.'

'And that fact would be?' Powerscourt asked very quietly.

'That Cosmo Colville was found in a chair, opposite his dead brother, with a gun in his hand.'

The Alchemist was happy in his work that day. The previous evening he had been to the opera and gloried in *The Magic Flute*. Now he was working on the creation of a series of pre-phylloxera wines for a grand dinner to be held in a couple of weeks at a top London hotel. The Alchemist often wondered where his profession – for he did not regard himself as a mere artisan – would have been without the disease that had wiped out so many of France's finest vineyards towards the end of the previous century. So many great wines were lost. But some survived, hidden away in obscure abbeys or interred in the cellars of the great châteaux. These fetched high prices. Engaged in this trade in France, working, as the Alchemist used to say to himself, to provide the market with what it so desperately wanted, had proved his undoing. The inspectors had caught him red-handed in a vast cellar under the Quai des Chartrons in Bordeaux. His superiors denied all knowledge of his activities. He was left as the centre and the chief victim of the scandal. He fled France in a fishing boat and took refuge in the vast obscurity of London's docks where strangers were commonplace and few questions were asked about a man's past. Very slowly and very carefully the Alchemist built up his business. He took great pains about secrecy. He refused to meet any clients or customers face to face. Orders had to be delivered by letter. Payment always had to be in cash. The Alchemist didn't even trust the banks.

He began the business of blending his new ancient vintages. The Alchemist never claimed to be offering the truly great vintages from before the phylloxera plague. Somebody, after all, might have actually tasted them. He picked respectable, steady, unremarkable châteaux that his customers would never have heard of, and so would have no idea of whether the wine they were drinking was genuine or not. They had nothing to compare it with, and without comparisons, as the

Alchemist knew only too well, the wisdom of the wine trade disappears as it has nothing to hold on to.

His was a solitary life, alternating between his workplace, his room in an anonymous part of north London and a chop house where he would eat his solitary supper. But he was not unhappy. He had no idea how long he might have been locked up in France, or how huge a fine might have been imposed on him. Loneliness for him was a price worth paying for freedom. He liked women, the Alchemist, but he was terrified of marrying one of them. A wife would always be eager to know the details of his activities, how well he was doing. Such knowledge could only bring him into trouble. He had great doubts about the ability of women to keep their mouths shut. When he remembered his two sisters and his mother, he always recalled what happened when you told one of them something that was meant to be a secret. The other two always knew within the hour. So the Alchemist restricted his activities with the opposite sex to one special prostitute in Soho who never asked him any questions but happily took his money.

By now the Alchemist had two reds ready that he thought might form part of his offerings for the dinner. Leave them to settle for a couple of days and then he would decide. He thought suddenly of the wide open and desolate spaces in the Auvergne, where civilization seemed alien, remote, places like the Aubrac with its strange cattle and vast skies and hardly any people. He had a great love of wide, wild open spaces, and was already planning a great holiday in a few years' time when he could visit the deserts of the Middle East and the mountains of America. Maybe he could ride right across the United States in a train and stop off on the way to make pilgrimages to the American wildernesses. He placed his two bottles carefully on a shelf and began humming another aria from *The Magic Flute*.

Nathaniel Colville looked like a patriarch. He was tall and well built with a slim white moustache and a great shock of white hair. He looked about seventy years old but his bearing was still erect, his eye steady. Powerscourt remembered Sir Pericles Freme and his less flamboyant white locks and thought he was surrounded by white-headed men. Nathaniel lived close to his brother in a beautiful house right on the river in a village called Moulsford. A gardener was working among the roses that led down to the Thames. A couple of rowing boats were drifting past towards Pangbourne. A pair of blue tits were conducting what sounded like a vigorous argument in the bushes. Nathaniel Colville showed Powerscourt into a seat by the fire.

'How very good of you to see me, Mr Colville,' said Powerscourt. 'This must be a very difficult time for you all.'

'It's good of you to come all this way,' said Nathaniel Colville. 'I don't suppose I shall be much use to you. I haven't had very much to do with the family business for years. I still get the dividends, of course, and I'm still meant to be writing the history of the firm. I'm supposed to have been doing that for the last eight years. I've got all the early records in a room at the top of the house but I don't even read them any more. I don't think I'm ever going to finish it now.'

'There's still time, plenty of time,' said Powerscourt, thinking ruefully of his own unfinished second volume on the Cathedrals of England, the notes and descriptions still mouldering in a cupboard in Markham Square. 'Tell me, Mr Colville, is there anything you can tell me about your nephews, Randolph and Cosmo? Anything you can remember about their early years, about their characters?'

Nathaniel Colville shook his head. 'I was thinking about that before you came, Lord Powerscourt. They were both perfectly normal little boys. They spent a lot of time, obviously, with my own children and another cousin when they were growing up. There was nothing that suggested one was going to be shot at his son's wedding and the other one arrested with a gun in his hand, nothing at all.' The old man shook his head slowly.

'Is there anything in the firm's history that might have left somebody bearing a grudge against them?'

'A vendetta come to Norfolk to take revenge for some sins committed long ago? I don't know anything of that sort but, as I said, I haven't had much to do with the business for a long time.'

'Were things very different in your days, Mr Colville, when the firm started up?' Powerscourt suspected that Nathaniel Colville might be happier with the past than the present.

'I know I'm old, Lord Powerscourt, God knows when you get to my age, you are reminded of it every day. But I think of those early years when we were establishing the business as a time of great happiness. We were doing something none of us had done before. We didn't really know what the rules were, if there were any rules. We took risks, we spent an awful lot of money advertising our wares in the newspapers once we were up and running. Nobody had ever done that before. We tried to do the best we could for our customers. We worked very hard. We were very intensely alive, if you know what I mean. There wasn't a great deal of time for children. Anyway we were away in France quite a lot of the time.'

'Do you think that times are less happy now? In the wine trade, I mean.'

'Do you remember the Jubilee, Lord Powerscourt? The second one, not the first? I remember watching the procession to St Paul's, the soldiers marching through London from all over the world, all come from parts of the British Empire, the royal carriages in procession with the little Queen at the end? I saw them all pass by from the windows of my club on Pall Mall and I remember thinking that this was the end of an era. Two days before, you see, we learned that one of our competitors had been offering champagne at two shillings a case less than we were. In the old days that would have been unthinkable. The rivals might put their stuff on the market at the same price. We all had to make a living after all. But now it was no longer live and let live, it was live and let die. I remember thinking very strongly that this was the end of an age. What have we had since? That fat adulterer on the throne. Women, suffragettes they call themselves, marching about the place throwing stones through shop windows and demanding votes for women. These dreadful motor cars belching smoke over us all – only the other day the gardener and the footman and I had to help pull some fool in his car out of the river down there. Brakes failed, the man said. God help us all. Right through my life, Lord Powerscourt, I've been interested in politics. I can't imagine saying today that things are better than they were at the time of the Jubilee. Entente Cordiale with our oldest enemy, the French, hoping to lure us into some terrible war of revenge with Germany over Alsace Lorraine. The Germans building up a vast navy and spoiling for a fight. Russia honeycombed with revolutionaries seeking a final reckoning with the Tsar – they had a damned good go at it only a couple of years back.'

'Has the wine trade become more and more competitive, Mr Colville?' Powerscourt was wondering if anything concrete was going to come out of his visit.

'Well, I'm not there now, but I would say it has, yes.' Nathaniel Colville laughed suddenly. 'My dear Lord Powerscourt, I realize I must have been sounding dreadfully reactionary just now. I'm not that bad. I try to do what the doctor tells me, regular exercise, moderation in all things. Did you learn Greek at school, Lord Powerscourt?'

Powerscourt nodded.

'Do you remember that they had a favourite saying back then, the Greeks I mean? Maiden agan. Nothing to excess. Think of it, man. Nothing to excess? Greeks? These were people who served up their guests children cooked in a stew at banquets, who went to war for twenty years because a king's wife ran off with another man, who ended up with their most restrained philosopher Aristotle educating a prince, Alexander, who wanted to conquer the whole bloody world.

Nothing to excess? Some day I'm going to tell my doctor what I've just told you but the right moment hasn't come yet.'

'Let me just go back to where I started, Mr Colville. Anything at all you can tell me about Randolph and Cosmo?'

The old man looked at Powerscourt carefully as if sizing him up, as if he were a colt he might buy at the sales. 'You seem a perfectly respectable sort of fellow to me,' he said finally. 'There is perhaps one thing you ought to know, though please don't tell any of my relations I told you.' He stopped and stared into his fire. 'It's about Randolph,' he said and paused again. It was as if he wasn't sure he could get the words out. 'They say he was a terrible man for the women, chased anything that took his fancy.'

'Before his marriage,' asked Powerscourt, 'or after?'

'Damn it, man, I only know what I hear. But I should say the answer to your question is both before and after. All the way through.'

8

Alfred Davis, general manager of Colville and Sons, was staring in disbelief at four sheets of paper on the table in front of him. The latest disaster to strike the Colville company was the non-arrival of a great consignment of wine from Burgundy, wine in every price range. The receipts in front of Alfred were the records of these deliveries in the previous years. Always they had left Burgundy in the second week of October and arrived in London a week or so later. Now there were no records at all. Every attempt to contact the firm of Chanson, Père et Fils, had failed. Alfred had first been made aware of the lack of incoming burgundy the evening before. He had spent most of his time since staring at the records of previous years. Alfred Davis did not wonder if anything had gone wrong at the wine merchants in France, a serious illness, a death perhaps which might have impeded business. He worried only about the firm of Colvilles. This consignment was meant to last them into the New Year. Another shipment usually came along in February. But Christmas, granted the long lead times involved in the trade, was almost upon them. Alfred did not know what he could do if the shipment simply failed to turn up at the docks. Mr Randolph had looked after the Burgundy business for years. No doubt he could have conjured some more wine out of those wily *négociants* and filled the gap. But Mr Randolph was rotting in his grave near the Thames and would trouble the wine trade no more. Alfred

91

could not imagine what damage the loss of the Burgundy wines would do the business at one of the busiest times in the wine merchant's year, Christmas and New Year.

There was a knock at his door. A junior porter told him that there was a Mr John Jackman, the younger Mr John Jackman, waiting to see him. Alfred shook his head. 'I can't see him now,' he said, 'not this morning, not today. He'll have to come back another time.'

'He says, sir,' the porter sounded apologetic, 'that he'll come back every day until he receives satisfaction.'

'He can come back every day till the end of time if he wants to,' said Davis, 'I don't see a time at present when I will be able to talk to him. Tell him there's no point. I've got nothing to say. There's nothing I can do.'

John Jackman senior had worked for Colvilles for over forty years. He ended up in charge of the wholesale distribution system. Shortly before he retired there was a row about his pension. Reports of great shouting matches and fists being thumped on tables circulated round all the Colville buildings. Jackman thought he had been conned out of what he had been promised. He said that Randolph and Cosmo were cheats, depriving their workers of what was rightfully theirs. If death and the prison cell had not intervened, Jackman had threatened to go to Walter and Nathaniel to plead his case. Alfred was not aware of the precise nature of the transactions and the various charges and counter charges. But as he stared down at the notes about the missing wine a truly terrible thought struck him. What if the Colvilles were reneging on all their promises about pensions? He had always been told that a generous provision would await him on his retirement and see him off into a trouble-free old age. What if that money never came? How would he and Bertha manage? He had a few savings, but not as much as he would have liked for Bertha was not good with money. Now another of his headaches was coming on and he had run out of pills. He remembered Bertha saying to him that very morning at the breakfast table in Kentish Town, 'You haven't been looking well at all, Alfred, not for weeks now. Why don't you change jobs? Ask Colvilles for a less stressful post or look for a position elsewhere?'

Alfred had almost shrieked his reply. 'Are you mad, woman? The Colvilles aren't running a hospital or a charity down there in the West End. If I said I wasn't up to the job, I'd be out of the door faster than you could draw the cork out of a bottle. Another position? At my age? Don't be ridiculous!'

Privately Bertha thought her husband was not up to the job, not in the present circumstances. Now, wondering yet again what to do about the missing burgundy, Alfred thought the same.

Powerscourt found Lady Lucy walking up and down the drawing room in Markham Square, her eyes red with tears.

'Lucy, my love, what's the matter?' Powerscourt held her tight.

'It's so silly, Francis. Here am I walking up and down this room just like you do. Only I know you're thinking when you do it, I can see it in your eyes, I'm just upset.'

'What's been upsetting you?'

Lady Lucy made her way to a chair by the fire. 'It's Milly,' she said, 'she's only just gone.'

'She of the Horrible Husband?'

'Indeed so, Francis. Things are worse than we thought, much worse. All her money has gone. Horrible Husband has debts that he's owned up to of three thousand pounds. Milly thinks there may be more. Only two people from the family have replied to my request that we club together to give her some money. So I wrote her a cheque right here in this room for one hundred pounds, Francis. I hope you think that's all right. It's just I couldn't bear the idea of those little children going hungry.'

Lady Lucy looked defensively at her husband. Perhaps he would be cross.

'Think nothing of it, Lucy. Where is the husband now? Is he still at home?'

'The real reason Milly came has nothing to with the money, Francis. This story doesn't come at first hand but I think it's reliable all the same. Milly thought you should know about it. Terrible Tim goes drinking in some sordid gambling and drinking den near Paddington station. He drinks quite a lot there with the husband of a great friend of Milly's called Trumper, Beauchamp Trumper. This Trumper told his wife that one day just before the wedding, Timothy had got more than usually drunk. He had begun to criticize the Colvilles. There was a lot of stuff, Beauchamp thought, about how he had been unfairly dismissed, his career ruined, his abilities questioned by those two Colvilles, Randolph and Cosmo. Beauchamp said it seemed to be the insults to his honour that made him most upset. Then, Francis – Beauchamp swears he remembers this bit perfectly – Tim said, "I tell you what I'm going to do to that arrogant sod Randolph Colville. I'm going to kill him. I bloody well am too."'

At that point they heard, more or less simultaneously, the ringing of the telephone and a series of whoops and war cries as the Powerscourt twins, Christopher and Juliet, five years old, hurtled down the stairs towards the noise. It was always the same now. Whenever the bell rang, wherever they were, whatever they were doing, Christopher and Juliet headed for their father's study at very high speed. They had once leapt out of the bath when the bell went off and shot down the stairs wrapped only in the scantiest of towels, passing one of Lucy's relations who happened to be a High Court judge on the way.

They seemed to believe that the telephone was like a sacred object in some primitive tribe, to be worshipped and revered. At first they had refused to accept that you could speak to another person through the instrument, or that another person could speak to you. When Powerscourt spoke to them once from a neighbour's telephone they had both dropped the instrument on the floor and fled upstairs, putting themselves straight to bed and holding whispered conferences from under the bedclothes.

On this occasion the twins reached the phone a lot earlier than their father. They took up their usual position, crouching on the floor and looking reverently at the instrument. When Powerscourt picked it up he was greeted by an unusually loud voice, even for his brother-in-law on the telephone.

'Francis!' boomed William Burke. The twins had never heard anybody speak so loudly through the telephone before. They thought the caller must be in the next room or outside in the street. Christopher and Juliet exchanged quick conspiratorial glances and clapped their hands over their ears. Then they fled the field to continue their life of crime elsewhere in the house.

'William, how good of you to call back so soon.' Powerscourt looked suspiciously at the study door in case the twins were lurking on the far side. A shriek from the upper floors told him they had gone.

'I haven't very much to say as yet,' Burke shouted cheerfully, 'and I haven't got very long. Mary's dragging me off to the opera again. Doesn't seem fair to me. I went a couple of years ago, for God's sake.'

'You might enjoy it, William,' said Powerscourt.

There was what sounded like a cross between a snort and a grunt at the other end. 'Back to the Colvilles, Francis. My man is out of town for a few days but I have managed to pick up a few tasty scraps for you.'

'Excellent, William, fire ahead.'

'The main thing is that a lot of people in the know say there is something very funny going on with the Colville money. Nobody knows exactly what, but there is general agreement among sensible men that there is a serious problem. One man thinks they run two sets of accounts, one real, seen by nobody but senior Colvilles, and another one for more widespread circulation. The most significant fact,' Burke ratcheted up the volume another three or four notches at this point, 'is that they've lost three senior accountants in the last five years.'

'Did you say three, William?'

'I did,' bellowed Burke.

'Did they walk of their own accord or were they pushed?'

'At least one walked out after three months in the job, saying, apparently, that he didn't want to be there when the balloon went up.'

'Names, William, can you get me names and addresses? Please?'

'I'll get them for you tomorrow, Francis. I've got to go. Damned cab at the door. Five hours of the wretched *Lucia di Lammermoor* coming up. It would all be over so much quicker if they didn't bloody well sing.'

Powerscourt made his way back to the drawing room. Lady Lucy seemed to have captured the twins and was reading them a story. She promised to read them another story in ten minutes if they went straight up to bed.

'I gather you've been talking to William Burke on the telephone, Francis?'

'William Burke says there is something funny with the Colville money. They've gone through three senior accountants in the last five years, apparently.'

'God bless my soul,' said Lady Lucy, whose knowledge of senior accountants was somewhat limited, but did include the view that they should stay in their position longer than twenty months each. 'I've been thinking about Milly's husband all the time, Francis. Suppose he did go to Norfolk intending to kill Randolph. Suppose you manage to rescue Cosmo Colville only to put Terrible Tim in Pentonville in his place. Suppose he has to go on trial for murder. It would be terrible for Milly after all she's been through.'

Powerscourt thought his wife had travelled quite a long way down the road of trial and retribution but she hadn't gone all the way. When would she reach the last journey, the apologetic priest, the pompous governor, the hangman and his assistant all on their way to the gallows? He was a pretty big man, Timothy Barrington White, he'd probably need a drop of seven and a half feet or so to finish him off.

'Francis,' Lady Lucy called him back from his reverie, 'if he was arrested, Terrible Tim, I mean, would you try to get him off? Anything to keep the scandal away.'

Powerscourt reflected that his wife wasn't exactly at the top of her form in this exchange. If Barrington White was arrested, it would mean that Cosmo Colville could walk free. If he then took on the responsibility of liberating Terrible Tim, somebody else would have to be arrested so that he too could walk free. Was Cosmo, after a couple of days of freedom, to return to his prison cell?

There was one definite fact where he could take action. He must speak to Beauchamp Trumper at the earliest opportunity. What if that fellow drinker of Tim's had been so alarmed by what he heard of Tim's drunken boasting that he would kill Randolph Colville, that he had warned the Colvilles to take care? If he had done so, one of the central mysteries of the case would be removed. Randolph Colville had taken his gun to the wedding because he thought somebody might try to kill his brother. Or himself.

Rain was falling in Fulham. It bounced off the top of the omnibuses and the roofs of the carriages. It bounced up off the pavement ensuring that the people were soaked from top to bottom. Small boys on their way home from school tried to shrink themselves inside their caps and hugged the side of the streets in a doomed attempt to keep dry. Lord Francis Powerscourt had his finest black umbrella high above his head, looking for the turning off this main road to the smaller Ringmer Avenue he believed should be the second turning on his left. London, he reflected, was growing bigger all the time, radiating outwards on all four parts of the compass. He wondered if it would ever stop.

Here was Ringmer Avenue at last and here was number sixteen, home to one James Chadwick, former senior accountant at Colvilles, who opened the door reluctantly.

'Good afternoon, Mr Chadwick, Powerscourt's the name. I wrote to tell you I proposed to call at this time today.'

'Come in then.' James Chadwick sounded as if he would have preferred to leave his visitor out in the rain. He showed Powerscourt into a small sitting room with a sofa and a couple of chairs and a good collection of books. Looking at it Powerscourt knew there was something wrong, something lacking. There was nothing warm or intimate about this place. It had all the humanity of a cell in the local jail. Powerscourt felt sure that there was no woman in the house. There might have been one here some time ago, but not now.

Powerscourt placed himself on the sofa. 'Thank you so much for seeing me, Mr Chadwick,' he began. 'How long is it now since you left Colvilles?'

'Four years nine months and two weeks,' said Chadwick, a hint of bitterness creeping into his voice.

'Were they good people to work for, Mr Chadwick? The Colvilles, I mean?'

'They were and they weren't, if you follow me. Good in some ways, not so good in others. Not that I can tell you very much about them. My work was confidential, you see.'

'I suggest, Mr Chadwick, that with one brother dead and the other one about to go on trial for his life, the time for confidentiality is past.'

'You know the oath the doctors swear, Lord Powerscourt?'

'The Hippocratic Oath?'

'That's the one. The section I'm thinking of says: All that may come to my knowledge in the exercise of my profession or in daily commerce with men, which ought not to be spread abroad, I will keep secret and will never reveal.'

'With the greatest respect, Mr Chadwick, that sentence is meant to apply to doctors, not to senior accountants. I can fully see the necessity for confidentiality under normal circumstances but these are not normal times. Come, I am not interested in every last detail of the Colville accounts. But I would be very interested to know how they got through three senior accountants inside five years.'

'Can you promise me that I won't have to give evidence in court?'

'I'm not sure I can promise you that, Mr Chadwick, but I can promise you that you won't have to go to court if you don't want to.'

Powerscourt looked again at James Chadwick. There was something seedy about the man. His shirt collar was on the verge of disintegration. His jacket was badly frayed at the elbows. The shoes had seen better days and the trousers were heavily stained. Powerscourt wondered if there had been a wife who had left, or passed away from some terrible illness or died in childbirth. He wondered too if money had become a problem. No sensible employer was likely to take on a man who dressed like this. They might as well take on a tramp from one of the great railway stations. He tried a different tack.

'Of course, if we find your information valuable there may be a question of a fee. I would have to talk to my colleagues about that.' Nightmare visions of the prosecuting counsel unleashed on James Chadwick flashed across his brain. 'Did you say you were paid for this information, Mr Chadwick? Perhaps you would like to tell the court how much? Gentlemen of the jury, it is for you to decide how much weight to attach to evidence which has been purchased as you might purchase a horse or a train ticket.'

The mention of money seemed to act as a tonic on the accountant. He sat up straight in his chair and fiddled with his tie as if that might restore it to health.

'I will tell you the bald points of my time with the Colvilles, an account I hope will still fall within the general guidelines of the Hippocratic Oath.'

James Chadwick paused briefly. One of the dirty curtains across his window flapped for a moment. Powerscourt wondered if he would be offered a cup of tea in this place. Probably not, he thought.

'I didn't think the accounts were properly organized before I got there, Lord Powerscourt. So I changed them so they followed the wines, if you follow me. Under the old regime everything was organized alphabetically. That might have been fine in earlier times, but it was hopelessly out of date when I got there. I changed the system so that it was organized by wine. Separate accounts for port, Madeira, claret, Bordeaux and so on. I could track all the money in these accounts at the end of every month. Over time, assuming the trade followed consistent patterns year on year, we could have predicted in May how much profit the firm would have made at the close of the year.'

'It sounds an admirable system, Mr Chadwick. You must have been proud of it.'

'It was admirable, and, yes, I was proud of it.'

'So what went wrong?'

'I'll show you what went wrong. I said I could track the money the firm was making or losing month by month. I knew by the end of the year what the final figures should be, I just had to add the monthly figures together. After that the figures went through Mr Randolph Colville and Mr Cosmo Colville to the main board who signed off on the final figures for the year's accounts.'

'That sounds perfectly proper to me, Mr Chadwick.'

'The difficulty lay in the gap, Lord Powerscourt. I won't give you exact figures, but the annual profit leaving my accounts might be three hundred thousand pounds. But the final figure in the final accounts would be in the order of two hundred and fifty thousand. Something in the order of fifty or sometimes one hundred thousand pounds was disappearing out of the Colville accounts every year. In good years it might have been worse, if you see what I mean.'

'Did you know who was doing the intercepting? Would they have been allowed to do this? Was it illegal?'

'I don't know who was doing the intercepting, but the most likely candidates had to be Mr Randolph and Mr Cosmo. Only Colvilles were allowed to hold shares in the company, you see. So whoever was doing the fraud was effectively stealing from his own family.'

'Did you mention this to anybody?'

'I mentioned it to Mr Randolph,' James Chadwick laughed bitterly, 'and I was fired the next day. I haven't had a full-time position since. The Colvilles put it about that I had helped myself to their money when in fact the problem was the other way round, Colville robbing Colville, not Chadwick robbing Colville.'

'God bless my soul,' said Powerscourt, 'you have had a hard time of it.' He was doing a series of calculations in his head. In the five years since James Chadwick left the firm, half a million pounds or more would have disappeared from the family firm, money that could have been spent on expansion, or larger dividends, or buying out your competitors. He had always thought that people were unlikely to murder for a bottle of Sauternes or a Chassagne Montrachet. But for half a million pounds? Or in revenge against those who had defrauded you out of such a sum? And what had the Colville thief done with the money? Where was it? As Powerscourt took his leave of James Chadwick and Ringmer Avenue he wondered if the other two senior accountants would tell him the same story. And if the theft led directly to murder and death.

Emily Colville, née Emily Nash, sat in the drawing room of her new house in Barnes close to Hammersmith Bridge. Emily had been married for less than a month and was already dubious about the supposed virtues of the married state. Their honeymoon to Rome and Florence had been postponed because of the murder of her father-in-law at the wedding reception. Emily missed Brympton. She missed the company of her younger brothers and sisters. She missed her horse and her dogs who, her father had assured her, would be waiting for her. Secretly, her father hoped that the animals would be a lure to bring her back home.

Many of the things that would have occupied newly married young women were not available to Emily. The all-important consolations of domestic bliss, the transition from doll's house to real house, the location of furniture and fittings, the vital questions of where to hang the pictures had all been taken care of as the house had been rented furnished and the owners, gone to New York for a year or two, had made it clear that they expected to find the house exactly as they had left it on their return. Every morning her husband Montague walked over Hammersmith Bridge and took the train to his Colville offices in the West End. Every evening he left his Colville office and returned to his house near the river. Emily stayed behind in what was, for her, in danger of turning into a Colville mausoleum. Other fashionable young women might have taken up votes for women and spent the occasional evening breaking the shop windows of Bond Street and Mayfair. Emily thought the suffragettes were faintly ludicrous and didn't care if she had the vote or not. Then there was charity and good works among the capital's innumerable poor. Sadly neither charity nor the poor appealed to Emily at all. She was restless, hungry for excitement. Her husband might be kind, reliable, steady, but the heady wine of romance did not flow in his veins. Sometimes Emily thought she was composed of two selves, one respectable, conventional like her parents, the other giddy, longing for escape and adventure and intrigue. It was the first Emily, not the second, who had married Montague. She sought consolation in the women's magazines but they only left her more dissatisfied than before. More and more she looked back to her summer adventures in Norfolk, the waiting, the secret messages that summoned her to these trysts in the little cottage. Only in these weeks in Barnes did she come to realize that forbidden activity brings its own excitement and that secret love is a most powerful aphrodisiac. Desperately, she wished for another message, scrabbling through the morning and afternoon posts in the hope that happiness might return.

9

Powerscourt had always thought that Brighton was the place where the pickpockets of London would go for their holidays. Latter-day Artful Dodgers and their companions could ply their trade in the crowds that thronged the station in summer and mingle profitably with holidaymakers on the sea front and the Palace Pier. Latter-day Fagins could supervise their flock from one of the smaller suites in one of Brighton's less reputable hotels. As his train drew into the station he saw that the crowds were not there in the autumn. Waiting for the passengers to leave he spotted the man he had come to see, former Detective Inspector Walter Baker, one-time fingerprint expert for Scotland Yard. Retired policemen and retired military men were usually easy to spot, something to do, Powerscourt thought, with all those hours standing to attention.

'How very kind of you to see me, Inspector Baker,' said Powerscourt, extending his hand with a smile.

'You don't need to bother with the Inspector any more,' said Baker, 'I've done with inspecting now, thank God. We could walk to my little house, if you like, or we could take a cab if you're in a hurry.'

There was a fine rain falling and a stiff breeze from the sea. 'I think I'd like to walk, if that's all right with you,' said Powerscourt and the two men set off down the hill past the clock tower towards the Palace Pier and the sea. Powerscourt filled Baker in on his problems with the murder and the gun as they went. Baker stopped by the railings at the bottom of the pier and stared out across the Channel. Powerscourt wondered what he was looking at, the structure nearly a mile long, the elegant struts and girders holding it in position, the various entertainments that lined its walkways, the squadrons of seagulls wheeling and squawking along the sides, the gun-metal grey of the water.

'I'd just like to think about it all for a moment, if I may, my lord,' said Baker apologetically. 'I'm a bit out of practice with fingerprints and I was never one of those policemen whose minds work like lightning and are often wrong. I'll have some questions for you when you reach my house. Not far now.'

Over to his left Powerscourt saw the beginnings of the Regency terraces of Kemptown. The wind had strengthened and was driving the few visitors off the pier or into the cafés. The former Inspector Baker let them into a small bow-fronted house in a neat terrace. There was a portrait of Queen Victoria on one side of the hall and another of Edward the Seventh on the opposite side. As he sat down in the little front parlour Powerscourt saw that he was in a temple devoted to the British Royal Family. Henry the Seventh, looking as if he might have been torn from a school textbook, was to the right of the door. The rest of the Tudors followed in line of ascent, the Virgin Queen in the Armada Portrait looking perfectly content as if this was her favourite among the many palaces she could call her own. George followed George, the Third looking as if he was rehearsing for losing his wits, the Prince Regent scowling at him from the next available slot on the wall. On and on the cavalcade went, culminating in a portrait of the Kaiser in some Ruritanian uniform with his consort, Victoria's daughter. On the bookshelves were various volumes relating to the Royal Family, and a whole series of knick-knacks of varying kinds, plates, medals, watches. It was rather like being at Lourdes, Powerscourt thought, with those terrible tourist shops dispensing holy trash to the sick and the dying.

'My goodness me, Mr Baker,' said Powerscourt, 'I had no idea you were so devoted to the Royal Family.'

'It's not me, my lord, it's Mabel, the wife. She's been collecting this stuff for years. There's a lot more of it upstairs. Whole bloody house is turning into a royal junk shop.'

'God bless my soul,' said Powerscourt. 'Such devotion!'

'I'll just see if I can persuade Mabel to make us some tea, my lord. I'll be back in a second.'

The tea, when it arrived, came in an Edward the Seventh Coronation teapot, and was served on Edward the Seventh Coronation saucers in Edward the Seventh teacups. Mrs Baker was breathing heavily as she performed her duties. Powerscourt thought she had the air of one about to confirm with her doctor that she did indeed have a serious illness.

'Lord Powerscourt,' she spoke with great reverence, 'seeing that you are a lord and all that, could I ask you. . .' Mrs Baker paused, her eyes fixed on Powerscourt's face. He thought he knew what was coming. He prepared the necessary lies. 'Have you, in your time as a lord, I mean, oh dear, maybe you've always been a lord, have you met. . .' She paused again, wondering, Powerscourt thought, whether she would be struck down if she uttered the names out loud, like one who dared speak the ninety-nine names of God. 'Have you met any of the Royal Family in your time?'

'I have as a matter of fact,' said Powerscourt, omitting to mention that one of his earliest cases in England after his return from India had involved examining the corpse of an important member of the family, his throat cut from ear to ear, his blood, not blue alas, but the normal red, lying in puddles on the floor in a Sandringham House bedroom. 'Very charming they were too, Mrs Baker.'

She purred with delight. Her husband, feeling perhaps that the due tax had been paid to the local authorities, reminded her that he needed to speak to Lord Powerscourt alone. Their business was important and confidential.

'Of course, dear,' she said. 'I'll leave you in peace now. But I would like to ask a question of our guest before he goes, if I may.'

'I think I may turn into a republican or an anarchist before my time is up.' Baker was running his fingers through the remains of his hair. 'One of those people who takes a pot shot at the Sovereign as they drive up the Mall on the way to some service or other. Since Mabel turned monarchist like this I've come to have increasing admiration for the Gunpowder Plotters and that fellow Catesby. Reckon they had the right idea – get rid of the whole lot of them in one go. Enough of this. Let us turn to your problem with the gun in Norfolk.'

The former policeman walked a few times up and down his little front room and eventually settled himself in front of an enormous cream-coloured plate in honour of Victoria's Diamond Jubilee.

'I can still remember how excited some people became when the fingerprinting came in, my lord.' Walter Baker was making a steeple with his fingers as he spoke. 'Some people could hardly believe it – that every single person had a set of fingerprints unique to them. We had one chap, a Detective Inspector I think he was, who was a devoted Baptist or Quaker or one of those funny religions, who said the fingerprints were God's filing system, the Good Lord's way of putting his mark on every one of his creatures. Cynics told the man it'd have to be a bloody big file, big enough to hold every single person on the planet. And did God remove the dead from the files, asked the cynics? Otherwise he'd have a system clogged up with people going right back to Adam and Eve themselves. Other people like me thought at the beginning that it was going to be a very useful tool in solving crimes and putting criminals away. Well, I still think it's useful, but I don't think it's as useful as we thought it might be.'

'And why is that, Mr Baker?' asked Powerscourt.

'It's like this, my lord. At the start when nobody knew how it all worked, the criminals didn't know what to do. Now they realize that all they have to do is to wear gloves. There's a couple of sergeants over in the East End who are keeping an unofficial record of the sales of fine gloves in Shoreditch and Whitechapel. They talk to the relevant shopkeepers and so on. Fine glove sales in those parts are going up at the rate of ten per cent a year. That might be the fashion but it might be something else.

'I don't know if the Norfolk police are using fingerprint analysis on the gun in this murder case of yours, but let's suppose they are. On the face of it, you might think it is all straightforward. If the living brother, Cosmo I believe you said he was called, had his fingerprints on the gun, you might think that was pretty serious. But then you tell me the gun probably came from the drawer in the desk in his brother's house where he was a regular visitor. At any rate the gun used to kill Randolph Colville was the same make and so on. It used the same ammunition. If it came from that drawer, it could well have had his fingerprints on it. Even if it came from somewhere else – in other words we might be talking about two different guns here – there could be perfectly innocent explanations for Cosmo's prints, if they are there. He could have picked it up off the floor or taken it from whoever was holding it at the time. A good defence counsel could run rings round the jury with fingerprint evidence in cases like this.'

'What happens,' said Powerscourt, 'if the gun is found to have other fingerprints on it? Prints that might be those of the murderer?'

'That gets very hypothetical, my lord. Think about it. On this gun there are Cosmo's fingerprints. If he has been holding the gun he must surely have left fingerprints. Fine. Now, gentlemen of the jury, says the defence barrister, hold on a minute, we have this other set of prints or two other sets of prints, also on the gun. We do not know who they belong to, these fingerprints, but they could well belong to the murderer, a man who spent no time at all in Brympton Hall but just long enough to kill his victim. It's not surprising we don't know who he is, he has got clean away.'

'Ah,' said Powerscourt, his fingers touching an imaginary gown, and addressing an imaginary judge, 'in my role as counsel for the prosecution, objection, my lord, objection. My learned friend is trying to present conjecture and guesswork as if they were fact. There may well be other sets of prints on the weapon, my lord, but we do not know who they belong to. For all we know they could belong to Mr Lloyd George or the Bishop of London. I submit, my lord, this is not evidence, it is mere conjecture.'

'Mr Defence Counsel?' Former Inspector Baker, now playing the part of the judge, had watched these games all too many times before.

'I was merely trying to let the jury know, my lord,' said Powerscourt, 'that there are other marks on the pistol which must have belonged to somebody else, and that the somebody else could well have been the murderer.'

Powerscourt turned into the judge, rising to his feet and turning from time to time to address an imaginary jury. 'Could well have been, Mr Defence Counsel,' he boomed, 'is not good enough. It is guesswork. Mr Foreman, gentlemen of the jury, I direct you to place no weight on these imaginary suppositions. They bear no credibility in this court. Objection sustained.'

Powerscourt and Walter laughed as they reached the end of their courtroom drama. 'Mr Baker,' said Powerscourt, 'I must confer with the real defence counsel before I decide what is for the best. But would you be willing to appear in court for us if necessary?'

'I would,' said Baker.

There was a sudden rustling noise by the door. Mrs Baker swept in, past Henry the Eighth and Queen Anne, and came to rest in front of a small picture of George the Second. 'Don't you let this Lord Powerscourt go without my question now, Walter.'

109

'And what, pray, is your question, madam?' asked Powerscourt.

'I want you to send a message to that Edward the Seventh for me,' she began.

'You mean the King?'

'I do. I want you to tell him that we, his loyal subjects of Brighton, wish him to have a Jubilee. Those two his mother had, Diamond and Golden, were the happiest days of my life. He's not looking well, that King. If he doesn't have a Jubilee soon he'll be dead before they have time to organize it. If he likes he can just have it down here in Brighton, he needn't bother with the rest of the country and all that Empire beyond the seas stuff. I'm sure we could find a foreigner or two to wave a flag at him if he thinks it's important. He could eat the big dinner in our Royal Pavilion. Maybe the Prince Regent and Mrs Fitzherbert could come back from the dead to join him. I'm sure they'd have a lot in common.'

'Have no fear, Mrs Baker,' said Powerscourt gravely, 'I shall make every effort to pass your request on to the appropriate authorities.'

'Look here, Vicary, I've had another idea.' Septimus Parry and Vicary Dodds were in conference about the progress and performance of their wine business, Piccadilly Wine, a recent arrival in the London area and a challenger to the supremacy of the Colvilles. Septimus Parry looked after the acquisition of the wine, Vicary Dodds looked after the accounts. Septimus stared up at the great blackboard where they kept a summary of their current stock. 'The thing is,' Septimus was a very slim young man, looking, his friends used to tell him, rather like a Spy cartoon, 'we've got all the conventional products on offer in our shops, port, claret, champagne, all of that stuff. What happens if we go for the cheapest red and maybe the cheapest white we can find? Genuine *vin ordinaire*, as drunk by the solid citizens of La Belle France, comes to England's capital.

The Entente Cordiale in a glass. Maybe I wouldn't actually use the word genuine now I come to think about it, but cheap is the way to sell it. That should bring the customers in. Then they save so much on our *vin ordinaire* that they buy a load of other wine as well. What do you think, Vicary?'

'I'm not sure I like the sound of your reservations about the word genuine, Septimus, but I'll let it pass for the present. Where do we get hold of this *vin ordinaire*?'

'Kind of you to ask,' said Septimus. 'I've got some samples here in my bag.'

He pulled out a bottle with no label that appeared to contain red. He fetched a couple of glasses and a corkscrew and poured it out. 'Don't think you need to swirl it around or give it a sniff, if you see what I mean. Straight down the hatch, that's the thing.'

Both young men took a respectable gulp of the liquid. Septimus did not seem affected one way or the other. Vicary Dodds turned rather pale. He coughed as if he were suffering from the final stages of consumption. Tears began trickling down his cheeks.

'My God, Septimus, where did you get this?'

'You don't like it then?'

'As you can see I'm not exactly wild about this consignment. If Christ had produced this for his miracle at the Feast of Cana they'd have been asking him to turn it back into water as fast as he could. Do you have any more poisonous mixtures in there?'

'As a matter of fact, I do, Vicary. Try your tears on this one.' Septimus whipped out another bottle and fetched some more glasses. Vicary tasted his incredibly slowly, a fraction of a mouthful at a time. This time he did not cough. No tears rolled down his cheeks. Instead he screwed his mouth into a rictus of dislike and peered incredulously into the glass.

'My God, Septimus, I think this one is even worse. I tell you what we could do with it. We could market this one as a means of giving up alcohol. Have you tried to give up the demon drink? Is alcohol ruining your life? Is your wife on at you all the time to forsake the juice of the vine and the products of the malt and the barley? This is the answer to your prayers. One tablespoonful of Piccadilly Wine's special elixir three times a day and you'll never want a drink again. I'm sure we could find some medicine man to give it the seal of approval.'

'Might not do a lot for the rest of the business, my friend,' said Septimus. 'Can't sell wines and spirits with one hand and try to turn them all teetotal with the other. We might go out of business rather quickly if the elixir proved a success.'

'I hadn't thought of that,' said Vicary sadly, staring hard at Septimus's bag. 'Don't tell me you've got another foul bottle in there, I don't think my taste buds would stand it.'

'Last one,' said Septimus, 'it's closing time after this.'

Vicary Dodds eyed the red substance with maximum suspicion, as if he were Socrates inspecting the hemlock that would kill him. At last, very reluctantly he took a small sip. A quizzical look crossed his features. He took another, slightly larger sip. Slowly, very slowly, a smile spread across his face.

'Good God, Septimus,' he said, 'this one isn't at all bad. A bit thin perhaps, but it's not going to send you mad or make you blind like those other two. Where on earth did you find them all?'

'Don't you trouble yourself about where they came from, Vicary. Let me just say that my contact said one of them might do rather well in Bulgaria and Rumania. Those Eastern Europeans like their wine a bit rough apparently, like their women. Anyway I could lay in enough of the final one to last a couple of weeks. Sort of trial run. What do you say?'

'Let's do it,' said Vicary Dodds, 'and let's throw some more mud in the Colvilles' eyes.'

'Let's not forget the white,' said Septimus, heading for the door. 'I'll bring a couple of bottles of that in next week.'

'White? Did you say white?' Vicary stared at his disappearing friend. 'I may need some time to build up my strength for a white like those. God save us all.'

Powerscourt thought it was one of the best-kept house fronts he had ever seen. The black door glistened and shone in the afternoon sun. The windows on either side looked as if somebody cleaned them once a week if not once a day. The orderly brickwork was immaculate. This little house in Weltje Road in Hammersmith, close to the Thames, was the home of his second Colville senior acountant, one Wilfred Jones. Apart from his name and his previous position Powerscourt knew nothing about him. The door was opened after he rang the bell twice by a fully clad yeoman warder of the Tower of London, resplendent in a red and dark blue uniform with spear in hand and Tudor bonnet on his head.

'I'm terribly sorry, I must have come to the wrong place,' said Powerscourt, beating the retreat.

'I don't think you have,' said the gentleman warder. 'I'm expecting a visitor but I'm damned if I can remember his name.'

'I presume you're expecting one of your colleagues from the Tower,' said Powerscourt, nearly out of earshot.

'I was an accountant once,' said the yeoman warder, 'before I went to work at the Tower. An accountant. I think that's what you have come to see me about. An accountant at Colvilles.'

Powerscourt began to retrace his steps. He had seen stranger transformations in his time than accountants turned into yeoman warders, but not in England.

'Wilfred Jones,' said the man, escorting Powerscourt into the front room of his house. Powerscourt wondered if it would be full of ceremonial swords and halberds and tabards and antique spears. It was not. It was full of sheet music, mainly religious works, Powerscourt observed, Handel's *Messiah*, Bach's St Matthew Passion, Beethoven's Ninth Symphony.

'I'm not holding you up or anything, Mr Jones? said Powerscourt. 'I mean, you're not meant to be on duty at this time, I hope?'

'No, I'm not,' said the warder, 'I'm not on duty for a little while yet.'

'Can I ask you, Mr Jones, how you have managed the transformation from senior accountant to yeoman warder? It's not a normal sort of journey.'

The accountant smiled. 'That's easy. The firm I was with before Colvilles used to do a lot of the accounts for the Tower. I was the man responsible for looking after them. I went on doing work for the warders after I went to Colvilles. When I departed from the drinks industry we came to an understanding: I would do the Tower accounts for nothing; they would make me a warder. It was all a bit unofficial but nobody seems to mind. I've always liked dressing up ever since I was a boy being Robin Hood and his Merry Men in the back garden. Now then. What can I tell you about the Colvilles?'

'I think you took over from James Chadwick, Mr Jones? I talked to him the other day.'

'Might I ask you, Lord Powerscourt, how he described the position in the firm?' Wilfred Jones was smoothing the front of his uniform across his knees. Powerscourt suspected he performed this little ritual so many times a day that he had virtually forgotten he was doing it.

'Two things mainly,' said Powerscourt, wondering suddenly if his accountant sang the Refiner's Fire from the *Messiah* in full yeoman warder uniform. 'That he rearranged the accounting system into categories, wine, port, gin, whisky and so forth. And that when he produced his annual figures, they were intercepted before they reached the full board, the figures I mean. Something like a hundred thousand pounds a year simply disappeared. Spirited away, he thought, by one lot of Colvilles who were defrauding another lot of Colvilles.'

The yeoman warder was twiddling his bonnet in his hands, picking nervously at the top.

'Chadwick did warn me about what happened to him,' he said, 'and they had obviously worked out new tactics for me. It was all fine until the end of the year. The division into types of drink went on. I prepared all those individual accounts in the normal way. Usually when you hand them over, they are provisional figures, you get the final set of accounts when the board and everybody else have had a go at them. I never saw the final accounts. It was as if I didn't exist or wasn't worth bothering with.'

'So what did you do?'

Jones laughed. 'I was angry, very angry. I told the two brothers that I was leaving, that I had never seen accounts or accountants treated in such a cavalier fashion. And that their behaviour was unethical and probably illegal.'

'What did they say?'

'They offered me extra money to stay on. Quite a lot of extra money, now, I think about it. Perhaps they didn't want it known abroad that they had lost another chief accountant.'

'So what did you think was going on, Mr Jones?' asked Powerscourt.

Jones looked solemn. Suddenly Powerscourt could see him on duty at the Tower in his uniform centuries before, the names of the recusants scratched into the walls of the cells by their fingernails, the escort for the doomed, Anne Boleyn or Thomas More or Lady Jane Grey, led across to the little patch of grass on Tower Hill, the executioner with the great axe, the blow to the neck, the screams of the dying, Guido Fawkes racked till he could no longer write his name.

'I had a number of theories, Lord Powerscourt, one of them rather far-fetched, I'm afraid. You know how in some old families – it may be dying out now, I'm not sure – there's often somebody who has to get served first at meal times. It might be a grandparent or a very old-fashioned father always keen to have the first serving of the roast beef or the Dover sole. It was as if there was somebody like that in the Colville tribe, somebody who had to be fed first with the money.

But why didn't the others complain? Perhaps they never knew. Maybe the money went on some common project of the family, that château they had near Bordeaux. But I checked that one out and all the payments came out of the French accounts. They didn't need to siphon the money off in London. Maybe Randolph and Cosmo were rewarded for being senior directors. But they were already paid more than the old boys Walter and Nathaniel anyway.'

'You said you had one rather far-fetched theory, Mr Jones. I don't think I've heard it yet.'

Jones laughed rather nervously and smoothed his uniform across his knees once more.

'Suppose somebody was blackmailing the Colvilles. Not just one Colville but the whole collective of Colvilles if you follow me. So it wasn't just a question of any individual member being at fault. The whole bloody lot of them were. So once a year, it's payday for the blackmailer. They all want a quiet life so they cough up this enormous sum every year. What do you think?'

'It's certainly ingenious,' said Powerscourt, preparing to take his leave, 'and it certainly makes some sense of it all. I just have one difficulty with it. I can't think what hidden crime would enable a man to blackmail the whole lot of them. It if it was just one family, it might be a child born out of wedlock or something like that. But all of them? I don't see it.'

Powerscourt wished Wilfred Jones good luck in his wardering and good voice in his singing as he left. As he headed back towards the tube station, the great bulk of Hammersmith Bridge towering above him, he wondered if the man wore his uniform all day. Perhaps he went to sleep in it, a snoring yeoman warder serenading the night sky of west London. But as he thought of the blackmail theory he realized that there was something else wrong with it. It was the wrong way round. In blackmail cases it was usually the blackmailer who gets killed as the victim tires of the endless payments. Suppose

Randolph Colville was being blackmailed. You would expect him to be the killer of the blackmailer, not to be the victim himself. Unless Randolph had decided to kill his blackmailer. Suppose there had been some sort of a struggle and Randolph rather than the blackmailer had been shot. But in that case, why was Cosmo holding the gun and still maintaining his vow of silence?

10

Charles Augustus Pugh was standing by his window, leaning forward for a better view of the perfectly manicured lawns of Gray's Inn. Advancing towards him, Powerscourt thought he looked like a cricket umpire stooping towards the other end and trying to establish whether the batsman was leg before wicket.

'Look at it, Powerscourt, it's a bloody disgrace.' He pointed to the sad remains of a blackbird which looked as if it had met a violent and bloody end, its head twisted over to one side, its insides opened out to the autumn air.

'Mark my words,' said Pugh, 'it's that bloody chambers cat the fools have brought in. I argued against it at the chambers meeting, I said we were a firm of barristers not a wildlife sanctuary or a bloody zoo, for Christ's sake. No good. I was voted down. Can you imagine? Some of the finest minds in legal London, and they want to have a cat. I ask you. They'll be drawing up rotas next for the barristers to put out the saucer of milk morning and evening. There are mice here, I grant you, but what's wrong with poison? We don't need a bloody cat.

'Never mind. Let us turn our attention to the Colvilles, one dead on his son's wedding day, one turned mute in the stone of Pentonville. The solicitors told me yesterday they'd tried again to persuade Cosmo to talk. No joy, not a word out of him. He'll bloody well have to speak in court to plead guilty or not guilty. Let's hope he hasn't forgotten how to get the words out. Do you have anything to report, Powerscourt? Any deus ex machina to solve all our problems?'

Powerscourt had already written about the fingerprints. 'I don't think I have anything at present that would get us out of our difficulties. There's something very odd about the money, though. One of the family solicitors told me very early on that Randolph Colville should have been worth a lot more than he actually was. Colvilles have got through three senior accountants in less than five years. They too tell of funny things going on with the money. Just before the final accounts are signed off, something in the order of one hundred thousand pounds a year simply disappears. Cosmo and the late Randolph seem to be instrumental in the disappearance of these Houdini funds. If you think about it, they're defrauding members of their own family – only family members can hold shares, you see. And the family don't make a fuss. Maybe there's blackmail in there, but you would have to think it's the whole clan who are being blackmailed. What do you make of it, Pugh?'

Two elegant black shoes descended from the desk as Charles Augustus Pugh began to walk up and down his room, pausing from time to time for emphasis as his thoughts unrolled. 'I think I like it. I didn't like the fingerprint angle very much. It would only be really effective if we found other fingerprints on it and we knew whose those were. But blackmail, my friend, blackmail might be better. It gives us motive for a start which we didn't have before. Juries like motives they can understand. Juries understand blackmail. Suppose one of these Colvilles learns about how they have been defrauded all these years. For some reason the fact of this missing money is very important for our man. Maybe there was a sick relative he couldn't send to Switzerland or America or somewhere or other. He gets hold of a gun, either Randolph's gun or one identical to it. Off he trots to the wedding and arranges to have a quiet word with Randolph before the festive board is actually rolled out. Bang, he shoots Randolph dead. He drops the gun on the floor and flees as unobtrusively as he can. Cosmo hears the bang and walks into the room. I say, he says to himself, isn't that Randolph's gun? So he picks it up, and then he is found with the gun in his hand and his murdered brother on the floor. Because he knows who the murderer is, Cosmo doesn't speak. He has to protect the killer. He has to keep quiet.'

Pugh sat down again and brushed a small speck of dust off his dark grey trousers. 'It's fine, of course, except we don't know who the blackmailer is or was or the nature of the blackmail itself. I can't believe it'll solve all our problems, Powerscourt, but I could do something with it if I had to. Can you line up these accountants to come to court? If we don't know who the real murderer is, all we can do is try to persuade the jury that there is doubt about a conviction, that the jury shouldn't feel comfortable sending Cosmo to the gallows. It's all we can do.'

Pugh stared over at his window. 'Bloody cat,' he said again. 'Do you know, they haven't even got a name for it yet? I think I'll make a suggestion at the next chambers meeting. I've wondered about Messalina or Cleopatra but I think we want something simpler.'

'What's that?' asked Powerscourt with a smile.

'It's a perfect description for the bloody animal's behaviour. Killer, that's what we should call her. Killer the cat, killer, now I think about it, rather like our unknown murdering friend up in Norfolk.'

Powerscourt found Sir Pericles Freme walking up and down his drawing room in Markham Square in a state of high excitement. It was with difficulty that he persuaded the man to sit down and take a cup of tea.

'I bring news, Powerscourt, news from the world of Colvilles. I did not receive the intelligence from them directly but I am assured it is correct.' Freme began rubbing his hands together and nodding his head up and down. 'Oh, yes!' he said. 'Oh, yes!'

'Please continue, Sir Pericles.'

Sir Pericles stared at Powerscourt for a moment as if collecting his thoughts. Certainly he sounded now less excited than he had before.

'In the wine business, as you know, everything is governed by the seasons. A time for harvest, a time for bottling, a time for planting. Round about now is the time Colvilles ship over their next consignment of white wine to see them through Christmas and the New Year. The winter is not quite upon us but if the wine does not come soon, the weather may cause problems. One of London's most distinguished merchants almost went under a few years ago when their vessel sank in the Bay of Biscay with a huge consignment of claret on board. Nobody has tried to ship anything in December since. But the Colville wine is still in Burgundy. It has not left the warehouses. It has not been pulled together ready for shipping.'

'Can't they buy some more? Won't there be some *négociants* in Beaune or in Dijon who can step into the breach?'

'There may well be,' said Freme, 'but it will take time and money, a lot of money. Word will have flashed round the vineyards that a big English customer has failed to take delivery of his consignment of Chablis and Meursault and so on. Colvilles will have paid for this lot of fine burgundy once. Now they will have to pay again. And there's worse, much worse.'

'How much worse?' said Powerscourt.

'The agent in Burgundy, a Monsieur Jean Pierre Drouhin, has disappeared. Nobody has seen him for ten days or so. You see, if he was there he could assemble all the Colville wine and organize the shipment in a couple of days, he knows where everything is. He has been with the Colvilles for ten years or more. But now he is not with them. He has vanished.'

'Does nobody know where he might have gone? Did he have a wife?'

'A pretty wife and two lovely children, they say.'

'Parents alive, parents not well, that sort of thing? Has he gone on a mission of mercy to the ancestral farm?'

'He would have told his wife if he was doing that, surely.'

'Another woman? Romance in Antibes or Biarritz, perhaps?'

'Nobody knows, Powerscourt, nobody knows anything at all.'

'You don't suppose he's dead, do you?' Powerscourt was spinning spiders' webs in his mind, wondering if there was any connection between death in Brympton, the missing money in Colvilles' accounts and the missing agent in Burgundy.

'The French police are investigating, of course.' Sir Pericles didn't sound as if he had great confidence in them. 'I must leave you now, I'm afraid. I have an appointment with a senior figure in Colvilles. Would you like a recipe, or a receipt, before I go?'

'Very much, Sir Pericles. Let me just fetch Lucy. She's devoted to the recipes.'

Freme pulled a little book out of his bag and settled a pair of spectacles on his nose.

'English sherry,' he began, 'here we go. "To every pound of good, moist sugar, put one quart of water. Boil it till it is clear. When cool (as near as possible to cold without being so) work it with new yeast, and add of strong beer in the height of working, the proportion of one quart in a gallon. Cover it up, and let it work the same as beer; when the fermentation begins to subside, tun it; and when it has been in the cask a fortnight or three weeks, add raisins, half a pound to a gallon, sugar candy and bitter almonds of each half an ounce to the gallon, and to nine gallons of wine half a pint of the best brandy. Paste a stiff brown paper over the bung hole and if necessary renew it. This wine will be fit to bottle after remaining one year in the cask; but if left longer will be improved. If suffered to remain three years in the cask and one in bottles it can scarcely be distinguished from good foreign wines, and for almost every purpose answers exactly as well."'

Powerscourt was making his way to the village of Moulsford on the Thames once more. He was going to call on Hermione, widow of the murdered Randolph Colville. He had felt it only polite to delay his visit until now when the death and the funeral were a little time in the past and the pain of bereavement, while still harsh, might not be as sharp as before. Looking up from his notebook he noticed that his train was slowing down. They were enveloped in white mist. Out of the left-hand window it hung in fronds or tendrils as if attached to an invisible washing line. Two ghostly horses stood still about fifty yards from his carriage, pale riders waiting to gallop off to some brighter future. On the other side the mist was packed close, so dense that you could only see for a couple of yards. The train was now advancing slowly through this other world. Powerscourt suddenly remembered coming out of the Hotel Danieli on the Venetian sea front early one morning and finding that the Basilica, the Doge's Palace, even the Lion of St Mark on his pillar had all disappeared in a dense Venetian fog. Only the water told you it was still there, he recalled, lapping ceaselessly against the quays. After a couple of minutes the mist vanished as quickly as it had arrived. A pale November sun broke through the clouds casting a light that danced on the blue waters of the Thames.

It was shortly after half past ten when a diminutive butler showed Powerscourt into an upstairs drawing room looking out over the river. On the left of the corridor at the top of the stairs he glimpsed a room that seemed to be full of guns of every description. Hermione Colville was sitting in a high-backed chair by a great window with a fine view over the Thames. She was dressed entirely in black. To her left, on a small circular table, was a large goblet. Behind that stood a bottle of wine, presumably white, in a cooler. Powerscourt

123

wondered briefly when she started drinking, this bereaved woman. Ten o'clock? Half past nine? Her voice, however, sounded perfectly sober.

'Good morning to you, Lord Powerscourt. How very kind of you to come and see me in my widow's weeds. I understand you are not having much success in your investigation so far. Is that correct?' She took another mouthful of her wine. Presumably, Powerscourt thought, she got the stuff cheap from Colvilles. Perhaps they sent it up from London in a barge. He wondered how much malice there was in her words.

'I am most grateful to you for seeing me this morning, Mrs Colville. It is true what you say about my investigation. So far it is not going as well as I would like.'

'Is that because it is a particularly difficult investigation or because you are not a particularly skilled investigator?'

Powerscourt smiled politely. What should have been a perfectly innocuous conversation was turning into a skirmish. 'I couldn't possibly say anything to that, Mrs Colville, but let me proceed with my business. Forgive me if I ask you about your husband at such a time as this but it often helps to talk to those closest to him. Could I ask first of all if you have a photograph of your husband I might borrow?'

Hermione Colville walked rather unsteadily to a little table by the side of the fireplace and gave him a family snapshot.

'Thank you so much,' said Powerscourt, 'I'm sure this will be a great help. In the weeks before his death, Mrs Colville, did he show any signs of anxiety? Would you have said he was worried about something? Did he have a problem on his mind?'

'No is the answer to all those questions. I cannot see what use they are to you or anybody else. They won't bring Randolph back.' She took another large mouthful from her glass and looked defiantly at her visitor.

'Would you have said your husband had any enemies, Mrs Colville? Perhaps I should say many enemies? People high up in business often do.'

'He didn't talk to me about things like that. We didn't have that kind of marriage, if you want to know.'

'No?' said Powerscourt.

'Well, he was away a lot in France. One of the children used to say he only had half a father because his papa was only here half the time.' She paused to take another mouthful and then rang a small bell. The diminutive butler appeared as if by magic and popped another opened bottle into the cooler. He slipped out as unobtrusively as he had come. The whole manoeuvre had taken less than thirty seconds.

'Did your husband have any money concerns, Mrs Colville? Any conversations about the times being bad for business?'

'I told you, Lord Powerscourt, we didn't have that sort of marriage.' Her words were beginning to sound slurred now. Powerscourt wondered if one bottle was going to make her drunk. Then it would be the second bottle and the slow descent into incoherence. Madam is not available in the afternoons, my lord. Maybe he had only got here just in time.

Powerscourt thought he would take a chance, draw a bow at a venture. 'What kind of marriage would you say you did have, Mrs Colville?'

She looked at him with contempt. She stared defiantly at the view outside her great window, a pair of oarsmen making their way downstream, a heron standing proudly on the bank. If you listened very carefully in that Colville drawing room you could just catch the distant screeching of the gulls. Hermione Colville took another glass of her wine. Powerscourt saw from the label that it was a Chablis. He didn't suppose Colvilles drank *vin ordinaire*.

'What kind of marriage did I have? How long have you got, Lord Powerscourt? It was all right at the beginning. I think most of them are all right at the beginning, or so I've been told. I've carried out a lot of research into marriages with the women of my acquaintance, you know. Sometimes I think I should have been made a Professor of Unhappy Marriage like that man who's Professor of Mind and Logic at University

College up in London. After a couple of years things begin to go off. Some husbands like little children. Most don't. Mine didn't. Being children themselves most husbands resent the amount and the extent of love their wives expend on their children. It's the love they can't stand, I think. The love pours out of the mothers into the children. The husbands don't think they get that sort of unconditional love any more. So some of them look elsewhere. Business keeps them in London overnight. In my case business took Randolph off to France a lot. He had to work very hard when he was there. He was always exhausted when he came home. Sometimes, now the children have left home – they can be so cruel, children, without ever realizing it – I feel like an empty wine bottle. My goodness has all gone, it's been spent, or consumed, or drunk. Now I'm just a glass shell waiting for the rubbish collection and a last few hours before being smashed to pieces.'

She paused for another drink. Her head was beginning to sway slightly. Powerscourt felt desperately sorry for her.

'So there you have it, Lord Powerscourt. Ours was a perfectly normal middle-class marriage. There are thousands more like it across the squares of Kensington and Chelsea and the grander houses of the Home Counties. Perfectly normal.' Hermione Colville began to weep, very gently and very quietly. The tears ran down her cheeks and on to her black silk shirt. Powerscourt fell into the male role in such occasions and offered his handkerchief as a substitute for comfort. There were a number of questions he wanted to ask but he felt the time was not right.

'We've often wondered, you know,' she looked at him through her tears, 'the women of my acquaintance and myself, whether we would have been happier if we had never married, if we'd never known the terrible unhappiness marriage sometimes brings. And do you know what most of us conclude? That in spite of everything, all the bad times, we would still rather have had to endure those than to live alone as a spinster in some damp little place in Battersea or go on living at home and watch our parents falling to pieces until they died.'

Powerscourt waited. There might be more to come yet. Would she speak of Randolph's wandering eye, he wondered? Did he dare ask? How should he phrase it?

She rang the bell again. 'Lord Powerscourt is just leaving us,' she said to the dwarf butler, as Powerscourt now referred to him in his mind. 'I think it's for the best,' she said to Powerscourt, trying to rise from her chair and falling back again. Powerscourt bowed to Hermione Colville and set out from the house towards the railway station. The air of Moulsford was refreshing, he thought. Especially when you were out of doors.

Powerscourt wondered about Mrs Colville in his train back to London. How much should he believe of what she had said? All of it? None of it? Was this In Vino Veritas? Or was it rather In Vino A Pack Of Lies? On the whole he subscribed to the latter theory, that most of what Hermione had said could be put down to a maudlin self-pity and an over-dramatized version of her position brought on by the increasing pull of the Chablis.

He wondered too about Timothy Barrington White, married to Lady Lucy's cousin Milly, and his friend Beauchamp Trumper at their drinking club near Paddington station. For Powerscourt had now reconciled himself to the kind of defence they would have to offer for Cosmo Colville. It was now unlikely that he was going to make one major discovery that would turn the prosecution case upside down and force them to withdraw. He thought of their position in building terms. He no longer felt that he would be able to produce a whole new floor, composed of sound boards and solid walls, large windows letting in the light. Instead, Powerscourt reckoned, they would have to come up with a mosaic of doubts and suspicions and uncertainties that might persuade the jury that they could not be certain Cosmo was the murderer. Into such a mosaic, rather like that in some long-abandoned Roman villa, Timothy Barrington White and his drinking companion might be profitably accommodated. First the friend would have to be persuaded to give evidence about Barrington White's threat to kill the Colvilles.

Then White would have to take the stand and answer questions about his previous rows with them. Charles Augustus Pugh would remind him of his threat. Pugh would then put it to White that he had, in fact, carried out his threat, that he had, indeed, only gone to the wedding to commit murder. White would deny it, of course, but some collateral damage might have been inflicted on the prosecution case.

There was, Powerscourt well knew, only one problem with his plan, maybe two. Lady Lucy would have to approve for a start. If he organized it with Pugh's people and Pugh's chambers without telling Lucy there would be hell to pay. He would, he decided, write to Pugh as soon as he could and ask his advice. Powerscourt suspected the whole scheme might be a waste of time. He approached the subject gingerly as he inspected an atlas of Norfolk for his trip later that day.

'Do you want me to organize this for you, Francis?' Lady Lucy said. 'Talk to the parties concerned and then tell Mr Pugh to sign them up or whatever it is he has to do?'

'Well,' said Powerscourt, 'let's wait and see what Pugh has to say.'

The conversation was cut short by the arrival of the twins. Ever since they could understand things they had been fascinated by maps. They stared at the page opened at the county of Norfolk. They understood that the lines of black ladders meant railways. On an earlier occasion, Powerscourt remembered, they had climbed up on the table and run their fingers along the railway symbol all the way from Plymouth to Inverness. On this occasion their interest lay elsewhere.

'Blue,' said Christopher.

'Blue,' said Juliet.

'Sea?' said Christopher, looking hopefully at his father.

The sea, in Powerscourt's experience, was the only thing known to have reduced the twins to total silence. That summer he and Lady Lucy had taken them to a great beach in Dorset and Powerscourt made them close their eyes until he gave the word. When the party was right at the top of the beach, the sea about four hundred yards away, Powerscourt told them to open their eyes. They looked at their parents. They looked at the sea. They looked at each other. They looked at the sea again. They stood perfectly still for over a minute without any fighting or kicking. Then with a great war whoop they held hands and hurtled off towards the water at full speed.

'All the way round the coast,' Powerscourt's finger ran in a great arc round the coast of Norfolk from Hunstanton to Lowestoft, 'there is the sea. North Sea, it's called.' He closed the atlas rapidly in case the twins worked out where he was going and asked to come too. He was saved by the voice of Cook offering fresh buns in the kitchen. He kissed Lady Lucy on the lips and set off for the railway station.

Powerscourt had arranged to meet Inspector Cooper at the Black Boys Hotel in Aylsham early that evening. He had taken the liberty of asking the young detective to bring copies of his two seating plans with him. He had pointed out that the defence could easily ask for them to be introduced as pieces of evidence at the trial. He thought again about the case against Cosmo with the gun in his hand. He still found it hard to believe that they could assemble a defence that could secure his acquittal. Piece by piece, he said to himself, scintilla of doubt followed by scintilla of doubt, undermining the jury's confidence like the incoming tide eroding a sandcastle on the beach.

'Good evening, Lord Powerscourt.' Inspector Cooper was there to greet him in the lounge of his hotel.

'I trust I find you well, Inspector,' said Powerscourt, shaking the young man's hand.

'More than well,' said Cooper, beaming broadly at his visitor.

'Has some happy event brightened up your life?' asked Powerscourt with a smile.

'It has indeed, my lord. I am engaged to be married, so I am, and that's a fact.'

'I take it this happened fairly recently?' said Powerscourt. 'May I wish you every happiness in your married life.'

'I asked Charlotte two Sundays ago. I was going to ask her on Christmas Eve, you know, but she looked so lovely that afternoon it sort of slipped out. Then I asked her father for her hand this Sunday gone. He was very happy for us.'

A rising police inspector would be a good match for your daughter, Powerscourt thought, a steadily growing income, sufficient money to support a family, a reliable pension at the end. A man might do worse for his daughter, a lot worse.

Powerscourt thought the Inspector had turned into a puppy, he was so happy. 'Forgive me for turning to business, Inspector, but were you able to find the time to have copies made of those two seating plans?'

'Of course,' said Inspector Cooper, fetching a large envelope from his briefcase. 'This is the one that relates to the moments before they left the garden and went upstairs, and this relates to where we think they were just before the shooting.' Each wedding guest, Powerscourt noted, was represented by a circle with a name inside. The large sheets of stiff paper were encrusted with circles.

'Thank you so much,' said Powerscourt, popping them back into their envelope for now. 'You don't happen to have addresses for all these people, do you, by any chance?'

'I don't but Mrs Nash does, I think. She had them all to send out the invitations. I was going to borrow her list when – when other matters intervened and the investigation was closed.'

'I hope to see Mrs Nash tomorrow as a matter of fact. Tell me, Inspector, has any fresh evidence come to light concerning this case? I presume you have been involved with other cases but there is often a trickle of fresh intelligence.'

'I have heard nothing,' said the young man. 'And how are your investigations proceeding, Lord Powerscourt? Have you cracked the case? Discovered the real murderer?'

Powerscourt decided there could be no harm in a little exaggeration. Nothing huge, just a little nudge that might, just might, persuade the prosecution that their case was already won and they could afford to be complacent.

'I am here this evening, as you see, Inspector. Tomorrow I carry out more inquiries. The day after that I shall return to London and carry out more. We have made no progress. The case remains exactly where it was when you were taken off it. The date for the trial may come this week. The defence barrister and I both wish we had never taken the business on. It does a man's career no service at all if is dogged by failure. I have never failed yet in a murder investigation, never. This case is going to be the first one. I am sure of it.'

11

Lord Francis Powerscourt wasn't absolutely sure what he hoped to find on his voyage round the hotels of northern Norfolk. If he was honest with himself, he was rather ashamed of what he was doing. It was all part of the attempt to build up a case for the defence. He hoped he would find a foreigner who had come to stay in one of these hotels. He hoped Charles Augustus Pugh could imply that the stranger had come for the wedding. Once persuade the jury that the stranger had penetrated the grounds of Brympton Hall and anything might be possible. Juries don't like foreigners very much, he remembered Pugh telling him about some earlier case. In some parts of the country they really don't like them at all.

The hotel manager in his own hotel, the Black Boys, at the corner of the main square in Aylsham, a mile and half from the Hall, remembered the night before the wedding well. The hotel was full, every last bed occupied. Mr Willoughby had booked all the rooms six weeks before. Were all the guests English? From London and around there? Powerscourt had asked. Oh, yes, the hotel-keeper had assured him. There had been some sort of sing-song after supper and the guests had all known the words, the hotel-keeper remembered that. No Frenchmen? Powerscourt had asked wistfully, no Italians? None of those, sir. What would them people want with a wedding in Norfolk anyway? Murder, Powerscourt said to himself, murder most foul, and he went in for his supper.

A few miles to the south was the Marsham Arms in Hevingham on the Norwich road, an ancient establishment even older than the Black Boys in Aylsham. It was the lady of the house who received him.

'The day you're asking about, sir, that'll be the day of the big wedding up at Brympton, the one with the murder, would it?'

Powerscourt assured her that it was. She bent down and pulled out a large visitors' book from a drawer underneath the table. 'Frederick and I always make sure we get the visitors to sign in. You can't be sure, of course, if they're signing with their real names or not. In the summer holidays you'd be surprised at how many strange people we get. A great number of people called Jones come for the weekend in the summer. It must be something in the air. Never mind. Fourth, fifth, sixth, here we are. We were nearly full that night, sir. Would you like to take a look for yourself?' She spun the book round and Powerscourt read a series of innocuous English names.

'No Frenchmen?' he asked. 'No foreigners?'

'No, sir, not that we don't often have some foreigners here. Very welcome we make them too, if I might say so.'

'I'm sure you do,' said Powerscourt cheerfully and went on his way.

North-east of Brympton Hall was the Manor House in North Walsham, a fine red-brick building that looked as if it been there for a couple of centuries. The proprietor introduced himself as Archibald Wilkins, a man of average height with pale brown hair and a broken nose and so thin it was painful to behold. He too pulled out a battered visitors' book. 'I remember that day well,' he said, 'we were short-staffed and I had to wait at table myself. I'd nearly forgotten how to do it. Here we are,' he swung the book round so Powerscourt could see it clearly, 'a pair of Robertses, four Donaldsons, a brace of Chadwicks and three Jardines, one about three years old. Any of them of interest to you, sir?' The man sounded hopeful that one of his customers might be in hot water of one sort or another.

'I'm afraid not, Mr Wilkins. You didn't have any foreigners here that night, did you? Frenchman? Italian? That sort of person?'

'I never did hold with them foreigners wandering about the place and staying in our hotels,' said Mr Wilkins, 'don't give them house room here, if you follow me. We usually send them over to the Saracen's Head over Erpingham way. They'll take anything over there. Come to think of it, them Saracens were bloody foreigners too, weren't they? They'd be well suited, over there.'

Powerscourt wished that Archibald Wilkins could be transferred to London and a position on the jury at the trial of Cosmo Colville. Such xenophobia could come in very useful. He had a list of nine hotels in the area in his pocket. He wondered if he would draw blank in all of them.

His next port of call was at the Bell at Cawston a few miles to the west of Aylsham on the Dereham Road. The landlord here was a great bear of a man in his mid-thirties with a mop of black hair and a black beard called Jack Gill. He offered Powerscourt a cup of tea in the empty saloon bar while he went to fetch his books from another part of the building.

'Fifth,' the black beard muttered to himself. 'We only had three guests that evening and they were all brothers having some sort of birthday reunion. Phelps, their name was, James, Jolyon and John Phelps, as if their parents could only cope with one letter of the alphabet.'

'You didn't have any foreigners that night, Frenchmen, Italians, that sort of thing?'

'I don't think so,' said Gill, staring suddenly at his visitors' book. 'Hilda!' he shouted suddenly. 'Hilda! Where the devil are you?' His voice echoed round the ground floor of the hotel.

Jack Gill took four strides over to the door that opened on to his garden. He was just about to shout once more when a pretty blonde woman, almost covered from head to toe in the biggest apron Powerscourt had ever seen, entered the saloon bar from the opposite side.

'You didn't have to shout, Jack,' she said sweetly, 'you know this is the day I do the baking in the afternoon.'

'Sorry about that,' said Gill. 'This gentleman is asking who we had here round about the time of the wedding and the murder up at the Hall.' Powerscourt hadn't mentioned it in a single establishment – all the hotel people had just assumed that was why he was here.

'Was that the time we had Philippe the Fair here?' Gill went on. 'His reservation was in the name of Legros, Pierre Legros, but I think it was false. He pretended not to understand when we mentioned the visitors' book and signing in, but I think he knew perfectly well what was wanted. He never did sign it. That's why I'm not sure exactly when he was here. Can you remember, my dear?'

Hilda scratched vigorously at her blonde hair. Flakes of flour floated to the ground. 'Do you know, Jack, I think it was then. He was here the same day the man from Norwich came about the drains. That was the day before the wedding, I'm fairly sure of it.'

'You're right,' said Gill, 'he came just after the drain man left and we were wondering if we could ever afford his bill.'

'What sort of man was he?' asked Powerscourt. 'Would I be right in assuming he was French?'

'He was French, with just a little English. There was something about him made me think he was a military man or had been a military man in his time. That erect bearing, beautifully polished shoes he had, I remember, as if he was going on parade.'

'Age?' said Powerscourt.

'Thirty, thirty-five?' said Jack Gill.

'And what did he do when he was here?' asked Powerscourt.

'Well, that's the thing,' said Gill. 'We hardly saw anything of him at all. He paid for his accommodation the minute he arrived. Then he went up to his room and we never saw him again, did we, Hilda, until you spotted him leaving in the morning.'

Powerscourt looked at the hotel-keeper's wife. 'He'd ordered a cab to take him away, sir, so he had. And he was all dressed up with the rest of his things in that little bag he was carrying so he wasn't going to come back here.'

'How was he all dressed up, Mrs Gill?'

'Well, sir, he looked as if he was going to a wedding. That Jim Cox who drove him was in here that night having a couple of pints of beer and he said he'd taken him over to Brympton Hall.'

'The cabbie didn't pick him up again after the ceremony?' asked Powerscourt.

'No, sir, he just left him there in the morning.'

'Could you describe him for me?'

'About five foot ten,' said Jack Gill.

'Very dark hair, almost black,' said Hilda Gill. 'We only called him Philippe the Fair because I thought I remembered some French king with that name.'

'Slim, he was,' Jack carried on.

'Clean-shaven,' said Hilda. 'Dark eyes. He looked like a man on a mission of some kind.'

And that, despite all his prompting, was the sum total of what Powerscourt could get out of them. He explained that they might have to come to court to give evidence about the arrival of Philippe the Fair.

'I've always wanted to see the Old Bailey,' Jack Gill said. 'But sure to God I never thought I'd have to go and appear there.'

Powerscourt found Georgina Nash sitting in her garden in the last of the sunshine. A couple of workmen were encamped round the fountain. Another seemed to have disappeared inside it head first.

'Good afternoon, Lord Powerscourt, how nice to see you again.'

'Thank you for taking the time to talk to me.'

136

'Let's go inside and have some tea,' said Georgina Nash, rising from her bench and taking a last wistful look at the fountain. 'I'm sure you'll remember that fountain wasn't working at the time of the wedding. They haven't fixed it yet. Willoughby says I'm getting obsessed about it.'

'I'm sure it will be working again soon. They can be tricky things, fountains.'

'Have you been making any progress, Lord Powerscourt? I gather that poor man is still locked up in Pentonville and not speaking a word. Do you have any news?'

'I have to say, Mrs Nash, that I have very little progress to report. I'm not doing well at this point. I do have one or two matters I would like to ask you about, but perhaps you could tell me first of all if anything new has come to light here about the events on the day of the wedding.'

'Well, we've had all sorts of people who were there on the day come to offer condolences, that sort of thing. I'm afraid we haven't had any strange-looking person turning up and announcing that he was the murderer.'

'I don't know if you remember, Mrs Nash, but you told me at the time that a wedding would be a very good place to commit a murder. If there were any strangers about, you said, the Nashes would think they were Colvilles and the Colvilles would think they were Nashes.'

'Did I really say that, Lord Powerscourt? That's rather clever, don't you think? I shall have to tell Willoughby. He believes I haven't got any brains at all.'

'The thing is, Mrs Nash,' said Powerscourt with a smile, 'that we have evidence there was a Frenchman here that day. He stayed the night before at the Bell over at Cawston where the landlord and his wife remember him. In the morning he took a cab all dressed up in his wedding clothes and came here, to the Hall.'

'What did he look like, Lord Powerscourt?' said Georgina Nash, looking alarmed at the thought of unknown Frenchmen wandering about her property. 'What was his name?'

'We don't have a name. He booked in at the hotel calling himself Legros but he didn't sign the visitors' book so I suspect it was a false name. Five feet ten, dark hair, almost black, dark eyes, some hint of a military look about him, the Bell at Cawston people thought. Can you remember such a man, Mrs Nash?'

Georgina Nash stared closely at Powerscourt. 'Dark hair, five foot ten, military look about him, I might have seen him but I can't be sure. There were plenty of military people about on the day. You see, even if I had come across him, I think I'd have thought he was a guest of the Colvilles – they've got wine interests all over Europe, so it's only natural they should invite a Frenchman or two. Sorry, Lord Powerscourt, that's not very helpful of me.'

'Could I just ask you to think very carefully, Mrs Nash, see if you can remember seeing such a man at the far end of your Great Hall where the murder happened?'

If Charles Augustus Pugh used such a technique, Powerscourt said to himself, he would most probably receive a fearful wigging from the judge for leading the witness.

'It's no good, Lord Powerscourt,' said Georgina Nash after a moment or two, 'I can't do it, I just can't.'

'Perhaps these might help you along,' said Powerscourt, producing the two seating plans he had obtained from Inspector Cooper and placing them on the low table.

'How fascinating,' said Georgina Nash, staring carefully at the Long Gallery seating plan and the garden plan, so carefully filled in, with names in bubbles by the matchstick wedding guests, the whole resembling the identifying key to the people in enormous paintings like Derby Day by artists like Frith, where a reproduction of the painting was made, with blank white spaces where the heads of the MPs or the spectators at Derby Day had been. Inside each head was a number and the numbers matched the names of the people in the main painting in a great panel on the side.

Georgina Nash shook her head slowly. 'It's no good,' she said finally, 'I can't do it.'

'Never mind, Mrs Nash, it's of no consequence. Could I ask a favour, a double favour of you? Do you have addresses of all these people in these seating plans? I'm sure you must have had them when you sent out the invitations but you may have thrown them away.'

'No,' said Georgina Nash, 'I have them still. I shall fetch them directly. What was the other half of your favour, Lord Powerscourt?'

'I thought you would have them,' said Powerscourt. 'The second favour is to ask if I could shoot upstairs and take another look at the Long Gallery while you are fetching the addresses?'

'Of course,' said Mrs Nash. 'You'll forgive me if I don't come with you. Neither Willoughby nor I have set foot in those rooms since the wedding.'

Powerscourt went out to the great staircase where the guests had gathered on that terrible day. He retraced the steps most of them would have taken, into the upper Anteroom with its French hunting tapestries and on into the Long Gallery itself. He headed straight for the far end, looking out over the lake. He checked the door on the right-hand side that opened on to the staircase leading to the garden where the guests had been taking their champagne. Up these, he said to himself, into the Peter the Great room, meet Randolph Colville in the state bedroom, pull out your pistol and shoot him dead. Make your escape back the way you had come. Or take the staircase in the corner of the state bedroom down and out into the west front and the gardens on the opposite side to the wedding party. From here you could vanish, or you could make your way round to the garden party and mingle with them until the time came to climb the stairs. Those two staircases, Powerscourt was sure, in some combination or other, must have provided the way in and the way out for the murderer. There were yet more staircases in the body of the house but he wasn't sure how many people would have known about them.

He strode rapidly from one staircase to the other. He stared at the gardens for a long time, his mind far away. He was returned to life by a great shout from Mrs Nash in her drawing room a floor below. 'Lord Powerscourt! Lord Powerscourt! Please come!'

She was standing by the window, mesmerized. Georgina Nash pressed a thick envelope into his hand. 'That has all the addresses you need,' she said, 'but look, Lord Powerscourt, look!' A hundred yards or so away, in the centre of the garden, the workmen had moved away from the fountain. A slow stream of water was climbing into the afternoon air. He felt her fingers tighten their grip on his arm.

'Watch,' she said. Even as she spoke, the mechanical devices operating the fountain sprang into full working order. The water shot twenty, then thirty, then forty feet into the air. The workmen cheered and waved their caps in the air. Georgina Nash shouted for joy. There were tears in her eyes as she looked at Powerscourt and said, 'My fountain! At last! After so long! At last!'

Johnny Fitzgerald came to breakfast in Markham Square the next morning. This was a most unusual event. Powerscourt could only remember Johnny coming for the eggs and bacon once, or possibly twice, in all the years they had lived in London. Only great events or great peril could bring Fitzgerald out at this hour. He was sitting on Lady Lucy's left hand, opposite the twins who were making valiant efforts to sit still.

'If you eat your breakfast properly,' he said, staring at them in mock severity, 'I might, just might, begin a little story for the pair of you after breakfast. Only the beginning of a story,' he emphasized as the twins began to consume toast at Olympic speed, 'you might get the next bit at bedtime.'

'Johnny,' said Powerscourt, 'how nice to see you at this early hour. It has special meaning because it is so unusual. You don't normally come for breakfast. You don't normally come for morning coffee. You don't normally come for lunch. Only very rarely do you come for tea and then it is unusually late, as if it might not be time for a glass of something. So tell us, my friend, is the world about to end? Have you cracked this case? Have you fallen in love?'

Johnny Fitzgerald laughed. 'I'm afraid I have to say no to all of those. I think my news had better wait till I have said a few words of story to our young friends across the table.' Christopher and Juliet were sitting upright in their chairs now, their arms folded across their chests, looking demurely in front of them, as if preparing to take part in an advertisement for perfectly behaved children. In front of them two large beaches of crumbs surrounded the plates where they had eaten their toast. Johnny Fitzgerald picked them up, one on each arm, and carried the twins out of the room. Lady Lucy smiled at her husband as the beginning of the story drifted down the stairs.

'This is the story of Drago the young dragon who got lost and separated from his parent dragons on a long journey across the sea.' Johnny breathed heavily and made hissing noises at this point. The twins squealed happily. 'Drago is tired now. His limbs ache from hours and hours of flying. In front of him he can see a great city where humans live and a river going through it. Drawing on the last of his strength and taking care not to blow any sheets of flame in front of him, Drago flies up the river and finally falls asleep on the riverbank. He does not know it, but Drago the young dragon has reached a place called Chelsea.' At that point Johnny emitted a huge hiss and fled the room, leaving the twins to the care of their nurse.

'Francis, Lucy.' Johnny helped himself to some more toast on his return. 'I have been doing a lot of drinking with the young men of Colvilles and some dockers and some chap who works in one of those big hotels behind Piccadilly, Whites, I think it's called. He's very keen on money, Francis, so I'm afraid I've had to humour him to get what I wanted. The news came almost by accident. He was telling me, this chap, about these big dinners they have once a month or so, pre-phylloxera dinners they're called, where all the wines served were made before the wine pest destroyed the French vineyards. Because they're so rare, these wines, they command high prices and these rich people, City types most of them, plenty of Old Etonians about, pay even higher prices to drink them.'

'Where do they come from, these wines?' asked Powerscourt. 'Pretty rare I'd have thought.'

'Good question, Francis, very good question. They're supposed to come from the cellars of abbeys or monasteries, or private houses where the master of the house or his butler was accustomed to laying down large quantities in the cellar during the good years. Nobody's touched them in the plague years. At this point, Francis, a pound changed hands. Then another. You'll not believe what I'm about to tell you, said my informant who called himself Fred, though I doubt if that is his real name.'

Johnny paused and took a sip of his tea. All this talk of wine and ancient vintages was making him thirsty and not for the produce of Assam or Darjeeling.

'What did the man called Fred say, Johnny?' said Lady Lucy, who remembered Johnny spinning out stories for so long that you almost wanted to scream.

'This is what he said.' Johnny lent forward to stare into Lady Lucy's face. 'The wine at these dinners is fake. It doesn't come from the cellars of some abandoned abbey or closed-down hotel. It's manufactured here in London, in a warehouse, where they have great stocks of pre-phylloxera labels from real châteaux they can replicate and all sorts of different wines they can blend together to produce the fakes. The chief forger has a strange name called the Necromancer or something like that. He's very secretive. Nobody knows his real name.'

'Surely the guests must smell a rat?' said Powerscourt. 'Surely they must suspect something is wrong?'

'Fred was rather sharp about that, Francis. I asked him precisely those questions. Think of it like this, he said. Sometimes I have to wait at table on these occasions. Everybody is dressed up. The table is beautifully laid out. You are told when you arrive which wines you are going to drink. These will not be the great wines of Bordeaux, the Lafites, the Latours, Margaux. Rather they will be decent second division wines most people will not have heard of. You have paid all this money. You are surrounded by fellow wine connoisseurs. Everything conspires to tell you these wines are real. It would never occur to you to think otherwise. The ambience, the candles, the silver, the elegant glasses all conspire to complete the illusion. And there's one other thing Fred pointed out. Very few people know a lot about wine. Nobody, but nobody would have tasted these wines before the onset of the phylloxera. So nobody would know what they were meant to taste like. So the dinners continue. The Necromancer produces the batch for the next event. The hotel must know what is going on but they and the forger are making a great deal of money.'

'Fascinating,' said Powerscourt. 'I don't suppose we know what the Necromancer uses to produce his fakes, do we? And I suspect you have more information for us, Johnny. I don't believe you would have broken the customs of a lifetime to come here for breakfast and tell us about forged prephylloxera vintages. I think there's more. And I think it must have to do with this Necromancer person. Who else does he provide for, Johnny? How extensive is his client list?'

Johnny Fitzgerald laughed. 'A hit,' he said, 'a very palpable hit. There is indeed more, though it is not all definite. Yes, the Necromancer has other customers. Yes, they include some of the leading wine merchants of London. Piccadilly Wine, a new and well-run competitor to the Colvilles in the London area, is believed to be a client. The Colvilles themselves? Nobody knows. I don't actually think Fred knows one way or the other. I could ask him to find out, of course, but I don't think reliable information is easy to find. It's not like you're dealing with Fortnum and Mason or the Army and Navy stores, if you see what I mean.'

'Do we know where the Necromancer lives? Or where he works? I wonder which law he is actually breaking. Anyway, Johnny, well done indeed. Think of the possibilities for blackmail all round. Consider the hotel with the dinners and the pre-plague wines. Roll up one morning and tell them you know the wines are all fakes and forgeries. For a small consideration, fifty pounds a dinner, hundred pounds a dinner, you will keep the knowledge to yourself. The potential shame and the potential scandal mean that you are almost certain to pay up. No hotel could bring it out into the open and appear in court. They'd be finished.'

'Surely there's something else,' said Lady Lucy. 'Suppose the Colvilles are also customers. Might not that be the key to the blackmail, if there is blackmail? Pay up or we'll tell the world that some of your wines don't come from France at all, but are cooked up in some Devil's Kitchen in a warehouse in Shoreditch. You'd pay up pretty quickly then, I should think.'

Johnny Fitzgerald rose. 'I'm most grateful for my breakfast. Now I must sleep. I shall give my full attention to the other customers of the man they call the Necromancer. I only have one other matter to attend to early this evening.'

'What's that, Johnny?' asked Lady Lucy.

'Why,' said Johnny very seriously, 'it concerns a young dragon called Drago who has lost his parents and fallen asleep on the riverbank in Chelsea. Do you think he should enter your house by the front door or by coming down the chimney breathing fire and smoke?'

12

It was just another boring morning in the life of Emily Colville in her little house in Barnes close to Hammersmith Bridge and the river Thames. The maid brought in the post as she sat sipping desultorily at a cup of coffee at the kitchen table. Montague had long since departed for the wines and spirits of Colvilles. There was a bill from her dressmaker in Chelsea. Really, the amount these people charged these days was outrageous. She hoped Montague wouldn't make a scene. She did dislike scenes so, they always gave her a headache. There was another bill from the place where she bought her shoes. That too seemed outrageous. Why was life so unkind to her? Then she noticed another, rather larger envelope in a hand she knew all too well. Emily stared at it and her heart began to beat faster. She hardly dared open it. She took a little walk into the dining room and back to the kitchen. At last she summoned her courage. She opened the letter with a trembling hand. It was the same as all those other letters she had received earlier that summer. There was no letter inside, only a sheet of music for a popular song of the time, 'Shine On Harvest Moon'. The cover showed a cornfield at night with a couple framed in moonlight at the top. Emily looked at the first page of the sheet music and she smiled. She shivered slightly as she worked out the code hidden among the clefs and the minims. She was to meet her lover in two days' time in the afternoon in the usual place. She would tell Montague she wished to see her parents for a day or two. Only she would leave on an earlier train and be waiting for her lover in the little house behind the lake in Norfolk.

Why do I always postpone the difficult interviews? Why can't I go and do them at the beginning? Powerscourt was berating himself. It's cowardice, pure and simple. Who knows, if I had conducted this interview earlier, the whole case might be over by now. A sensible investigator like Mr Sherlock Holmes would not have been smoking opium and playing the violin in 221B Baker Street. He would have summoned a brougham and driven straight to Wisteria Lodge and taken the interview in hand. Come to think of it, Powerscourt's internal monologue went on, 221B Baker Street is only a couple of hundred yards away. He was walking across St John's Wood to the house of Mrs Cosmo Colville, wife of the man incarcerated in Pentonville prison who had scarcely, as far as anybody knew, spoken a single word since he was found opposite the dead body of his brother, with what seemed to be his brother's gun in his hand. Her reply to his note had been encouraging: 'Of course you must come and see me. I would be delighted to welcome you to my house. Might I suggest three o'clock on Wednesday?'

So far it had not been a good day for Lord Francis Powerscourt. A note had come for him first thing that morning from Charles Augustus Pugh.

'Trumper, Barrington White,' it said. 'Horse won't run. No legs. Barrington White goes into witness box. Denies everything. We have no proof of anything at all. Waste of time. Only causes drop in our share price, already at dangerously low levels. Regards. Pugh.'

A military butler showed him into a well-proportioned drawing room with great sofas and prints and pictures covering the walls. Isabella Colville was sitting in an armchair to the left of the fire. She motioned Powerscourt to its twin on the other side. She was a tall, slim woman, with pale hair that was almost blonde and faint lines that might have been caused by worry and strain on her forehead, wearing a long dark grey skirt with a blue blouse that showed off the colour of her hair.

'Lord Powerscourt, let me say first of all how grateful we are for what you are doing. It is much appreciated, you know.'

Powerscourt waved his hands slightly and shook his head, 'I thank you for your kind words, Mrs Colville. I wish I could say that I had done enough so far to deserve them. I fear I have not. Not yet at any rate.'

'But there's always time, isn't there. Somebody who knew about one of your earlier cases, Lord Powerscourt, told me the other day that sometimes the answer comes to you in a flash. There's a sheet of lightning or something like that in your brain and all the pieces of the puzzle fall into place.'

'You're too kind,' said Powerscourt. 'Let's all pray for lightning.' They laughed.

'Now then,' said Isabella Colville, 'I've been thinking about this conversation, Lord Powerscourt. You must feel free to ask me absolutely anything you want. I don't mind if it seems rude or in bad taste. You see, that's my husband and the father of my children in that horrible prison. I'll do anything I can to help get him out. I gather you've seen my sister-in-law over at Pangbourne? Could I ask you what time of day it was?'

'I arrived about half past ten,' said Powerscourt, reluctant to criticize her sister-in-law.

'I wish you had talked to me beforehand. The hour between nine and ten is the only safe one in the day. I've told the lawyers that. Otherwise the Chablis flows on and on like the Mississippi river. I'm not judging her, mind you. My husband may not be in ideal circumstances but at least he's still alive.'

'When did you last see him, your husband I mean?'

'Yesterday afternoon.'

'Did he say anything?'

'Not a word, not one.'

'So what do you talk about? Do you tell him the latest news?'

'I do.' Isabella Colville smiled for a moment. 'I decided early on that it's like talking to some old person who's near death's door and has lost the power of speech. But they can still make sense of most of what you tell them. I do find I prattle on a bit but it's the best I can do.'

'So what kind of things do you talk to him about?'

'Well, I tell him what news I have of the children – they've left home now but they're always keen for the latest about their father. I tell him about what news I have of the other Colvilles. I tell him about the house – yesterday I had to inform him that the footman had dropped a valuable vase on the kitchen floor where it smashed to pieces. Talking of other Colvilles, you should go and see a cousin of ours who worked for the firm for a long time. He grew up with Randolph and Cosmo. He and his wife live in Ealing now.'

Powerscourt could see her now in that Spartan cell in Pentonville, her face bright as if she were talking to a small child, reeling off the latest family and domestic gossip, hoping for a word or a reaction that never came. And hovering behind the silence, the secret on the far side of the prison visiting room, the prison chaplain, the prison governor, the prison hangman, the noose and the drop.

'Tell me, Mrs Colville, do you get any reaction at all? A smile? A kiss when you arrive? An embrace when you leave?'

Isabella Colville shook her head rather sadly. 'No, there's none of that. Hold on a minute though, that's not quite true. His eyes are eloquent sometimes, as if he's trying to tell me something. That he cares, perhaps. I don't know.'

Powerscourt had always known how he wanted to end their interview, and in some ways he wished he could ask those questions now. But he stuck to his original plan.

'Tell me about your husband, Mrs Colville,' he was speaking very quietly, 'what sort of a man is he?'

She paused for a moment. 'It's odd, isn't it,' she said, 'how difficult it is to answer that question about somebody you know so well. Let me begin with his work, that's probably the easiest thing.'

She paused again and looked into the fire. 'Conscientious, that's how I would describe his attitude to his work. Conservative, maybe even a little old-fashioned. He inherited that whole Bordeaux network from his father and his uncle, you see, the growers, the *négociants*, the shippers, the owners. He took great care to maintain good relations with all of them. Indeed, as far as I know, and I never followed the wine business very carefully, most of the people he deals with are the same people or the sons of the same people his father dealt with. As far as I know, some of these other wine merchants are forever looking out for new suppliers, changing their shippers, taking a chance on some new grower with revolutionary new ways of doing things, always in a ferment of excitement. That wasn't Cosmo's way. He didn't like ferment very much. He didn't like change. He didn't like excitement.'

'Was his work the most important thing in his life? Some of these second-generation merchants in wine or tea or things like that develop interests which become the mainspring of their lives. Shire horses, maybe, art collecting, that sort of thing. Was your husband one of those?'

'I think that's difficult. The business was very important to him. He might not have liked it very much, but it was what he inherited from his father. He had to maintain what he had and pass it on in his turn. The real passion in his life was cricket. That's what he really cared about. That's why, I'm sure you will have noticed, we live where we do, so close to Lord's Cricket Ground. Cosmo has an enormous collection of paintings and prints of Lord's in his study and on the back stairs. He did say that we could have a cricket-free area in here. He was quite thoughtful in that way.'

'And in other ways, was he not so thoughtful perhaps?'

'I wouldn't say that, Lord Powerscourt. He was very dutiful. He always remembered everybody's birthday.'

Powerscourt was now close to the end he had planned

beforehand. 'Duty, Mrs Colville, would doing his duty sum up his attitude to life and his role in it?'

'Duty? Duty?' Isabella Colville held the word up to the light, as it were, and looked at it carefully. 'I suppose you could say that. Duty or responsibility, yes, you could.'

'And what form of duty would compel your husband not to speak a word in his own defence or to explain what had been going on in the Peter the Great room and the state bedroom up at Brympton Hall on the day of the wedding?'

Isabella Colville looked at him helplessly. 'I don't know,' she whispered, 'I really don't know.'

'Let me try a few suggestions on you, Mrs Colville. Family honour perhaps? Suppose there was some terrible scandal about to break that would be bad for the Colvilles and could be ruinous for the business?'

'He cared profoundly about anything concerning family honour or scandal that could ruin the family name. He said so in that terrible family row the week before the wedding.'

Isabella Colville paused. She began to turn pink, then red. She looked down at the floor and stammered, 'I didn't mean to say that. It was a mistake.' Two desperate eyes now looked up at Powerscourt. He felt as if somebody had just placed something very slippery – a scallop perhaps, or a Dover sole – in his hand and he must not let it go.

'Perhaps,' he said in his mildest voice, 'you could tell me a little more about the family row. Just the broad outline, of course.'

Isabella Colville shook her head. Powerscourt decided to try sternness.

'I do not wish to remind you of certain unpleasant facts, Mrs Colville, but this knowledge could help release your husband from Pentonville. Unless something material can be presented by the defence the chances are that he will be found guilty. And you know as well as I do what that means.'

'It concerns the family, it's private,' she said. 'I can't see how it has anything to do with the trial.'

'With the greatest respect, Mrs Colville, I think that's a matter for myself and the defence counsel Mr Pugh to decide.'

'It's family, it's private.'

'Nothing is private in a murder trial, Mrs Colville.'

'This is,' she said defiantly.

'Very well,' said Powerscourt, 'we'll leave it there for now, Mrs Colville. But you are free to change your mind at any time. You have my address. Please don't hesitate to get in touch at any time of day or night. It could save your husband's life.'

Powerscourt was thinking of honour on his way back to Chelsea. Was honour, in this most modern age, still capable of bringing a man to a display of honourable silence that could kill him, like Cosmo Colville? He thought of Falstaff's more cynical or more realistic view of it in *Henry IV*, 'What is honour? A word. What is that word honour? Air. Who hath it? He that died o' Wednesday.'

It was not yet clear on which day of the week Cosmo would die, but die he would unless he, Powerscourt, could pull off a miracle. As he passed down the northern end of Baker Street, close to where 221B would have been, he sent a message to Sherlock Holmes, asking for assistance.

Lady Lucy was reading the Obituary columns of *The Times* when Powerscourt returned to Markham Square 'Francis,' she said, 'you've just missed Sir Pericles. He only left the house five minutes ago.'

'And what did he have to say, Lucy?'

'He seems to have got his lines of communication into Colvilles working like clockwork,' Lady Lucy said. 'He says they've hired a *négociant* in Burgundy to supervise the despatch of all that Colville wine.'

'There's still going to be a gap, isn't there? Between the current lot running out and the next lot arriving. I wonder what they'll do about that,' said Powerscourt. 'Perhaps they'll give the Necromancer a call.'

151

'Do you think they'd do that? Employ a sort of wine forger, Francis?'

'Well, that posh hotel where they have the pre-phylloxera dinners is happy to serve his wares.'

'So they are, but the question is, do they know they are buying a heap of fakes, the hotel people, or do they buy them from some apparently respectable wine merchant, supposing them to be real?'

'Maybe I should go and talk to the wine department of Whites Hotel.'

'Never mind that, Francis, tell me what Mrs Colville had to say for herself.'

Powerscourt told her everything, the frankness at the beginning, her description of Cosmo's character, and then the news of the family row before the wedding.

'Did she say how long the row was before the wedding? Days? Weeks?'

'She said it was a week before the wedding. Now then, Lucy, I think we should run through what we know so far. Some fresh line of inquiry may come to us. Time is running short, after all. Let's begin with the murder itself. What do you think was going on?'

'Let's think of our French friend, the one who stayed in Norfolk the night before the wedding. Suppose he has some score to settle with Randolph that has to do with the Colville wine business in Burgundy. He reaches the Hall, finds the gun, shoots Randolph and disappears, leaving the gun lying on the floor for Cosmo to pick up.'

'But the gun, Lucy, how did the gun get there?'

'How about this. After the family row Randolph was so worried about the possibility of family fights and family violence that he took the gun along to keep the peace if necessary. The Frenchman forced him to hand it over and shot Randolph.'

'But how did the Frenchman know there was going to be a gun there?' said Powerscourt. 'He can't have been exchanging

152

messages with Randolph across the bloody Channel, can he? Maybe the gun had dropped out of somebody's pocket. That's not much good either. I don't think it would stand up to cross-examination in court, do you?'

'No, I don't, Francis. Surely if you were a Frenchman with murderous intent you would bring your own weapon with you. You wouldn't want to take a chance on finding one lying around at a wedding.'

'You're absolutely right. We're going round in circles so we are. Why don't we look at it another way, Lucy. I hoped I could run through with Mrs Colville the various reasons that might have persuaded Cosmo to pick up the gun and to keep quiet. We know about family honour, family scandal. What else?'

'Suppose he was being chivalrous. Suppose there was a woman involved and he wanted to protect her.'

'Possible, but which woman? Isabella Colville? Well, maybe he would do it for her. I can't see him doing it for anybody else. I'm afraid there is another explanation that fits the bill perfectly,' said Powerscourt. 'Let's go back to the family row. Let's suppose that an argument between Randolph and Cosmo is at the centre of it. The row grows even more heated and even more poisonous in the days leading up to the wedding. So Randolph takes his gun along, either in self-defence or because he intends to shoot Cosmo. They arrange to meet in the state bedroom at the far end of the Nashes' Long Gallery. Either there is a scuffle and Randolph gets shot. Or Cosmo grabs the gun and kills Randolph just before the butler chap comes into the room. He can't throw the gun away, so he hangs on to it.'

'But why,' said Lady Lucy, 'does he keep quiet? Why doesn't he speak?'

'Ah ha,' said Powerscourt, 'this is where the row comes in. If he speaks he will have to explain, sooner or later, what the row was about, if not to the police, then under oath to counsel in court. That would bring disgrace on the name of Colville and ruin to the business. The grey hairs of the remaining old gentleman who raised Colvilles to fame and fortune will turn white. His last years will be spent in shame and sorrow. All of that must flash through Cosmo's brain. He is a man of conscience, after all, susceptible to the call of duty. He keeps his mouth shut.'

'You mean, the police have got the right man all along, Francis?'

'I wouldn't go as far as to say that, Lucy. It's interesting, I think, that we haven't yet come up with a more convincing explanation of the shooting of Randolph Colville.' Powerscourt wandered over to the window and looked out at the traffic in Markham Square. Way over to his left there was a rumble of cabs and buses progressing along the King's Road towards Sloane Square. Two small boys were kicking a stone along the pavement.

'That's not the only mystery we haven't solved, Lucy. There's the question of the blackmailer, if there is a blackmailer. There's Randolph's missing money and the tens of thousands those accountants found disappearing from the Colvilles' accounts.'

Powerscourt paused and looked back at the traffic again. 'I don't think this is doing us any good. We'll make ourselves confused and depressed. I'm sure I could find some lights of hope if I set my mind to it, but just at the moment hope in this case seems rather far away. Why don't I take you out to dinner, Lucy? There's a new restaurant just opened in Lower Sloane Street. They say the seafood is excellent.'

Tristram Bennett, a Colville on his mother's side, had decided that it was his destiny to save the family. A couple of days before his tryst with Emily he was making his way towards the Colville Head Office behind Oxford Street. He looked down at his tie from time to time. He wasn't sure that these were the clothes a sober wine merchant should be seen wearing in the heart of the West End. The suit was not a quiet suit. It did not speak of respectability. With its long jacket and wide labels it had a faint air of Regency about it, as if Tristram was on his way to some coffee house in Covent Garden. The shirt was loud and the tie was raffish. Trying to remember when he had last worn this outfit, Tristram recalled that it was on a visit to a club off Park Lane where people gambled for high stakes. He had been wondering about Emily Colville on the way. She was very young and very pretty, but had he had the best of her? She didn't have enough money to help support his lifestyle and she wasn't always available. Maybe he should just give her up. As he crossed the Colville threshold he remembered that he might come across Emily's husband Montague, toiling in some lowly position among the wines and spirits. Montague was never going to set the world on fire, Tristram said to himself, not even the limited world of London's wine. Montague was one of those regular souls who would work away for years, with only limited doses of promotion, perfectly happy to fill his days in the station and the manner he had been called to. Such a life, however, was not for Tristram. He would, as he often told himself when on the verge of some great adventure, rather die in glory on the battlefield than serve a lifetime in the counting house.

He swept into the Colville Head Office, across the great room where the clerks laboured to keep paper track of all those different bottles and cases that circled the globe, and up to Alfred Davis's office.

'Good morning , Davis,' he said, 'I've come to restore order here. Things have got out of hand since the unfortunate events at the wedding. Take me to Mr Randolph's room, if you would. I'll make a start there.'

The one thing instilled into Davis and his fellows was that obedience to any Colville demand was automatic, unquestioning, instant. In such a spirit, centuries before, the servants of the emperors in Rome must have opened doors and bottles and laid out the clothes of their masters. The Colville code, unfortunately, like that of the emperors, had made no allowance for bad Colvilles but Alfred was not to know that. He took Tristram down a floor and showed him into the large office where Randolph had worked. Tristram sat at the desk by the window and told Davis he could go now. When he, Tristram, wanted him, he would send a message. He went over to the door and made sure it was firmly shut. Then he began his morning's work with Randolph's diary. Nothing very interesting there. Tristram had imagined endless invitations to wine or port tastings at discreet hotels off Park Lane, lunches in expensive restaurants with leading members of the wine trade, men from Berry Bros. & Rudd, or Justerini & Brooks perhaps. Instead he found a very mundane list, meetings with wine shippers, meetings with wine merchants who dealt in bulk transport, meetings with bottlers and bottle manufacturers and advertising men. This was not the stuff of high romance, Tristram said to himself, wearying of the mundane. He turned instead to two large files of Randolph's correspondence. Anybody looking at Tristram at this point would not have described him as a man dabbling around for fun in somebody else's business. They would have said he was a man definitely looking for something. And he was. Randolph, after all, had served him well for a number of years. The payments were small. They always came on time. There was never any hint of fuss. Randolph's demise had left a hole in Tristram's income, a fairly small hole, but a hole nonetheless. As he peered through Randolph's letters, or the letters to Randolph, he was looking for a replacement, another target who would pay up without any trouble.

Tristram Bennett did not find what he was looking for that morning. Shortly before twelve o'clock he sent word to Alfred Davis that he was going to lunch. He checked his tie was in the right position in the mirror and set off for his club. He had no doubt that sooner or later, in Randolph's correspondence, or in the late-night drunken confidences at his card parties, he would find another victim. Another Randolph.

13

Powerscourt glowered at the telegram which had just arrived in Markham Square. He had never liked telegrams. He vaguely remembered some malevolent deity from the gods and goddesses of ancient Greece who only brought bad news. He slit it open. 'Another tragedy has come to Brympton Hall. William Stebbings, sixteen years old, has disappeared. He was the junior footman running errands for Charlie Healey in the Long Gallery on the day of the murder. Please come. Please stay with us at the Hall. Georgina Nash.'

'My God!' said Powerscourt. 'Lucy! Lucy!' She glided into the hall, holding a twin in each hand. They stared anxiously at their papa. He didn't look well, the twins thought. Perhaps he would have to go to bed during the day and lie down, a terrible fate if you were a twin.

'I've got to go to Norfolk, Lucy. A junior footman has gone missing at Brympton Hall. He was right in the middle of the action at the time of the murder. Maybe he saw more than he told us or the police. God knows what's happened to him. Only sixteen years old, poor boy.'

'Can you see what this means, Francis? I've only just thought of it. Suppose this poor little boy has been killed. Whoever did it, it can't have been Cosmo, he's locked up in Pentonville, he hasn't been allowed out for weeks.'

'So, if we suppose that we have two linked murders here,' said Powerscourt, 'then Cosmo's off the hook. Somebody else must have done the second one, Cosmo couldn't have done it, and so, as night follows day, Cosmo couldn't have committed the first murder either. Or probably couldn't have done the first one. That would be a pretty problem for the prosecution. But, Lucy, I think it only works for Cosmo if this young man is dead and we shouldn't be thinking that, not for a moment. I must go now, I'll get back as soon as I can.'

Six hours later, as the light was fading, Powerscourt arrived at Brympton Hall and found Georgina Nash staring out at the gardens in her downstairs drawing room.

'Lord Powerscourt, how good of you to come. This is all too terrible.'

'Good evening to you, Mrs Nash. Is there any news? Has the young man turned up?'

'No, he has not. There's no sign of him at all. The police are here, searching the house and grounds. Willoughby is leading a search party around the lake. We've had one corpse here already, and now this.'

Georgina Nash looked as though she might be about to cry.

'Do we know when he was last seen?' said Powerscourt. 'How long has he been missing?'

'I think he was last seen after supper in the servants' quarters yesterday evening. He said he was going up to his room. William shares a room on the top floor with the other trainee footman, Oliver Fox, but Oliver's away at present. So nobody noticed until he didn't come down to breakfast. I'm going to find our butler Charlie Healey, if he's not out with one of the search parties, he knows more about William than anybody.'

Powerscourt stared out into the gardens behind the south front. He smiled when he saw that the fountain, source of so much anxiety to Georgina Nash until it was finally repaired, was still working properly, great bursts of water shooting into the evening sky.

Charlie Healey looked about forty years old. Powerscourt could tell at once that Charlie had been in the British Army. He vaguely recalled being told that he had fought with great distinction in the Boer War.

'Good evening, Mr Healey,' Powerscourt began. 'This is a bad business.'

'It is indeed, sir. I pray to God we can find him.'

'Tell me about William Stebbings if you would. What sort of a young man was he?'

Charlie had given his account twice already today to different varieties of policemen.

'Well, sir, he was a very good young man, if you know what I mean. He was hard-working and polite and always keen to learn. When he'd finishing learning how to be a footman, sir, he would have been a credit to anyone's household.'

'Did he want to be a footman? Or did he have other plans?'

'Funny you should ask that, my lord,' said Charlie Healey. 'He did have other plans for later on, if you follow me, and he was kind enough to ask my advice.'

'So what did he hope to do?' asked Powerscourt.

'Well,' said Charlie Healey, pausing as if not sure he should mention this in front of Mrs Nash, 'he was in love with those great ships, the ones that cross the Atlantic on the White Star Line and the fleets of the other great shipping companies like Cunard. *Mauretania, Lusitania, Carmania.* . . the names of those huge vessels were music in William's ears. His plan, my lord, Mrs Nash, was to get lots of experience working as a footman. Then he was going to apply for a job as a steward on one of them big ships. After that he thought he could get promoted up from steward to senior steward and maybe even purser. That was William's dream. One day he told me that he might even see if he could transfer from being a steward to being a sailor. Maybe he'd have ended up Captain, who knows.'

Charlie smiled at the end of his account. 'You don't suppose, Charlie,' said Powerscourt, 'that his dream might have got the better of him? That he's run away to sea?'

'I have thought about that, my lord. It's possible. Inspector Cooper had the same idea and he's sent word to Southampton and Liverpool and all the places those big ships sail from asking them to look out for William.'

'What about his room?' said Powerscourt. 'Has he taken all his clothes? Would it be possible for me to have a look, Mrs Nash?'

'Of course you can, Lord Powerscourt. Charlie will take you up there now. Remember to mind your head in the attics.'

Charlie Healey and Powerscourt had a brief military conversation on the way to the top floor, discovering each other's regiment and dates of service. Charlie was most impressed when he learnt that Powerscourt had been Head of Military Intelligence for the British Army in South Africa. 'Why, my lord,' he said, 'we must have been there at the same time even though we never met. Just fancy that.'

The first two floors of Brympton Hall were full of large elegant spaces like the drawing room downstairs or the Long Gallery on the first floor. Up here it was as if the architect and the builders had run out of room. The second floor was a rabbit warren of little rooms, attic rooms, twisting staircases and even one room directly underneath the clock tower with a kind of balcony looking out over the front drive that seemed to Powerscourt like the perfect place for suicide.

'Just round this corner, my lord,' said Charlie Healey, showing them into a small room above the Long Gallery with low windows and a sloping ceiling overlooking the garden. If you twisted your neck, Powerscourt discovered, you could just catch a corner of Georgina Nash's fountain. There were two single beds lined up against opposite walls. Each bed had a small cupboard beside it. There was a tall cupboard for clothes at the far end.

'Feel free to look into William's cupboard, the one on the left of the door,' said Charlie Healey. 'The only thing that seems to have gone is the money, but I have no idea how much he had, or if he had anything at all. He bought an expensive present

160

for his father's birthday last month, that might have cleaned him out completely.'

'And the clothes? Have they gone?'

'As far as we know, they're still here. He didn't have very much in the way of clothes, William. Most of them looked to have been inherited from his brothers, there were plenty of elder brothers.'

'And he was last seen after supper yesterday evening, 'said Powerscourt, 'and his disappearance was only spotted after breakfast this morning, am I right, Charlie?

'You are, my lord. We eat our meals together in the servants' quarters in the basement. Cook was always trying to get William to have second helpings. He was thin, you see, and she thought he needed fattening up.'

'If William wanted to go out, did he have to tell you where he was going, when he would be back, that sort of thing?'

'All the servants could go where they wanted in their free time. Sometimes they told me if they could find me. I'd gone out myself yesterday evening so maybe William tried to tell me but wasn't able to do so.'

'Were there any visitors expected? Did anybody see any strangers in the grounds or approaching the house?'

'Inspector Cooper asked that one too, my lord. I don't think so. Inspector Cooper did say that the Hall was so full of doors and staircases that you could get a whole football team in and out and nobody would notice.'

Powerscourt sat down on William's bed and tried to imagine that he was sixteen years old and obsessed with ocean liners. What would William have done? Where would he have gone? Did it have to do with the murder?

'Forgive me for asking, my lord,' said Charlie Healey, 'but is William's disappearance very important? To your investigation, I mean. It's not every day after all that Norfolk sees all these policemen arriving on the case, closely followed by a top investigator from London. I presume it must have to do with the earlier murder.'

'This interest does have to do with the earlier murder, Charlie,' said Powerscourt, 'you're quite right. Can I tell you the reason in confidence?'

Charlie Healey nodded. He was an avid reader of mystery and detective stories in his leisure time, and was particularly devoted to *The Moonstone* and *The Woman in White* by Wilkie Collins.

'My role in this case,' Powerscourt was checking the space behind the pillow in William Stebbings' bed in case it contained buried treasure, 'is to secure the acquittal of Cosmo Colville, the man you apprehended in the state bedroom with a gun in his hand. Now – forgive me this horrible thought, but I can assure you it is the same thought that has led Inspector Cooper and his men here on their search mission in the grounds – if young William has been murdered, one assumption must be that it is because of what he saw at the time of the murder. Maybe he didn't realize how important it was since most of the people were strangers to him. Murderers often kill a second time because somebody has seen them committing the first murder or has some piece of information which links them to the killing. Are you with me so far, Charlie?'

'Clear as a bell, my lord.'

'Now then, this is the crucial point. If this is murder, and it is linked to the earlier one at the wedding, there is one person who couldn't possibly have done it.'

'Cosmo Colville,' said Charlie with an air of triumph.

'And,' said Powerscourt, 'if Cosmo didn't commit the second one, he's unlikely to have committed the first one either.'

'I can see why everybody has rushed up here,' said Charlie.

'Could I ask you a favour, Charlie? Again it must be in the strictest confidence.'

Charlie nodded once more. Really, he said to himself, I'm quite enjoying this. It's as good as a detective story.

'Let's suppose,' said Powerscourt, 'that in one of the families involved in this case, there has been a tremendous row.

162

Doors slamming, people stomping out of houses, real physical violence not far away. I can ask all of the people involved what the row was about and they will all tell me the row was private. Family matter. None of your business – you can imagine the sort of thing.'

Charlie Healey was trying to work out which family Powerscourt was referring to. He thought it must be a Colville but which particular Colville family he did not know. Maybe the row had engulfed them all.

'There are other people in the house who must know what the row was about, the servants. But they're not going to betray their employers. They'd lose their job if it became known. Is there a way round it, Charlie?'

Charlie stared out of the little window at the gathering gloom engulfing the garden. 'That's very tricky, sir, trying to talk to the servants. It'd be hard for you to get into the house without somebody telling the Master or the Mistress you were there and then they'd throw you out. Offering money has the same disadvantages. The only way you might do it, my lord, is to catch them away from the house altogether in a pub or a café, for example, if they have a regular place they go to. Most people in service like going to the pub every now and then. It gets them out of the house. I'm sorry, sir, if that's not very helpful.'

Powerscourt smiled. 'It's very helpful, Charlie. I have a friend, you see, who works with me on all my cases. He's an expert in persuading people to talk, usually in the King's Head or the Coach and Horses after he has poured giant's helpings of beer or whisky down them. I hadn't thought of him until now.'

They made their way downstairs to the drawing room once more. Inspector Cooper was telling Mrs Nash that he hoped to return in the morning. He assured them that word would be sent to all the surrounding towns and villages about William Stebbings. Willoughby Nash, the strain showing in the lines on his face, said that his party would also carry on in the

163

morning where they had left off that evening. The invisible figure of a sixteen-year-old boy, always polite, keen to learn about his position, fascinated by great sailing ships, hovered, about the room. Powerscourt wondered if the old adage was true, that the longer it took to find a missing person, the more likely it was that they were dead.

He had only one suggestion for Inspector Cooper the following morning before he set out for London: to contact William's school, and more specifically, his friends in his last year or two. Might he have gone off on some adventure with one of his old school friends? It was, he told the Inspector and Mrs Nash, a long shot, but it was the best he could do. He left Pugh's address as well as his own with Georgina Nash. Could she please send on any news to both of them once it came? Shaking hands with Inspector Cooper at the front door, Powerscourt thought the young man's eyes were full of foreboding. Maybe he thought William Stebbings was dead.

At two o'clock the following afternoon Powerscourt presented himself at the reception desk of Whites Hotel, one of London's most discreet establishments, nestling in the streets between St James's Square and Piccadilly. Other establishments in the capital trumpeted their services across the sides of the buses or in the pages of the newspapers and the magazines that the rich and fashionable read. Whites, if asked, would have regarded that as rather vulgar. Whites was where Lady Lucy's mother stayed when the Powerscourts were out of town and she needed a hotel in London. Unlike other hotels, White's did not send out regular bulletins to the press about who was staying in its elegant rooms. Anything that happened once you had crossed the threshold was private. The regular clients – and there were considerable numbers of those – behaved in White's as they would have done when they were in their own homes. The cynics pointed out that the code of White's Hotel made it the perfect place for the conduct of illicit affairs. Once you were safely ensconced within its walls and within its bedrooms, you were safe from exposure and scandal.

Whites was the hotel where the pre-phylloxera dinners were held. Presumably the clients were keen to indulge their passion for these wines at a place where no publicity was likely to leak out. Maybe even their own wives didn't know where they had gone on these evenings, or of the size of the bills. Powerscourt asked for the general manager and was shown into a small room behind the reception desk. The walls were lined with prints of the great houses of England, Blenheim, Longleat and Wilton House on one wall, Holkham Hall and Castle Howard on the other.

Two or three minutes later a very neat little man, five feet six inches tall and clean shaven in his frock coat, who looked as if he was polished twice a day, announced himself as George Brandon, general manager of Whites Hotel.

'And how might I be of service to you today, Lord Powerscourt?'

Powerscourt wondered, not for the first time, if the Lord in his name meant that he received speedier service than a mere Mister. He reflected ruefully that he would never find out. 'Thank you for seeing me so quickly, Mr Brandon. I am most grateful. I am seeking information and guidance on pre-phylloxera wines. I understand that you hold dinners here from time to time when such wines are served.'

George Brandon smiled. 'You have come to the right place, Lord Powerscourt. Would you like me to arrange to have you added to our list of clients? I don't think that would be a problem.'

'Would that it were so easy, Mr Brandon! Nothing would give me greater pleasure than to join your connoisseurs and their ancient vintages around the table. Let me be frank with you. We are talking of a dinner, a celebration, for a relative who is approaching his eightieth birthday. Indeed it may be touch and go whether he reaches that happy day or not. I fear that some of the younger and more flippant members of the family have been placing wagers on whether the old boy will see his birthday or not. He lives in a crumbling Tudor mansion in the depths of Somerset. His doctors will not let him out as far as Bath, let alone the West End of London.'

'I see,' said George Brandon. He rubbed his chin for a moment or two. 'Let me see what we might be able to do, Lord Powerscourt. On very special occasions we put in motion a very special travel service for special clients. A luxurious, upholstered cab to take them to the station. A special train, equipped with its own doctors and nurses, to bring them up to London. A special motor car, also furnished with medical staff, to bring the clients to the hotel. The pre-phylloxera dinner on a scale and of a complexity to suit the client. A night under supervision in one of our Edward the Seventh suites. The journey in reverse the following day. We activated the service only last month, Lord Powerscourt, for an American millionaire who was taken ill in Yorkshire. It was very satisfactory.'

'What was wrong with the American gentleman?' asked Powerscourt.

'I fear he was somewhat over-concerned about his health. He had a pain in his chest and thought his heart was going to stop.'

'And was it?'

'The doctors said his heart was in fine condition. They said he had probably pulled a muscle, coughing from an over-generous intake of cigarettes.'

'I see. Let me return to Somerset, Mr Brandon. Even with your superb travelling hospital, as it were, I do not think the family would be happy bringing the old gentleman to London. Let me apologize to you. What I meant to ask you right at the beginning was for the name of your wine merchants. I have been diverted by the quality of your service and the range of what you can supply.'

Powerscourt smiled at the little hotel manager. George Brandon rubbed his hands together again.

166

'I should be happy to oblige. All I would ask, Lord Powerscourt, is that you would consider our services for any special occasions in the future. We should be only too happy to oblige. Now then, the name of the pre-phylloxera wine merchant is Piccadilly Wine, of Sackville Street, behind Regent Street. You should ask for Septimus Parry – he's the gentleman we deal with.'

Powerscourt wondered if Brandon carried the names and addresses of all his principal suppliers – florists, butchers, greengrocers, bakers, tea merchants – round in his head. 'Might I ask if these gentlemen supply all your wines, or just the special ones?'

George Brandon smiled. 'They just supply the pre-phylloxera wines. They came to us in the first instance a couple of years ago. They said they had found large stocks of these pre-plague vintages. They more or less threw themselves on our mercy as to what to do with them. Piccadilly knew there were people who would pay a great deal of money to drink these wines but they didn't know how to find them. Fortunately we were able to help on that score.'

And Piccadilly Wine, in the person of one Septimus Parry, had finessed themselves into a position where they would be able to charge the very top prices, with a band of drinkers assembled by Whites Hotel. God only knew how much they charged for a bottle of the stuff.

'Mr Brandon, I am most grateful to you. I will detain you no longer. I shall set out for Piccadilly Wine at once.'

Twenty minutes later Lord Francis Powerscourt was shown into the office of Piccadilly Wine. There were two large desks, an enormous map of France on the wall and two young men, Vicary Dodds, attending to his account books with great care and total concentration in his suit of sober grey, and Septimus Parry, leafing idly through some wine catalogues from France in a suit that looked as if its owner should have been taking bets in the enclosure at Newmarket.

'Good afternoon to you, sir,' said Septimus. 'How may we be of service?'

'A very good afternoon to you too,' Powerscourt replied. 'I am interested in buying some of your pre-phylloxera wines.'

Was it just a normal reaction, Powerscourt wondered, or did Septimus Parry put up his guard at the mention of the word pre-phylloxera? Even Vicary Dodds, keeper of the eternal verities of the account books, put down his pencil and inspected his visitor. Certainly Septimus's manner from now on was more reserved than it had been when he came in.

'Who told you we sold these wines?' said Septimus.

'I've just been informed about them by George Brandon at Whites Hotel.'

'I see,' said Septimus. He only realized later that a more devious wine merchant would not have been satisfied with Powerscourt's answer. George Brandon might have confirmed to Powerscourt that these dinners with these wines existed, but it was unlikely that he would have volunteered the information. Powerscourt must have heard about them from somebody else. But who?

'We do have access to some of these wines, Lord Powerscourt, but might I ask about the occasion for which they are needed and the quantities required?'

'Of course you may, Mr Parry. There is an elderly gentleman in our family approaching his eightieth birthday. He lives in the depths of Somerset. He is not very strong or very well. His doctors are not sure if he will reach this birthday. In his youth,' Powerscourt knew he was embroidering the life and times of the old gentleman every time he spoke, 'our elderly friend was a great connoisseur of French wines, burgundy and Bordeaux in particular. Most people prefer one or the other, Bordeaux or burgundy. The old boy liked them both. He would travel there in his holidays and taste them on the spot. You know as well as I do, gentlemen, of the terrible ravages of phylloxera that ran for thirty years or so from the 1860s. Over time all the great vineyards had to be replanted. Our elderly gentleman,' Powerscourt thought he had better give him a name fairly soon, 'saw one important part of his life taken away from him, his love of these great French wines. The replacements and their produce he did not care for. He said they might as well come from Morocco as far as he was concerned. Then, somewhere, he can't remember where, his memory is going so fast, he read of the existence of pre-phylloxera wines in France, and a limited quantity in England. Gentlemen, I am sure you can see why I am here. The chance to bring back to an old man some of the joys of his youth. The chance to let the old gentleman taste once more the wines that he loved so well. The chance to brighten his last days and let him approach the final one floating in a lake of Château Lafite or Château Latour.'

Septimus Parry smiled. 'I can almost see the old gentleman, tottering slowly round his house, taking a few hesitant steps in the garden. I regret to have to tell you that we have no Latour and no Lafite. That is not to say there is none of it in England – there is – but we cannot persuade the owners to part with it for any amount of money. Just let us know how many red and how many white you would like, what quantities of Bordeaux and burgundy would suit you and we will do the rest.'

'You don't have a *carte des vins*, a wine list?'

'Not as such,' said Septimus, feeling rather anxious now. 'As I say, we ask the clients what they would like, in general terms.'

'Is that not rather unusual?' said Powerscourt. 'You mean my old relative can't even have a bottle of his favourite Nuits St Georges?'

'I think we could manage that, Lord Powerscourt. You see, the way it works at Whites Hotel is that we supply the wines at our discretion. Their chef plans the meal round the particular vintages we are going to provide and everybody is happy. So if you let us know the colour and the quantity we can set to straight away.'

Powerscourt wondered if the young man knew that he, Powerscourt, suspected that the wines were fake, that they weren't playing an elaborate game of charades. 'I should be most interested to know,' he said, 'how you discovered these wines. And how nobody else has discovered them. That's rather a coup, I should say.'

'It was luck, really,' said Septimus, running his fingers through his hair. 'I've got this great-uncle, he's dead now, but he was a great lover of wine. Every year Berry Bros. & Rudd would send him their pick of the best clarets and the best burgundies of that year. In the early 1860s he saw the writing on the wall – he thought that sooner or later the phylloxera insect would munch its way through all the vineyards of France, starting in the south and going all the way up to Champagne. So he doubled the size of his order. Soon the cellar was full to bursting with this stuff. Then, before he had time to drink a tenth of it, he died. His son wasn't interested in wine at all, hardly touched it. I knew his son, third in line from the man who bought all the wine, at Oxford. So when we started the business, Vicary and I, we got in touch with this chap. His family knew two or three others who also had supplies. Then we got into touch with Whites to organize the dinners.'

'How fascinating!' said Powerscourt. 'I should love to go and see the cellars where these treasures are kept. Is there any chance of a visit?'

'I'm afraid not, Lord Powerscourt,' said Septimus, sending the ball back across the net once more. 'If it was up to me we could go there this very day, but the owners don't like people trampling all over their house as they put it. They're very strict about their privacy.'

'Very well,' said Powerscourt. 'I can't see a wine list, I can't see the place where the bottles are stored – what can I see, Mr Parry?'

Septimus laughed. 'You come back tomorrow, Lord Powerscourt, and bring us a list for you to choose from. I promise you.'

Powerscourt said he would return and set off on his way back to Markham Square. As he went he reflected that there was only one part of Septimus Parry's story that might be true but probably wasn't. The house in the country with the wine lover forty years before ordering his supplies from Berry Bros. & Rudd, that was possible, but probably untrue. This evening Septimus would have a meeting with the Necromancer where they would agree the wines to be faked. Powerscourt looked forward very much to tasting them. And he sent urgent word to Johnny Fitzgerald to ask him to follow Septimus Parry wherever he went the following afternoon. He, Powerscourt, was going to call on Piccadilly Wine in the early afternoon. Maybe Septimus Parry would lead him to the Necromancer.

14

After three days Tristram Bennett tired of being the replacement for his murdered cousin Randolph. Life as a wine merchant was not quite what he had expected. Tristram had imagined that Colville retainers would appear at regular intervals throughout the day, bringing tea or coffee or drinks. They did not appear. Instead a wide variety of messengers appeared with things for him to read, things for him to sign, people in the trade he must talk to. These conversations did not go easily. For although Tristram had absorbed a certain amount about the wine business in his time with the firm, he was not capable of an opinion on the likely vintage quality in Burgundy or whether they should change shippers for the delivery of their Sancerre. To all difficult questions he told his visitors he would get back to them. He rather wished he could return to his undemanding position in East Anglia.

He wondered what to do about Emily Colville. If Tristram was going to continue his affair, he would have to find a house or a flat to rent close to Emily's place in Barnes. He knew she would never yield to him in the house she shared with her husband. In Norfolk the rent on the little cottage with the thatched roof had been tiny. In London it would be rather more, but he knew he did not dare mention money to Emily or she would accuse him of putting gold before love. This, in fact, was a proposition that Tristram would gladly have subscribed to, even if not in female company.

It was the formal invitation that finished his incipient career as a wine merchant. It came shortly before lunch on the third day. It was an invitation to the Annual Dinner of the Wine Merchants and Vintners Society of London, to be held in the Vintners Hall in the City. Formal Dress, it said on the bottom line. Tristram was no puritan in questions of food and drink, but he could imagine the whole scene. Row upon row of tables bedecked with flowers and bottles of wine. The men, all in their fifties and sixties, balding, braying and boasting about their wine business or their wives or their children, growing redder and redder as the evening went on, progressing from the colour of rose to the colour of beetroot. And then the speeches! All too long, all too pompous, all too self-obsessed, all too vain. Whatever else the wine business might hold, this was not for Tristram. He did tell Davis before he left for his club in the middle of his last afternoon that Randolph's position was not for him. He was going back to Norfolk.

Lord Francis Powerscourt was going to the west London suburb of Ealing on the Piccadilly line. He was thinking as he went about the links between the Necromancer in his warehouse, if that, indeed, was where he lived, Whites Hotel and Piccadilly Wine where he proposed to call later in the day. He found the history of these strange wines, real or faked, absolutely fascinating and he knew he would follow the story with great interest. But for the life of him he could not see how it might lead to murder. Faked wines would easily lend themselves to blackmail. The announcement that Colvilles or Piccadilly had been trafficking in these illicit substances would be bad for a day or two. But a sensible firm would quickly put out a statement that a bad apple had been identified and removed, that business was returning to normal and the loyal customers who had been with Colvilles or Piccadilly all these years could sleep easy in their beds as all Colville wines were now genuine.

Thomas Colville opened the door of 27 Inkerman Avenue in person. He was in his late forties or early fifties with a great beard and a handlebar moustache.

'Good morning to you, Lord Powerscourt, welcome to 27 Inkerman Avenue. The battle may be long over but the house still stands!' He laughed lightly at his own joke. 'Come in and sit down, I'll rouse Ethel up from wherever she's hiding!'

A few minutes later they were all seated comfortably in the Colville parlour with prints of famous racehorses on the walls, drinking Ethel's tea and eating Ethel's biscuits. 'You must ask whatever you want, Lord Powerscourt. Randolph and Cosmo might not be my very best friends but I wouldn't wish their fate on anybody.'

'I think you knew them as children, Mr Colville. What were they like then?'

'Pretty bloody, if the truth be told,' said Thomas Colville. 'The adults all thought that three cousins roughly the same age should get on together and play nicely, as they used to put it. How little did they know!'

'What happened, Mr Colville?' asked Powerscourt.

'There was a lot of bullying, hair pulling, kicking, various forms of physical and mental torture, really. The odd thing is that Randolph didn't seem to have any moral sense at all. He thought this kind of behaviour was perfectly normal and that he was only exercising his God-given rights in carrying on like this.'

'What about Cosmo? Did he take the same view as Randolph?'

'Well, he was more normal, if I can put it like that. I think he knew the difference between right and wrong. He would tell Randolph every now and then to stop what he was doing.'

'If it was all so grim, why didn't you tell your parents? They could have stopped you going to the Colvilles, surely.'

'You know what small boys are like, Lord Powerscourt. My parents were too much in awe of their richer relations to dare take me away.'

'So what happened when the two others went away to school?' asked Powerscourt. 'Life must have been somewhat easier then.'

'During term-time it was, but the holidays were worse, much worse. Randolph had come across all kinds of bullying at school so he simply brought the techniques home with him. I was hung up on trees in the garden. The two of them took great pleasure holding me upside down and forcing my head in the lavatory bowl and then flushing it. Any animals or insects they could catch were given a hard time – birds had their wings pulled off, butterflies cut in two, that sort of thing.'

'Great God!' said Powerscourt. 'How dreadful. Could I ask you, Mr Colville, why it was after all this humiliation that you went to work for the family firm? Surely you must have known that there might well be more grief, years more grief from these two.'

'Once a Colville, always a Colville,' said Thomas with a smile. 'My parents wanted me to join the firm. They still suffered from the illusion that Randolph and Cosmo and I got on very well. So they thought I would be well looked after and would prosper in the business.'

'Not so?' said Powerscourt. 'Not well looked after? Not prospering?'

'Very little prospering,' said Thomas, 'very little indeed. You see, the one thing I had always shown an aptitude for was maths. Adding up, dividing, algebra, all those equations with $2x + 4 = 3y - 2$ were all meat and drink to me. So I asked to work in the accounts department. Randolph, who had manoeuvred himself into a position where he was in charge of my future, sent me to the bottling plant instead. When I'd learnt all there was to know there I applied for a transfer, to the accounts department, naturally. This time I was sent to the labelling section and very boring it was too. After ten or twelve years I'd been round every department bar one, and that was where they did the sums.'

'And what was Cosmo doing while all this was going on? Was he aiding and abetting his brother?'

'That's the curious thing,' said Thomas. 'As Randolph turned into more and more of a bully, Cosmo became a more normal member of the human race. He wasn't Francis of Assisi or anything like that but he was decent and kind and sometimes considerate.'

'Before we talk about why you left, Mr Colville, could I ask if you were the only one singled out for horrible treatment by Randolph? Or were there others?'

'I was not alone. No, sir. There were plenty more singled out for bullying, some of it much worse than what I received.'

'Could I ask Mrs Colville how she coped with all these difficult times?' said Powerscourt.

'We got through, Lord Powerscourt. We got through. There were times when I just wanted to walk into the Head Office and tell everybody I saw what a brute Randolph Colville was.'

'You left, Mr Colville, ten years ago, I think. Do you keep up with any of the people you knew when you were working for the firm?'

'One or two close friends, that's all. Oddly enough there's one chap come to work in the brewery where I do the accounts, Fuller's in Chiswick. But I hear bits and pieces every now and then.'

'I want to ask you both a question, and I want you to think very carefully about the answer. Do you think that the bullying could get so bad that somebody might decide to kill Randolph?'

Thomas ate a couple of biscuits and then a couple more. It was Ethel who answered first.

'I do think it is possible, Lord Powerscourt. I think Thomas is a fairly even-tempered sort of man in spite of everything he has had to put with. But if you were a redhead with a temper, like my younger brother, you could well decide to kill him. I just wonder about the timing, though. If he had been really horrible to you, and you had a gun to hand somewhere in the offices, you could go and kill him in a fit of fury, so incensed you scarcely knew what you were doing. But leave the office, take a train to Norfolk, get your hands on a gun, I'm not sure. I think common sense would intervene somewhere along the way.'

'I think what you say is very sensible, Ethel,' said Thomas Colville, 'but I've been trying to remember exactly how I felt after some of these outrages. I think there are, maybe, different sorts of anger. There's the hot anger Ethel was talking about but there's also a kind of cold anger which can last for days or weeks. I'm sure there were times when I could have got on the Norfolk train and killed Randolph Colville.'

'You've both been very honest with me,' said Lord Powerscourt. 'Could I ask you one last favour? If you or your friends can think of anybody who might have gone to kill Randolph, could you let me know? I would be most grateful.'

As Powerscourt left, Thomas Colville handed him a bottle of beer. Fuller Smith and Turner, 1845, it said on the label. 'This is the beer from the place where I work now,' said Thomas. 'It's a bloody sight better than any of the rubbish you can buy in Colvilles off-licences!'

Emily Colville enjoyed the secrecy involved in meeting her lover. Now she had escaped the boring and the humdrum into the mysterious world of romance. Her cab took her from Norwich station, the blinds tightly closed in case she should meet her relations, and round the back of Brympton Hall to the tiny cottage in the woods behind the lake. It looked as though it came from a fairy tale with a round shape and a thatched roof on the top. From such a place elves or fairies might have ventured forth to dance in the woods at midnight, lit by the moon and the stars.

Emily took out her key and settled in the tiny living room to wait for her lover. She busied herself with preparing a fire, for the tiny cottage was cold from lack of use. Her heart sang as she carried in the logs and began arranging them in the grate. Surely, this was real life. Surely this was far better then organizing tiresome elements of domestic duty, asking the servants to polish the spoons or checking that there were enough pillowcases in the linen cupboard. She checked her watch and remembered the picture of 'Shine On Harvest Moon' on the front of the sheet music, the code that had brought her here. He must come soon. Emily had brought the sheet music with her. It sat in a heap of other popular songs by the window. The code was very simple. Emily thought she should offer it to the Foreign Office where she was sure they had need of codes and ciphers of every description in the intelligence war with the Germans. The code was based on the musical keys. A meant Monday, B meant Tuesday, C meant Wednesday and so on. Flat meant morning and sharp meant afternoon. It was such a lovely secret. Emily liked secrets. She was the only person in the country who knew the secret behind Tristram's mild blackmail of Randolph Colville and she was never going to tell that to anybody.

Tristram Bennett, the man Emily was waiting for, was in no hurry to find his lady. Keep them waiting, that was his motto. After the first success, Tristram believed, the women would be more ardent if they had to sit around wondering if he was ever going to come. So he stretched his legs out in the front parlour of the Nelson Arms a couple of hundred yards from the tiny cottage and ordered a second glass of brandy and another large cigar.

Tristram Bennett was the eldest son of Beatrice, daughter of Walter Colville, younger sister of Randolph and Cosmo. His parents had sent him to Harrow where he had one of those middling sort of school careers, middle of the class, middling in athletics, middling popular with his fellows. The one thing his contemporaries could have told you about him was that he had a passion, some might have called it a mania, for gambling. Tristram's doting mama had great hopes of him entering the Church and rising through the lower ranks to become a bishop. He would look so handsome, she thought, in bishop's robes and a mitre. Her husband put a stop to all that by repeating what Tristram's housemaster had said, that of course the Church of England was a broad church which would take all manner of persons into its bosom, but a man who might take as the text for his sermon the list of runners and riders in the three-thirty at Sandown Park might not be welcomed with open arms. Beatrice took a violent dislike to the housemaster and continued her policy of secret subventions to her sons's already generous allowance. It was decided that the Army might prove a better career than the Church Militant and Tristram joined the Blues and Royals. It might have been his charm, it might have been his good looks, it might have been the way those two qualities combined in his dashing uniform, but at this stage Tristram discovered he was very attractive to women. The ones dearest to his heart were the rich ones who would think nothing of helping him out with his gambling debts in return for his helping them into their beds.

Just into his thirties now there was still no sign of a wife. Or rather, there were plenty of signs of wives, but they all belonged to other people. Tristram's father wondered sometimes if the boy might never marry at all but turn into one of those ageing rakes who frequented the less reputable London clubs. His mother, devoted to the last, thought it was only a matter of time before Tristram marched up the aisle with a daughter of the aristocracy perhaps, or the daughter of some great trading concern with innumerable investments in the Funds.

Tristram's job was as East Anglia development manager for the family firm of Colville. He was to seek out possible areas of expansion for the company. So far Tristram had enjoyed only limited success. He had persuaded Fakenham Racecourse to make Colvilles their chief supplier of wines and spirits. Recommending the change to the Committee the Secretary told them that Tristram had lost so much money gambling at the racecourse that losing his custom would cause an outcry if not a revolt among the bookmaking fraternity. He had similar success with the Norfolk Club, a rather stuffy establishment in Upper King Street, Norwich where gentlemen were encouraged to play cards for money on Fridays and Saturdays. Once again the size of his losses was instrumental in obtaining the commission.

Now it was time to go. Tristram finished his cigar and strolled down the road to Emily's cottage. He was glad to see she had bothered to light a fire.

'Tristram,' she said, looking at him carefully, 'you're so late. I thought you weren't coming. I thought you'd forgotten.'

'How could I forget you?' said Tristram, taking her in his arms. 'That simply wouldn't be possible.'

'I haven't seen you since before my wedding, Tristram. You didn't come. Why was that?'

'I thought I might spoil it for you,' said Tristram, who had, in fact, spent Emily's wedding day in the arms of a rich widow in Cromer.

Emily thought of saying that he had spoiled her wedding already but she desisted. It wouldn't do to upset Tristram, he could turn very moody. 'How long have you got here today? How is business?'

Tristram propelled her gently up the stairs. 'I've got plenty of time today, Emily, and in a minute I'm going to tell you the latest news on the problems of the Colville family. After all, you're part of us now.'

Early the same afternoon Powerscourt presented himself at the offices of Piccadilly Wine once more. He thought a villainous-looking tramp winked at him from across the street but he couldn't be sure. Vicary Dodds was still pursuing the firm's numbers through his account books and Septimus Parry was making notes about recent vintages in Bordeaux. 'Lord Powerscourt,' said Septimus, 'how good to see you again.

Now then, somewhere here is a list of the pre-phylloxera wines we propose to marry up with your own list for your elderly relative's celebration. He's still well, I take it? Not succumbing to the flu or anything like that? Brain still working normally? Able to stand up unaided?'

Powerscourt knew from this inquiry that Septimus believed the aged relation in the depths of Somerset was an invention, a Bunbury. He produced a sheet of paper with his requests. 'Now then,' Septimus said, 'let's see, you'd like some Bordeaux. We don't offer much choice on these occasions. We do have Château Figeac, a *grand cru* from Bordeaux with a delightful fragrance and gentleness of texture, and Château Gazin, a Pomerol from Bordeaux, grown next to the legendary Château Petrus. From Burgundy you would like the old gentleman's favourite Nuits St Georges and Aloxe Corton from the village of that name at the northern end of the Côte de Beaune, we can supply both of those. White burgundy you would like, well, we have some Meursault from one of the bigger villages in the Côte d'Or and Puligny Montrachet, two of the most famous wine names in the world, and we can throw in a Sancerre and a Pouilly Fumé from the Loire Valley, if you like. If those seem agreeable to you we need to know the quantities for each bottle and we shall send you the bill after the wines have been enjoyed, not before.'

Powerscourt marked a number next to each type of bottle asking for two of everything on offer except for four of the Nuits St Georges and four of the Puligny Montrachet.

Septimus handed him another sheet with details of the normal offerings of Piccadilly Wine for him to take home. 'The pre-phylloxera ones should be ready tomorrow. We'll send them round to your house,' he said. 'But in the meantime, let us present you with a sample.' Parry bent down behind his desk and came up with a couple of bottles. 'We thought these might whet you appetite, Lord Powerscourt, pre-phylloxera Nuits St Georges and pre–phylloxera Pouilly Fumé. I hope you enjoy them.'

Septimus Parry watched Powerscourt walk to the end of the street and turn left towards Chelsea.

'I wonder what he wants,' he said, 'the man who calls himself Lord Powerscourt. Do you think that's his real name, Vicary?'

'I don't think that's his real name for a moment,' said Vicary. 'If you were a Lord Powerscourt, even an Irish peer Lord Powerscourt, what on earth are you doing grubbing around in the world of pre-phylloxera wine? The man must be an impostor. We'd better watch our step, Septimus.'

'Even the Customs wouldn't investigate a suspicious business with a man pretending to be a peer,' said Septimus. 'But he's going to get a shock when he opens the bottles, our fraudulent friend. I took the labels off and put some of ours on instead. But what he thinks is going to be fake pre-phylloxera wine isn't going to be anything of the kind. They may not be pre-phylloxera, but they're the oldest bottles of those two wines from one of London's oldest wine merchants. When Lord Powerscourt and his friends get the corkscrew working they'll find they're drinking Justerini & Brooks' finest. That should confuse them just a bit.'

A few moments after Powerscourt's departure Septimus Parry stepped out briskly into the London streets to deliver the order. His mind was too busy to notice the stooped figure of the tramp with the dirty hair who followed him fifty yards behind. As Septimus boarded a Bakerloo line train going south at Piccadilly Circus the tramp was two carriages away, looking closely at the exits when the train pulled in at a station. At Embankment Septimus changed on to the District and Circle line, again pursued by the faithful tramp. Johnny thought he knew the general area they were going to now. It seemed unlikely to him that wine forgers would be operating in the heart of the City of London. Their terrain would be further east, somewhere in the sprawling docks. They passed

Tower Hill. The tramp almost missed Septimus alighting rapidly from his train at Shadwell but he caught sight of him half a minute later striding up one side of Shadwell Basin, and disappearing into an enormous warehouse on Newlands Quay.

The inevitable seagulls were performing their ritual pavane around the shipping in the basin. Men could be seen loading and unloading different-sized vessels. The enormous warehouse betrayed no sign of ownership. It was six storeys high and had small barred windows at regular intervals. Johnny Fitzgerald crouched down by the door and strained to hear any conversation between Septimus and the Necromancer, for he was sure the Necromancer was the man Septimus had come to see. However hard he tried he could hear nothing. The door looked solid. Suddenly it was flung open and he was dragged inside the warehouse and pulled unceremoniously into a small section in the corner. Johnny saw that there were rows and rows of shelves lined with bottles of every size known to the wine trade. The two men tied him roughly to a chair.

'This is the fellow I told you about,' said Septimus, 'the one who followed me from the office down here.'

'You must be Mr Septimus Parry,' said Johnny, staring intently at the muzzle of a gun in his companion's hand, pointing directly toward his stomach. 'And you, sir, you with the gun,' Johnny turned his gaze up from the gun to the face, 'must be the Necromancer.'

The mention of the word necromancer seemed to cause fury. 'I am not known as the Necromancer!' he snarled. 'They are mere conjurers, penny magicians on minor feast days, fortune tellers by the hedgerows, soothsayers of the future for simple minds. I am known as the Alchemist. Alchemists were famed for transmuting base metals into gold as I do with crude wines being converted into noble vintages with great names. And you,' he began waving the gun about in what Johnny thought was a rather dangerous fashion, 'who the hell are you?'

Johnny made no reply. Septimus was looking rather nervous now. What had begun as a lark could turn very nasty at any moment. 'Are you by any chance an associate of the man who calls himself Powerscourt?'

Johnny thought that Septimus would be unlikely to resort to violence on his own. But he wasn't sure about the other one. Above everything else, he realized, he had to remain as a tramp. If they thought he was an intimate colleague of Powerscourt he might be in great danger from the man with the gun.

'Look here,' said the Alchemist, 'I don't think you fully understand your position. I am perfectly happy to put a bullet into any part of your filthy anatomy I choose if you don't co-operate. Tramps disappear all the time. In this part of London,' he waved the gun airily in the direction of the river, 'nobody even knows they've gone. Now, you'd better start telling us the truth. Are you employed by the man who calls himself Powerscourt?'

'Every now and then,' said Johnny.

'What does that mean?' snapped the Alchemist. 'Once a week, once a month, once a year?'

'More than once a year, less than once a month,' said Johnny, 'three or four times a year maybe. It's always when he wants somebody followed.'

'So when, before today, was the last time you worked for him?'

'Just before Easter,' said Johnny, observing that the gun now seemed to be pointing at his knees.

'Very well,' said the Alchemist. 'There is nothing I can do, short of killing you, to prevent you telling your master what you have seen. I do not want you here any more. The man they call Powerscourt is ruining my life. My entire life depends on secrecy, on nobody knowing what I look like or where I work. You and your employer have ruined that. Don't think I won't get my own back. Now get out and don't come back. And tell your master,' the Alchemist snarled as he shoved Johnny towards the door, 'that he hasn't heard the last of me.'

The Alchemist was shaking with fury as he kicked Johnny out of the warehouse and into the street. He sat down on a stool by one of his great shelves and put his head in his hands. 'Everything I've worked for, gone. My work. My anonymity which I have done so much to preserve, blown away like gossamer down. My office, the very place where I do my work, now known to the tramp who must surely work for the authorities. I am finished, Septimus, finished! Just tell me, tell me before you go, what is this Powerscourt's address?'

Powerscourt was annoyed that he hadn't managed to get any closer to the Necromancer. Maybe Johnny would pull it off this very day. He remembered Johnny saying that the man valued his privacy above everything else. What did he have to hide? Powerscourt had a deep suspicion of forgers, fakers and counterfeiters of every sort. In one of his previous cases he had encountered a forger called Orlando Blane who had caused chaos in the London art world with the accuracy of his reproductions. Orlando too had links with Norfolk, producing his Gainsboroughs or his Joshua Reynoldses or his Giovanni Bellinis in an abandoned Jacobean mansion close to Cromer and the sea. He felt that the fakers and the forgers debased the natural order, that they brought something squalid and sordid into a world where beauty should reign supreme, that their works poisoned the art world. Not that Powerscourt had any illusions about the art dealers and the auctioneers and the art experts. Many of them, he knew, were little better than the forgers when it came to morality. And what of his own first offering from the Necromancer, those two bottles nestling in their bag? Should he taste them immediately he reached home? Probably not, he decided. He would wait until tomorrow when the rest of the consignment arrived. He would summon Sir Pericles Freme and his finest palate to join him and Lady Lucy in the first tasting of the pre-phylloxera wines.

A hundred miles to the north Georgina Nash was walking up her drive with its massive yew hedges towards the main road that skirted round Brympton Hall. Every day now she performed this melancholy ritual five or six times during the hours of daylight. When she reached the main road, with the church on her left where the doomed marriage took place a month or so before, she would stand and stare, now to the left, now to the right. Sometimes she would walk for half a mile or so in either direction, hoping desperately that the next person to come round the bend would be young William Stebbings. It was now three days since his disappearance, and the Nash family were, if anything, even more upset than they had been on the day he went missing. Inspector Cooper continued with his searches but he had informed them sadly that morning that he and his men could only search for one more day. Then they would be reassigned to other duties. Looking at the Inspector's face in the kitchen at nine o'clock that day Georgina Nash could see that the Inspector thought William was dead. Her husband Willoughby continued his searches with some of the gardeners when he could spare the time from his legal business in Norwich. He too, she felt, was losing faith in William being alive.

Georgina turned round and made her way back towards the Hall. The afternoon light was beginning to fade. She had thought and thought about what William might have seen in her Long Gallery on the day of the murder. Had he seen the murderer leave the state bedroom and press the gun into Cosmo's hand? Had he seen something which he didn't think was important, but which was of vital importance for the murderer? Had one or other of those possibilities led to his death, the murderer creeping into the Hall under cover of darkness and luring the boy outside to strangle him by the lake and throw the body into the water, pockets filled with stones? Her butler, Charlie Healey, a man with wide experience of violent death in the Boer War, didn't think much of these theories. Somehow Georgina Nash didn't believe in them either. Her permanent image of William was of the boy, five or six weeks ago, standing behind one of the guests' chairs at one of the rare formal dinner parties she and Willoughby gave, holding himself perfectly still, looking very handsome in his black suit and white shirt, ready to help with the serving or removal of dishes as required. Hidden away in William's cupboard they had found a magazine full of pictures and engravings of the great transatlantic liners where he hoped to serve as a steward sometime in the future. Looking through the illustrations of the state cabins with their unimaginable luxury on the top deck, the vast and ornate drawing rooms and libraries and dining rooms, Georgina could see where the appeal lay for the young man. She was back by the Hall now. She heard footsteps coming, loud footsteps, coming on the road from Aylsham. Perhaps it was William. Her heart leapt. She was sure it was him! He was back at last!

But when the figure came round the bend she saw it was only the vicar, come to open up the Church for evensong.

Lady Lucy had organized the Powerscourt dining room with considerable care. Three places were laid at the top end of the table nearest the hall. There were no knives or spoons, but half a dozen glasses, three for red wine and three for white, and a tumbler for water. By the side of each place was a large French saucepan for the participants to spit their wine into. Lady Lucy didn't feel they were perfect, the large saucepans, but they would suffice. She wondered if somewhere in London you could buy special glasses for the special substances of the man they called the Necromancer. Francis had put the list of pre-phylloxera wines in the centre of the table.

As they took their places with Powerscourt at the head of the table, Sir Pericles on his right and Lady Lucy on his left, Freme was rubbing his hands together in anticipation.

'I can't tell you how much I am looking forward to this. So many times in my life I have drunk wine that I knew to be fake. Undrinkable stuff composed of water and raisins and elder berries from some slum in the East End, diluted claret, watered down with low-grade red from Languedoc brewed up in some warehouse in the south of France, unspeakable burgundy made with apple juice and brandy cooked up in a seedy cellar in Hamburg, I think I've seen them all. But to know every bottle is a fake before you start tasting, that is a great joy. Powerscourt, how to you intend to proceed?'

'I do have a plan of campaign, as a matter of fact. I think we should start with the Nuits St Georges they gave me the other day, before today's delivery. Couple of sips of that and then compare it with the ones that came today.'

'Capital!' said Sir Pericles Freme and smiled broadly at Lady Lucy. Powerscourt was busy with the corkscrew. He poured three small helpings into their glasses. 'To the Necromancer,' he said, sipping at his wine. Sir Pericles took a small sip of his Nuits St Georges and spat expertly into his saucepan. He looked at Powerscourt like a man who cannot quite believe what he is tasting. 'Would you both oblige me by taking another sip of this one you brought from the shop? I am somewhat confused.'

All three were served another small helping by Powerscourt acting as wine waiter. All three spat carefully into their saucepans. Lady Lucy suspected that the business of spitting wine into saucepans at one's own dining table would not have met with her mother's approval. She wondered which of the many words of disapproval in her mother's wide vocabulary of words of disapproval would have been employed for the practice. Disagreeable? Demeaning? Unworthy? Vulgar? Common? Common, she decided, that would have been the adjective of choice. Sir Pericles, she noticed, looked like a man who has just been given an enormous and impossible piece of mental arithmetic.

'I'll be damned, Powerscourt! Excuse my language, Lady Lucy. Could you put the right cork back in that bottle? You have the right cork? Good. You see, I don't think that this Nuits St Georges is a forgery at all. I think it's the real thing. I'll take it round to one or two people I know after we've finished here. It's the rich taste, the body of the wine. I'm sure it's real. Come, let us try one of the Nuits St Georges that came today.' Sir Pericles examined the label with great care, even producing a small magnifying glass from his jacket pocket for a closer look. 'They sometimes make silly mistakes with the labels, these forgers. We had some Château Margaux years ago labelled Château Margo, as if the spelling had been done phonetically. Last year, I remember, we had a large consignment of Chablis with the year 1909 on the label. Time travelling Chablis perhaps. I'm sure H.G. Wells would have enjoyed a bottle or two.'

Once again Powerscourt poured out three small glasses of the Necromancer's burgundy. 'Try to remember the taste of the one before,' Sir Pericles said quickly before anybody drank. They took cautious sips of the wine.

'What do you think, Lady Lucy?' asked Sir Pericles 'What do you make of it?'

'Well,' said Lucy, 'it's definitely not the same as the one before. But it's not absolutely disgusting, though I thought I detected a faint hint of a nasty aftertaste. If you told me at a posh dinner at Whites Hotel that this was pre-phylloxera Nuits St Georges I'd probably believe you. I've only ever tasted one bottle of pre-phylloxera wine and that was a Château Lafite with my grandfather shortly before he died. I have to say I can't remember the taste or the bouquet at all. Is that very bad of me?'

'Not at all,' said Sir Pericles, 'perfectly normal. What about you, Powerscourt?'

'I agree with Lucy,' said Powerscourt loyally.

'Let's try one more red, one of the Bordeaux, I think. Then we'd better taste the Pouilly Fumé you brought from the shop, Powerscourt. You've kept it separate from the others?'

Powerscourt pointed to a small cabinet by the wall where one bottle had been placed. He opened the Château Figeac from Bordeaux and poured a small amount into clean glasses.

'Well,' said Sir Pericles, 'certainly not the real thing, but not bad, not bad at all. I suspect our friend has got hold of some cheaper claret from a lesser Château and diluted it with red from the Languedoc and maybe a shot of brandy. But I should say the fellow knows his blending well, how to mix the things up in the most convincing manner. Now then, last but not least, that Pouilly Fumé, if you please.'

He sipped very slowly at his glass of white. This time he didn't spit it out. 'If I was a betting man,' said Freme,' I think I'd put money on this Pouilly Fumé being the real thing. I think they were trying to confuse you.' He finished his glass. 'Lady Lucy, your thoughts?'

'Delicious,' she said, 'absolutely delicious. We must order some for the cellar. You're not going to tell me, Sir Pericles, that this one is a forgery?'

'I'm not, it's not,' said Freme, 'I think I'll take that bottle away with me too, if I may. Our friend the Necromancer has not done badly, mind you. It's easy to see how those dinners at Whites Hotel have kept going. I think I'd give him six or seven marks out of ten. Now then, this is my last word.'

He pulled a little notebook out of his pocket and began to read: '"White elder wine, very like sweet muscadine from southern France: Boil eighteen pounds of white powder sugar, with six gallons of water and two whites of egg well beaten; then skim it and put in a quarter of a peck of elder berries from the tree that bears white berries; don't keep them on the fire. When near cold, stir it, and put in six spoonfuls of lemon juice, four or five of yeast and beat well into the liquor; stir it every day; put six pounds of the best raisins, stoned, into the cask and tun the wine. Stop it close and bottle in six months."'

15

The Alchemist was fuming with rage. Ever since he arrived in London he had taken great care to defend his privacy. Nobody knew where he worked, the great space in the warehouse filled with bottles of every type and size, locks and bars on the doors. Now he and Septimus Parry had discovered that somebody calling himself Lord Francis Powerscourt and his tame tramp knew his identity and the place where he worked. The most important thing in the Alchemist's life in London was his isolation, his solitary existence between his lodgings in north London and his bench at the warehouse in the docks. Parry had told him that he did not think Powerscourt was the man's real name. Neither he nor Vicary Dodds believed a real lord would waste his time ordering pre-phylloxera wines that he suspected might be fakes before he even tasted them. The whole story about the elderly relative in darkest Somerset was, in Septimus's view, a charade, a story that wasn't true and wasn't to be believed. Informed opinion at Piccadilly Wine reckoned the man called Powerscourt must be a government agent of some sort, come to check on the shipping manifests of the wine perhaps, or from one of the innumerable agencies that made it their business to raise taxes for the government.

The Alchemist was due to attend the opera that evening but he didn't go. He was too upset and too angry, even for Wagner. Terrible fates unwound themselves in his mind, incarceration in the Tower perhaps, exiled to some other terrible prison, an English equivalent of Château d'If maybe, deportation to France where his earlier crimes would catch up with him. The Alchemist had learnt the rudiments of his trade in the back streets of Marseilles. They knew what to do with their enemies there, those tough little Corsicans, men from Bastia and Ajaccio and Calvi. One of them had even given him lessons in the use of the knife and the garrotte. The Alchemist had never thought he would need to employ these murderous techniques on his own account. Now, he thought, in a wet November in London, the time had come to defend his privacy and his honour.

Charles Augustus Pugh was seated at his desk in Gray's Inn. His feet, for once, were on the ground, not resting on his desk. His hands were attending to some piece of paper rather than wrapped round the back of his neck.

'Damn and blast!' he said to Powerscourt, just settling himself in on the other side of the formidable desk. 'I mean, seriously damn and blast!' He opened a low drawer rather furtively and produced a packet of cheroots and a box of matches. 'Not meant to have one of these before six o'clock in the evening. Manage it most days. I've always said a chap should be allowed a few sins every now and then to make his virtues brighter the rest of the time. Would you agree with that, my friend?'

'Absolutely,' said Powerscourt, wondering what fresh catastrophe had reduced Pugh to his tobacco at ten o'clock in the morning. A quick glance out of the window revealed no hecatomb of dead birds or dismembered mammals that might have been massacred by the Pugh chambers cat.

'The gun,' said Pugh, blowing a great cloud of smoke past Powerscourt, 'you will remember the gun in the state bedroom, held by Cosmo, believed to have been the weapon used to kill Randolph?' Powerscourt nodded. 'My God, this cheroot tastes good. Maybe you have to smoke them earlier and earlier in the day.' He took another contented puff. Powerscourt looked expectant.

'And you will recall, my dear Powerscourt, that you yourself toiled mightily to find a couple of fingerprint experts who might be willing to give evidence, travelling as far as the louche purlieus of Brighton to find one of these gentlemen? And indeed you did find such a man. So I had our solicitors write to the Norfolk Constabulary, copied to the prosecution solicitors, naturally, to ask if one of our own experts might look at the fingerprints on the gun and give his opinion to the court. The law officers of East Anglia, I fear, took some time to reply. Now I know why. This is the relevant portion of their answer: "The Norfolk Constabulary does not, at present, have its own fingerprint service. In any cases where we consider fingerprint evidence necessary, we send the relevant materials to the Metropolitan Police in London and they look after our interests as they would those of their own officers. Unfortunately" – I'll say this is unfortunate, Powerscourt, wait for it, my friend – "the gun found in the possession of Mr Cosmo Colville was brought back to Fakenham police station. It was not tagged or stored in a safe place. A new cleaning woman, unacquainted with the customs of the force and the need for integrity in the storing of evidence, dusted the gun the very day it was taken to Fakenham. She told the station sergeant that she didn't like dirty and dusty objects cluttering up the place. It looks much better now it's cleaned up, that gun, she told the officer in charge. There's not a print left on the thing now. It's as clear of fingerprints as the day it left the factory." God save us all.'

'Heaven deliver us from Norfolk cleaning women,' said Powerscourt, 'especially the ones from Fakenham. How bad is it, Pugh?'

'Well, suppose there were no prints other than those of Cosmo Colville on the gun. We could have argued that he wiped the gun with his own handkerchief to protect the murderer, that it was entirely consistent with his policy of being prepared to lay down his life for another. And if there had been anybody else's fingerprints, then they would obviously have been those of the murderer. So far, my lord,' Pugh pulled at the sleeve of an imaginary gown, 'we have not been able to find the owner of these other prints. Perhaps he is in hiding or has fled abroad. But, gentlemen of the jury, I would remind you of your duty not to convict my client if you think there is any doubt at all about his guilt. I put it to you that these other fingerprints are themselves eloquent witnesses to the dangers of a conviction and the need for a more prudent acquittal.'

Pugh took another satisfying pull of his cheroot. 'I could have wittered away for quite a long time in that vein, Powerscourt, you know. It might have done some good.'

'Is there anything at all you can do with the gun, Pugh?'

'Well,' he grinned slightly, 'I've subpoenaed the cleaning woman for a start. I want her to say that nobody had told her about not cleaning certain things, that she regarded everything in the station as fair game for her dusters, that if the Ark of the Covenant itself had dropped into the yard at the back of the premises, she'd have been on to that in a flash, brush and dusters in hand. I shall imply that the Norfolk police were negligent. I shall point out that their incompetence has made it impossible for my client to have a fair trial and that the case should be thrown out because of the tampering with the evidence.'

'Don't suppose there's any chance of that?' said Powerscourt.

'No, there isn't,' said Pugh, blowing an enormous cloud of smoke towards the ceiling, 'but it's worth a try. The thing is, I don't think many of these judges understand fingerprints. One of them told me after a case not long ago that he believed they changed every time a person washed his hands. Stood to reason, his lordship said, all that water running over the skin, it's bound to change the patterns.'

'You are bound to be a much better judge than I of what

194

might weigh with the jury, Pugh. Now the fingerprint evidence is gone, what are we left with?'

'Don't underestimate the cleaning lady, Powerscourt. I have high hopes of the cleaning lady. I shall recall the elderly police person before her. She may show up the Norfolk Constabulary for a collection of fools who couldn't look after things properly, and ipso facto, were unlikely to have arrested the right man. Mind you, they may get some director person up from the Theatre Royal in Norwich to coach her. I've known provincial police forces do stranger things in my time.'

'The mysterious Frenchman,' said Powerscourt, 'how do you rate him?'

'Ah,' said Pugh, 'if anything I like the mysterious Frenchman even more than I like the cleaning lady of Fakenham. That couple from the hotel are going to appear for the defence. Tell me this, Powerscourt, you have been writing to lots of people who were near to where the murder was committed in the Long Gallery, is that not so? And none of them remember a Frenchman?'

'Not one,' said Powerscourt.

'I just wonder if we shouldn't shift the focus. Look at it this way. If our theory is correct, and the mysterious Frenchman was the murderer, then I don't think he would have gone back into the crowd after he'd done the deed. He'd have cleared off as fast as he could, down the stairs from the state bedroom and legged it round the empty side of the Hall. So he wouldn't have been up there in the Long Gallery for any of your correspondents to see. Why don't we try the other seating plan, the one taken in the garden before they went into the house, and see if any of those people remember a Frenchman or a stranger. He's bound to have been lurking about then. He had to get into the house to commit the murder after all.'

'Right,' said Powerscourt, 'we'll write to them all.'

'What about the vanished under footman or trainee coachman or whatever he was,' said Pugh. 'Has he turned up yet?'

'William Stebbings,' Powerscourt replied, 'trainee footman, close to the butler and the murder scene at Brympton Hall. No sign of him as yet. I think the Nashes are beginning to lose hope.'

'I'm sure you know as well as I do, Powerscourt,' said Charles Augustus Pugh, 'horrible thing to say, but he's more use to us dead than alive. God forgive me, but if he was murdered I could almost guarantee to get Cosmo off.'

Powerscourt nodded across the desk. 'Lucy and I were saying the same thing only the other day. I'd like to pick your brain on a slightly different tack, if I may. It doesn't help us in the short term with the defence, mind you.'

'As things stand at present,' said Pugh, now nearing the end of his cheroot, 'we don't have enough to save Cosmo. Unless we can work a miracle, he's going to swing. Tell me what you want to pick my brain about.'

'It's this,' said Powerscourt, 'why is Cosmo refusing to say a word? Nobody's made any sense of that so far. Let's leave women out of it for a moment. What on earth would persuade a conservative character like Cosmo to play the hero? Does he know who the murderer is? Does he refuse to give somebody away? Is it a question of honour in some way? Did some dark secret of the Colvilles have to remain a secret? Family honour and all that? I can just about see Cosmo taking that line, you know. Like a lot of people who aren't necessarily very clever, I'm sure he could be very obstinate when it came to what he saw as his interests or his family's interests. Did the secret have to do with the family row? God knows, Pugh, I'm sure I don't.'

'I'm sure the notion of honour, probably family honour, is a runner. But your theory worked on an assumption that women had nothing to do with it. I seem to remember you telling me that one of his relations said Randolph was a ladies' man throughout his lifetime, before and after his marriage. Who might he have been carrying on with who could have brought dishonour and disgrace to his family? The wife of a Colville? The wife of a competitor? Some pretty twenty-year-old serving maid? Somebody whose lowly origins would have brought disgrace to the family? But how could that lead to his death? Unless he promised money, marriage and all that to the girl and then changed his mind. Then she shoots him. That's no good at all, Powerscourt. It remains the very centre of this case, that little tableau in the state bedroom, Randolph lying dead on the floor, Cosmo sitting opposite him with a gun in his hand, refusing to speak. If we could unravel that we could get Cosmo off, but we can't.'

Johnny Fitzgerald dropped into Markham Square late that afternoon. He refused all offers of tea. He had further news to report, though none of it, he would be the first to admit, likely to lead to an acquittal.

'My first piece of news ,' he began, 'has to do with the man we used to call the Necromancer.'

'Used to call the Necromancer?' Powerscourt cut in. 'Is he dead?'

'No, he's not dead. I followed that Septimus Parry to a warehouse in Shadwell. Huge forbidding place, about six or seven floors. Maybe they're all filled with fake wines. Anyway I was trying to listen at the door when they pulled me in. I was, thank God, a tramp for the afternoon, rather than myself. I had to confess to working for a Lord Francis Powerscourt every now and then, before they kicked me out. Literally. I've got a bloody great bruise on my leg. The thing is he's not called Necromancer at all. He's called the Alchemist. He was very cross that his fakery had been discovered. He uttered some dire threats against you, Francis.'

'He'll get over it,' said Powerscourt, 'I'm not too worried about a few threats from a forger. He'll probably find another corner of another warehouse tomorrow, I shouldn't wonder. What news of Colvilles, Johnny?'

'I think I've finally discovered what all the young men there are frightened of,' Johnny said, stretching himself out full-length on a Powerscourt sofa. 'They think the firm is going to go bust. It was bad enough, they said, with Randolph and Cosmo alive. Neither of them ever paid very much attention to the future. Their main concern was that things should go on as they had done in the past. But now they're both gone, there's nobody with any grip left in the place. There's an old general manager who's apparently no use to anybody at all. There's a young relation called Tristram who tried to move into Randolph's shoes and Randolph's office recently but he was more interested in going out to lunch than he was in the business. He's cleared off now. What they should do is to advertise for a first rate man from one of the other wine merchants and pay him handsomely to drag Colvilles back from the brink. One of the young men told me the place was running on collective memory, nothing else.'

'I don't suppose,' said Powerscourt, 'that any of the young men had any information about dark secrets that might lie beneath the surface?'

Johnny Fitzgerald shook his head. 'I tried them all, all the bad words. Family rows, blackmail – I went on and on about blackmail – adultery, mistresses, fallen women. None of them registered. One of them told me they were too far from the centre to pick up any of that, and he was probably right.'

Johnny looked sternly at the cupboard in the centre of the opposite wall. That was where the Powerscourt wine usually dwelt. But the doors were firmly closed today.

'I think they may be a bit naughty, the Colvilles,' he said, 'but probably not any naughtier than everybody else.'

'What sort of crimes are they up to, Johnny?' asked Lady Lucy, very aware of the keen interest her guest was taking in the closed cupboard by the wall.

'Bit loose with the labels was what my man said. Stuff comes up in a wine train from the south, wagon after wagon full of cheap Languedoc red, gets bottled in Dijon or Beaune and then labelled as Bourgogne Cuvée or some such name. Much more expensive now. My man says everybody's doing it. This chap, he comes from Beaune by the way, had another story to tell. The Colvilles have a very close relationship with a man called Thevenet, Louis Thevenet, a grower in the Mâconnais to the south of Beaune. He's rather a whiz at wine making, our Louis, and when he produces a really cracking wine every two or three years the Colvilles buy the lot, get out the labels again and call it Meursault, which sells for more than four times the price of the Mâcon. It all adds up. They've also bought up a large parcel of land just inside the official boundary of Puligny Montrachet. Clean the land up, plant your vines, wait for them to grow and then you've got your very own world-class white wine at world-class prices. And there's one other thing I've got to report. I've found the pub in St John's Wood where the Colville servants drink. It's called the Jolly Cricketers, oddly enough. I tried the subject of family rows in there two nights running and got absolutely nowhere. They're not saying a word.'

'All this fiddling about with the wines, it's still not enough to kill for,' said Powerscourt, wondering if he would ever get to the bottom of the mystery of two brothers, one dead and unable to speak, one alive and refusing to speak, and one gun which took the life of the elder.

Johnny Fitzgerald looked at his watch and sprang to his feet. 'Francis, Lady Lucy, forgive me, I'm going to be late. I've got to go to a meeting with my publishers about the bird book. Bloody man said he'd found a problem with it.'

Half an hour later Johnny's place in the Powerscourt drawing room was taken by the dapper figure of Sir Pericles Freme, dropped by in a hurry, as he put it, to impart one piece of important news and one rather odd piece of gossip.

'The important thing,' he began, checking that the crease on his trousers was still immaculate, 'is this. Colvilles are in danger of going broke, going out of business. The business hasn't been run properly for a long time. It's going to seed really, like a field that hasn't been cared for in years. Pity, really. In their day they were a fine business.'

Powerscourt wondered how impending bankruptcy might provide a motive for murder but he couldn't see it.

'Could anything save them? The return of Cosmo maybe? A general increase in levels of thirst in the population at large?'

Sir Pericles smiled. 'Fresh management might do the trick. A substantial injection of funds might keep them afloat but they'd still have to put their house in order.'

'And the gossip, Sir Pericles?' asked Powerscourt hopefully. He had known many cases where the gossip had been more useful than the facts in solving the mystery.

'Simply this,' replied Freme. 'That chap from Beaune, the one who looked after the Colville interests and has since disappeared, dammit, I've forgotten the fellow's name.'

'Drouhin,' said Powerscourt, 'Jean Pierre Drouhin.'

'Of course it is,' said Sir Pericles. 'Anyway, it seems the fellow is completely ambidextrous, able to sign his name with both hands, write at the same time on both sides of a notebook, all kinds of tricks. Just thought I'd mention it.'

With that Sir Pericles departed into the night.

Neither Powerscourt nor Sir Pericles noticed a figure lurking in the shadows a few doors away from the Powerscourt house in Markham Square. The coat was drawn up and the hat was pulled down over the forehead. The figure appeared to have its eyes locked on the Powerscourt's front door.

Lady Lucy looked closely at her husband after Sir Pericles had left. He was walking up and down the drawing room again and his face looked as though he had travelled in his mind to some far distant place. Something was nagging at him, some connection he couldn't quite place. Without a doubt it had to do with what Freme had just said, but was it the facts or the gossip that were swirling round his brain? He sat down by the fire and looked at Lady Lucy as if he hardly knew her. Then he came back.

'Lucy,' he began, 'I think there was somebody else in this case who was ambidextrous but I can't for the life of me remember who it was.'

'Somebody in Norfolk perhaps, Francis? Some Colville relation? Someone to do with the wine business?'

Powerscourt shook his head. Lucy was close, surely, but she hadn't quite pulled it off. Suddenly he knew where he had heard it before. It was at Randolph's funeral and the remark had come from a neighbour who had watched Randolph play tennis some years before without a backhand ever being employed. The thing was impossible, surely. Powerscourt shot down the stairs to his study where he had a file of information about the case. With difficulty he managed to raise Georgina Nash on the telephone. She was another great shouter down the line as if her words had to travel the entire length of the train tracks between Norwich and London. After checking in her wedding notebook she reported that Jean Pierre Drouhin and his wife had indeed been invited to the happy occasion, but had declined. The reply was in a man's hand. She provided an address in Beaune. Lord Francis Powerscourt, she informed her husband as he tucked into a large helping of oysters later that evening, appeared to be losing his wits.

Mrs Cosmo Colville's telephone manner was more regular, coming as it did from a much closer place near Lord's Cricket Ground. Now she came to think of it, she said, she didn't think she had ever met this Mr Drouhin. He didn't seem to cross the Channel very often. On the one occasion when she and Cosmo had made an appointment to visit this Jean Pierre when on holiday in France, he had been called away to a sick relative in Montpellier. As she put the receiver down she also reflected that Powerscourt seemed to be chasing at straws.

'Lucy!' Powerscourt was back in the drawing room. 'It may be a wild goose chase. There's less than one chance in ten that I am right. Never mind. There's not a moment to lose! We must catch the first boat out of Dover in the morning. There will be a train to take us there tonight if we hurry.'

Lady Lucy knew where they were going. She had been there before. As they walked as fast as they could to pick up a taxi in the King's Road, the watching figure slipped his moorings and followed them, about ten or twelve paces behind. When they climbed into a taxi to Victoria the figure was less than fifty yards behind. He was close enough in the ticket queue to hear where they were going. The Alchemist swore briefly when he realized that his prey were travelling to the one country he dare not visit. Then he remembered his little brother Marcel in Lyon. He would send him a telegram first thing in the morning. The neighbours in his fashionable street thought he was a successful businessman, the Alchemist's brother. All his children's friends knew him as a very generous man, always prepared to pay for charities and treats for his daughters' classmates. The police of Lyon, however, would have told you a rather different story. In their view Marcel was one of the most violent gangsters in France.

Ten minutes after the Powerscourts' departure a note was dropped through the door. It came from Charles Augustus Pugh. '"Time, like an ever rolling stream,"' it began, '"bears all its sons away." Or, in this instance, it has borne away the trial due before Cosmo's. The case has fallen apart. Cosmo's appearance in court is scheduled for next Thursday, six days from now. God help us all.'

16

Powerscourt had never known a Channel crossing like it. The captain, it transpired later, had serious reservations about setting forth but had been overruled by the managers of the shipping line. Now the boat, apparently so large and so solid on the quayside at Dover, had turned into a matchstick box, rising and falling in the great swells of the angry sea, its metal shrieking and battered in the fury of the waves. The passengers were confined to the great cabin where they clung on to the seats that were fixed to the floor or held on to the railings by the bar. Anybody on deck would have been swept away to certain death in the swirling embrace of the angry waters. Up on his bridge the captain peered ahead, seeking any respite in the storm. There were several small children on board and they huddled sadly into their mothers' coats, their faces drawn and pale, asking from time to time when it was going to end or were they all going to die and go to heaven.

Lady Lucy had never been seasick on board ship until today. A nauseous mixture of sea water and vomit swirled round the little table where she and her Francis tried to make a shelter from the tempest. She remembered suddenly that Powerscourt's first wife Caroline and their little son Thomas had been drowned in a terrible storm in the Irish Sea years before. She hoped Francis wasn't going to meet his first wife again after another maritime disaster. Perhaps, she thought, they have a special section in heaven for people drowned at sea. At least she presumed her husband would be going to heaven. Looking at him now, she saw that his eyes were closed and his lips moving. She wondered if he was praying or reciting some of his favourite poetry. Tennyson's Ulysses, she remembered, had a pretty rough time on the seas of Greece, taking ten years after the Trojan Wars to reach the craggy island of Ithaca that he called home.

It took over three hours to cross the first ten miles of the English Channel. There was nobody on board now who had not been sick. Many were throwing up for the fifth or sixth time and had little left in their stomachs. The captain sent word that he thought the last stages of the journey might be easier than the first. There was a sort of embryonic hospital in the corner of the great cabin now, populated by people who had broken an arm or a leg sliding across the floor, unable to stop before they crashed into some immovable object.

Just when you could dimly see the French coast, a thin pencil line of land that wasn't moving or sliding or falling over, it began to rain. It rained, as Lady Lucy said afterwards, as if it were the last downfall ever on earth, as if all the rivers and all the oceans of the world had to give up their water for it to be hurled down on to the English Channel. It lashed down in torrents so dense you could only see a couple of yards in front of your face. Any other shipping close by would have been a grave hazard. Powerscourt looked at his watch from time to time, realizing that all their train connections had, quite literally, been blown apart. He might not have been aware of the latest Pugh deadline, now in Markham Square, but he was sure the start of the trial could not be very far away. And here he was, miles away from London on a mission that ninety-nine people out of a hundred would have described as a wild goose chase.

Nearly eight hours after they set out from Dover their ship docked at Calais. The passengers, some still shaking from their ordeal, others wrapped round husbands or wives, small children held very tight in their parents' arms, descended the gang plank gingerly and wobbled about helplessly on the unmoving dry land. The captain was waiting to greet them at the bottom, rather like a vicar come to shake hands with his congregation after service on Sunday. He proffered his apologies, assuring everybody that he would never have set forth if he had known the conditions were going to be so harsh. The passengers thanked him for bringing them safely from England to France. Powerscourt found a train bound for Paris that was leaving in twenty minutes. The man in the ticket office said they would have to wait until the next day, a Sunday, to reach Beaune.

Tristram Bennett was back in the tiny cottage behind Brympton Hall. He was lying in bed, completely naked except for an enormous cigar. Emily was lying beside him, her hands folded behind her head, eyes closed, a dreamy look on her face, her shock of red hair bright against the pillows. Tristram had been thinking seriously about his own position in Colvilles and the dues he was owed by society in general. He had been hurt by various episodes in his youth when he felt people, particularly schoolmasters, had not paid him the respect due to a man of his abilities. There had been that refusal to take his going into the Church seriously. On another occasion they had laughed when his mother suggested putting him in for the Diplomatic Service. Only a month ago he had heard of a contemporary of his at school who had just been made a director of a leading bank in the City of London. And here he was, languishing away as junior manager for Colvilles in East Anglia, a post that had provided insufficient scope for his genius.

Emily was not quite asleep. She was dreaming of a great ball where she had gone with Tristram. Now he had left her to play cards and she was besieged by a host of beautiful young men, asking her to dance. The champagne was flowing freely. Through the great windows you could see the garden glowing in the lights strung between the trees and the young couples strolling arm in arm along the paths. This was where she belonged, Emily thought, as she was led away to the dance floor by a young hussar with a slight scar on his cheek that made him seem even more romantic.

'I tell you what I'm going to do,' said Tristram, taking a long pull at his cigar. 'The firm is now as full of holes as one of those Swiss cheeses. Randolph gone, the fool Cosmo locked up and not speaking for something he didn't do, the old boy Nathaniel out of his depth and past it. Don't you agree, Emily? You've watched what's been going on.'

'Oh yes,' said Emily although it was hard to tell whether she was speaking to an imaginary lover in her reverie or the real one on her right-hand side.

'They've never given me a chance,' Tristram went on. 'Just because I was unlucky enough to back a few wrong horses and put my money on the losing cards once or twice doesn't mean I haven't got a financial brain. Oh no. It just needs a chance. And I won't get a chance to do that mouldering up here with the donkey rides on the beach and the boats messing about on those ridiculous Broads.

'I'm going to sell my shares, all of them, and set myself up as an independent investor with the proceeds. How about that, Emily?'

Emily was still dancing with the hussar with the scar. 'That sounds very nice, Tristram,' she said.

Now it was Tristram's turn to dream, staring out of the little window at the upper branches of the trees waving in the wind. He saw himself at a large desk in a large office in the City, signing cheques and bankers' drafts, looking for new investment opportunities. His firm would expand, possibly, into casinos and luxury hotels and horse racing. Surely, he thought, you couldn't lose if you owned the bookies or the roulette wheel. 'Yes, Mr Bennett,' 'What good taste you have, Mr Bennett,' 'Thank you, Mr Bennett.' He was completely incapable of seeing himself as others saw him. He had, after all, been the only boy in his school who had been totally on the side of Malvolio through all his troubles at the court of Olivia in Shakespeare's Illyria. They were both sick with self-love, the lovers, dreaming their way to running Colvilles or enjoying the most perfect romance.

A thin sunshine illuminated the last stage of the Powerscourts' journey from Dijon to Beaune the following morning. They were following the route of the Côte de Nuits in the heart of Burgundy, one of the most famous wine routes in the world. Powerscourt remembered travelling the same path years before with his father when his three sisters had been left in London with their mother while the men went off to taste the wines of France. Louis the Fourteenth, his father told him, had been devoted to the Côte de Nuits, Madame de Pompadour had more expensive tastes with Romanée Conti, and Napoleon never set forth on campaign without a decent supply of Chambertin. Lady Lucy had fallen asleep, still weary from the ordeals of yesterday. Stretching away on the south- and east-facing slopes the vines reached out in ordered rows like soldiers on parade. The villages with the numinous names, Powerscourt remembered, Marsannay la Côte and Gevrey Chambertin, Chambolle Musigny and Nuits St Georges, Vougeot and Reulle Vergy, Vosne Romanée and Aloxe Corton all had a number of features in common. They all seemed to be virtually uninhabited, windows shuttered, gates to the store rooms locked and barred. Sometimes an occasional peasant could be seen tending the vines as they stretched across the hillside but nobody could describe the art of the *vigneron* as being arduous. And every now and then there was a sudden glimpse of hidden wealth, an imposing new house, a brand new car, a Citroën come to grace the hills and the sleepy villages of Burgundy.

The Alchemist's brother Marcel had not heard of the terrible storm in the Channel. He had expected Powerscourt to arrive in Beaune the day before. One of his men, Jean Jacques, a slim young man with only a couple of teeth left from street fighting, had been posted at the railway station for most of the day to vet the arrivals. The Alchemist had sent descriptions of Powerscourt and Lady Lucy over from London.

'They're not coming, boss,' Jean Jacques had told Marcel at the end of the day. 'They're probably still in London. We could head back to Lyon.' Jean Jacques thought he had a girl in Lyon.

'Don't hurt yourself trying to think, Jean Jacques,' had been Marcel's reply, 'just get yourself back down the station first thing in the morning.'

Powerscourt overheard his neighbours on the train talking in a very excited fashion. Most French conversations, he would have admitted readily, took place in an excited fashion but this was something more. After a moment or two he looked at the date on his newspaper. He stared out at the vines of Comblanchien going past his window. He looked again at the prosperous pair conducting the conversation. They were both in their Sunday best, boots polished, dark waistcoats and great jackets to conceal their girth, hair washed and moustaches waxed. Powerscourt didn't think they were going to church. Gradually it came back to him. He remembered the hotel-keeper telling his father and himself about it late one night at their hotel in Meursault when the other guests had gone to bed. He remembered even more clearly the very special bottle the hotel-keeper had fetched from his cellar to keep them company. Powerscourt told Lucy the story as soon as she woke up.

'This is a special day in Beaune, Lucy, one of the most special days in the year. Hundreds of years ago, in the middle of the fourteen hundreds or somewhere around there, a Chancellor of Burgundy and his wife decided to endow a hospital for the sick here in Beaune. It was going to look after everybody, rich or poor. They'd just had a lot of plagues in these parts, I seem to remember. Nicolas Rolin, that was the man's name. Anyway, he endowed his hospital not with money but with vineyards. And not just any old vineyard but ones that sat between Aloxe Corton and Meursault, two of the finest wines in Burgundy, or anywhere in the world come to that. I think the hospital may have been left other parcels of land and vineyards over the years.'

'What's all that got to do with today, Francis? There's nothing special going on in the wine world today, is there?'

'There is here,' said her husband triumphantly. 'On the third Sunday in November the Hospices de Beaune – that's the all-purpose name for the hospital and its various sections – have an auction where they sell off all their wines from that year. It's considered a great honour to have acquired one of these great vintages and sometimes the wine goes for far more than anybody expected. But this is the important thing, Lucy. All the money raised at the Hospices de Beaune auction goes to pay for the hospital, the nurses, the doctors, everything is paid for out of the funds realized at the wine auction. And today is the third Sunday in November.'

'What happens if they have a bad year, Francis?' asked Lady Lucy.

'No idea,' said her husband cheerfully, 'I expect they keep some over from the good years.'

Beaune station was packed with visitors when they arrived. Small local trains seemed to have been bringing in more people from the surrounding villages. Lady Lucy noticed Jean Jacques staring with particular interest at her husband and resolved to make appointments with the dentist for all her family as soon as she reached home.

'Would I be right in thinking, Francis, that you would like to go to this auction?'

Powerscourt laughed. 'I would, definitely. It can't take very long and we don't have to stay till the end. It would be a bit like being in London on the day of a Coronation and not going to see the parades and the procession. This notice here says the auction is to start at eleven o'clock in the courtyard of the

Hôtel Dieu. I presume God's hotel must be part of the hospice. We just have to follow the crowd.'

They made their way through streets devoted to the complexities of wine making, shops selling staves to hold the vines, bottle makers, barrel makers, label makers, exporters, blenders, even some shops selling the wine itself. Twice more Lady Lucy noticed the man with no teeth drawing very close to them. His eyes seemed to be locked for the moment on Powerscourt's back.

The Hôtel Dieu had an innocuous-looking frontage. As they handed over what seemed to be an enormous sum of money to gain entrance to the courtyard they saw that they were in an extraordinary building complex. It was long and rectangular in shape. A balcony ran all the way round the first floor. The wings to the left and rear had spectacular roofs of coloured glazed tiles of yellow and blue and red broken up by double rows of dormer windows. Powerscourt thought they had been transported back hundreds of years. A King Henry or a King Edward might ride past on some magnificent horse. Beautiful ladies of the court in long dresses might peep out of the windows. At a high table on the balcony at the opposite end from the entrance there sat four middle-aged men. One was wearing the robes of the Mayor. Another, dressed in white, might have been the superintendent of the hospital. In the very centre, another official-looking figure sat as if he were the centre of attention, the gavel in his hand, his eyes scanning the potential customers on the balcony and in the courtyard below. The table was decorated with bottles of wine, red to the left and white to the right. Right at the front of the table a couple of Nebuchadnezzars holding twenty bottles each kept watch on the proceedings. Powerscourt rather wished that Chancellor Rolin and his wife could return in their fifteenth-century garments to preside over it all. Lady Lucy broke into his reverie and whispered close to his ear.

'Francis, there's a man behind us. I think he's following you. He's been behind us all the way from the railway station.

You can recognize him from the teeth, or rather the lack of them. He can't be more than twenty-five but he's hardly got any left. Teeth, I mean.'

'Would you say,' said Powerscourt, 'that his intentions were friendly or unfriendly?'

'Unfriendly, Francis, definitely unfriendly.'

'I'd better see if I can give him the slip,' said Powerscourt, peering about him for ways of escape. Years of experience told him that there was little point in waiting for meetings with unfriendly powers. 'You stay put here, my love, no point in the two of us falling into enemy hands. If it takes some time I'll see you back at the hotel. It's just round the corner.'

Some ten feet to his left there was a large double door. One half of it was slightly ajar, as if people inside were trying to keep an eye on the auction. Firing a fusillade of *excusez-mois* and *pardons*, Powerscourt slipped through the people in front of him and shot through the door. He disturbed a flock of nuns who had obviously taken temporary leave of their charges to watch the auction. He started to run. After a moment or two he heard another pair of boots behind him. He shot round a corner and almost collided with another nun, dressed in sober grey like the others, helping a man on crutches. Then round another corner and he was in one of the most extraordinary rooms he had ever seen. His impressions of the Grand Salle passed in a kaleidoscope of size and colour. An enormous room well over two hundred feet long. Fifty feet high and fifty feet wide. A great timber roof in the shape of an upturned keel. Gargoyles and monsters in green at the end of the beams. Ranged along the sides, fourteen to a row, long wooden compartments with beds covered in red blankets and white sheets, set back a couple of feet from the walls. In the beds, some sitting up, some asleep or dozing, some with their curtains drawn closed, the patients of the biggest ward of the Hospices de Beaune, the Salle des Pauvres, the Room of the Poor. Moving quietly around the huge space, the nuns, one or two carrying medicines, others helping the sick to the bathrooms, the lucky ones waiting in attendance on the doctors who sat by their patients and reviewed their treatment. Powerscourt thought it was the most unlikely place for a chase he had ever been in. But the footsteps were behind him again. The nuns at the double doors couldn't have held the man with no teeth up for very long. He shot behind the left-hand row of beds and tiptoed slowly up the ward. An elderly lady peered at him indignantly from what he thought must be bed number seven or eight and was about to speak when he held his fingers to his lips and made the sign of the cross. That seemed to keep her quiet for the time being. He heard the footsteps, slower now. A man with both arms in plaster turned slowly in his bed and stared at Powerscourt. Powerscourt resisted the urge to write another message on the man's plaster and tiptoed on. Halfway up the line of beds there was a break and sufficient room to let Powerscourt or a nurse through into the main thoroughfare. He tiptoed quickly into the gap and wished he hadn't.

The man following him was walking quite slowly up the Salle des Pauvres, peering behind the beds on either side. Powerscourt could stay where he was or he could run. He ran. He shot up to the ends of the row, behind the beds with the red blankets, inspected in astonishment by the patients, one reading her missal, another inspecting herself in a mirror, then out past a painting of the Last Judgement on his left and into the next ward. This was much smaller, with half a dozen beds and some very ill patients indeed. Two of them were chalky white in the face and looked as though they might not last the day. Two more were asleep or dead already. Powerscourt sprinted on. Advancing towards him now was an elderly nun in the regulation grey carrying a tray of medicines. The tray seemed to be rather large and she was holding it well in front of her. When she saw Powerscourt she opened her mouth as if she was going to speak or perhaps to scream. Then, almost in slow motion, the tray slipped from her grasp and a whole flotilla of medicines fell to the floor, pills white and pills red, lotions, potions, mixtures, medicines of every shape and size. They slithered across the floor, forming a slippery sheet that might cause anybody coming her way to fall into this viscous soup of medicines. Powerscourt didn't stop to find out if his pursuer retained his grip on the floor. He was almost through the next room which seemed to be filled with elderly women when he saw a phalanx of nursing power advancing towards him. In the lead, resplendent in white, was a formidable woman of about forty years of age. Powerscourt thought she must be a sister at least, maybe the Matron herself. She stared in disbelief at the running man come to invade her hospital and disturb the repose of her patients and then she began to speak in one of those imperious voices that have grown used to being obeyed.

'What on earth do you think you are doing, charging round our hospital in this way?' she began.

Powerscourt felt the time for serious discussion with nursing sisters or even Matrons was not now. Maybe another time.

'Terribly sorry, ma'am,' he said. 'Chap following me, you see. Very bad teeth. Maybe you could do something for him now he's here. Can't stop at the moment. Terribly sorry. *Au revoir.*'

And with that he was gone. He fled through a room where the walls were lined with tapestries and a sombre couple on the wall in Renaissance costume who were, he presumed, Chancellor Rolin and his wife, still keeping watch over their hospice after four hundred and fifty years. Behind him he could hear voices raised in anger. Maybe the man with no teeth had been arrested by the nursing sorority and was even now having his mouth examined. But he didn't wait to find out. On he sprinted through the kitchens and here lay disaster. Lunch was being carried to the wards by a group of six nurses lining up two abreast to take delivery of the meals and carry the trays to the wards. Powerscourt noticed

213

that chicken with roast potatoes and vegetables was on the menu today for those with the will and the teeth to eat it. But there was scarcely any room to move past the nurses. A grey stove was in the way with a steaming double oven between him and the wall. This was no time for dignity, Powerscourt said to himself. There was only one way out. He dropped to the floor and crawled through between the legs of the nuns, reciting the Lord's Prayer as he went. He thought it might provide a diversion and stop them screaming. It wasn't completely successful. A volley of Hail Marys followed him out of the kitchen and into a corridor. He thought he might have come round in a circle and emerged on the other side of the courtyard. He could hear the noise of the auction growing louder, punctuated by the enormous bangs of the auctioneer's gavel and the cheers of the crowd who might, he thought, have been sampling the wares on offer. One small room at the end that might have been an office was dominated by sacred paintings on the walls and a trio of nuns writing things in enormous dark ledgers at high desks. They too looked as if they were about to speak but they were too late. Powerscourt was already opening the door. I'm through, he said to himself. Whatever was going on with that toothless youth is over. I can find Lucy at the hotel and we can do what we came for.

But Powerscourt was not through. He came out at the very back of the courtyard, closest to the door into the street. He couldn't see Lady Lucy. The crowd were concentrating on the auction, many of them rather tipsy by now. He hadn't known it but he was up against two or maybe more enemies on this day. As he emerged, blinking slightly in the sunshine, an enormous man seized him by the arm. Looking at him for the first time Powerscourt thought he was shaped exactly like a barrel with an enormous chest. He could have done sterling work in the front row of a rugby scrum. Powerscourt wondered if he had in fact been manufactured by some master cooper in his quarters in Santenay or Pommard and brought to life by the patron saints of Burgundy.

'You're to come with me,' said the barrel, 'and don't make any trouble.' Powerscourt felt what he presumed was the point of a knife jabbing into his ribs. He knew he could never win in a fight with this man. He would be crushed. As he was guided out of the courtyard he wondered where they were taking him.

Lady Lucy felt rather lonely when her husband disappeared through the double doors. She watched as the man with no teeth set off in pursuit. At this stage she was not particularly worried. She had seen Francis go off so often on strange missions but he always returned. She wished Johnny Fitzgerald was with him. He always served as guardian angel on these occasions. She had two indices of anxiety that she carried with her. One was the level of danger for Francis, rated on a scale of one to ten. Today in Beaune didn't count for much more than a two or a three. There was another index, totally out of her control. This was the knot of anxiety that formed in her stomach when she felt he was really in peril. It grew tighter and tighter when she was really scared for him. So far the knot had not put in an appearance. There was another reason for feeling lonely here in the beautiful courtyard. Most of these people were countrymen. Their hands were calloused from working in the fields or hauling bottles and barrels around the cellars and the storerooms of Burgundy. There were one or two more sophisticated clients here, men in elegant suits with buttonholes who might have come from Paris or Lyon to bid for the great hotels and restaurants. But they were all male. The voices of the suffragettes and the marching protesters demanding equal rights for women did not seem to have reached Beaune yet. Everybody here this morning was male, every last one of them. As the shouts of the bidders grew louder and traded insults with their rivals, Lady Lucy slipped away to their hotel, the Ducs de Bourgogne tucked away in a little square a couple of hundred yards away. Francis would find her there.

Powerscourt was pleased to see, but did not show his pleasure, that the man with no teeth, who he now gathered was called Jean Jacques, must have fallen foul of the nurse with the medicines back at the hotel. His trousers were stained in a strange medley of colours, red and green and a chalky white. A strange smell, a compound of dispensary and chemical factory, rose from them. And he must have twisted his leg as he fell, for he was limping painfully. Powerscourt thought of suggesting that he should have stayed in the hospital but thought better of it.

They were joined by a third man, in his early thirties, with a mean face and a vivid scar on his right cheek. The others referred to him as boss at all times. Powerscourt felt sure that his rule was maintained through fear rather than brotherly love. 'We're taking him to the barn first of all,' he said. The two others, No Teeth and Barrel as Powerscourt mentally referred to them, maintained a discreet guard through the streets of Beaune. Powerscourt noticed that one enterprising wine merchant had already filled his windows with bottles whose labels had Hospices de Beaune on the top with the titles of the particular wines, Corton Charlemagne or Beaune, underneath. The citizens, barred from the auction by the high entry fee or the lack of space, were making up for their loss in the shop, carrying off bottles by the dozen in enormous panniers on the front of their bicycles.

They were on the very outskirts of the town when Scarface took them off the main road and on to a little track that led through the fields. Half a mile away there was a farmhouse with an enormous barn fifty yards or so behind it. Just inside the doorway they halted while instructions were given. In the shadows at the back of the barn Powerscourt could see a very strange device. It was very old and looked as though it had survived from some earlier times. It was in the shape of an H or the goal posts at rugby except that the section above the cross bar was quite short and there was another beam of the same size just above the ground. And the beams were far thicker. At the top was a long beam, six or seven feet long and three or four feet wide. This beam was attached to the lower one, of similar size, running along the bottom of the H. Linked to the two vertical columns that joined the top and bottom were a series of short wooden arms that could be used to raise and lower the upper beam until it could touch the lower one if required.

'*Pressoir!*' said Barrel with a note of reverence. '*Ancien pressoir! Formidable!*'

Then Powerscourt understood and he was terrified. The device must have been used to press the juice out of the grapes in the olden times. The grapes would have been held in some sort of container, probably made of cloth rather than wood, and arranged on the lowest horizontal beam. The top section would be lowered further and further down to crush the fruit until all the juice was extracted. There must have been a series of buckets or other containers by the sides to hold the grape juice. Or, in a less peaceful world, a man could be squeezed or pressed between the two beams until all the blood had run out of his body.

'Tie him up,' said Scarface. 'On the lower beam, naturally.'

In less than a minute Powerscourt found himself lying on the bottom beam, secured to the contraption with thick rope. He wondered what they proposed to do with the upper beam. He did not have long to wait. There was a series of grunts and curses as the two men tried to work the levers that would lower the upper section.

'They're stuck,' said Jean Jacques. 'Nobody's oiled the damned things for a couple of hundred years.'

'Nonsense,' said Barrel, 'they were working earlier this summer. Damn it, I saw them myself.'

With that he gave a tremendous heave. Powerscourt could

see the muscles straining in his face. With a thick squeak the left-hand lever began to work. Looking at the beam descending towards him Powerscourt began to pray. Then, as if working in sympathy, the other one limped slowly into action. The two men looked on as the upper section of the press grew closer and closer to Powerscourt's chest.

'Hey, boss,' said Barrel cheerfully, 'do you want any juice this morning?'

17

The knot returned to Lady Lucy as she picked her way through a large helping of roast chicken in the hotel dining room. It was slight at first, the knot, then it gathered strength as her lunch progressed. By the time she reached the cheese it was as tight as she had ever known it. Where was Francis? Who were these people who pursued him into the Hôtel Dieu and must be holding him prisoner somewhere by now? Why were they after him? As she reviewed the case of the murdered Colville in her mind she could not think of anybody who might want to harm her husband. Perhaps he had not told her about a whole new raft of enemies. Perhaps he did not know of them himself. Perhaps they had risen up from some old investigation years before, but for the life of her she could not think who such people might be. She wondered if she should go back to the hospital and ask the nuns what they had seen. Then she remembered what Francis had always told her. If I get lost or taken prisoner, he always said, don't go charging round the place trying to find me. You may be taken prisoner too. Please stay put where I know I can find you. That will be for the best. And so, sipping at a bitter coffee, Lady Lucy sat in the dining room of the Hôtel des Ducs de Bourgogne wondering where her husband was. She wished Johnny Fitzgerald was with him. Somewhere she knew she had the telegraphic address of her brother-in-law William Burke in London. He would be able to find Johnny but even if she sent the cable first thing in the morning when London offices would be open again it would be at least two days before Johnny Fitzgerald could reach Beaune. The knot seemed to be growing worse. Lady Lucy was determined about one thing. She wasn't going to cry. Not yet anyway. And certainly not in the hotel dining room.

Marcel came to inspect Powerscourt, lashed to the beam like a prisoner on a galley slave. He tested the knots that held him in place. He motioned for the upper beam to be lowered slightly until it pressed harder on Powerscourt's chest.

'I don't think we want any juice for the moment,' he told his men. 'We just need to be sure Monsieur here cannot escape.' He glances at the ropes again. He patted the upper beam with his right hand.

'Right,' he said. 'We can leave Monsieur here for a little while. Have no fear, sir, we shall return.'

Barrel looked closely at Powerscourt as they left. Powerscourt could see the disappointment in his face, disappointment that there had been no juice pressed that afternoon, disappointment that Powerscourt's blood had not been forced out of his body into the square buckets lined up in rows on either side of the beam. Powerscourt suddenly remembered the torturers in the basement cells of the Russian secret police, the Okhrana, in St Petersburg he had met on a previous case. There the mouths of the victims had been taped up so that the neighbours could not complain about the screams. Barrel, he thought, might have a great future in the Okhrana. But here they hadn't bothered to tape up his mouth. The barn was miles from anywhere. Nobody in Beaune would hear him scream, nobody at all.

With determined and painful wriggling he found he could move an inch or so to his right. It didn't do him any good, of course, but it gave him the illusion of control. He wondered yet again who his captors were and where they came from.

He tried in vain to establish a link between them and the case of Randolph Colville. He was, however, optimistic on one count. He didn't think they were going to kill him. If they had been, they would surely have done so by now. Five or six great turns on the levers and he would have been crushed to a pulp. He hoped that if they were going to press him to death they would be quick about it. A real Okhrana man would be able to drag the process out for hours until there was no breath left to scream and no bones in your body left unbroken. He thought of Lady Lucy abandoned in a strange city. He prayed that she was in the hotel, not tracing his movements and running into danger herself. He thought suddenly of the long drawing room on the first floor of Markham Square, the sunlight streaming in on summer days, the books on either side of the fireplace, Lady Lucy's favourite pictures on the walls, Lady Lucy herself reading a story to the twins. The contrast with his present surroundings was almost too much to bear. He tried to remember some of the worst predicaments he had found himself in on previous cases. If he twisted his head as far as he was able he could just see the light coming in the barn door, but it was beginning to fade and he didn't like to think about what might happen in the dark.

Lady Lucy was now sitting in a small desk in her room at the hotel. She wrote some letters. She tried once more to make progress with the latest Joseph Conrad but found it difficult. She had taken a photo of her husband she always carried with her and propped it up on the little table by her side of the bed. She prayed that Francis would come back to take his place on the other side. She prayed to God that He would bring Francis back from his time of trouble. She prayed that they might be reunited with their children before too long. She asked for forgiveness for the sins she had committed and any others that she might have committed but not known about. 'Keep him safe, Oh Lord, please keep him safe.'

Marcel and his thugs returned just as the light was fading. Marcel was carrying a battered suitcase.

'Take him down,' he said, 'quickly, while we can still see what we are doing.'

'No juice at all, boss?' asked Barrel. 'Not even a cupful, or better still, seeing where we are, a bottleful?'

'No, no,' said Marcel. 'We've got other plans for our friend here.' With that he bestowed on Powerscourt a ghastly smile. 'Get him out of those clothes. I've got something appropriate for where he's going in the bag here.'

Powerscourt needed no assistance. He climbed out of his London suit and put on the clothes of a French peasant, a pair of dark trousers that might once have been blue, a filthy shirt and a sweater with holes in both arms. He managed to conceal about his person a large amount of money that had been in the trousers of his suit. He stood still for inspection.

'Rub some earth in his hair, would you, please? And scuff up those shoes, we don't want him looking as though he's just walked down the Champs-Elysées.'

Jean Jacques produced a pair of scissors and proceeded to chop random tufts out of Powerscourt's hair. The final result was a bedraggled peasant, complete with a cut on his forehead from the scissors.

'Good,' said Marcel. 'He'll do. If you try to escape, monsieur,' he addressed the latest recruit to the French peasantry, 'I shall shoot you. If you do not try to escape, I shall not shoot you. Do I make myself clear?'

They set off down the little track back towards the main road. At the junction Marcel led them to the right, away from the lights being turned on in Beaune. Powerscourt reflected sadly that they were taking him further away from Lucy. Marcel was in the lead, Powerscourt second, with the other two close behind. On either side of the road the vines stretched far into the distance. Powerscourt wondered if they belonged to the Hospices de Beaune and if their produce had been auctioned in that beautiful courtyard so very long ago that morning. A cart passed them, going towards the city, driven by a silent crone. A dog barked somewhere ahead of them. Looming up ahead on the right Powerscourt could see a large building some distance from the road. As they grew nearer he thought it might be a barracks. Rows and rows of small windows were set back slightly from the walls. Closer still and he noticed that all the windows, without exception, were barred. Was it a prison? There was no sign that he could see on the outside to tell him the building's function. They turned off the main road and proceeded to the front door, a massive creation that looked to Powerscourt as if its principal purpose was to keep the insiders in rather than the visitors out.

Marcel pulled firmly on the rope. A surly porter who looked as if was expecting them let them in. He showed them to a small waiting area with no chairs. Then Powerscourt knew where he was. A very official-looking sign on the wall welcomed them to the Maison d'Aliénés, Département de Côte d'Or. No visitors, it proclaimed, unless by prior arrangement. This was the local lunatic asylum, also known as Maison de Fous. The Madhouse. Welcome to Bedlam.

The porter indicated that Jean Jacques and Barrel were to remain in the waiting area. He brought Powerscourt and Marcel to an office off on the left of the main corridor. He knocked firmly on the door.

'Come in,' said a tired voice on the other side. They were placed on two chairs opposite a wide desk littered with files. The only decoration in the room, apart from the grey paint on the walls, was a great etching of the Palace of Versailles. Perhaps they were all mad in there too, Powerscourt thought, Marie Antoinette playing with her pretend dairy at Le Petit Trianon, the courtiers measuring out their importance across

223

the château floors, a court inhabited entirely by lunatics until they were swept aside by the wilder lunacy of the Revolution. A sign facing them announced that they were in the presence of Dr Charles Belfort, Professor of Medicine at the University of Dijon and Director of the Maison d'Aliénés. He was a small tubby man with a slim moustache and greying hair. A younger medical man stood sentry behind him.

'This is the man you spoke of earlier today, monsieur?' he said to Marcel. The doctor looked Powerscourt up and down distastefully. There was a faint smell of countryside and cowdung coming from his new clothes.

'It is, sir,' said Marcel.

The doctor rummaged briefly in his papers. 'And this is the letter from Dr Rives, the distinguished general practitioner from Beaune?'

'It is,' said Marcel.

'Monsieur,' the doctor turned to Powerscourt, 'could you please tell us your name?'

'My name is Francis Powerscourt.' He was damned if was going to call this ridiculous little man sir.

'And do you have any titles, monsieur?'

'Titles?' asked Powerscourt. 'What titles?' Was the man asking him if he was Lord Mayor of London or the Keeper of the Privy Purse?

'I was wondering if you thought you were a member of the aristocracy perhaps?'

It was now that the severity of his plight struck home. God knows what Dr Rives had said in his letter, written for him by Marcel presumably, but here he was, his hair looking like a scarecrow, his clothes stinking of the farmyard, his flies undone because Marcel had cut the buttons off, a scar across his face, his shoes with holes in them and filthy fingernails, about to announce himself as a Peer of the Realm.

'My full title,' said Powerscourt rather sadly, 'is Lord Francis Powerscourt. I am an Irish peer.'

'An Irish peer?' said the doctor, as if this was the most interesting thing he had heard all day. 'And tell me, pray, how do they differ from English peers or Scottish peers or Welsh peers? We have grown beyond all this nonsense here in France.'

Powerscourt just restrained himself from pointing out that Dr Belfort's fellow countrymen had cut most of their peers' heads off on the guillotine. 'It is a purely honorary title. Irish peers are not allowed to vote in the British House of Lords.' Powerscourt remembered suddenly the French governess who had lived in his parents' house when he was aged between two and fifteen. Her mission was to make all the Powerscourt children fluent in French. She succeeded so well that his accent would pass for that of a native. He sounded like a true Frenchman.

'Really?' said the doctor in a condescending voice. 'How very interesting for you all. How unusual. And tell me, do you work for a living? Do you have an occupation?'

'I am an investigator. People in England employ me to solve cases of mystery and murder.' Even as he spoke Powerscourt knew he was in real trouble. The man didn't believe a word he said. The investigating was only going to make it worse.

'I see,' said Dr Belfort, casting a meaningful glance at his young companion. 'So you are Sherlock Holmes, is it not so, leaving Baker Street for the delights of Burgundy?'

'You could put it like that, I suppose,' said Powerscourt, wondering desperately if he could find a way out of this horrible place.

'We have three Sherlock Holmeses in here already,' said the doctor. 'An elderly one, a red-headed one, and one who talks to Dr Watson all the time. Perhaps you will be able to hold meaningful conversations with them. No?'

Powerscourt remained silent. 'And what brings you to Beaune, Mr Investigator? The Case of the Poisoned Meursault? The Curious Affair at the Hôtel Dieu, perhaps?'

Powerscourt sighed. 'I am looking into a murder case. We

believe the wrong man has been charged. I need to go back to work at once or else an innocent man may be sent to the gallows.'

'Of course you must go back to work. Of course. I'm sure you'll be able to work very well on the top floor here.'

With that the doctor began writing furiously in a large black notebook. 'We have seen cases of the paranoid delusions, the illusions of self-importance like this before, have we not?' He looked over his shoulder at his young assistant as he spoke. 'But rarely one where the various fantasies fit so well together, I think.' He talked about Powerscourt as if he were not in the room. Powerscourt remembered English doctors doing exactly the same thing in London. It was a different form of mental illness. The patients only exist in the minds of the doctors. They have no independent life of their own.

Dr Belfort rang a bell on the side of the desk. Another member of the staff of the Maison d'Aliénés appeared, clad entirely in pale blue smock and trousers.

'Third floor,' he pointed to Powerscourt. 'Solitary. Same medicine as the rest of them up there. Regular observation for now.'

As Powerscourt was led away Marcel stood aside for him at the door. Marcel looked him straight in the eye. 'The compliments of the Alchemist, monsieur.' With that he left the room. The warder took him into the reception area and down a long corridor which seemed even longer than it was because of the lack of any decoration on the walls. There were weak electric lights overhead casting feeble shadows on the wooden floor. Weird noises that might have been screams of ecstasy or terror made their way into the corridor.

Back in his office Dr Belfort dismissed Marcel and thanked him for performing his public duty. 'The really irritating thing,' he said to his assistant, 'about these poor patients of ours is how fervently they believe in their own fantasies. The man's real name, according to the doctor, is Albert Bouchet. Lived around Beaune all his life apparently. But if that peasant who thought he was an Irish peer had been dressed up in fancy clothes we might, we just might have believed him.'

'I think you underestimate yourself, sir,' said the young man. 'I'm sure you'd have rumbled him whatever he'd been wearing.'

There was a staircase to their left at the end of the corridor. Powerscourt stopped cursing the Alchemist and suddenly remembered a very sad poem, written by a man called John Clare who was locked up in Northampton General Lunatic Asylum for over twenty years.

> I am: yet what I am none cares or knows,
> My friends forsake me like a memory lost;
> I am the self consumer of my woes,
> They rise and vanish in oblivious host,
> Like shades in love and death's oblivion lost;
> And yet I am, and live with shadows tossed.

Powerscourt wondered about the inhabitants of this prison disguised as a mental hospital. He tried to work out how the Alchemist had managed to have him locked up in this mad-house. He thought of the three Sherlock Holmeses, deprived of opium and the solid sense of Dr Watson and Mrs Hudson's cooking. Were there Napoleons strutting round these dismal corridors, triumphant after Austerlitz, worried after Borodino or the retreat from Moscow, despairing on the bleak rock of St Helena before they were fifty years old? Mad poets perhaps, Baudelaires of the insane world, spouting decadent but meaningless verse in their Spartan cells? *Philosophe* lunatics preaching the rational virtues of The Enlightenment to a few colleagues in the asylum canteen?

> Into the nothingness of scorn and noise,
> Into the living sea of waking dreams,
> Where there is neither sense of life nor joys
> But the vast shipwreck of my life's esteems:

> And e'en the dearest – that I loved the best –
> Are strange – nay, rather stranger than the rest.

They were on the second floor now, twenty pairs of eyes, alerted by the sound of boot on wood, staring through their peepholes at the latest arrival. Welcome to the Maison de Fous. Welcome to Hell. Powerscourt remembered one doctor telling him how easy it can be to have people declared insane. Convince the relevant people that somebody is mad and then everybody else will believe it. We all know he's mad. It's common knowledge. This doctor had terrifying stories of the wrong people being locked up, in Ireland, or in France, or even in England. It was very difficult to liberate victims such as these because nobody knew they had been locked away in the first place.

They were on the third floor now. The warder was sifting his way through an enormous pile of keys. At last he found the right one and pushed Powerscourt into his cell.

'There you go,' he said, not unkindly, 'you're home at last.'

> I long for scenes where man has never trod,
> A place where woman never smiled or wept:
> There to abide with my Creator, God,
> And sleep as I in childhood sweetly slept:
> Untroubling and untroubled where I lie,
> The grass below – above the vaulted sky.

By late afternoon Lady Lucy Powerscourt was seriously worried. Maybe it was her nerves, maybe it was the local cooking, but the chicken she had at lunchtime had not agreed with her. Stomach pains were added to the knot of anxiety that possessed her. She had walked for an hour round the hotel square, reasoning that if Francis were to return they must surely see each other beneath the plane trees. Beaune had gone quiet by late afternoon. Lady Lucy wondered what the French did for the rest of Sunday. They went to church, of course. Then they had an enormous lunch with as many relatives as they could lay their hands on. And then? Perhaps they all went to sleep from the smallest baby to the oldest *grandmére*. The worst thing, she kept telling herself as she contemplated French family life, was that, unlike them, she had nobody to talk to. In London she could have picked up the telephone and talked to her relatives for the rest of the day. She could have located Johnny Fitzgerald and poured out her worries to him. She had discovered the telegraphic address of William Burke but she wasn't quite sure what to do with it. She knew men sent telegraphic messages to each other all the time, often concerning the movements of share prices or the winners of important horse races. But the telegraph was an alien male world that she did not understand. Late in the afternoon she enlisted the help of a young man on the hotel reception who had been sending telegraphs all afternoon, triumphant messages of purchases of the contents of the wine auction to the hotels and grand restaurants of Paris. Olivier, for such was the young man's name, undertook to send her message. It would, he assured her, be with Mr William Burke in his bank first thing in the morning.

'Francis missing,' she wrote. She had some distant memory that you weren't meant to use too many words. 'Please tell Johnny Fitzgerald and Mr Pugh. Replies to this number. Most urgent.'

She felt slightly better after the despatch. She might not be winning the war, but at least she had sent for reinforcements. Not for the first time that day she wondered what Francis would have wanted her to do. And where he was. And if he was still alive.

As the street lights were illuminated in the fashionable district of Holland Park in west London Sir Jasper Bentinck KC sat at his desk on the top floor of his house overlooking the great

229

wide open spaces across the road. It was his custom at this time to read through the most pressing of his forthcoming cases. Monday and Tuesday, he was appearing for the Crown in Rex versus Griffiths, a straightforward case of fraud. Later in the week he was leading for the prosecution in Rex versus Colville. Sir Jasper had read the papers some weeks before the committal hearing and been astonished at the lack of any proper defence. Charles Augustus Pugh, he saw, was to be the counsel for the defence at the Old Bailey and Pugh was not a man to let his clients down. He also had a reputation for springing surprise witnesses on the court at the very last minute. Sir Jasper lit a large cigar and stared upwards at his ceiling. He remained in this position for some fifteen minutes, searching through the evidence in his mind for what might be the weak link in the prosecution's case, some unexplored avenue where the defence might yet rally their forces for a surprise victory. Try as he might, Sir Jasper could find no holes in his case. He was not a man given to self-doubt or self-criticism, Sir Jasper. Leading barristers from the Middle Temple or any other Temple seldom are. If he could find no weakness in the case, then there was no weakness in it.

Lord Francis Powerscourt was wondering about the catering arrangements in his new establishment. There were no lists pasted on the back of the door informing clients about the times of meals, particularly breakfast, and the time by which they must vacate their room on their day of departure. Somehow he doubted there was much information available anywhere here about days of departure. Probably there was none at all. Nor were there any menus to be seen. He wondered if the solitaries like himself were given room service for their meals while the rest of the customers, accommodated, he suspected, in vast undecorated dormitories, ate equally cheerless food in some huge canteen. He wondered if the food in a French asylum would be better than in an English one. Did they serve a glass or two of wine with lunch and dinner, surely part of the ancient ancestral inheritance of every Frenchman in this part of the world?

Powerscourt began to pace around his cell. It was not large, about twelve feet by eight. There was one small window looking out over the dark. He pulled as hard as he could on the bars but they yielded nothing at all. There was a slit in the door on to the corridor, designed to let people look in rather than the other way round. The door itself was sturdy and the hinges that bound it to the wall were strong. The floorboards, he discovered, lying flat on them for ease of inspection, were joined together with some adhesive that would not give way to human hand or, he suspected, to human hand with hammer. No plank to batter a warder could be constructed out of this floor. There was nothing for him in the walls either. He tried knocking as hard as he could on the two sides of his cell but there was no reply. There was a crude bucket in the corner that would be useless as a weapon. There remained the bed. Powerscourt pulled off the mattress. It was thicker than he would have expected. Maybe the inmates were encouraged to sleep as long as possible and cause less work for the warders. He remembered suddenly the doctor prescribing for him the same medicine as the rest of the third floor. Were they all solitaries on this floor? And what should he do with the medicine when it came? He felt sure it would be some powerful form of slow-you-down-and-make-you-sleepy medicine, probably designed to turn him into a semi-automaton in a week or so, capable of a few bodily functions, incapable of thought. He suspected this was the target condition as far as the doctors were concerned, a collection of patients who had been turned into zombies. All he could think of doing with the medicine was to try to hold it in the back of his mouth until the warder had gone and then spit it into the bucket.

Five minutes later he was trying to prise one iron leg away from the body of his bed and finding it impossible. He heard footsteps approaching up the corridor outside. He threw the mattress back on the bed and sat on it. An elderly man, clad in that blue uniform of the warders, stood in the doorway. Behind him, Powerscourt could just see, he had a primitive sort of trolley. The man was about Powerscourt's height with no moustache and a bald head.

'Good evening,' said the warder in a guarded sort of voice.

'Good evening to you,' said Powerscourt cheerfully. Remember the nursery rules, always be polite to the servants and visiting tradesmen like chimney sweeps.

'Now then,' said the warder, reaching for something on his trolley, 'these are for you.' He tossed Powerscourt a pair of pale green trousers, a worn vest, a green shirt and a green jumper. 'You must have this on when somebody calls in the morning. They'll take what you're wearing now into safe-keeping. And you must wear this at all times.' He tossed Powerscourt a small disc on a string with a number on it. 'That's your hospital number, you see,' the warder said, 'so we know who you are.'

Powerscourt had been making a careful examination of the man's keys. He carried an enormous bunch of them attached to a ring on his belt. Each one, he saw, had a small tag beside it.

'Settling in all right, are you?' The warder believed in being as polite to the patients as he could. That was what his local priest Father Jugie had told him when he discovered the warder's occupation. 'They are all God's children, they are all worthy of his grace. The good Lord does not mind if they speak to him in a different language.'

'I can't complain,' said Powerscourt. 'I'm not sure about the food, mind you. I haven't actually had any yet.'

'I'll be back with that in about a quarter of an hour. I have to give the medicine out first. I've got yours just here. This'll calm you down, it calms everybody down.'

He handed over a large beaker filled with a cloudy liquid. Powerscourt smiled at the warder and took it into his mouth. He did not swallow but went back to lie on his bed.

He thought it would be easier to avoid conversation if he was lying down. The stuff was beginning to burn the back of his mouth. He wasn't sure how much longer he could hold it 'See you in a moment,' said the warder and shuffled off on his rounds. Powerscourt strode to his bucket and spat into it. He wondered if the stuff could weaken you even by being in your mouth for a few minutes. A quarter of an hour later the warder, who he discovered was called Jean, brought his supper, a stringy piece of meat that might once have been pork and some overcooked vegetables. There was no wine. As he lay down to sleep Patient Number 35601 reflected that it had indeed been an interesting day. He wondered about Lady Lucy. He decided to stop fretting about the Alchemist as there was nothing he could do about him now. Escape, that was the thing. Escape, before the medicine turned him into one of the waking dead. Escape in time to pursue his inquiries in Beaune. And as he drifted off to sleep he remembered that from the morning there were only a few days left before the trial of Cosmo Colville. Powerscourt fell asleep with the warder's belt drifting across his brain, huge bunches of keys floating through his mind, enormous keys two or three feet long, long thin keys, pencil slim and several inches long, ordinary-looking keys that might open your own front door, tiny delicate keys for opening drawers or secret caskets. On that belt, he felt sure, were the keys of his kingdom, twelve feet by eight, one rough bed, one bucket in the corner, one small window to the outside world, one slit in a door for your enemies to make sure you were still incarcerated. Welcome to the Maison d'Aliénés.

18

Lady Lucy Powerscourt dozed fitfully through the night in her Beaune hotel. No Dukes of Burgundy after whom the establishment was named came to visit her in her dreams. Sometimes her right arm reached for the space where her husband would have been, but Francis was not there. Some of the time she thought Francis was still alive. The rest of the time she thought he was dead. These fears had crossed her mind often in the past when she felt his life was in danger. How would she tell the children? How would the twins survive, growing up without a father? Would they be damaged in some way? She wondered about the funeral arrangements. Would there be some sort of Memorial Service for him, graced by various forgers and burglars and a whole host of characters Francis had saved from prison or the gallows? And where would he want to be buried, laid to rest? She suspected if she were honest that he might like to join his parents in a Powerscourt grave in a Protestant cemetery in his native Ireland. Then I could not be with him at the end, she said to herself, we'd end up in different cemeteries hundreds of miles apart and I couldn't bear it. For the first time that day she began to cry.

It was a short paragraph in the newspapers that did it. Nathaniel Colville was just finishing his breakfast when it caught his eye. He was to tell friends later that it was almost a miracle he saw it at all for he scarcely bothered to read the newspapers any more. 'Trouble at wine merchant' the headline said. It was part of a daily column that conveyed slightly gossipy information to its readers. 'We are given to understand,' Nathaniel read on, 'that times are not easy for the firm of Colvilles where one of the partners has been murdered and the other is awaiting trial for the deed in Pentonville prison. No figure of substance has, as yet, appeared to take their place in the direction of the firm.'

Nathaniel put down his piece of toast. Trouble at wine merchant indeed. No figure of substance. It was monstrous. There was nothing a man could sue for but the innuendoes were as broad as daylight. The man could almost have put his message up in lights at Piccadilly Circus. Nathaniel shouted for his dog and set forth to walk off his wrath in the back garden. This garden had once been the envy of the other Colvilles. It was enormous. There was a tennis court on one side and a croquet lawn on the other. Banks of roses used to circle the vast expanse of grass. Ranks of fruit trees and bushes were organized at the bottom. Flowers whose names Nathaniel never knew came up every year to grace his garden. Now the senior gardener was on his last legs and the younger one was not much better. He was over seventy and while the spirit might have been willing the flesh was undoubtedly weak. If you knew where to look you could usually spot him asleep in the early afternoons, snoring quietly behind the raspberries. The grass on the tennis court was overgrown, baselines and tram lines scarcely visible now. It was almost halfway up the croquet hoops on the other side, so deep that the balls themselves would have been hard to see. Nathaniel's dog Bacchus much preferred the wilderness to the order that had prevailed before. He would disappear into the wilder sections of the garden and leap up and down in pursuit of insects. Nathaniel decided this morning that his garden had become the mirror image of his life. Lack of organization.

Bad planning. No strategic direction. The problems here were the same as those at the firm. Trouble at wine merchant indeed! Damn the journalists! Damn the newspapers! I may be seventy-two years old, Nathaniel said to himself, but I'm not too ancient to get on top of things. I'm going to pay off these two old fellows and employ some new gardeners. I'm going to put on my best suit and hat and go down to Colvilles this very morning. I'm going to take charge. And I'm going to find somebody to help me in the meantime. And then I'll find some bright young fellow from some other firm to come and run the place. Colvilles were not born to provide idle tittle-tattle in the financial pages.

He strode back to his house and scribbled a short note. A footman was despatched to deliver it to the Chelsea residence of Sir Pericles Freme. Nathaniel had known him years ago and though he might not be able to secure his services full-time Freme could still join the board of Colvilles in an advisory capacity. He would not be alone. Nathaniel Colville had never felt happy doing business alone. All his life he had worked closely with his brother Walter. Now he would have a new companion in arms.

An hour later Nathaniel and Sir Pericles were installed in the Colville Head Office They brought with them an air of confidence, of experience. These were men who knew what they were doing. Inside forty-eight hours morale had improved dramatically. Colvilles, people in the trade said, are back in business.

Powerscourt slept surprisingly well in his hospital cell. He awoke to find that the outlines of a plan were forming in his mind. He rejected his first option, bribery. He had in his pocket as many francs as a warder here might earn in six months. The warder might help him escape, or he might tell the authorities and then Powerscourt would be a marked man, locked up somewhere even more forbidding, the knock-out drops in his daily medicine increased to a giant's dose. He wondered at first about violence, about why nobody attacked the warders, about the violence that might be needed to overpower the guard and steal his keys. Surely some of the prisoners must be big and burly, bodies strengthened by years of manual labour, well able to overcome a warder before breakfast. Then he remembered the knock-out medicines. What had the warder said to him yesterday evening? 'This'll calm you down, it calms everybody down.' The hospital authorities must have worked out how much medicine was needed to incapacitate every size and shape of patient they were likely to encounter. Maybe they had a book full of details with patients calibrated by age, weight, height, occupation. Extra large doses for blacksmiths and prize fighters. They didn't have to worry, the authorities, about violence from the inmates. The madmen were incapable of it. Powerscourt tried to work out if that huge key ring the man carried contained the keys for all the doors in the hospital. He remembered from the way in that he had gone straight from the reception area to the third floor without any gates or barriers in the way. Did the man have the key to the front door? If not, did he have the key of some other exit, back door, side door, tradesmen's entrance, madmen's gate?

Lady Lucy's breakfast consisted of warm croissants and jam and delicious hot chocolate. Her husband's consisted of a hard roll and a glass of cold water. Powerscourt managed not to swallow the medicine again, but he knew he would not be able to keep this up for very long. The morning warder was different from the one he had talked to the evening before. He too was old, leading Powerscourt to speculate that they might be able to pay the elder ones less than the younger men. But sooner or later a more watchful warder would keep looking at him to make sure he had swallowed his dose or ask him to open his mouth. He would have to escape today or it might be too late. Evening would be better than daytime. It was dark between five and six in Burgundy in November. The last round of medicine came at about half past five. Powerscourt settled down to wait. He lay on his bed and tried to remember as much as he could about the journey to his cell the day before, about the locks on the front door. If he had known then what he knew now he would have taken a much greater interest in his surroundings. He wondered if they were given any exercise in this French prison. He saw in his mind's eye one of those enclosed courtyards so dear to the hearts of English prison architects where the inmates trudged round and round under the watchful eyes of the guards in a ghastly arabesque, not allowed to speak to each other, unable to see anything of the real world except the stone blocks of their prison house and the little patch of blue that prisoners call the sky. Lunch time came and a further round of medicine, once more deposited in the bucket when the guard had left.

Powerscourt was now thinking about a weapon. He had his fists, of course, and they might well suffice to incapacitate the warder. He tried swinging the bed without the mattress but it was cumbersome and slow. He lay down once more and thought about his problem. His first plan had involved taking the warder's uniform as a disguise on his way out of the hospital but he wasn't sure one man without a weapon could force another to remove the outer layer of his clothes. The keys? Were they heavy enough to threaten a man's face? Would they be credible? How about the belt? He wondered what they would do to him if he beat up a warder and didn't manage to escape. He didn't like to think about that. Shortly after lunch he lay down on his bed once more and made plans for his future.

Lady Lucy certainly had a more varied morning than her husband. A cable from William Burke arrived shortly after breakfast, informing her that Johnny Fitzgerald and Charles

Augustus Pugh had been informed of her husband's disappearance. Johnny Fitzgerald, he reported, had set off immediately for Beaune and hoped to be there late the following day. Burke had taken it upon himself to telephone Lord Rosebery, a close friend of the Powerscourt family and a former Prime Minister. Rosebery had hurried round to his old stomping ground, the Foreign Office. Shortly before eleven o'clock a telephone call from the British Embassy in Paris informed Lady Lucy that a Second Secretary was setting off for Beaune within the hour. Half an hour after that a handsome young French police inspector arrived and took from Lady Lucy all the details she could remember about her husband's last hours in Beaune. He would begin his inquiries, he told her, with the Hospices de Beaune. A cousin of his was a sister in the hospital and should be able to help. Lady Lucy marvelled at all this movement and activity marshalled on her behalf. She suspected that Francis would manage his escape all on his own.

The light was beginning to fade and Powerscourt began to laugh. A visitor from the external world might have deduced that this one was indeed mad, pacing the floor of his twelve foot by eight cell, peering occasionally out of the window. And laughing. Perhaps he needed some medicine. In fact Powerscourt had just realized something about the keys on the warder's ring. There had just been time that morning for Powerscourt to see a row of medicine phials on the trolley he brought with him. That surely meant that the warder had the keys to all the doors that held the patients on this floor due to take their daily dose. That also meant that once Powerscourt had the keys he could open all the other doors. He could let the patients out and lead a great escape, a mass break-out from the Maison d'Aliénés. It would be tremendous. Then he wondered how wise it would be to release a band of lunatics into the French countryside. Maybe some of them were capable of violence or worse. Then he told himself that the rapists and the vicious criminals would be held in a prison rather than locked up in the Maison de Fous. And if the patients he might liberate were really mentally ill, wandering in their wits, paranoid, not sure who they were, would it be fair to those patients to return them to the hostile world that had caused them to break down in the first place? Would he have a better chance of success on his own or with a platoon of the insane for company?

The Second Secretary from the British Embassy in Paris arrived at Lady Lucy's hotel in time for tea. He was a most fashionable young man, discreetly fashionable, Lady Lucy thought, surveying the expensive shirt and the slim gold cuff links and the highly polished shoes. She wondered if he did the polishing himself. Perhaps there was a sort of shoe-shine wallah inside the Embassy retained to ensure that the British diplomatic corps had the brightest footwear in Paris. He took a small cup of lemon tea with Lady Lucy, Piers Montagu, before departing for the Town Hall and the Mayor. He firmly believed, he told Lady Lucy, that the Mayor held the key to all French towns and cities. He was a strategic point, said Piers, in the manner of the Château of Hougoumont at the Battle of Waterloo. Hold the Château, or the Mayor, and success was assured.

The young Inspector learnt little from the sister at the Hôtel Dieu. Nobody had seen any of the people involved in the chase the previous day before. They were all strangers. They could not be citizens of Beaune, surely, or we would have seen them about the town. You would not forget the man with no teeth for instance or the round man who was his companion. During the afternoon the policeman rang round some places in Beaune where the stranger might have been seen, the hotels, the restaurants, such *chambres d'hôte* as were on the telephone. There were no reports of an English milord anywhere. He rang the Maison d'Aliénés only because it was on the approved list of places to call in the hunt for missing persons. The administrative office told him that there had only been one new admission in the previous twenty-four hours, a Burgundy peasant called Albert Bouchet.

Emily Colville had turned into a different person. Or rather, Emily thought she had turned into a different person, a better person. It had all started with a present, a present from Montague, brought home from town one cold evening some weeks before. It was unusual for Montague to give presents, and even more unusual for him to give a present of this sort. It was oblong, and quite heavy, and seemed to Emily as her fingers crossed over the slight gaps in the surface to be in three different parts.

'Aren't you going to open it then?' Montague asked with a smile.

'Of course,' she replied, and worked her way to three volumes of a book called *Middlemarch* written by somebody called George Eliot. It was the first time she had ever seen her husband with a book.

'Have you read this?' she asked her husband.

'Don't be ridiculous,' said Montague, 'my great aunt Philippa thought you might like it.'

'Great Aunt Philippa, I see,' said Emily. She had only met this great aunt once, an old lady more interested in the arts than in the world of commerce. This Philippa thought that life with Montague might be a little dull for a quick intelligent girl like Emily. George Eliot might fill the gap for a while. But George Eliot had done more than fill the gap. George Eliot made a convert. The new Emily longed to be good. She held imaginary conversations with Dorothea Brooke. The prize of goodness was always in her sights. And when she had finished *Middlemarch*, she told herself, she would be twice as good after reading *The Mill on the Floss*, twice as good again after *Felix Holt, The Radical*. A great parade of virtue stretched out before her now.

By nightfall Powerscourt was ready. He had managed to tear his sheets into strips that could be used if necessary to tie the warder up. He had placed his bed underneath the window. He had very few advantages in this business. Darkness might be one of them. He waited on the far side of the door. Over the next forty minutes he prayed that the warder would continue the pattern set by all of them on their rounds, morning or evening. Find the key. You could hear the clinking on the other side of the wall. Put it in the keyhole. Turn it in the lock. Open the door. Turn back to your trolley. Pick up the medicine. Come into the room. Powerscourt would be waiting.

He felt nervous, as he used to feel nervous before a battle. In this encounter he had only one chance. There would only be five or ten seconds where he had to get it right. If he failed, he dreaded to think what might happen to him. Maybe they would transfer him to some other ghastly hospital and Lady Lucy would not know he had gone.

He heard the keys jangling now. Not his door, but the one next door. There was a brief conversation while the man took his medicine. Then the key went back in the door. Powerscourt's turn now. Open the door and look inside. Powerscourt saw that his guess had been right. The warder took a couple of steps into the room and stood still, staring into the gloom. The door, kicked by Powerscourt using both feet with all his force from a sitting position on the ground, caught him full in the face. The warder began to fall backwards into the corridor. In a second Powerscourt was on him, pulling him back into the cell, slamming the man's head into the wall until he passed out and slumped to the floor. Powerscourt checked he was still alive – death and the guillotine had little appeal – and closed the door. He taped up the warder's mouth so any calls for assistance would not be heard. He pulled off the jacket and the belt with the keys. Getting the trousers off the warder was incredibly difficult for a man on his own. Powerscourt remembered some funeral attendant telling him once how difficult it was to undress the dead. At last he had the trousers to go with the jacket. The warder began making faint groaning noises as if he might be about to wake up. Powerscourt used up his last two sections of sheet and tied up his wrists and his ankles. He put on his new clothes and inspected the keys. Then he stepped into the corridor and locked what had been his door. 'You'll find the bucket in the corner,' he whispered to the trussed warder before he left. He had decided against liberating any of his fellow inmates. They might start singing on their way to the front door or wander off on their own. Indiscipline, he thought, might be rife in the ranks of the *aliénés*. He pushed the trolley down the corridor until he came to the stairs. Each floor, he saw, had a trolley of its own, waiting for the staff to place their trays. He wondered how many patients would miss their evening dose. Then he remembered that there was, according to the warder, a fifteen-minute gap at his cell between the medicine and the evening meal. He had less than ten minutes to get out.

He made his way down the stairs carefully, listening intently for any movement from somebody in authority. Occasional groans drifted out into the corridor from distressed inmates, more *aliéné* than their fellows. He was on the first-floor landing now, a small window with bars on at the end facing the outside world. Down the last flight of stairs, tiptoe to the front door, inspect the keys. He had one key with the legend Front Door on its tag. There were three locks in the door. He unlocked the central lock which he hoped might be the main one. The door did not open. Growing slightly frantic he tried his key in the other locks in the hope that one key might be able to open all three. It couldn't. Powerscourt tried pushing the door but it did not move an inch. The bolts at the top and bottom were still undone. Somebody must come along later to draw them. Would the somebody have the keys as well?

He heard voices now. One of them was shouting. 'Jean, Jean, where the devil are you? The supper's ready to go round. Come along, for God's sake.'

Powerscourt didn't think Jean was going to wake up very soon. He wondered if they would realize what had happened to their fellow warder, that they would have to open the doors of every single cell until they found him. It seemed possible to Powerscourt that they would assume Jean had gone home early, or had been taken ill and gone to lie down somewhere. Maybe they wouldn't realize he was locked in one of the cells, unable to speak, and in that case they wouldn't come looking for him. A prisoner escaping was just impossible. It had never happened before.

The events of the next ten minutes confirmed to Powerscourt that they had no idea that one of their charges was at large. They shouted messages for Jean, some of them rather rude, and they returned to their own quarters. Powerscourt crept into the room where the doctor had talked to him, close to the front door. Even in here the windows were barred. He padded round the room, removing a doctor's white coat from a hook on the door and some bandages from a drawer in the desk. To the side of the window was an enormous closet, large enough to hold a man. There was a bathroom to the side and from a little window in there Powerscourt had a view of the path leading up to the main gate. His plan now depended on somebody coming up to the front door and being able to open it. He put on his doctor's coat and felt safer inside it. He put a couple of large pens in the top pocket. He put a stethoscope round his neck just in case. Everything in here depends on the colour of your clothes, he said to himself. Dress or be dressed in pale green and they'll pour medicine down your throat two or three times a day. Pale blue and you're a warder with vast powers over the patients. But a white coat? You're virtually God.

He checked the time on the clock on the wall. The bastards had taken his watch and he didn't think now was an ideal time to ask for it back. It had probably been sold already somewhere in the back streets of Beaune. Eight minutes to eight. He thought any more staff clocking on would come on the hour or the half-hour. Maybe a few minutes earlier to be on the safe side. Peering out of the bathroom window, Powerscourt saw that nothing moved for now. There was nobody in sight. He wondered if he should explore other parts of the hospital in search of windows with no bars or doors with no keys. He decided against because he might open a door on to a room full of warders and be sent straight back to the cells with extra dosage for having knocked out Jean. He checked that he could breathe if he was concealed inside the cupboard for a while.

Eight fifteen came. Eight thirty. Powerscourt was back on duty at the bathroom window, rubbing at the glass from time to time. He wondered about Lady Lucy and hoped she was bearing up. He hoped she had remembered to send a message to William Burke. If anybody could organize reinforcements it was Burke. Powerscourt thought his brother-in-law would have made a most efficient adjutant in the Army. He wondered about the theory that had brought them to France. It didn't seem that important now, he told himself, until he remembered the forthcoming trial of Cosmo Colville on a capital charge.

At twenty to nine he heard footsteps. But they were on the inside, the footsteps, not outside, and there were voices too. Two people were heading for the front door. Powerscourt had a split second to make his decision. He waited until he saw the door opening. He patted the stethoscope round his neck and fastened his coat buttons all the way to the top and strode out into the corridor.

'Good evening, gentlemen,' he said cheerfully, 'time to go home at last, I see. Even we doctors must rest.' He was halfway out the door now, one of the men busy with keys in the locks.

'Good evening, doctor,' the men said in unison, peeling off to the side of the building to pick up their bicycles.

Powerscourt didn't risk any more conversation. He was out. He was free. It had been brief, his stay in the Maison des Aliénés, but it had been one of the more disagreeable experiences of his life. That and the monstrous *pressoir* where you felt your limbs could be crushed at any moment. A few stars were visible in the night sky. The two cyclists must have gone in the other direction, away from Beaune, south towards Chalon sur Saône. In the distance the low hills of Burgundy were dark against the night. Powerscourt felt glad to be breathing proper air again after the stale fug back in the hospital. Looking behind him he could just make out its great bulk, dark except for a couple of lighted windows on the ground floor. Ahead, over to his left, was Beaune and Lady Lucy and a welcome in a French hotel. He was just enjoying a mental glass of beer when the world behind him went mad. All the lights in the hospital had been turned on. Darkness was banished from every floor. A powerful bell was ringing continuously as if the Maison d'Aliénés was an ocean liner in distress. 'Man the lifeboats! We've struck an iceberg!'

Powerscourt wondered if they would send out a search party of warders. Either Jean had made his escape, or the two on the bicycles had returned to the asylum to reveal that they had met a strange man pretending to be a doctor at the front door. He could just see three figures emerging from the door and come trotting after him. Powerscourt wrapped his white coat round his waist and ran as fast as he could towards Beaune, checking behind him as he went. The gap appeared to be closing. He was in the street that led out of the town now. He plunged into the side streets, aiming for where he thought the centre of Beaune should be. He felt in his pocket for his money. It was still there. He saw a sign for the station and hurried towards it. Surely stations would have taxis in them, even this late. He put his white coat back on. Now he was in the station square, great puffs of smoke rising into the night sky from the Paris express. As he made his way towards it he crossed the path of a group of six gendarmes, commanded by a sergeant.

'Forgive me, doctor,' said the sergeant, 'there is an escaped lunatic at large. He made his way out of the Maison de Fous back there. Forty years of age or thereabouts. Brown hair. Have you seen such a man, doctor?'

'I do believe I might have seen him just now, sergeant. Running away from Beaune on the Chalon road. If you're quick, you'll catch him. Good luck!'

The sergeant and his men marched off at the double. Dr Powerscourt hurried off to the station and hailed the first cab he saw. 'Hôtel des Ducs de Bourgogne, if you please,' he said, sinking into the red upholstery. As the cab rattled its way north into the town, Powerscourt saw yet more Beaune policemen marching towards the asylum. Even here you could still hear the bell.

He gave the cabbie a generous tip. 'Would you like to earn some easy money, monsieur?' he said, riffling through a bundle of French banknotes.

'Of course,' said the cabbie, 'but not if I have to break the law and go to prison.'

'You need have no fear on that score. All you have to do is to forget that you brought me here. If anybody should ask, say nothing. Deny it. Here.'

Powerscourt handed over the equivalent of a week's earnings if not more.

'Thank you, sir,' said the cabbie. He held his finger to his lips. 'Mum's the word.'

19

The man at the front desk told Powerscourt that Lady Lucy was in room twenty, at the end of the corridor on the first floor. He was just about to ask his dishevelled visitor a question, but the man had gone, bounding up the stairs two at a time.

When he knocked on the door of the room Lady Lucy thought it must be one of the porters bringing another message. 'Come in' she said, rather sadly, standing at the window, looking out over the square. When she turned round she saw that she was looking at a scarecrow. The white coat had long since lost its freshness. There were great stains across the front. The pale green trousers beneath looked as though they might belong to an attendant in a Turkish bath. The hair was tousled and uneven with patches that were almost bare sitting next to the natural curls. The scar on the face, left by Jean Jacques's scissors, was still there. But if it was a scarecrow it was her scarecrow. She had, after all, married the scarecrow. She had lived with the scarecrow and loved the scarecrow for longer than she cared to remember.

'Francis!' she cried and rushed across the floor to embrace him. 'I am so pleased to see you!'

Powerscourt held her very tight. 'I hope you haven't been too worried,' he said. 'I usually manage to come back in the end.'

'What have you been doing, my love? Why are you wearing these dreadful clothes? And what's happened to your poor hair? It looks as if some wild animal has been pulling lumps out of it!'

Powerscourt explained about Marcel's gang and his abduction to the *pressoir* and the lunatic asylum. It was, he told her, all the revenge of the Alchemist for ruining his privacy in London. His hair, he explained, had been cut off by one of the thugs who had virtually no teeth.

'I'm so pleased you are back,' she said, holding tightly on to her scarecrow. 'The hotel people have been very good about things like telegrams, and there's a helpful young man here from the British Embassy in Paris. And Johnny Fitzgerald is on his way.'

'Very good,' said Powerscourt. 'Could I tell you what I'd like to do, Lucy? Right now, I need a bath. Washing facilities haven't been too good in the company I've been keeping. Then I can get into some decent clothes. And then we can see what the food is like in this hotel. Where I've been it was rather primitive. And then I can tell you the rest of what's happened and we can make our plans for tomorrow.'

As Powerscourt and Lady Lucy slept the church bells marked the passing of another day. There were two days left before Cosmo Colville was due to stand trial in the dock in Court Number Two of the Old Bailey on a charge of murder.

Shortly before three o'clock the next afternoon a cab took Powerscourt and Lady Lucy to the little village of Givray, up in the hills outside Beaune. The house of Monsieur Jean Pierre Drouhin, the Colville wine merchant who had disappeared, was at one end of a pleasant square. Lady Lucy had insisted on sending a note in the morning, saying they had come on Colville business and proposed calling on Madame Drouhin after lunch. The house itself was a handsome eighteenth-century building. Inspecting it as he got down from the cab Powerscourt thought that in England such a house would look masculine, wearing metaphorical braces and starched collars and a smart waistcoat. Here in France the building was feminine, adorned with imaginary ringlets and flounces and bonnets.

Madame Drouhin opened the door. She was a pretty woman in her early thirties with light brown eyes and very dark hair, dressed in sober grey. She led them up to the drawing room on the first floor with a fine view of the boulangerie across the street.

'It's very kind of you to spare us the time,' said Powerscourt, smiling at the lady. 'As we said in the note, we have come about your husband. Could you tell us how long ago he disappeared?'

'Of course,' replied Madame Drouhin. 'It's now a month and a half since he vanished.'

'Did he behave strangely before he went?' Lady Lucy said. 'Was there anything odd about him then? Even the best of husbands,' she glanced loyally at Powerscourt, 'can have their strange moods, they can withdraw into themselves if you like.'

'I don't think there was anything strange about his going. He said he had to go to England on business. There was nothing unusual about that. He went to London a lot. He must have spent nearly half the year there, now I come to think about it. But he never wrote this time – normally he was a good if irregular correspondent. He just got on the train in Beaune one morning and disappeared out of our lives.'

'And since then, madame,' said Powerscourt, 'you haven't heard anything at all? Not even a letter or a card?'

'Nothing, monsieur, not a word.'

'And had your husband, madame,' Lady Lucy was trying to sound as sympathetic as she could, 'ever disappeared like this before? Gone to visit his family perhaps?'

'Often he has left us,' said Madame Drouhin, 'but he has always told us where he was going and written to us while he was there. It was usually London or near London that he went to.'

For twenty minutes or more Powerscourt and Lady Lucy questioned Madame Drouhin about her husband and his movements. Finally Powerscourt felt he could delay no longer.

'Can I ask you a question, Madame Drouhin?' Powerscourt was leaning forward in his chair. 'It may seem rather odd if the answer is No. Could your husband write equally well with both hands?'

'How interesting that you should know that,' she said with a smile. 'Yes, he could. The children were always fascinated by it.'

Powerscourt had been looking carefully round the room. On a small table by the window there were some photographs but he couldn't see them clearly.

'There's something wrong, isn't there,' said Madame Drouhin. 'That's why you're here. There must be something wrong, very wrong.' She looked at Lady Lucy with pleading eyes.

'I'm afraid there is,' she said. 'Francis will tell you.'

Powerscourt pulled a photograph out of his pocket, the one Mrs Colville had given him while she was still sober. 'Is that your husband, madame?'

'Of course it is,' she said. Randolph Colville was standing next to a punt by the side of the Thames with a boater on his head, smiling happily at the world. By his side was a handsome woman of about forty-five, some years older than Madame Drouhin. In front of them were a couple of children with determined smiles for the camera.

'How very English,' said Madame Drouhin with a note of bitterness in her voice. 'On the outside we have the smiles, inside we have the cold hearts and the betrayal.'

'Do you know who these other people are in the photograph, madame?' Powerscourt was speaking very softly.

'I do not know,' she replied and her voice was filled with despair, 'but I can guess. That is the English wife of

251

Mr Drouhin, and those must be two of the children he had with her.'

'You knew?' said Powerscourt. 'You knew your husband had two wives?'

'I did. I have known for some time.' Silence fell in the handsome room as Powerscourt and Lady Lucy digested this astonishing piece of information. Bigamy. They had suspected it might be here but to find it in reality was stunning. And terrible. Bigamy. A unique arrangement whereby one man could betray two women at the same time twenty-four hours a day. A clock on the mantelpiece announced that it was half past three. Outside in the square a group of starlings were holding a concert in the trees. Powerscourt felt so very very sorry for Madame Drouhin, so dignified with them this afternoon.

'When did you find out?' said Powerscourt, astonished that Madame Drouhin already knew.

'It must have been about two months ago, maybe more.'

'May I ask how you found out?'

'It was silly, really, silly of Jean Pierre, I mean. He left a letter from his first wife in the back pocket of his trousers one day. He left his trousers on the floor as he usually did. The piece of paper virtually fell out when I picked them up. Normally you'd never find anything at all in Jean Pierre's pockets. He was always very careful. Not surprising really with two different lives to lead. I took the letter to the schoolmaster and he told me what it said. All kinds of things about his life made sense to me then. Those regular trips to England for a start. There are a number of other merchants round here, you see, who have the same sort of business with other houses in London like the Colvilles. They only go to London two or three times in a whole year, these other merchants. My Jean Pierre was going ten or twelve times. Often I have suspected that he must have a woman over there. Only now do I realize that it wasn't just a wife but a whole family as well.'

'How did he take it? When you confronted him with the letter, I mean?' Lady Lucy was feeling full of sympathy for a woman so badly wronged by a member of the opposite sex.

'His first reaction was to laugh. I found that strange. Then he said that he had always thought he might get caught at some time on either side of the Channel. I think he found that element of danger exciting. He said he still loved me and our children. He wasn't going to run away from his responsibilities.'

It was one thing, Powerscourt thought, to travel to France and tell somebody they were married to a bigamist. Then you had to tell them that their husband was dead. Not to tell Madame Drouhin would have been too cruel.

'I fear there is more bad news, madame,' he said.

She looked him straight in the eye. 'You're going to tell me he's dead, aren't you?'

'I'm afraid I am.'

'I'm not surprised,' she said, 'I think I've known he was dead for about three weeks now. I couldn't think of any other explanation. Always before there were letters. Always. This time there were none. That bastard from up the road has got to him at last. I knew it, I knew it!' Madame Drouhin paused for a moment while she contemplated the bastard from up the road.

'My wife and I extend to you our most sincere condolences.' said Powerscourt.

Madame Drouhin folded her hands over and over again in her lap. She looked at them both in turn, as if in supplication.

'Can you tell me how he died?'

Powerscourt gave a heavily censored version of what had happened. The unfortunate event, he said, took place at a house in Norfolk. He did not say that there was a wedding in progress. He made no mention of wedding guests either. Jean Pierre had been shot, he told her. He decided to mention the dead man's brother being found in the same room with a gun in his hand, and that the brother Cosmo was about to stand trial for murder in London any day now, and that he, Powerscourt, was trying to secure the release of Cosmo. Madame Drouhin only asked one question. The killing itself, the arrest of the brother did not seem to interest her very much.

'What was he called? In England, I mean. My husband.'

'He was called Colville, madame, Randolph Colville.'

That seemed to please her. 'Colville.' She rolled the strange English word round her tongue. 'Randolph Colville. So he was one of the family. No wonder he always seemed to have so much money. He bought an enormous amount of land over here, you know. Vineyards, mostly.'

Powerscourt wondered if this was where the missing Colville money had gone, beautiful houses on the edge of the Burgundy hills, another wife to maintain, another life to lead, another family to feed and support.

'Forgive me, madame, we have no wish to disturb you any more at this time. We shall make our departure in a moment. Just now you referred to somebody as that bastard down the road who has got him at last. Could I ask who that somebody is?'

Madame Drouhin got up and walked over to the windows. 'This is difficult for me, very difficult,' she began, still facing the square. 'I'm sure you can understand that any man with two wives is going to have an eye for the ladies. That's how he got into marital difficulties in the first place, being unable to resist the charms of another woman. Jean Pierre or Randolph in the English version was a relentless pursuer of women. I imagine he had been like that since he was about sixteen years old. Chase anything in a skirt, as my grandmother used to put it. Don't get me wrong. I'm not saying he was committing adultery all the way from here to Dijon. It was just a kiss here, an embrace there and he was on his way. Sometimes I'm sure he would have liked to go further. Anyway, the point of this story is that in the street that runs into the bottom of the square here there lives a very pretty young wife of about twenty-five years. Yvette is her name, Yvette Planchon. It was she who told me this story.'

Powerscourt thought suddenly that Randolph's targets seemed to drop ten years each time.

'Jean Pierre was very struck with this girl. Her husband was believed to be away in North Africa. He was a soldier, a sergeant in the Army. Eventually the young wife gives in to Jean Pierre's flirting. She gives him a kiss in their kitchen. She told me later that she thought he might go away after one kiss and leave her in peace, But then, dear me, in the middle of the kiss the husband walks in. He has unexpected leave from his regimental duties. He swears that he will take the traditional Frenchman's revenge against my husband. He does not believe Yvette when she tells him it was only a kiss. They were never in the bedroom upstairs, never. Yvette's husband does not believe her. He is very jealous. He is consumed with jealousy. He tells my Jean Pierre he is going to kill him. Jean Pierre flees out the kitchen door pursued by the jealous husband with a poker in his hand.'

'What is the traditional Frenchman's revenge, madame?' asked Lady Lucy.

'Why, in some parts of the country it still holds good. The French male believes he has the right to kill a man who has interfered with his wife without penalty. You can't be sent to jail or the guillotine, you get off scot free. It's as simple as that.'

'God bless my soul,' said Lady Lucy. 'It does seem rather extreme.'

'Does it still apply in these parts?' asked Powerscourt, wondering about court cases where defendants could be given a sort of automatic acquittal for murdering their wives' lovers.

'I'm afraid I don't know the answer to that,' said Madame Drouhin. Powerscourt thought there was no chance he would be able to persuade any of these women to cross the Channel with him and give evidence in an English court. Could he, perhaps, find a lawyer who would take a signed statement from them? But first they had to meet Yvette.

'Madame,' said Powerscourt, 'could you give us the name of the house where Yvette lives? We would like to hear her story for ourselves.'

'I will take you to her myself,' said Madame Drouhin. 'You have been very kind to me, coming all this way with the unhappy information.'

A couple of moments later the strange party of three, the French widow, the Irish peer and his wife, were seated round Yvette's kitchen table where Yvette was doing something culinary with a chicken. She was so mortified by her behaviour with the man she thought of as Madame Drouhin's husband that she would hardly speak of it at all. It was Lady Lucy who solved the problem, narrating what she believed to have happened and asking Yvette to nod her head or to say yes in agreement. When they were past the dangerous rapids of the kissing Powerscourt asked her where her husband was now.

'I do not know, monsieur. He went away after the events of that unhappy day and I have not seen him since.'

'Has he gone back to the Army? Perhaps his leave was very short.'

'I do not know, monsieur. He had not been in touch with me since that day.'

'Really?' said Powerscourt. 'You don't happen to know, madame, if your husband went over to England at all?'

'Once again I just don't know, monsieur. My Philippe is very impulsive, he is always changing his plans.'

'And do you think he meant it when he said he was going to kill Monsieur Drouhin?'

'Oh yes, I did believe it, he is a very violent man, my husband. He is perfectly capable of killing somebody. They teach you how to do those things in the Army. That is what armies are for, after all, killing people. May I ask you a question, monsieur? Do you know where my husband is? Do you know where Madame Drouhin's husband is? This is not a good time for wives in Givray, I think.'

Powerscourt smiled. 'We do not know where your husband is. Madame's husband, as she has suspected for some time, is dead. He was shot over in England. We are not sure who killed him. We have been hired to try to find out who the real murderer is. We think the police have arrested the wrong man and the trial is due to start any day now.'

Yvette grew pale. 'So you think my husband went all the way to England and shot Monsieur Drouhin? That is what you are thinking, is it not?'

'I have to tell you, madame,' said Powerscourt, 'that we have absolutely no idea who killed Monsieur Drouhin, no idea at all.'

Powerscourt took a surreptitious look at his watch. The afternoon was nearly over. The two women had been through enough strain and emotional upset for one day. Signed statements would have to wait until the morning. He hoped they weren't going to miss the court case altogether.

'Ladies, thank you so much for your assistance this afternoon. I would like to return in the morning. I would like to ask for further help concerning this forthcoming court case in England. It is obviously impossible for you to cross the Channel and attend the trial in person, but I will find a local lawyer and we can prepare statements summarizing your position for you to sign in his presence in the morning. That will be very helpful for our court case.'

'The finest lawyer in Givray, monsieur, is Antoine Foucard whose offices are just up the street from here,' said Madame Drouhin, pointing helpfully in the right direction.

Powerscourt bowed slightly. 'In that case, may we thank you both for your time this afternoon, and, Madame Drouhin, our condolences once again on your sad loss.'

Ten minutes later the Powerscourts were on their way back to the hotel. The lawyer had proved a most accommodating young man who promised to meet them in the morning. He said he would bring a copy of the marriage certificate for they had one on file in their offices. Powerscourt had said that he would bring prepared statements for the two women to sign. He thought it would save time.

Georgina Nash was completing her walk round the lake at the back of Brympton Hall. Every day for weeks past, whatever the weather, she had donned her wellingtons and set off with a couple of dogs for a trip up the road outside the house or a circuit of the lake. There was much on her mind. She still worried about the murder committed in her own house at her own daughter's wedding those weeks before. She felt they had all been coarsened by it. It was, she thought sometimes in her more fanciful moments, as if they would never be clean again. She worried about Emily and her miraculous escape after the fling with Tristram. Georgina wasn't sure that she herself would have chosen to marry Montague Colville, so decent, so well brought up, so stupid, so gullible that Emily had him plucked and trussed and ready at the altar less than six weeks after they met. She worried that Emily would get bored. Emily got bored very easily. She wondered about her husband Willoughby, so concerned that their position in Norfolk society might have taken a battering after weddings interrupted by gunshot. And she worried about the missing under footman William, gone from his post for days now, his cheerful face no longer on parade around the Hall. With every passing day she grew more certain that he was dead.

The dogs began barking furiously, shooting ahead of her and racing through the passageway to the long main drive in front of the house. They carried on barking and Georgina heard a voice talking to them now. It was a young man's voice. He was obviously good with animals. Then she saw him. It was William, emerging from the gloom of a Norfolk dusk to return to his post at Brympton Hall. Georgina smiled with happiness and strode out to meet him. He was kneeling down with the dogs, stroking them firmly. Georgina knew that she should be cross, angry, the scorned employer, but she couldn't do it when she looked at the boy's face. He had been crying and very recently too. She brought him into the drawing room and sent for some tea. William had never actually sat down in this room before.

'William,' she said, 'I'm so glad to see you. I'm sure everybody here will be glad to have you back. But what happened? Why did you not send word? It's days now you've been gone. We thought you might be dead.'

William pulled a crumpled telegram from his pocket and smoothed it out as best he could. 'This came for me very early in the morning the day I left,' he said. 'Nobody else was about. Please read it. I don't think I could read it again.'

'Mother severely ill. Please come at once. Father.' Georgina Nash read it to herself and looked up at the young man.

'I was in such a state when I got that, I just rushed off. I know now I should have left a note. When I got home, my mother was very ill. There was some terrible influenza going round and she had caught it worse than most. The doctor told me he was so glad I had been able to come. He didn't think she would last another twenty-four hours.' William paused while a cup of tea was poured for him. He looked up into the reassuring face of the butler Charlie Healey.

'William's just been telling me about the terrible time he's been having,' Georgina Nash said to her butler. Charlie Healey smiled at William and withdrew.

William looked close to tears once more. 'If you'd rather wait and tell me another time, I'm perfectly happy to do that,' said Georgina.

'No,' said William gulping at his tea, 'it'll be bad whenever I tell you.' He paused and looked up at a sumptuous Gainsborough of a previous chatelaine of Brympton, Lady Caroline Suffield. She too seemed to be smiling down at him.

'Neither my father nor I knew exactly when she passed away, it must have been one or two in the morning. We thought at first she'd just gone to sleep, she looked so peace-ful, as if the pain had been taken away. Then she seemed to lose colour. Then we knew.'

Mrs Nash gave him another cup of tea. 'I was so upset I never thought of sending word back here,' William said sadly, 'and there was so much to do what with the funeral and all. It was the next morning I sent the telegram here saying what had happened. Or at least I think I sent the telegram. I'd never sent one before and I got a bit confused in the post office about the money and that.'

'It never got here,' said Georgina Nash. 'Never mind. The main thing is you're safe now.'

'I've nearly finished now,' said the young man. 'We had the funeral this morning and that was awful. It didn't seem real, as if it were happening to somebody else. My father seemed to feel a bit better when it was over. "We're through with it all now, thank God," he said to me as I was leaving. "Your mother would want us all to get on with our lives."' William Stebbings stopped. 'So here I am,' he said and burst into tears once more. Georgina Nash comforted the young man as best she could. Then she hurried off to send word to her husband and telegraph to Powerscourt and Pugh to give them the good news.

'What do you make of all that, Francis?' asked Lady Lucy as they rattled back towards Beaune.

'It's the only case I've ever come across with a bigamist at the heart of it,' said Powerscourt. 'Easy to see how he got caught, I suppose. I'm sure I leave bits of paper and letters hanging out of my pockets all the time. I shall have to be more careful in future. But it doesn't look as if the bigamy killed him.'

'Surely it did in a way,' said Lady Lucy. 'If he hadn't been a bigamist he wouldn't have been in France to come across the pretty young wife down the road. And if he hadn't had the tendencies of a bigamist he wouldn't have carried on with her like that.' Lady Lucy looked across at her husband and considered some of his qualities. Absent-minded, yes, sometimes selfish when on a case, yes, forgetful, yes, too interested in cricket, yes, bigamist or even capable of bigamy, absolutely not. 'Do you think her husband the sergeant did it?'

'We'll have to ask her tomorrow where the husband is based. Then we can send a cable asking when he was there and when he wasn't. Pretend for a moment, Lucy, that they now have women on juries. It's a triumph for the suffragette cause. You're on the jury trying Cosmo Colville. The defence come along with a story about a flirtation in France, a stolen kiss, a promise to kill our bigamist friend, who is indeed murdered. A Frenchman came to Norfolk, stayed overnight in a hotel the day before the wedding, set off in the morning to attend said nuptials. The contention of the defence is that Yvette Planchon's husband was that hotel guest. He didn't attend the wedding service in case he was noticed and remembered, but he managed to make his way into the house and kill Randolph before the wedding lunch. Would you believe it, Lucy?'

'We come back to the gun, surely, Francis.' Lady Lucy was frowning at her new responsibilities as a jurywoman. 'How did the Frenchman get hold of the gun?'

'There's an answer to that, surely. Randolph remembers the death threat from this volatile French person. Randolph brings the gun in case the Frenchman turns up. But the point here is this, Lucy. Would you believe the story about the Frenchman from Burgundy? Or rather would you believe it enough not to believe in the prosecution version, if you see what I mean?'

'I'm not sure, Francis. I'm not sure at all. I think I wouldn't really believe either of them, which means I'd be for an acquittal, I suppose. The evidence against the Frenchman is pretty flimsy when you think about it. Nobody remembers actually seeing him at the wedding. It would be different surely if they

261

had. None of those people on the seating plan you wrote to remembered seeing a Frenchman either, did they?'

'No, they didn't, but I don't think that's conclusive. Nobody ever knows all the guests at weddings.'

'One more question, Francis. Why did Randolph Colville change his name in France? Why didn't he just carry on being Colville? There are plenty of English people with English names living in France after all.'

'I don't know the answer to that, Lucy,' said Powerscourt, 'but I can guess. Plenty of English people pass through Burgundy for one reason or another. Randolph Colville, they say to themselves? I was at school with the fellow. I've bought a lot of wine from him. I wonder how he's getting on. Fancy him ending up here of all places. I'll pop over and see him this evening. One or two of those and you're finished. A visitor from the Home Counties – one is enough – reports back to his friends that he's seen Randolph Colville in France when they saw him only last week at the races in Epsom. Too risky, I'd say. That's why I think he changed his name.'

They had now reached their hotel. As they walked up the steps to the entrance they were greeted by a loud shout from a figure holding the largest glass of red wine that Powerscourt had ever seen.

'Francis! Lucy! How very nice to see you!' Looking completely unruffled from his hectic charge across France, Johnny Fitzgerald had come to pay his respects. There was a good deal of mutual embracing and kissing on both cheeks.

'Johnny,' said Powerscourt, 'stay here a moment for me. Don't move.'

He shot into the hotel and communed with the man at reception for some minutes.

'Johnny,' he said, returning to join his friend, 'I hope you haven't unpacked or anything.'

'Course I haven't unpacked yet,' said Johnny, 'I'm not a bloody butler, for God's sake. What's all this about, Francis?'

'It is now six forty-five, my friend. At twenty minutes past seven the last Paris express stops in Beaune. There is a night train to Calais, for some reason. Most irregular but never mind.'

'And why, pray, do I have to get on another train and then another one after that? I've only just got off the last one.'

'While you fetch your bag, Johnny, I am going to write down for you the main points of what we have discovered here. It is most germane to the trial of Cosmo Colville. We don't know when the trial starts. It could have started already. It is most important that Charles Augustus Pugh receives my note at the earliest possible moment. It could mean the difference between victory and defeat. It's too sensitive to entrust it to the cable companies. The information could fall into the wrong hands. Lucy will go with you and tell you what we've found out while you fetch your bags.'

Five minutes later Johnny Fitzgerald was tucked up in another cab, bound for the station. The cabbie was astonished for it was the same man who had brought him from the station to the hotel less than an hour before. In his breast pocket he had two pages of Powerscourt's finest handwriting with the details of their discoveries. He leant out of the window as he left, waving his enormous glass at them.

'Could you sort out the cost of this glass with the barman, Francis? Haven't been able to finish it yet, damned thing's so big it must hold about the same amount as a bloody bottle.'

20

On the outside Charles Augustus Pugh appeared confident, sure of his ground as he strode into Court Two of the Old Bailey on the opening day of the trial of Cosmo Colville for the murder of his brother. He smiled at the chief counsel for the prosecution, Sir Jasper Bentinck, and made a slight bow to the judge, Mr Justice Black. The court was full, with the members of the public crammed into their seats and looking forward to the show. It was not every day after all that you could see a senior member of one of London's leading wine merchants on trial for the murder of his brother. Pugh turned from his table to whisper something to his junior, an industrious young man recently arrived in the Pugh chambers by the name of Napier.

Inwardly, Pugh felt more unhappy about this case than he had about any of his previous outings as principal counsel for the defence. He had little fresh evidence and what he had did not inspire him. He was going to have to proceed through a policy of innuendo and suggestion which was alien to his nature. He was going to have to make his appeal to the Doubting Thomas side of the jury rather than the Sir Lancelot. His principal collaborator in this trial, Lord Francis Powerscourt, had vanished into the hills and vineyards of Burgundy and had not returned. Pugh had begun work on this case with high hopes that Powerscourt might pull an enormous rabbit out of a hat at the very last moment as he had the last time the two of them had worked together. Today there was no sign of anything at all, not even a minute mouse with a minuscule tail.

The area reserved for members of the public was crammed. So was the area reserved for the gentlemen of the press. Many members of the public were regular consumers of the Colville products and had come to see the one who had killed his brother. Others had heard rumours of the defendant who had not spoken a word since the murder and had come to Court Two of the Old Bailey to inspect a man whose silence might cost him his life. The pressmen too had heard, of course, of Cosmo's silence. Their collective memory, even when fortified by Colvilles' finest in the Bunch of Grapes at the end of Fleet Street, could not recall such a silent witness in living memory.

Pugh turned to inspect the jury. They seemed younger than the normal run of juries, he thought. They sat up in their place looking very serious, conscious perhaps that over the next few days they held a man's life in their hands.

Sir Jasper rose to begin the case for the prosecution. He called Georgina Nash as chatelaine of the great house where the events had taken place.

'Mrs Nash. Could you tell the gentlemen of the jury what was happening at your house on the day in question?'

'Of course,' she replied. 'There was a wedding, my daughter's wedding.'

'And could you tell us who your daughter was marrying, Mrs Nash?'

'She was marrying Montague Colville, son of Mr Randolph Colville and Mrs Hermione Colville.'

'Did the service go off satisfactorily, Mrs Nash? And could you tell us how many guests were in attendance? Not a precise figure, you understand, just a general idea.'

'The service was fine. The bride was late, but brides often are. I think I cried but then mothers often do at weddings, I believe. And we had a hundred guests or so.'

'So what happened after the service, Mrs Nash? Perhaps you could give an idea of the sequence of events leading up to the murder.'

'After the service everybody came back to the house. We served them champagne in the garden. I remember feeling rather cross because the gardeners hadn't fixed the fountain. It's a very impressive fountain when it's working properly. It sits in the middle of the lawn where everybody can see it. I must have asked those gardeners three or four times.'

'Mrs Nash,' Sir Jasper was at his most emollient, 'I don't think we need concern ourselves about the fountain today.'

'Sorry, Sir Jasper.' Georgina Nash looked at the judge, unsure if she should apologize to him too, but she pressed on. 'I think the champagne lasted about half an hour. Then we began to bring people up to the Long Gallery where the food was to be served. There were two seating plans on display in the garden for people to see where they were going and another two indoors, one in the Great Hall and another at the top of the stairs.'

'In my experience, Mrs Nash, not that I possess a Long Gallery like yours in my modest home, these manoeuvres involving large numbers of people can take a long time, far longer than one would think.'

Charles Augustus Pugh scribbled a quick note to his junior Richard Napier. 'Bentinck's modest home runs over five floors in Holland Park,' the message said. 'Enormous garden the size of three or four tennis courts. Platoons of servants. Must be worth a bloody fortune.'

Georgina Nash carried on: 'How right you are, Sir Jasper.' She smiled a bright smile at him. Pugh thought you could almost hear Sir Jasper purr. 'It did take a long time, far longer than I had thought.'

'So here we are, Mrs Nash, a grand wedding in a grand country house, the guests sipping their champagne in the garden then making their way up to the Long Gallery for the wedding lunch. Perhaps you could tell us, Mrs Nash, how you first became aware of the unfortunate incident which has brought us here today. Were all the guests seated by then?'

'No, they were not, Sir Jasper. Some of them were still milling about looking for their places. I remember thinking how noisy it all was. Then there was a sharp bang from the rooms at the end of the Long Gallery which I later gathered was the gun being fired.'

'And how were you informed of what had happened, Mrs Nash?'

Georgina Nash paused. 'The first I knew about it was when Charlie Healey, our butler, rushed in looking very strained. He whispered something to my husband. Willoughby told me what had happened, about Mr Randolph Colville lying dead on the floor and Mr Cosmo Colville sitting on a chair holding the gun. Everything became something of a blur after that. I felt so sorry for my daughter with her big day ruined and for the guests, many of whom had come a long way.'

'Quite so, Mrs Nash, quite so.' Sir Jasper made it sound as if he himself had been one of the unfortunate long distance travellers whose celebration of a wedding turned into a wake. He pressed on with a few more questions about the arrival of the police before he sat down.

Pugh had originally intended to let the early witnesses go, not to ask any questions at all. But the lack of weapons in his armoury left him no choice but to cross-examine them all. Doubt, he said to himself, doubt. I can't possibly persuade them that Cosmo didn't do it, I just need to plant some doubt. Enough doubt and I might get an acquittal if we're lucky.

'Mrs Nash,' he began, trying to sound as friendly as he could, 'did you say you had a hundred guests at this wedding? And how many of them were known to you personally, the guests I mean?'

'I'm not sure I understand you,' said Georgina Nash. 'Are you suggesting that I didn't know who I'd invited to my own daughter's wedding?'

'Not at all, Mrs Nash, I can't have been making myself clear.

267

Let me try again. I suggest that if there were a hundred guests, half were on your side and half on the Colville side. Roughly speaking that is. So you would probably have known all the guests invited on your side, and some, but probably not the majority, of those invited through the Colvilles. Would that be right?'

'I see what you mean,' said Georgina Nash. 'Yes, that is more or less right.'

'So, of the hundred guests drinking your champagne and looking for their tables in your Long Gallery, there might be about forty you did not know and had never met?'

'If you choose to put it like that I suppose that must be the case.'

Georgina Nash didn't sound happy at being represented as the principal hostess at a party of a hundred where forty of them were completely unknown to her.

'So these people could have been English or French or of any nationality at all?' Pugh was determined to introduce the notion of a villainous Frenchman, garlic-chewing if possible, beret-wearing, onion-carrying, frog's-legs-munching, into the minds of the jury.

'I'm pretty sure they were all English, British anyway,' Georgina Nash said loyally.

Pugh made a non-committal sort of noise that hinted at disbelief, a sound referred to by his junior as a muted grunt. 'Could you enlighten us, Mrs Nash, about the various entrances and exits to the Long Gallery? It is the contention of the defence that a person or persons unknown may have made their way into your grand room, killed the unfortunate Mr Colville and made his escape long before the police arrived on the scene. Could you enlighten us about the principal ways in and out? We don't need to know about the back stairs.'

'Well,' said Georgina Nash, 'the principal way in is up the main staircase in the Great Hall – that's the route the guests were taking. Then there's a smaller staircase at the far end of the Long Gallery near the lake. And there's another little staircase out of the state bedroom itself, now I come to think of it.'

'So, Mrs Nash,' said Pugh, taking delivery of a diagram of the first floor of Brympton Hall from Richard Napier and pointing to the relevant sections as he referred to them. 'Here is the main staircase, slightly set back from the Long Gallery, here is the little staircase at the other end of the room, and here is another, a third staircase, in the very room where the murder was committed.' Pugh had moved right over to the jury benches and showed them the various staircases on his diagram. He left the illustration with the foreman of the jury in case they needed to refer to it in the future.

Mrs Nash did not say anything. She was beginning to feel that this whole business of giving evidence was rather distasteful. Pugh pressed on. 'Let me try, Mrs Nash, if I may, to pull together some of the strands of your evidence. On your own account, there were approximately forty people roaming around at your wedding reception that you had never seen before. And we have seen from the diagram of your beautiful house that there are three separate ways in and out of the relevant rooms a murderer among the forty unknowns could have used to kill Randolph Colville and make his escape.'

'Objection, my lord.' Sir Jasper was on his feet. 'This is pure speculation, my lord, almost fantasy. My learned friend has no more proper evidence for saying these things than I would have for saying the earth is flat.'

'Mr Pugh?' A judicial pencil span rapidly through judicial fingers.

'I was merely trying to point out to the members of the jury that Mr Colville could have been murdered in a completely different fashion to that put forward by the prosecution.'

'Objection overruled,' said the judge, 'but try to confine your comments to the facts in future, Mr Pugh. Carry on.'

'I have no further questions for this witness,' said Pugh, bowing slightly to Mrs Nash. He had, he thought, done as much damage as he was capable of to the prosecution case.

But his victory over the objection, he suspected, was Pyrrhic. These tactics of suggestion and innuendo were all he had until Powerscourt returned. Maybe they would still be all he had after Powerscourt returned.

Sir Jasper moved majestically on. Charlie Healey, the Nash butler, was in the witness box now, being guided through his role on the day of the murder. Pugh waited until the police had been called and Charlie's role returned to that of attendant lord rather than major player. Sir Jasper looked particularly pleased with himself as he sat down.

'Am I right in thinking, Mr Healey,' said Pugh genially, 'that you were a military man before you turned butler?'

'I was, sir. I was a sergeant in the Blues and Royals.'

'A most responsible position, I'm sure. I want to concentrate on the events immediately before and after the murder, if I may.'

'Very good, sir.' Charlie Healey looked at Pugh as if he were a detachment of hostile cavalry dimly seen in the distance but approaching fast.

'Can you tell us exactly where you were when you heard the shot, Mr Healey?'

'I was at the far end of the Long Gallery, trying to get people seated in their proper places, sir.'

'And with your military experience, you knew immediately that it was gunshot?'

'I did, sir,' said Charlie Healey, wondering where this elegantly dressed lawyer was trying to take him.

'But let us be clear on this point, Mr Healey. You didn't see the gun, you didn't see anybody pull the trigger.'

'I did not, sir.'

'And at this point, you told my learned friend, you hurried as fast as you could towards the direction of the gunfire.'

'I did, sir,' said Charlie, 'I wanted to make sure there weren't any more shots.'

'Quite right, Mr Healey, quite right. Perhaps you could tell the court precisely what you saw when you went into the state bedroom on the far side of the house from the Long Gallery.'

'Yes, sir,' said Charlie. 'It was like a tableau, so it was, everything sort of frozen. Mr Randolph Colville lying on the floor, looking very dead with blood trickling out on to the carpet, and Mr Cosmo locked into the chair opposite with the gun in his hand. I managed to get the gun off him and sent word to the master about what had happened.'

'I'm sure you behaved very properly, Mr Healey,' said Pugh, who suspected that a witness like Charlie would make a very good impression on the jury. 'But could we just be clear on a couple of points? You saw the defendant with the gun in his hand. But you didn't see him fire it, did you?'

'No, sir, I did not.'

'And, to the best of your knowledge, the gun could have been fired by some other person or persons unknown who made good their escape down the stairs in the state bedroom, so convenient as that was the room where the murder was committed. Is that not the case, Mr Healey?'

'If you put it like that,' said Charlie defensively, 'then I suppose it could have happened in that way.'

'Let me try to sum up your position for the benefit of the gentlemen of the jury, Mr Healey. You didn't see anybody fire the gun. You didn't see the defendant fire the gun. A completely different person could have fired the gun and fled down the stairs leaving the defendant to follow the noise of the gunshot and find his brother dead. Is that not so?'

Charlie Healey did not choose to reply.

'No more questions,' said Pugh and sat down.

Powerscourt and Lady Lucy were eating lunch in the buffet of the Gare du Nord in Paris. Lady Lucy was looking anxiously at the weather. 'I do hope we're not going to have a crossing like the one we had on the way over, Francis.'

'That's not possible, my love.' Powerscourt was making his way through an enormous lamb chop. 'I'm sure those kinds of storm only happen about once every five years or so.'

'Johnny Fitzgerald should be back in London by now.' Lady Lucy was having moules, a growing mountain of empty shells threatening to spill out of the bowl. 'That should cheer Mr Pugh up at any rate.'

'I'm not sure that what we're bringing is a great deal of use,' said her husband, relapsing into miserable mode. 'I'm sure he was going to make a lot of the mysterious foreigner going to the wedding anyway. We've just managed to put some flesh on the bones for him. We've got a name and address.'

'I'm sure he'll be able to get Mr Colville acquitted now,' said Lady Lucy loyally. 'I'm certain of it.'

Sir Jasper took a long time on his examination of Detective Chief Inspector Weir. This was because of the length of time Weir took thinking about his answers before he spoke. Pugh could feel his irritation rising. His junior kept sending him messages as the afternoon went on. The young man had a remarkable talent for drawing life-like sketches of the people about him. He had already produced a choleric Judge Black with both hands wrapped round an enormous pencil, and the foreman of the jury, one hand to his forehead, lines of worry etched across his face.

When Sir Jasper had finally finished with the policeman, Pugh rose to his feet with a broad smile on his face. He had just had an idea and there wasn't time to bounce it past his junior, unusually mature in his judgements for one of his age.

'Tell me, Detective Chief Inspector, how long is it now before your retirement?'

Weir also smiled a mighty smile. 'Why, sir, it's six weeks and two days now.'

'And you plan to stay in Norfolk with Mrs Weir?' Pugh prayed that there was indeed a Mrs Weir and that she was not either bedridden or suffering from a terminal disease. Close inspection of the Detective Chief Inspector seemed to indicate an officer who was well looked after, beautifully ironed shirt, trousers pressed to perfection. 'A little cottage near the coast, perhaps, for the retirement years?'

Weir's reply showed that Pugh's guess had been correct. There was a Mrs Weir, thank God, neither confined to bed, nor heading for the coffin.

'How did you guess, sir?' said Weir. 'We've bought a place near Blakeney, up on the coast.'

Pugh reckoned he had one more question before Sir Jasper exploded to his left or the judge exploded to his front.

'And I suppose that the planning of the move and so on takes up a lot of your time, and of course of Mrs Weir's too.'

'It does indeed, sir. It's amazing how much of my time it takes.' Pugh's junior suddenly abandoned his pose of bored lethargy interrupted by portraiture and wrote something down at great speed. He waited for the right moment to hand it to his superior.

'But come, Detective Chief Inspector, we must not waste the court's time with pleasantries about your retirement, however enjoyable they may be. I would like to ask you, if I may, about the principles you follow in making an arrest.'

'I'm not quite sure what you mean, sir,' said Weir, scratching his head and looking perplexed.

'Well,' said Pugh airily, 'some men in your profession concentrate initially on motive. Once they see who might profit from someone else's death, they concentrate their attention on that person, searching for when and how they might have killed their victim. Others don't care much about motive, they concentrate on who could have done the murder at the time it was committed and look for motive after that. Does that help, Detective Chief Inspector?'

'I see what you're getting at now, sir. I would say I rely on experience. I must have investigated well over fifty murders in my time with the force, so I have. You get a good sense of how they're done after that.'

'I see,' said Pugh, still in charming mode. 'I would like to remind you of the evidence of Mrs Nash, which I'm sure you know. She told the court there were about forty people wandering about at her daughter's wedding who were unknown to her, to Mrs Nash that is, not the daughter. Might that not give cause for doubt? Just a little doubt perhaps, but doubt nonetheless as to whether the defendant was the murderer? And Mrs Nash also referred to the three staircases, one in the murder room itself, which could be used to reach the state bedroom where the dead man lay. Do those two facts not make you doubtful about your arrest?'

'God bless my soul, sir, surely you're ignoring the most important evidence of all. There sat the defendant with the gun in his hand, the gun used to kill Mr Randolph. There was Mr Randolph lying dead on the floor. Nobody else was reported as going in or out of that room. It was an open and shut case.'

'So are you just ignoring the facts that might cause you doubt, Detective Chief Inspector?'

'Certainly not, sir. I'm just relying on experience. When you're nearly sixty-five, you learn to trust your instincts.'

'And instinct in this case might prove more powerful than reason?'

'Not at all, sir. But when you see a dead man on the floor, another man opposite with a gun in his hand which has come from the dead man's house, then I think that is an open and shut case.'

Pugh felt he wasn't making much progress with his cross-examination so far. He thought he was losing support with the jury. One or two them, particularly the one in the dark blue waistcoat, were casting hostile glances at him. He did have one weapon to bring into play.

He moved over to the exhibit table and picked up the gun.

He brought it back to his place and ran his fingers along the sides.

'Could we talk about the gun, Detective Chief Inspector? This is not the real gun used in the murder, gentlemen of the jury, but it is the same make and the same size. I do not need to remind you jurymen of the recent advances in the science of fingerprinting, the ability to use one man's fingerprints to establish whether or not he has been in contact with a particular gun or safe or something similar. We have recently seen, indeed, a conviction for murder here in London based on fingerprint evidence. It is the perfect means of discovering whether a particular individual has handled something like a gun for he would have left fingerprints all over it if he had.'

'Now then, Detective Chief Inspector, does the Norfolk Constabulary have its own forensic and fingerprinting service?'

'No, sir, it does not.' Pugh's junior thought that Weir was beginning to shrink slowly in front of them. He picked up his pencil and began another sketch.

'You're not telling us that your force chooses to ignore fingerprints altogether, are you?'

'Certainly not,' said Weir.

'How, pray, do you manage to avail yourselves of the resource of a fingerprint service when you don't have one?'

'We use the Metropolitan Police Force's fingerprint bureau, sir. We send the stuff down to London when we need to.'

'So I presume the gun in this case was despatched down to the Met's fingerprint people?'

'I'm afraid it was not,' said Weir, almost whispering now.

'So what happened to it then?' Pugh was now holding the gun up for the jury to see.

'It went to Fakenham,' Weir muttered as if the mere mention of the word Fakenham was enough to explain everything.

'Speak up, man, speak up for the court. They can scarcely hear you in the back row of the jury.' Pugh was booming now, the initiative with him for the first time in the case so far.

'It went to Fakenham,' said the policeman again in a slightly louder voice.

'Fakenham?' said Pugh. 'Fakenham? What is so important about Fakenham? Does the place have magic powers, a well that heals the sick perhaps? An East Anglian Lourdes?'

'There was an accident in the police station at Fakenham.' Detective Chief Inspector Weir was whispering again.

'What sort of accident?' barked Pugh. 'I do not recall seeing any reports in the newspapers of accidents in the Fakenham police station at this time.'

'The cleaning woman was new.' Weir had grown almost inaudible again.

'And?' said Pugh, leaning forward to catch the words.

'Speak up, man, I can hardly hear you.' The judge too was leaning forward to pick up what Weir was saying.

The policeman looked at Sir Jasper with desperation in his eyes, as if Sir Jasper could save him from this ordeal.

'She wiped the gun clean, the new cleaning lady,' Weir said at last. 'She said later that the gun looked very dirty with all those smudges on it. She said the police deserved a nice clean station when they came to work.'

'That's as may be, Detective Chief Inspector, Norfolk policemen going to work in a tidy station.' Pugh's junior knew by now that his master had a number of different modes of operation in court: charming, ironic, sarcastic, we're all men of the world together in this, angry, indignant, on his high horse. Now, here in Court Number Two of the Old Bailey, Richard Napier was certain his master was definitely mounted on his high horse, and pawing the ground.

'What about the defendant? The man in the dock opposite you, Chief Inspector? Does he not have rights too? More important rights maybe than the absence of dust and the removal of a few smudges in the Fakenham police station? A fingerprint test on that gun could have cleared his name. There could have been other prints from other hands which had also held the weapon and might have pointed it at the

276

defendant's brother and pulled the trigger. I suggest the Norfolk Constabulary and their auxiliaries have done my client a most serious disservice. He has been deprived of his rights as a citizen and a taxpayer. Do you have anything you wish to say, Detective Chief Inspector?'

'I'm truly sorry about the cleaning lady,' said Weir.

Pugh knew that he had to keep hold of the advantage if he could. He suspected that a different tone might work better, for he thought the jury would be with Weir by instinct. The jury did not come from the criminal classes. They did not come from the middle classes. They came from that vast segment of the population in between who worked hard, went to church and hoped their children would have a better life than they had. Such people were predisposed to trust policemen.

'Gentlemen of the jury, Detective Chief Inspector, I want to put a little hypothesis before you about the conduct of this case.' Pugh was sounding conciliatory, a friend to all the world. Richard Napier thought his master was definitely up to something. He, Napier, would not have trusted a conciliatory Pugh as far as he could throw him.

'I put it to you, Detective Chief Inspector, that in these last months of your long career you were more interested in your retirement than in seeing justice done in this case. "It's amazing how much of my time it takes." That's how you described your retirement a few moments ago. Is that not so?'

'I have always done my duty,' said the Detective Chief Inspector, falling back on a saying that had served him well in the past.

'Do you agree, Detective Chief Inspector, that in your younger days you would not have brought this case to court, because there was not sufficient certainty about the evidence? That is a fact, is it not?'

Weir might not have been the brightest boy in the school but he could see very clearly that if he went along with this proposition the whole case would collapse around him.

'That's all very interesting, sir. I'm not sure I can keep up with all your clever theories. I repeat what I said just now, sir. I have always done my duty.'

'No further questions,' said Pugh.

In the room reserved for witnesses a Mrs Bertha Wilcox was going over her evidence for the twentieth time. She felt she was more nervous than she had been at any time since her wedding day. But she was not called into the witness box that day or the next. Charles Augustus Pugh had snatched a quick look at her during a recess and decided not to call her, even though he had subpoenaed her to come to the Old Bailey in the first place. He thought her demeanour and her occupation were such that the jury would automatically be on her side. On this occasion that did not suit Charles Augustus Pugh. Mrs Wilcox was the cleaning lady from the police station in Fakenham.

21

Charles Augustus Pugh had been looking directly at the jury during most of his encounter with Detective Chief Inspector Weir. He thought he might have won on points, that one or maybe two members of the jury could have been added to the few he thought might vote for an acquittal. His junior, not as experienced at reading juries as Pugh, but no slouch nonetheless, reckoned that three or possibly four were in the acquittal camp. They might, mind you, he told Pugh later that day, be lured back into the conviction team fairly easily.

Pugh was surprised to see Inspector Albert Cooper in the witness box. There was his youth and his youthful appearance for a start. Then there was the fact, as Powerscourt had briefed Pugh before, that Cooper did not think there should have been an arrest at all. He did not think the evidence was strong enough for a conviction. Powerscourt had approached the matter with extreme cynicism.

'If he doesn't appear,' he had told Pugh over lunch at his club in Pall Mall, 'then it means he's an honest man. They have failed to nobble him.'

'They being?' asked Pugh.

'His immediate superiors, their immediate superiors, their immediate superiors, the Superintendents and the Commanders and the Chief Constable in person. Not necessarily in that order.'

'And if he does appear?' asked Pugh.

'Some or maybe all those superiors will have got to him. Maybe not to him, maybe to that girl he's going to marry. His parents, her parents perhaps. Why should Albert throw up such a promising career for a few doubts about an arrest? If every police officer followed his doubts about arresting people then the prisons would be empty and the courthouses all boarded up. God knows how the senior officers in the Norfolk police will do it, but they'll certainly try.'

Sir Jasper Bentinck found Detective Inspector Cooper a much better witness than his immediate superior. There weren't the pauses for a start. Cooper brought an air of freshness into the courtroom, of youth and hope. He told the story of the aftermath of the murder very well, not omitting the complaints about his age. Sir Jasper did not bother to ask about any doubts Cooper might have had about an arrest. Pugh was wondering right up to the point where the examination in chief came to an end about whether to cross-examine or not. Of all the witnesses so far, Cooper was making the best impression on the jury. Georgina Nash came from a different world. The Detective Chief Inspector was too old and too slow. This young man, so quick and so bright, was the one for them. Pugh thought one or two of his recent converts to an acquittal vote might have defected back to the other side. Napier had sent him a note suggesting no cross-examination at all.

In the end Pugh couldn't resist. If Powerscourt's realpolitik in the Pall Mall club was right, then Cooper might prove a godsend. It was worth a try.

'Detective Inspector Cooper,' an emollient, a charming Pugh began. 'I believe you have made the acquaintance of a colleague of mine, Lord Francis Powerscourt, who has been investigating this case?'

'I have indeed,' said Cooper, smiling back at the defence barrister.

'Lord Powerscourt told me right at the beginning of the case that Mrs Nash over there informed him that you thought

Detective Chief Inspector Weir was going to arrest the wrong man. Is that the case?'

Albert Cooper thought about all the arguments brought to bear on him not to repeat his doubts at the trial. Weir himself had spoken to Charlotte when he was out, trying to persuade her to persuade him to deny it. He remembered the ploy that had finally brought him round. The Chief Constable himself had told his parents that if he didn't do what he was told, his career in the Norfolk Constabulary or any other Constabulary would be over for ever. His mother, never strong, had grown ill. It was his father saying that he couldn't bear to see his mother going downhill that finally turned him. What, asked his father, were a few white lies compared with his mother's health?

'That's quite right,' said Detective Inspector Cooper cheerfully, 'I did think that at the beginning of the case.'

'Could you tell the court what persuaded you into that judgement?' Pugh was still emollient.

'Well, sir, it seemed to me to be too obvious that the defendant had done it. It was as if somebody meant us to think like that.'

'Really?' said Pugh. 'And what made you change your mind?'

'I think there were two things, sir. Chief Inspector Weir is a detective of great experience. He has been investigating murders in Norfolk since before I was born. You have to take account of things like that, especially when you've only just been promoted like I had been at the time.'

'And the second reason?'

'I think I was influenced by the fact that there didn't seem to me to be any other explanation. None of the guests at the wedding came up with anything and as time went by no other explanation presented itself.'

'I see,' said Pugh. 'I put it to you, Detective Inspector, that your superiors put considerable pressure on you to change your mind. How much more convenient to have all the officers in the case singing the same tune. Did they talk to you about your future prospects? Did they put pressure on your family to make you come round?'

'I don't know what you mean,' said Inspector Cooper, but he had turned a shade of deep red.

Charles Augustus Pugh remained on his feet for half a minute or so, staring at Detective Inspector Cooper. Then he turned abruptly on his heel and sat down.

'No further questions,' he said.

Sir Jasper rose quickly to his feet, aware of the damage that might have been done to his case.

'Detective Inspector Cooper, could you just confirm one or two points for the gentlemen of the jury? It is your belief that the defendant, Cosmo Colville, murdered his brother Randolph at Brympton Hall at a wedding in October of this year?'

'It is,' said Cooper, the red fading from his cheeks.

'And you reached that opinion entirely on your own with no external pressure?'

Mistake, thought Pugh. The young man can control what he says but not what happens to the colour of his face.

'I did,' said Albert Cooper, the colour rising up his cheeks again.

Sir Jasper was quick to react. 'No further questions,' he said, and it so happened that right at that very moment he fell victim to a coughing fit that involved a great deal of noise and apologies to the judge while this storm raged about him. The fit also led to the production of a quite magnificent red handkerchief from his trouser pocket, an enormous kerchief about the size of a tea towel which appeared to bring some relief. Under cover of this display Albert Cooper was able to slip away with the gentlemen of the jury unaware of whether he had turned pink once more or not. Out of the corner of his eye Pugh caught an angry glower on the face of Detective Chief Inspector Weir, as though the young man had let them down. You could control his words but you couldn't control the colour on his face. Weir in angry mode, thought Pugh, did have a remarkable similarity to an aged warhorse.

It was just after four o'clock now. Outside the lamps were being lit. A couple of hundred yards away the choir of St Paul's Cathedral were preparing for the daily ritual of evensong. Sir Jasper thought he had chosen his last witness well. Willoughby Nash, husband of Georgina, owner of Brympton Hall, leading solicitor in the city of Norwich, chairman of this and director of that in the city where he worked, captain and leading run scorer for Aylsham Cricket Club, was a man of substance, a man of weight. Even in the alien territory of the witness box of the Old Bailey, seldom, if ever, the scene of courtroom encounters for the solicitors of Norwich, Willoughby Nash radiated an easy power. Sir Jasper hoped that he would prove a fitting final witness for the close of the prosecution case.

'Mr Nash.' Sir Jasper seemed to have recovered from his coughing fit by now. 'Perhaps you could give us your account of the day of the murder. You were at the very centre of events after all.'

Willoughby Nash looked at the gentlemen of the jury as if he might be about to sell them at an auction and needed to determine the appropriate prices.

'Yes,' he said, 'of course. There was nothing untoward about the wedding itself apart from the fact that the organist fellow didn't play what he'd been told to play. After that people milled around at the front of the church as they usually do, trying to kiss the bride or shake hands with the groom. Eventually they all drifted into the gardens at the rear – Brympton has gardens to the front as well as the back, being such a large house – and we served them champagne.'

Sir Jasper was now holding his hand up, rather in the manner of a traffic policeman.

'Forgive me, Mr Nash, were there any strangers you could see, milling about in the crowds?'

Sir Jasper thought that the only viable defence Pugh might be able to run would be The Mysterious Stranger and he was determined to nip it in the bud if he could.

'Strangers?' said Willoughby Nash, and he began stroking his chin. 'Well, as my wife told you this morning, there were some people one didn't know. It's not possible to have made the acquaintance of all the groom's family before these occasions, but the Colville people looked absolutely fine to me. Quite a lot of them you'd be happy to go hunting with. A lot of medals on display, one or two people who'd obviously been wounded in the Boer War. You'd be hard pressed to find a more respectable body of people. I'd have been more than happy to propose the lot of them for my own club in Norwich.'

'I see,' said Sir Jasper, asking himself briefly if Willoughby Nash would propose him for the club. 'Could you tell us now about the sequence of events leading up to the murder?'

Pugh suddenly noticed the prisoner in the dock opposite Willoughby Nash, the low wooden walls keeping him in, the stairs just visible to bring Cosmo Colville up and down from the holding cells below. He had been slumped in his chair for most of the day. Now he was leaning forward intently as if this was the witness he was most interested in.

'Of course.' Any slight nervousness Nash might have had at the beginning had gone now. Pugh wondered if this witness might not be too grand for the jury. They might prefer plainer men and plainer fare.

'There was a lot of trouble getting the guests to sit down in their proper places,' Willoughby Nash went on. 'I thought at the time it was rather like trying to get the horses lined up in the correct order before a race at Fakenham or Ascot or one of those places. There's always some damned filly that won't get into line. This jostling was still going on, guests not yet in their proper stalls if you follow me, when I heard the shot. It's an unmistakable noise even if it was a bit muffled with the people all talking at the top of their voices. Next thing I know our butler Charlie Healey takes me to the room with the body and the silent figure of Cosmo Colville. We sent for a doctor and the police and all that sort of thing.'

Sir Jasper's hand had risen slightly once more in the stop the traffic position.

'And what was your impression, there on the spot? What did you think had happened, Mr Nash?'

'Well,' said the owner of Brympton Hall, 'call me simple, call me naïve, but I know what I thought then. It seemed to me to be perfectly obvious. I said to Georgina after the doctor had taken a look at the corpse and before the police arrived, "Cosmo's killed his brother," I said. "Randolph's lying on the floor with blood running out of him like it might run out of a side of beef cooked rare, and Cosmo's sitting in that chair like someone's just cast a spell over him." As I said before, that was my opinion then and it remains so to this day. All these theories about strangers and so on aren't worth a brass farthing.'

Pugh had been wondering for some time if he should cross-examine or not. Another note arrived from Richard Napier. 'The trouble is that there is really only one word for knowledge in the English language. In this case the knowledge that Randolph is dead in English seems to be the same sort of knowledge as Cosmo killed him. But it's not. Could you try Plato? Episteme is knowledge, Randolph is dead, doxa is opinion. Cosmo killed him is doxa. Socrates often droned on about the difference. Too difficult for the jury? Flatter them into thinking they're more intelligent than they are?' Pugh looked across at his junior. He could suddenly see him lying on the grass by the Cam, volume of Plato in hand, progressing serenely towards his double first in Philosophy before he changed over to the law.

'Just to sum up. . .' Sir Jasper was keen to keep Willoughby Nash out of the clutches of Charles Augustus Pugh for as long as possible. This judge was always anxious to get away at close of play. 'You've made it very clear what your views were on the day of the murder. In all the events since, the visits from the police and the detectives and so on, you say you haven't changed your mind?'

'No, sir. Just take a look at the facts on the ground. No guessing and speculating like these shifty young men who write for the newspapers nowadays. Get on the horse and head for the fox, that's what I always say. No point wondering if you've got the wrong mount. Waste of time.'

Charles Augustus Pugh decided to take a chance. It was risky, he thought, rather like bringing the spinners on after only four overs on a fast wicket suited to the quick bowlers.

'Gentlemen of the jury, I would like to remind you, if I may, subject to his lordship having no objections, of one particular element in the wisdom of the ancient Greek philosopher called Plato which I believe has bearing on this case.'

Pugh looked attentively at the judge. 'As long as your detour doesn't last too long, Mr Pugh,' said Mr Justice Black, smiling slightly. 'I always liked Plato at school, but that man Socrates sometimes went on too long.'

'Thank you, my lord,' said Pugh, aware that Sir Jasper was rattling with fury beside him like a ship's boiler.

'I just want to remind you, gentlemen of the jury, of the distinction Plato drew between knowledge and opinion. Episteme in Greek meant knowledge, hard knowledge, hard facts. Randolph Colville is dead, that is episteme, the doctors and the pathologists would confirm it. Opinion for the Greeks was doxa. Opinion was what people believed to be true. It might be or it might not. Doxa, opinion, did not have the same weight as episteme, knowledge. Cosmo Colville killed his brother is opinion, doxa.

'So, Mr Nash, do you accept Plato's distinctions between different sorts of knowledge? And would you accept that Randolph is dead is not in the same category of knowledge as Cosmo killed him?'

Willoughby Nash had seen too many courtroom dramas in his own city to fall into the trap of trading philosophical niceties with the lead counsel for the defence.

'You can stick to Plato, Mr Pugh. I thought his works were boring and unintelligible when I had to read them at university. I thought Cosmo killed him, as I said, and I still do. You just had to look at him sitting in that chair with the gun in his hand and a faraway look in his eye to realize what was going on.'

Not even Plato, Pugh reflected, could change Willoughby Nash's mind. He wondered if the man's bombastic manner might put the jury off. Perhaps they wouldn't want to be on the same side. He wondered if he could launch one last question that might show the man in the worst possible light. He was aware of the judge shuffling his papers and gathering up his collection of pencils great and small.

'And what, Mr Nash,' he asked, 'do you think of the people who read the matter differently from yourself, who think that while it is perfectly possible that the defendant killed his brother, nonetheless we have no definite proof that he did so and therefore he should be given the benefit of the doubt?'

Willoughby Nash had had enough. Questions to his wife that lacked what he thought of as the proper respect. Some damn Greek philosopher dragged into the case to confuse things. Willoughby Nash knew perfectly well what he would have done if he had been a member of the jury of Athenian citizens who tried Socrates for corrupting the young. He would have voted for the prosecution, for the death penalty and the richly deserved glass of the fatal hemlock. He would, furthermore, have burnt all the books written by that man Plato as well if he could. The life of the nation's young, he felt, would be better and happier without philosophy of any kind.

Out of the corner of his eye Pugh suddenly spotted a man in a dark blue coat slipping into the back of the court. Reinforcements were arriving and he hoped they were not too late to save the day. Johnny Fitzgerald had come to the Old Bailey.

'I think such people are fools.' Willoughby Nash thought the court could do with a strong dose of common sense. He felt like making a derogatory reference to the suffragettes but found he couldn't make the connection. 'Let's face facts. You find a man with a piece of your silver in his hand creeping out of your house. He is a burglar. Some footballer kicks the ball into the back of the net on a football field. That is a goal. You find a man holding a gun opposite his brother who is lying dead on the floor. He is a murderer. He should pay the penalty. Society must have rules or we should all descend into anarchy.'

Willoughby Nash stared defiantly at the jury. He glowered at Charles Augustus Pugh. The judge completed the tidying of his desk and the formation of his armada of pencils. They were to meet again, he reminded the court, on Monday morning at half past nine of the clock. With that he went to his rooms. Sir Jasper Bentinck smiled at Pugh and headed off to his modest home. Pugh and his junior headed for Gray's Inn to confer with Johnny Fitzgerald.

Pugh hung his gown on the back of the door of his chambers. Then he opened a bottle of Aloxe Corton and handed a glass to Johnny Fizgerald.

'Bought a case of this stuff the other day when I heard Powerscourt was invading Burgundy,' he said cheerfully. 'Not a very good day in court, I fear. Not necessarily bad, but I would say things were going more in Sir Jasper's direction than in ours. Would you agree with that, young man?'

Richard Napier sipped appreciatively at his wine.

'I think you'd have to say, sir, that they have built up a considerable first innings lead. Not that we can't come back, mind you.'

'You arrive, Johnny,' Pugh looked across at Johnny who was now draped across a small sofa, 'like that messenger chappie who came from Marshal Blücher to tell Wellington that the Prussians were coming to help him at Waterloo. What news of Powerscourt?'

'He should be here tomorrow,' Johnny said, digging about in his inside pocket for Powerscourt's pieces of paper. 'He gave me this, for me to give to you with the main points he's discovered over there.'

'And what are the chief points?' said Pugh, beginning to peruse the document.

'It's quite dramatic, really. We've found a man who swore he would kill Randolph Colville. He must be the fellow who checked into that hotel in Norfolk and set off for the wedding the next morning.' Johnny took another pull at his Aloxe Corton. 'And Randolph was a bigamist. He had another wife and another family tucked up in a pretty house near Beaune.'

'A bigamist, did you say? A second wife? Like he was a Musselman or one of those Mormons from Utah? God bless my soul! I never heard of such a thing in all my years at the Bar. Pretty, was she, Number Two, I mean?'

'I never saw her. I don't think I heard Francis describe her one way or the other. Younger than Number One he said.'

'Look here, Johnny, we need to think of the practicalities of the court,' said Pugh, scratching his head and passing the first page over to his junior. 'I don't think Francis's note is going to be admissible in evidence. You don't suppose he has packed the two ladies into a railway carriage to confront the judge and Sir Jasper on Monday morning? No? Even then it would be the devil's own job to have their evidence accepted.'

'I was just coming to that,' said Johnny, staring hard at his glass, 'Francis was hoping to get signed statements out of both of them, witnessed by some local lawyer and looking as official as possible. That's why he's coming back a bit later than me.'

'That's something,' said Pugh. 'You say Francis is coming back tomorrow? If not then, Sunday?' He scribbled something on a piece of paper. 'I've just got one of these telephone machines. Perhaps he could ring me as soon as he gets back and we can arrange to meet. I'm going to have to rethink my entire plan of campaign. It's as if some kind person at the War Office has sent you another fifteen thousand troops the day before a battle, but you've no idea how reliable they're going to be. Now then, young man,' he turned to his junior, 'I'm afraid we're working late, you and I. Can you see if you can find some precedents for the late admission of evidence and the various procedures that have to be gone through? If Sir Jasper decides to cut up rough we may not be able to use any of this. God knows what the judge will make of it. He's not an adventurous man, Mr Justice Black. If we can find a precedent it'll be easier for him.'

'Does it matter how long ago it was, sir?' Richard Napier was collecting his notebook for a long vigil in the Gray's Inn Library.

'Well, don't go as far back as the trial of bloody Socrates,' said Pugh, recalling his junior's suggestion that afternoon. 'Anything modern should do.'

As Johnny Fitzgerald took his leave of the lawyers he glanced at the bottle. In the middle of the label it said 'Corton – Charlemagne, Grand Cru.' And above that in a slightly larger typeface was the legend, 'Hospices de Beaune'.

22

Powerscourt and Lady Lucy didn't reach London on Saturday. They still hadn't reached London by six o'clock on Sunday evening. By that stage Charles Augustus Pugh had rung the telephone exchange three times to check that his line was working. He had called on the Powerscourts' house in Markham Square at four o'clock in the afternoon only to be told that the master and mistress had not returned. At last, a few minutes before seven, Pugh's telephone rang. It was Powerscourt. He, Pugh, would set out for Chelsea immediately.

'My God, Powerscourt, you look as though you've been in the wars,' said Pugh, inspecting his friend at the top of the staircase to the drawing room.

'I'm fine now,' said Powerscourt with a smile, 'last rites not needed for a while yet.'

'Well,' said Pugh, 'you must tell me the whole story when we've got more time.'

'I'll buy you lunch. How's that? Now then, these are the French documents, my friend,' said Powerscourt. 'Lucy translated them while we were waiting for the train in Paris. The local lawyer thought it would help if he got the Mayor's signature as well. They look as though you could get married or buried with them they've got so many stamps on the page.'

Pugh read them very fast. 'I'll get them typed up first thing in the morning. That junior of mine is rather an expert with the typewriters though he doesn't advertise the fact in case he's turned into a glorified clerk. It's amazing what you can do with a philosophy degree these days. But I think we need something more. We need a signature from some responsible person here to say the translation's accurate and can be relied on.'

'Lucy's word not good enough?' said Powerscourt.

'Lady Lucy's word is good enough for anything,' said Pugh loyally, 'we just need something the prosecution can't argue with.'

'French Ambassador?' suggested Powerscourt. 'I've met the fellow a couple of times.'

'He's foreign,' Pugh put in. 'Juries don't like foreign.'

'How about Rosebery?' asked Lady Lucy. 'He's a former Prime Minister, after all.'

'How's his French?' said Pugh.

'Don't think it matters much about his French, actually,' said Lady Lucy. 'It's very good but the prosecution won't want to cross-examine a man of his eminence, former Foreign Secretary and all that. Would you like me to drop him a note?'

'Please do,' said Pugh. 'Now then, I want to hear what you think. It seems to me that all this stuff about bigamy isn't going to wash in court. As far as we know, the Colvilles on this side of the Channel don't know about the extra wife down there among the vineyards. Johnny Fitzgerald told me he didn't find a hint of bigamy when he poured drinks down the Colville servants in St John's Wood and Pangbourne, fishing for gossip about the family row. I don't think I can just put one of the Colville women in the witness box and start asking them about bigamy. The judge wouldn't allow the question. So I think we have to go with the sergeant. That is, if we are even allowed the sergeant.'

'What do you mean, Pugh, no sergeant?' asked Powerscourt. Was it for this that he had gone to France to be chased round a hospital floating in wine, tied on to a terrifying *pressoir* and locked up in a French lunatic asylum?

'Well,' said Pugh, leaving his chair and draping himself over the Powerscourt mantelpiece, 'I've never been in a murder trial with evidence this late before. I'm not absolutely sure about the procedure. I should have brought young Napier with me. He's very hot on procedure, probably reads it up in bed last thing at night in his best pyjamas after a blast of Aristotle. Never mind. This is what I think happens. I have to inform the judge and the prosecution team that the defence have fresh evidence they would like to submit, even at this late hour. Grovel grovel grovel. I would be most grateful for your considered opinions as you can fit into five minutes. Then the judge can do one of two things. He can clear the court, tell everybody including the jury to come back in an hour or something like that. We carry on the argument from our normal positions. Or, if he feels he wants his home comforts, bigger pencils, softer chairs in the case of Mr Justice Black, he takes Sir Jasper's team and my team back to his rooms to discuss the matter.'

'And what,' asked Powerscourt, 'is the argument about?'

'Basically, it's about whether to admit the new evidence or not,' said Pugh. 'We're in Sir Jasper's hands, really. If he says this is most improper, these statements have no value, there are no real witnesses for me to cross-examine in the normal way, why are the two women not here, then that will bear heavily with the judge. He can either throw it out, or insist that the two witnesses appear in his court by such and such a date. If he follows the strict letter of the law and the proper procedures we might fare rather badly.'

'Could we launch an appeal, if they won't admit our evidence and Cosmo is convicted?' said Lady Lucy, who disliked losing as much as her husband.

'Don't even think about appeals at this stage, Lady Lucy. One thing at a time.'

'Which way do you think Sir Jasper will jump, Pugh?' said Powerscourt.

'I wish I knew,' said Pugh. 'If he wants to win the case very badly then he'll be very difficult and it will be hard for the judge to admit our new evidence. We'll just have to wait until the morning.'

'Do you think Francis will have to give evidence?'

'He might well have to,' said Pugh. 'White shirts, highly polished black shoes the order of the day. Nothing fancy. Nothing to irritate the bloody judge.'

Powerscourt left Markham Square early the next morning for a last-minute conference with Pugh. The court was due to sit at nine thirty. Lady Lucy had promised herself one important task involving the twins' hair when Rhys, the Powerscourt butler, made his normal apologetic shuffle into the room, holding a letter in his hand.

'This just came in the post, my lady. From France. I thought it might be important, my lady.'

'Hold on a minute while I look at it,' said Lady Lucy, glancing anxiously at the clock which showed the hour of five past nine.

'Dear Lord Powerscourt,' she read, translating as she went, 'I hope your journey back to London was uneventful. In all the turmoil about my husband and his sad end I forgot to tell you one thing. I don't know if it's important or not but I felt I should let you know. I tried to contact you at the railway station before you left but your train had gone. I wrote to the other wife, the one in England, to tell her her husband had a French wife living as well as an English one. The letter should have reached her about ten days before the fateful wedding. The letter from the English wife I found in Jean Pierre's pocket was written on headed notepaper so I had the address. The schoolmaster wrote it in English for me. What he must think of us all! I asked her what she wanted to do with her husband. I said I was perfectly happy to keep him if she didn't mind. He is so happy in Burgundy with his wines. I have had no reply. Yours etc.'

'My God,' said Lady Lucy. 'You have done well, Rhys, this

changes everything. Now then, can you get me a cab right away? And a driver who knows the back routes to the Old Bailey? There is hardly any time left.'

It was ten past nine when the cab set forth from Chelsea. Lady Lucy was thinking hard as the vehicle swung out of Markham Square and into the King's Road. Rhys had done well again, she felt. This was not one of those ponderous cabs capable of taking four people at a time. It was a two-seater, more like a fly or a phaeton, and the young man driving it seemed to know his business.

'What time do you have to be at the Old Bailey, Lady P?' he shouted back to her through the glass panels separating driver from passenger.

Lady Lucy couldn't help smiling. Nobody had called her Lady P in years.

'Half past nine,' she said. 'It's very important.'

'Christ,' said the young man, swearing violently at a couple of pedestrians who threatened to hold them up. 'I'm going to try the Embankment route,' he yelled, turning at full speed into Sloane Street and down towards the river. 'I checked with one or two of the other drivers,' he said, 'and they all said it's very crowded further north.'

Lady Lucy thought she could see things clearly now for the first time since her involvement in this case began. She remembered hearing about the great family row at the Colvilles shortly before the wedding. The letter from France must have arrived by then. Accusations, recriminations, cries of betrayal. And Randolph? What did he say to his tormentors? Maybe by now he had simply run out of lies. They had just passed the Royal Hospital Chelsea, one or two aged pensioners in their red coats wandering down towards the Thames, and the driver had performed another hair-raising manoeuvre with supreme skill. At what point Randolph had decided to kill himself Lady Lucy could only guess. It was now eighteen minutes past nine. Maybe I should always travel across London like this, she thought, in a graceful little vehicle with Jehu himself come back from the dead to take the reins.

Charles Augustus Pugh was on edge that morning. He had smoked two cheroots in his chambers before they set off for the court. His young man Richard Napier had rings under his eyes from long hours spent in the Gray's Inn Library searching for precedents. All three were wearing immaculate white shirts and polished black shoes. Just before they reached the Old Bailey Pugh stopped suddenly and waved his arms violently in the morning air.

'My friends,' he said, putting an arm round each of his companions, 'there will be no half measures today. Either we shall succeed beyond our wildest dreams and Cosmo Colville will walk a free man tonight. Or the judge will throw our documents in the bin and the unfortunate Cosmo will be a day closer to the hangman and the rope. There can be no middle way. But come, my friends, let us be of good cheer. England expects that every man this day will do his duty.' With that Pugh laughed his enormous laugh and led them into Court Number Two of the Old Bailey.

Lady Lucy's driver had overtaken everything he could on his madcap journey through the streets of London. They were just past Westminster Bridge now, Whitehall and Horse Guards Parade a street away to their left. It was twenty-three minutes past nine. Lady Lucy could hear the cabbie muttering to himself about the traffic around Charing Cross.

'If they didn't have those bloody trains, Lady P, they wouldn't have so much bloody traffic,' he yelled, pulling out to overtake an omnibus, 'stands to reason.'

'Are we going to make it?' Lady Lucy shouted through the noise.

'Get clean through Charing Cross and we might just do it,' said the cabbie cheerfully.

'Whoops,' he yelled, pulling sharply on his brakes as an old-fashioned four-seater stopped suddenly in front of him. 'What the hell do you think you're doing?'

Lady Lucy was wondering about Randolph Colville's last hours. Presumably he had taken the gun with him to the wedding. Maybe it was the sight of all those people at the reception who would shortly learn of his shame and his disgrace that pushed him over the edge. At least he had waited for his son to get married. Poor man, she thought, as the cabbie let out a shout of triumph after negotiating the perils of Charing Cross. Poor Randolph, blowing his brains out in that remote bedroom while the champagne flowed and the oysters were being carried up from the kitchens down below. The driver carried on up the Embankment and up Middle Temple Lane to the Strand. Fleet Street now and the passing of Temple Bar, gateway to the City of London. Twenty-seven minutes past nine. Lady Lucy could see St Paul's and its dome, towering over London like the Colossus towered over Rhodes in ancient times. She checked the letter was still in her bag and ran through her translation once again.

The court was very full that morning. Society ladies jostled with the gentlemen of the press as they settled in their seats. Powerscourt wondered if Pugh had tipped them off. Sir Jasper made another of his little bows to the defence team. Pugh had told him as soon as he saw him of his fresh evidence and his proposal to ask the court to consider allowing it. He handed Sir Jasper his copy of the relevant papers and sent another copy to the judge. It was twenty-eight minutes past nine.

Then disaster struck Lady Lucy's mission of mercy. A cart had overturned in the middle of the road at the bottom of Ludgate

Hill. Barrels were lying about all over the street. Porters and policemen were trying to restore order.

'Damn!' said the cabbie. 'I think we've had it, Lady P. I'm going to have to turn into these side streets. One large vehicle coming the other way and you can get stuck for half an hour.' He turned round at full speed, the little machine tilting over like a yacht turning in a stiff breeze, and then he shot right into Farringdon Road.

In Court Two the day had an unusual beginning. Mr Justice Black sent word that the jury were to be kept in the jury room. There was, the judge informed them, a question of law which had to be settled. A couple of minutes later Mr Justice Black sent word that he wished to see both legal teams and their supporters in his rooms. The Clerk of the Court told the witnesses and the spectators and the journalists that the court was adjourned until eleven o'clock.

The cabbie had turned into the Old Bailey at last. They were only three minutes late. Lady Lucy pressed an enormous sum of money into the cabbie's hand.

'Run for it, Lady P!' he shouted. 'Good luck!'

Lady Lucy made her way through the throng of people who appeared to be leaving rather than entering the court-room. She could just see Charles Augustus Pugh about to exit through a side door.

'Mr Pugh!' she shouted. 'Stop a moment! There's more evidence.' She was now almost at his side, waving the letter in her hand. 'This letter came from France this morning. It's from the French wife. She wrote to the English wife before that great row they had, telling Mrs Colville, English version, that she, Madame Drouhin, was Madame Colville, French version. Sometime before the wedding it would have been.'

'Written in French or English?' They could both hear a cry of 'Mr Pugh, where are you?' coming from the behind the door.

'French,' said Lady Lucy.

'Try to get it translated and typed up if you can,' said Pugh, opening the door, 'and send it in as soon as possible through the Clerk of the Court.' With that he ran at full speed towards the judge's rooms.

Mr Justice Black was settled deep into his chair as the lawyers began to file in, defence solicitors on the side of Charles Augustus Pugh, the last to arrive, Detective Chief Inspector Weir for Sir Jasper. The judge was the proud possessor of a handsome room in the new Old Bailey, a fire burning in his grate, bookshelves lined with legal documents, a forbidding desk for his lordship with a couple of humble chairs on the opposite side. So far Mr Justice Black was still in the genial mood he had at the start of the day.

'Mr Pugh,' he said firmly. When he learnt of the circumstances of the judge's weekend a year later, Powerscourt was to say that the judge's weekend was the most important single event in that day at the Old Bailey. The judge was a keen, and very successful, bridge player. He had spent Saturday evening at his club playing for rather high stakes. He had won a great deal of money. The memory of that last finesse to secure the final rubber would stay with him for a long time. Claret, that was how he planned to spend his winnings. The judge was very fond of claret. He had brought with him that day the latest catalogue from Berry Bros. & Rudd to read on the train.

'My lord,' said Pugh, 'I beg the court's forgiveness for what I am about to request and I convey my apologies to you for the inconvenience I may be about to cause.'

'Get on with it, for God's sake,' his junior whispered to himself and began a drawing of the foreman of the jury.

'My lord,' Pugh went on, 'the defence would like to ask the court to consider admitting fresh evidence it wishes to put before the court. This evidence only reached London on Sunday evening. It is, I believe, germane to the very substance of this case. I have given a copy of the papers to my learned friend, Sir Jasper, and to yourself.'

Pugh sat down. The judge peered at Pugh.

'This is irregular, Mr Pugh, most irregular.' Pugh wondered for a moment if he was simply going to throw the new evidence out without even hearing it.

'Mr Pugh,' the judge began, 'you will forgive us, Sir Jasper and I, while we read these new documents.'

'The page with the English translation is under the page with the French, my lord. The French wedding certificate is in your bundle, my lord. And before you start reading, forgive me, but I have yet another document relevant to the proceedings. It only came from France this morning, my lord. The Clerk will bring it in once the translation and typing is complete, my lord.'

'When documents come from France,' said the judge, searching for his glasses, 'they come not as single spies, but in battalions.'

Mr Justice Black read the pieces of paper. Then he read them again.

'Correct me if I am wrong, Mr Pugh. Your new evidence tells us that Randolph Colville was a bigamist, with a second wife living in Burgundy. And, furthermore, that he was flirting with another Frenchwoman whose husband caught them kissing and threatened to kill Randolph Colville. God bless my soul. It does make you wonder about their morals over there, it really does.'

Pugh restrained himself from saying that the same or worse could be said about English morals over here. There was a knock at the door. The Clerk of the Court shuffled in and handed over copies of the letter.

'Battalions, gentlemen, battalions,' said the judge grimly and read the final piece of evidence from Beaune.

'There is a precedent, my lord, for documents arriving late

being admitted as evidence. Regina versus Spick, my lord, 1897. Late financial information from America was accepted by Mr Justice Williams in that case.' Pugh did not bother to point out that his young assistant had discovered five other cases where the late evidence had not been admitted before tumbling on Spick at a quarter to two in the morning.

The judge muttered to himself as if precedents were not going to hold much weight with him. 'Mr Pugh,' Mr Justice Black laid his glasses on a pile of papers on his desk, the one concealing the wine catalogue, 'what can you tell us about the provenance of these documents?'

'Well,' said Pugh, 'the defence has been fortunate to have at its disposal a private investigator who went to Burgundy, discovered the other wife and tried to give their testimony such legitimacy as he could. You will note that the first two are signed in the presence of a French lawyer and the Mayor of Beaune? And there is the marriage certificate, of course.'

'Did you say private investigator?' asked the judge. He made it sound like the lowest forms of rat catcher.

'I did, my lord, he is a most distinguished man in his field, called Powerscourt.'

'Powerscourt, did you say, Mr Pugh? Lord Francis Powerscourt?' asked Sir Jasper.

'The same, Sir Jasper. He is without, if you would like to question him.'

'Forgive me, Mr Pugh,' said the judge, 'I should like to hear from Sir Jasper about the attitude of the prosecution to these documents. I have to say I regard it as most irregular. There are no witnesses. The proper course would be for me to adjourn the trial for forty-eight hours and send a reliable man over to Burgundy who can confirm that these statements are reliable. Or I could throw them out altogether. Sir Jasper?'

'My lord, my initial reaction is one of suspicion. These documents could all be forgeries after all. I see that the note from Lord Rosebery vouchsafes the veracity of the translations but not the veracity of the documents themselves. Where are the witnesses, my lord? Why are these two ladies not in court to give their evidence? Why is there nobody for me to cross-examine to establish the truth? That, after all, has always been a fundamental right of counsel in English law going back centuries.'

Richard Napier was making a lightning sketch of Sir Jasper now, Bentinck in Full Flow he had decided to call it.

'I think we can launch a limited investigation into the truth of the documents right here in this court, my lord.' Sir Jasper was sounding very efficient now, a man rising to the occasion. 'I believe we have the wife of the defendant and the wife of the victim in the witness room, both of whom took part in family discussions on these matters. I propose to request Detective Chief Inspector Weir here to ask the two ladies if they believe this new material to be true, and if they object to this evidence coming out in court.

'I must confess an interest here, my lord. I have not had the privilege of meeting Lord Francis Powerscourt in person. But I know many people who have. Indeed I recall our former Prime Minister Lord Salisbury speaking most highly of his integrity and his abilities in my hearing shortly before he died, Lord Salisbury that is, not Lord Powerscourt. Perhaps, my lord, if we could summon him here he might be able to help me.'

'By all means,' said Mr Justice Black in cheerful mode at the memory of his winning contract of six spades redoubled in the penultimate rubber. 'Bring him in when Sir Jasper has finished his conversation with the Chief Inspector.'

Richard Napier went off to find Powerscourt. Pugh suddenly saw that Powerscourt, although he would not be aware of it, might hold the whole case in his hands. If he could convince Sir Jasper that the documents were genuine, then the prosecution would accept them and the judge would have little option but to agree with that decision. If Sir Jasper was not convinced, then there would be no documents and the case would almost certainly be lost.

Another chair was brought forward opposite the judge. Powerscourt bowed to him and shook hands with Sir Jasper.

'Good of you to join us, Lord Powerscourt,' Sir Jasper began. 'I would like to ask you a few questions about these documents if I may.'

'By all means,' Powerscourt replied, turning slightly in his chair to face the prosecution counsel.

'Could I begin by asking what took you to France in the first place? Did you suspect that Randolph Colville might be running a separate establishment over there?'

'May I say something about the different ways of operating between barristers and judges and private investigators?' said Powerscourt. 'You gentlemen here in these august surroundings are dealing with the full majesty of the law. You need facts. You need evidence. You need to be able to cross-examine witnesses to test the truth of their statements. With me it is very different. I went to Burgundy on a hunch, on instinct. It was, admittedly, a hunch of several different parts. Randolph Colville was ambidextrous, totally so. He could play tennis without ever using a backhand. The Colville man in Burgundy disappeared around the time of the murder. He was often asked to England but never came. When representatives of the firm who knew Randolph Colville went to Beaune, he was always away on business. This man in France was also ambidextrous, able to write his name with both hands at the same time. It seemed to me that they might be one and the same person.'

'Are you telling us,' Sir Jasper sounded incredulous, 'that you were not aware of the bigamy factor until you went there?'

'I was guessing, Sir Jasper. I took a recent photograph from his English wife's house with me so that the wife and the other woman could confirm his identity.'

'Let me ask you two related questions, if I may,' said Sir Jasper. 'Was it impossible for the two women to come and give evidence? And are you certain this marriage certificate is genuine?'

'I tried, believe me, Sir Jasper, to persuade one or both of them to come to London. The wife was too upset. She was, after all, married to a man who was married already. Her children, their children, had lost their father and, possibly, their future. She was going to travel as soon as she could to her mother's house somewhere in the Auvergne. The other lady could not face the shame of telling a court in another country what she had done in her own. And she was waiting for her husband the sergeant to come back. You mention marriage certificates, Sir Jasper. I have brought the one in the possession of the lawyer Antoine Foucard from Givray who witnessed the statements of the two women. His father had been the lawyer responsible for the wedding. His father had been a guest at the reception. When I showed him the photo of Randolph Colville by the Thames he was in no doubt it was Jean Pierre Drouhin. Madame Drouhin was reluctant to let me take her copy away as she thought she would need it in any arguments with the legal gentlemen about the will. The one I have brought is the one from the lawyer's office. I am certain it is genuine.'

Detective Chief Inspector Weir had found an empty office to talk to the two Mrs Colvilles. He explained that the defence were trying to bring new evidence to bear concerning the bigamous behaviour of Randolph Colville.

'When did you first hear of this bigamy business?' asked Weir.

'I'll handle this, Hermione,' said Isabella Colville. 'We first heard about ten days before the wedding.'

'But you didn't see fit to inform the authorities?' said Weir sternly.

'No, we didn't,' said Isabella, 'we didn't think it was any of their business.'

'I must ask you this, ladies, did you believe it was true, this information about the other wife in France? That there was another Mrs Colville, as it were?'

'Of course it was true, it is true.' Isabella Colville sounded indignant. 'Randolph didn't deny it, he never said it wasn't true. He admitted the whole thing, for heaven's sake.'

'Could I ask, Lord Powerscourt, if you were operating through a translator in these discussions in Burgundy?' said Sir Jasper.

'No, I was not, Sir Jasper. I am fluent in French and my wife Lady Lucy speaks it perfectly. She is, if I could coin a phrase, linguistically ambidextrous between French and English.'

Sir Jasper glanced at his watch. It was now ten past ten, fifty minutes to go before the court re-assembled.

'One last question, Lord Powerscourt. This is all most irregular. What can you say to convince me that these statements are genuine, that we are not being hoodwinked by a couple of crafty Frenchwomen out to feather their nests in some way or other?'

'Gentlemen,' said Powerscourt addressing the judge and Sir Jasper, 'in my profession, as in yours, you acquire over the years an acute sense of when people are lying to you. I am absolutely convinced that the two women were telling the truth, that their statements are genuine. If you asked me to go into the witness box behind us and swear under oath that they were true I would gladly do so.'

'Thank you,' said Sir Jasper, 'thank you very much.'

'I must put one other point to you, ladies.' Weir was well used to being treated as a fool by now. 'Do you have any objection to this information coming out in court? About the bigamy, I mean.'

Mrs Isabella Colville paused. She knew there were people who suspected that her husband Cosmo was keeping his silence because of some secret, and if those people knew about her brother-in-law's bigamy, they might assume that the bigamy was the cause of the silence. Would Cosmo want her to admit the bigamy into court proceedings? Would it bring shame on the Colville name? Suddenly she remembered the look on Charles Augustus Pugh's face and the tone of his voice the previous Friday when she asked him outside the Old Bailey about her husband's chances. His words were optimistic. His face and his voice were not.

'It's the defence that's asking for it, isn't it, Detective Chief Inspector?' Scandal or no scandal, Isabella Colville wanted her husband back. 'Well, it's my husband who's on trial. If his defence team want it, then I think they should have it. Absolutely. No objections here.'

Sir Jasper and the rest of the lawyers listened gravely to the Detective Chief Inspector's account of his interview.

'Gentlemen,' said the judge, 'I would welcome a brief summary from both of you of your own position. Mr Pugh?'

'My lord,' said Pugh, 'I have very little to say. I believe Lord Powerscourt put the case for the acceptance of the French evidence very clearly. We believe that the signed documents and the marriage certificate are sufficient proof that the women of Givray are telling the truth. We have just heard that the Colville women here are convinced the bigamy is true – the husband never denied it after all – and they have no objections to the matter coming out in court. Of course the defence would like to see the new evidence included. But that is not my decision, my lord. It is for you and Sir Jasper and the defence is most grateful for the way the matter has been handled. I remain in your debt, my lord, for your willingness to look at this late request. We shall, of course, accept your judgement.'

'Sir Jasper?'

'I have to say, my lord, that I am torn. On the one hand we have the lack of witnesses, the fact that there is nobody for me to cross-examine. And yet. And yet.'

Sir Jasper was not a dyed-in-the-wool reactionary like some

of his colleagues. As a young man, fresh from Oxford at the elegant buildings of Lincoln's Inn, he had fallen in love with the law. He had lit metaphorical candles in all the temples of the legal system. Those candles had long since gone out, guttered and blackened as his disillusion grew with the passing years. Exaggeration had a lot to with it. The police, he felt, exaggerated their evidence and left out the bits that did not suit their case. The barristers exaggerated their vanity, locked into an adversarial system that confused the force of advocacy with the reality of their cases and the cause of justice. Judges and juries grew confused, cynical of the evidence and the barristers who presented it. Three years ago Sir Jasper himself had been involved in a miscarriage of justice. He had appeared for the prosecution in a case where a man was hanged, only for it to be discovered three weeks later that he was innocent, by which time it was too late. That case had weighed heavily with him ever since.

'I must say,' he went on, 'that I attach great weight to the testimony of Lord Powerscourt. What particularly impressed me was his willingness to put his career and his considerable reputation on the line by going into the witness box. I also attach weight to the marriage certificate for I believe it to be genuine. And we have just heard from Detective Chief Inspector Weir, my lord, that the two Mrs Colvilles, who learnt of the bigamy some ten days before the wedding, are absolutely certain that it is true. And they have no objection to the bigamy evidence being brought into open court. I believe, my lord, that we always have an obligation to maintain the traditions of the law, for without order there is nothing. But we also have an obligation to be fair, to hear all the arguments and all the evidence even when they may have arrived by singularly unorthodox means.'

Sir Jasper paused. Pugh sat perfectly still, looking at his papers. Powerscourt was looking at Sir Jasper. Pugh's junior had abandoned his sketching for the moment, staring at the prosecution counsel.

'On balance,' Sir Jasper concluded, 'the prosecution has no objection to the admittance of these documents. I leave the matter, my lord, in your capable hands.'

'Thank you, gentlemen,' said Mr Justice Black. 'It is now twenty-five minutes past ten. I suggest the legal teams take an adjournment. If you, Sir Jasper and Mr Pugh, care to return at ten to eleven I shall inform you of my decision. That should give you a little time to prepare for any new circumstances we may find ourselves in.'

The legal teams shuffled out. The jury and the gentlemen of the press were drifting back into court. Pugh and Powerscourt collected Lady Lucy and filled her in on what had happened in the judge's rooms. They held an impromptu conference on the pavement outside away from the public and the newspapermen.

'Do you think he's going to admit it, Powerscourt?' said Pugh.

'Yes, I think he will.'

'Do we run with the mysterious Frenchman? Or the suicide?'

'Suicide surely,' said Lady Lucy. 'He couldn't take the shame, poor man.'

'There's one thing we haven't realized,' said Powerscourt. 'I've only just seen it this minute. Sir Jasper may have seemed rather magnanimous in there, but I wonder if he's just being cunning.'

'What do you mean?' asked Pugh.

'Well,' said Powerscourt, 'think about the new evidence. It shows that there was bigamy and that the Colvilles on this side of the water were aware of it. Indeed they had a massive family row about it.'

'So?' said Charles Augustus Pugh.

'Simply this,' said Powerscourt. 'The one thing the prosecution case have never had is a reliable motive for Cosmo murdering his brother. Now they have one. The family are desperately keen to preserve the good name of Colville. They do not want the bigamy to be known abroad. Randolph has disgraced the family. Once he is dead the whole story might never get out. Cosmo shoots his brother to preserve the family honour and is just about to make his escape down one of those back stairs. Then the butler steps in. It's highly unlikely the police would have arrested Cosmo if he hadn't been found in that unfortunate position. He'd have got away and come in round the front door with the stragglers. Just bad luck he got caught. Remember the police never heard a whisper about the bigamy.'

'Christ!' said Pugh. 'I've got to reappear before the judge. I have to say, I have no idea what to do when the court resumes. Send me a note if inspiration strikes you, Powerscourt.'

23

The judge was back in Court Two at exactly eleven o'clock. There was a hum of expectancy round the room. Word had seeped out about the reason for the adjournment. What, people had been asking themselves for the past hour and a half, was this new evidence? Some thought it must relate to some fraud or other outrage in the Colville wine business. Others believed that it had to do with the defendant, that he had a secret history of violent behaviour which had only just been discovered. Most of all, the spectators and the jurymen agreed, they felt they had a right, as free-born Englishmen and ratepayers, to know what the new evidence was. They prayed that the judge was not going to let them down.

Mr Justice Black called the court to order. He coughed lightly and waited until his court was completely still.

'Gentlemen of the jury,' he began, 'an hour and half ago I adjourned this court while we considered whether or not to admit new evidence from the defence. Unusual though the circumstances are, I have decided, after consultations with Sir Jasper Bentinck and Mr Charles Pugh here, to admit the new material. Mr Pugh, perhaps you could read the evidence out to the court so the shorthand writers can enter it into the record.'

Pugh adjusted his glasses and began to read. In each case he mentioned the date and the names of the witnesses at the top. He spoke with no emotion in his voice at all. His tone was neutral, what his junior, who had heard it before, referred to as Pugh's railway station announcer's voice. When he revealed the bigamy there was pandemonium in court. One or two of the newspapermen wrote instant news stories and had their runners take them to their offices at full speed. They might just make the lunchtime editions. The society ladies were beside themselves. 'I've never heard of such a thing!' 'Fancy leaving a letter like that in your back pocket! Only a man would do that!' One word ran through the court like a fire in barn of straw: 'Bigamy, bigamy, bigamy!'

'Silence! Silence in court!' Mr Justice Black looked livid, as if one of his famed finesses at the bridge table had failed to come off. 'Any more noise and I shall clear the court of spectators and newspapermen alike! Mr Pugh.'

The barrister from Gray's Inn carried on. He was on the second piece of evidence from Beaune now where Madame Yvette Planchon told of the stolen kiss, the unexpected arrival of her husband the sergeant, his threat to kill Randolph Colville and his disappearance from the scene.

Powerscourt was staring at the shorthand writers at the table below the judge. They, unlike everybody else in Court Two, had remained impassive as the new evidence was disclosed. Perhaps they had heard it all before. Powerscourt's mind was racing. Yet another interpretation of events at Brympton Hall had just flashed through his brain. He picked up his pen and wrote a very brief message. He folded it carefully twice and wrote Pugh on the front. As his colleague made his way through the letter that had arrived from Beaune that morning with the astonishing news that the Colvilles in England knew about the other Colville wife in France, he leant forward and slipped it into the hand of Richard Napier, leaning back from his bench. Lady Lucy, sitting beside her husband with Cosmo's solicitor on her other side, looked at him expectantly. Powerscourt spoke not a word.

Pugh had finished. He placed the three documents on the exhibit table where the gun was still lying as it had throughout the trial.

'Call Mrs Colville, Mrs Cosmo Colville.' Napier slipped the note into his hand. Pugh read it while the new witness made her way to the box. He squashed it up and put it in his pocket, then he turned and glanced enigmatically at Powerscourt.

'Mrs Colville,' he began, 'Would you say that you were a close family?'

'Yes,' she said, 'we always have been.'

'So perhaps you could tell the court, Mrs Colville, when you first became aware that your brother-in-law was a bigamist with a second wife in France?'

She blushed deeply. She seemed to find it difficult to give an answer. She began folding and refolding her hands. Powerscourt thought that had she been Lady Macbeth she would have been washing those hands by now.

'Come, Mrs Colville,' said Pugh in his politest tones, 'I'm sure you can give us an answer.'

'It must have been fairly close to the wedding,' she said finally.

'And did all the Colvilles attend the meeting?'

'No,' she was whispering now, 'the first meeting was just the two brothers, Randolph and Cosmo, and their wives. We told the others in the days that followed. Everybody in the family knew by the time of the wedding.'

'I wouldn't want the intimate details of what was said at that first meeting, Mrs Colville, but perhaps you could just give us the broad picture.' The more intelligent members of the jury realized that intimate details were exactly what Charles Augustus Pugh did want but knew he wouldn't get if he asked for them directly.

Mrs Colville was now looking very distressed indeed. Only when Powerscourt turned round almost one hundred and eighty degrees did he see part of the reason. Cosmo Colville had hardly moved a muscle during the trial so far. But now he was sitting directly opposite his wife, he, Cosmo, in the dock, she in the witness box. The eye-lines of the court had been constructed for precisely this purpose. Before the arrival

312

of gas lighting a mirrored reflector was placed above the prisoner in the dock to reflect light from the windows on to the faces of the accused. This, Pugh had told Powerscourt years before, allowed the court to examine the facial expressions of the prisoners during testimony. Cosmo was now bent forward in the dock, his hands leaning on the little wooden wall and making gestures to his wife on the other side of Court Two. These gestures seemed to be causing considerable distress. Powerscourt wondered how long it would be before the judge noticed them.

'Mrs Colville,' Pugh said in his mildest tones, 'I can appreciate how distressing this must be for you, but I would remind you that you are under oath in a court of law. Could you please answer my question?'

Out of the corner of his eye Powerscourt saw that the dumb show in the dock was continuing. Cosmo might have chosen not to give evidence but he was trying his hardest to influence the court by other means.

'I'm sorry,' said Mrs Colville, 'everybody was very cross, very angry. People said Randolph had ruined the family name, that Colville Wine would become a laughing stock. The firm might even go out of business.'

The judge had finally caught sight of Cosmo. 'Prisoner at the bar,' he said sternly, 'please stop making signs to your wife. If I see you doing it once more you will be taken below to the holding cells and kept there until the end of this trial. I would remind you that this is a court of law, not some School for Semaphore.' He turned back to the witness box. 'Pray continue, Mrs Colville, Mr Pugh.'

'And what,' Pugh went on, any note of criticism or reproof removed from his voice, 'was the reaction of your brother-in-law, Mr Randolph Colville?'

She paused. 'If anything,' she said finally, 'he was the most upset of all of us. He kept saying, over and over and over, that he had destroyed the good name of Colville and ruined the lives of his family.'

'I see,' said Pugh, 'and did that attitude continue when the other members of the family were informed?'

'If anything, it grew worse,' Mrs Colville replied, now looking at the jury, now at Pugh. 'We kept telling him that there was no need for him to attend these terrible meetings. He could have gone for a walk or kept to his room. But he wouldn't have it. He felt he owed it to all his relations to be there in person to be attacked and humiliated.'

'Terrible meetings, you said, Mrs Colville?'

'Well, there was a lot of shouting. One of the uncles said Randolph deserved a horse whipping.'

Powerscourt could see where Pugh was heading. Any minute now, he said to himself, he's going to mention the S word. Or maybe he'll try to bring Mrs Colville to say it.

'And had Randolph's attitude changed at all by the time of the wedding, Mrs Colville?'

'I'm afraid not,' she replied, 'if anything it got worse.'

Now, Powerscourt thought, surely he must say it now.

'Mrs Colville, would you agree with me that your brother-in-law Mr Randolph Colville was weighed down by his circumstances?'

'Yes, I would.'

'And would you agree with me that he found it hard to see a way out of his predicament?'

'I don't think he could see any way out at all.'

'And over the ten days or so between the bigamy information reaching England and the wedding itself, did his mood improve at all?'

'No, it didn't. If anything it got worse.'

'In view of what we know now, Mrs Colville, what is your view about Mr Randolph Colville's conduct?'

Mrs Colville paused. She looked up at the dock where her husband was watching carefully. 'I'm afraid to say, Mr Pugh, I think now as I thought then that it all got too much for the poor man. The shame and the disgrace drove him to suicide.'

Pugh was quick to reply. 'Suicide, Mrs Colville? Are you sure?'

The word was out now. Suicide in shorthand was entered in a dozen reporter's notebooks.

'Yes, I am,' she said. 'Watching him through those ten days there was a very strong sense that he thought his options had run out, that he had come to the end of the road. So, yes, I think it is possible, indeed probable, that he committed suicide.'

Powerscourt had been watching Mrs Cosmo Colville intently for the last few minutes. He could have sworn that for a split second after the mention of suicide her face lit up with happiness. Then her surroundings pulled her back to the normal pose of conventional regret. If Randolph had indeed committed suicide, and the jury believed that, then her husband would be a free man, able to leave the gaunt surroundings of Pentonville for the delights of St John's Wood and Lord's Cricket Ground.

'No further questions, my lord,' said Pugh, consulting his notes and giving the jury time to take in Mrs Colville's evidence.

'Please call Mrs Randolph Colville,' said Pugh. Almost a hundred pairs of eyes followed Hermione Colville on her long journey towards the witness box.

'Mrs Colville,' Pugh began, 'we have heard from your sister-in-law about the mental condition of your late husband in the days before his death. Would you agree with her about his state of mind?'

Mrs Randolph Colville glanced quickly over to Sir Jasper. 'I would agree,' she said.

'And would you agree with her that it is possible he committed suicide?'

'I would, yes,' she said.

'Did he mention it in conversation, that he might take his own life?'

'I'm afraid there was no conversation in those days. We were not speaking to each other.'

315

'And was that,' said Pugh, taking a small sip of water, 'because he wasn't speaking to you or because you weren't speaking to him?'

'I'm sorry to say I wasn't speaking to him. I was so angry. The last words we exchanged were a discussion about who should walk the dogs the evening before that letter arrived.'

'Perhaps you could tell us, Mrs Colville, about your own state of mind in the period following the arrival of the letter from France?'

She stopped and looked up at the prisoner in the dock.

'Some of the time,' she said, 'I was out of my mind with rage. I was angry with Randolph, so angry that I could scarcely look at him. He'd betrayed us all. I was angry at that French whore. But I knew I had to reorder my life. There was no point in being angry all the time.'

Charles Augustus Pugh took a deep breath. Now or never. Cry havoc and let slip the dogs of war.

'Mrs Colville,' he said, 'I want to put a proposition to you if I may. We have heard from your sister and from yourself this morning about the possibility of suicide, that Randolph Colville took his own life. It certainly seems to fit some of the available evidence. If the jury were to believe it they would have to acquit the defendant. It would be in both your interests, an acquittal. Your sister-in-law would regain her husband. You would regain your brother-in-law. Mr Cosmo Colville would presumably regain his voice as well as his freedom. Is that not the case, Mrs Colville?'

'I suppose it is, yes.'

Pugh paused and picked up a piece of stiff cardboard from the table of exhibits. 'But I want to put to you, Mrs Colville, a rather different sequence of events.'

Mrs Colville looked yet again at Cosmo Colville. There was a desperate pleading in her eyes. There was no signal in reply. Everyone had gone completely silent in court. The eyes of judge, jury, pressmen, spectators were fixed on the slim figure in the witness box whose last conversation with her dead husband had been about who should walk the dogs.

'I put it to you, Mrs Colville, that on the morning of the wedding, you were indeed out of your mind with rage. Your husband had betrayed you. It wasn't as if he betrayed you with some compliant mistress hidden away in the Home Counties. Randolph had betrayed you with another woman in another country. Not only had he betrayed you, he had actually married this other woman in Beaune. You were left, only half a wife. Is that not so?'

'If you say so.'

'Your future and that of your family were on the very edge of ruin. Your children would be known for ever after as the children of the bigamist. So, you went to the room in your house where the guns are kept. I have heard accounts of this room, gentlemen of the jury. There are enough firearms in there to equip a small regiment. You picked out the pistol because you knew how it worked. Is that not the case?'

Mrs Colville did not reply. A look that might have been fear flashed across her face.

Pugh paused and took another sip of his water. Lady Lucy was holding her husband's hand very tightly, her eyes fixed on Hermione Colville. Richard Napier appeared to be making a sketch of the scales of justice that sat on top of the Old Bailey roof.

'You kept the pistol in your bag all the way on that journey to Norfolk. You attended the wedding. You took a glass of champagne in the Nashes' garden, Dutch courage amid the flower beds and the broken fountain.

'I put it to you, Mrs Colville,' Pugh's eyes were locked on to the face of the woman in the witness box, 'that at some time in the half-hour between the end of the service and the wedding breakfast, you carried out a quick reconnaissance of the first floor of Brympton Hall. I presume that you thought the state bedroom was a good distance away from the room where the food was to be served.'

317

Pugh held out his diagram of the first floor of Brympton Hall for the jury.

'Gentlemen,' he said, 'here is the Long Gallery, looking out over the gardens. Here is the state bedroom round the corner, where the murder took place. Here and here,' he pointed to the stairs to the garden at the end of the Long Gallery and the other stairs down from the state bedroom, were the entrances and exits open to those who did not want to come up by the Grand Staircase back here.

'I put it to you, Mrs Colville, that you managed to speak to your husband to lure him up the staircase into the state bedroom. You pulled the pistol out of your bag. You shot him. You dropped the pistol on the ground and rushed out of the house down the staircase in the state bedroom, along the opposite side of the Hall to where the champagne had been served, and back into the house to join the rest of the guests by the main entrance near the main staircase. Aroused by the shot, Cosmo arrives to see what's going on. He picks up the gun off the floor and sits down on the chair while he works out what to do. There he is found. There he is arrested while you are preparing to eat your wedding breakfast a couple of rooms away. There, Mrs Colville, that's how it was, isn't it?'

She was sobbing now. 'No, that's not how it was,' Hermione Colville managed to say, 'not the last bit anyway.'

'Tell us about it,' said Pugh.

'Cosmo came in just as I was leaving,' she said, the tears running down her cheeks. 'I still had the gun in my hand. Cosmo took it. "Give me that," he said, "and get back down those stairs as fast as you can."'

There were shouts of 'No! No! No!' from the bar of the court.

For the first time since the trial began Mr Justice Black raised his voice. 'Mrs Colville! Mrs Colville! Please pay attention! You do not have to answer any further questions that might incriminate yourself in any future proceedings. Do you understand?'

318

Mrs Randolph Colville nodded sadly. Cosmo looked as though he was trying to climb out of the dock into the main body of the court. The warders manhandled him roughly back into his chair. A great sigh ran through the court. Mrs Randolph Colville had collapsed in a chair, watched over by two sturdy policemen. Lady Lucy was trembling. Detective Chief Inspector Weir was striding across the court for a conference with Sir Jasper. The newspapermen were elbowing their way towards the entrance as fast as they could. Some of them muttered to each other that they hadn't seen such a sensational case this century. Pugh was sitting down, talking quietly with his junior, other barristers and solicitors whispering their congratulations. Powerscourt felt only pity for this poor woman, driven halfway out of her mind by her husband's crimes.

Emily Colville nudged her mother gently in the ribs. 'That's what I told you on the night of the wedding, Mama,' she whispered. Emily did not see fit to tell her mother that she had known for years about Randolph's other wife in France. That, after all, was what Tristram had been blackmailing him about.

Georgina Nash leaned over to whisper back. 'What did you tell me on the night of the wedding, Emily?'

'Why, Mama, I told you I had seen Mrs Colville, Mrs Randolph Colville, running down the stairs out of the state bedroom after the shot. Where the murder was.'

Georgina Nash stared at her daughter. Of course. That was what she had tried to remember about that awful day. That was what she had intended to tell Lord Powerscourt only it had slipped out of her mind. And at some point between the wedding and today, she realized, she had forgotten that she had forgotten. She wondered how much work and trouble and expense might have been avoided if her memory hadn't let her down. The whole affair began with Emily's wedding. It was ending now with Emily telling her that she had seen the murderer leaving the scene of the crime. Should she tell Lord Powerscourt? There didn't seem much point now. It was over.

Pugh leant back and whispered to Powerscourt and Lady Lucy: 'I wonder if some sharp solicitor advised her on how to tell her story. You see, if she goes on with the line of being out of her mind with anger and grief, it could go well for her. Her counsel could argue that she didn't know what she was doing, that she was suffering from a kind of temporary insanity. I don't think it would get her off, but they wouldn't hang her.'

Sir Jasper Bentinck was rising to his feet now. 'My lord,' he began, speaking loudly to rise above the noise in court, 'I have just been having a conference with Detective Chief Inspector Weir of the Norfolk Constabulary. I have to inform your lordship that in the light of recent events the Crown no longer believes in the case against the defendant Mr Colville.'

The judge beckoned Pugh and Sir Jasper over to his position for a brief conversation. Then he banged his gavel very firmly on his desk.

'Gentlemen of the jury, you have heard what Sir Jasper has just told us, that the Crown have lost faith in their case. That means they do not believe Mr Colville is guilty. But even in these circumstances, the law must have a verdict. Mr Cosmo Colville has been on trial here on the most serious charge a man may face in an English court, that of murder. The Crown no longer believe Mr Colville to be guilty. But he must be seen to be Not Guilty. That is why I am going to send you out now to consider your verdict. Only you can put Mr Colville back into society as an innocent man. I recommend most strongly that you give your verdict in favour of the defence, a verdict of Not Guilty.'

The judge nodded at the foreman, who led the jury out. He stared at the spectators and the remaining newspapermen, as if daring them to speak. Pugh was taking sips of his water, holding a whispered conversation with his junior who sent Powerscourt a note.

'Can't stop for drink afterwards. New case.'

'Markham Square, six o'clock,' Powerscourt replied. 'We'll contact everybody.'

Yet another note arrived for Powerscourt saying the judge would like a word in his rooms when the trial was over. The jury were returning now. Lady Lucy worked out that it had taken about four minutes to save a man from the gallows. The sombre litany rang out across Court Number Two of the Old Bailey as it had done for centuries.

'Gentlemen of the jury,' said the Clerk, 'have you reached your verdict?'

'We have.'

'Do you find the defendant Cosmo Colville guilty or not guilty on the charge of murder?'

'Not guilty.'

Mrs Randolph Colville fainted clean away. Perhaps she knew she would be next. She was led away by the two policemen when she came round. Cosmo Colville was weeping in the dock, the warders astonished that a man just released from the death penalty should take his freedom so hard. The judge spent some time collecting his things. Pugh and his junior shook hands with Powerscourt and Lady Lucy and promised to come to the party. Detective Chief Inspector Weir of the Norfolk Constabulary felt angry with himself. This was the first murder case in over thirty years where he had lost. Perhaps he should have listened more carefully to young Cooper and his ideas. Georgina and Willoughby Nash were pleased that their house would fade from the news. Two of the newspapers had used diagrams of Brympton Hall and the layout of the rooms to explain the case to their readers. Now they were returning to the old anonymity that should surround their home.

Powerscourt was wondering what the judge wanted to see him about. Had he committed some faux pas in the course of the case? Should he not have sent any of those notes to Charles Augustus Pugh? The Clerk of the Court ushered him into the presence of the majesty of the law.

'Ah, Powerscourt,' said Mr Justice Black, 'how good of you to come and see me. Minor matter, actually, more a question of family history really. Aren't you a Cambridge man? Trinity Hall if I'm not mistaken? Cricket?'

Powerscourt admitted the charge was true.

'My youngest brother was up at the same time as you,' the judge went on, 'I saw you both batting together in a match against St John's. He made twenty-nine and you were undefeated on thirty-seven. I was watching that day, God knows how many years ago it was. I knew I'd seen you before.'

Powerscourt bowed slightly and headed for the door. 'One last thing, Powerscourt. You're not a bridge player by any chance, are you? Four Spades? Three No Trumps? That sort of thing? It's my partner, you see. We've been together for years. Then he dropped down dead yesterday. Collapsed into the roast beef at the Garrick. Always good, mind you, the roast beef at the Garrick. Good way to go.'

Powerscourt admitted that he was not proficient at bridge. As he made his way towards the street he wondered what sort of tariff might await the judge's partner. Three months for the wrong lead perhaps. One year's hard labour for failing to count trumps. Three years in Pentonville for not reading your partner's signals correctly.

By three o'clock that afternoon the Powerscourts were ensconced in the drawing room in Markham Square. Powerscourt was wondering about taking Lucy to Rome once things had calmed down.

'Francis,' she said, 'can I ask you a question?'

'Of course, my love, fire ahead.'

'That note you sent to Mr Pugh, before he cross-examined the Colville women in court this morning, what did it say?'

'I think I said we couldn't be sure of winning with the suicide argument. Sir Jasper, after all, could have used the family disgrace as a motive for Cosmo to kill his brother. There is a different murderer, I said. *Cherchez la femme.*'

'I see,' said Lady Lucy. 'Did it come to you that late on, that Mrs Colville was the killer?'

'I should have seen it much earlier,' said Powerscourt, 'in so many cases the husband or the wife is the murderer of the other.'

'And the money, Francis? All that money that disappeared out of the Colville company accounts?'

'Well, I think I know what happened to that,' Powerscourt replied. 'You remember the French wife over in Burgundy saying her husband had been buying a lot of land, vineyards, that sort of thing? I don't know if he put it in his French name or in the company name but that's where the money went.'

He paused for a moment. 'There is one thing I'm not sure about, and that is the mysterious Frenchman, the one who spent the night in Cawston and took a cab over to Brympton Hall for the wedding the next morning. I'm sure he was real, those two in the hotel were trustworthy people. Perhaps he lost his nerve in a strange place where he didn't understand a word anybody said to him. Perhaps he thought he would be exposed and ran away before he was caught.'

Johnny Fitzgerald was the first to arrive at the Powerscourt party that evening. He began complaining about his publishers as he broke into a bottle of Chambertin. 'Honestly, Francis, you'd think they could do better, wouldn't you. I gave them the bloody manuscript about Birds of the North three months ago. Then they lost a third of the damned thing. Didn't lose any of the drawings, thank God. I've just reconstituted the text and the drawings, it took me five whole days and I've missed your trial. You seem to have routed the Philistines pretty successfully.'

Lady Lucy was welcoming Pugh and his young junior Napier, closely followed by Nathaniel Colville, patriarch of the clan, with a bottle in his hand.

'I've been trying to put some sense into young Cosmo,' Nathaniel said to Lady Lucy. 'Ridiculous business, blubbing in court like a bloody woman. At least he's going to show up for the party, must make a change from being cooped up down in Pentonville.'

'Pugh!' said Powerscourt, and he shook the lawyer firmly by the hand. 'Congratulations! You pulled it off, by God!'

'I say it again, my friend,' Pugh was smiling an enormous smile, 'I merely fired the bullets. But you provided them.'

Pugh was virtually engulfed by guests offering him their congratulations. Lady Lucy thought it was slightly unfair.

'Could I ask you a question, Lord Powerscourt?' Richard Napier, Pugh's junior, had all the earnestness of the young. 'Don't you think it would have been better all round if the verdict had been suicide? Cosmo is set free. Mrs Hermione Colville returns to her unhappy existence, lubricated with the Chablis by the Thames. Nobody loses.'

'Are you saying, Richard,' said Powerscourt, 'that you believe we have ended up with the wrong verdict?'

'Not at all. It would just have been better all round if the suicide verdict had won out. That way Mrs Colville might not be hanged or go to prison. No more trials either. Surely it is better for the living to remain living and what people call justice to be pushed to one side?'

'I'm for justice myself,' said Powerscourt. 'Come, young man, you'd better have a glass of Chambertin.'

The room filled up. Powerscourt wondered if the multitude of Colvilles reminded Lucy of one of her own family's tribal gatherings. He suspected the Colvilles might be even more numerous. Sir Pericles Freme had brought a white piece of paper which he entrusted to Rhys, the Powerscourt butler. Powerscourt could catch snatches of conversation between Cosmo, his uncle, Freme and Richard Napier for the younger generation.

'The point is, Cosmo,' said Nathaniel, 'it's completely wrong to think that the firm of Colville will be deserted by its clients. Freme and I will take care of that.'

'Think of it as an opportunity,' Freme put in. 'You know what they say, all publicity is good publicity. You have been all over the newspapers for two or three days, Cosmo. Think how much it would cost to buy all that.'

'This is not how it was meant to be,' said Cosmo. 'When I picked up that gun, I thought I could deflect all the attention on to myself. I could take the blame. We could keep all the stuff about the bigamy out of the papers. I didn't mind being hanged as long as the good name of Colville was preserved and nobody knew about the French Mrs Colville. I couldn't stand the thought of Hermione going on trial and what might follow. She's had enough to put up with over the years, God knows. I reckoned without that man Powerscourt, mind you. I don't know whether to thank him or curse him, even now.'

'That's all in the past, Cosmo,' his uncle boomed, 'we must look to the future. The firm's fifty years old now. We must go on. Even if I'm not going to see the end of the next fifty, I'm going to make sure we're in bloody good shape for the anniversary.'

'I say we must work out a new advertising campaign while people remember the headlines,' said Sir Pericles.

'Colvilles,' young Napier said, 'wine to die for, perhaps. Try Colvilles, last drink before you go.'

Powerscourt and Pugh were having a final conversation about the case. 'Do you know who we have to thank for our good fortune, Pugh?'

'Who?' said Pugh.

'I'll tell you,' Powerscourt replied, 'it's that cleaning woman from Fakenham police station, that's who it is. If the police thought they might have a real fingerprint then even Chief Inspector Weir would have sent it off to the Met. So there would have been two sets of prints, one lot belonging to Mrs Randolph Colville who could say she dusted the gun a week or so before. The servants aren't allowed to touch the guns in case they kill themselves. And, of course, Cosmo's prints, clear as daylight. That would have been pretty hard work for us, I think.'

By eight o'clock the guests had departed. Powerscourt was going to take Lady Lucy out to dinner to celebrate the end of the case. She was adjusting her hair in the mirror.

There was a knock on the door. Rhys crept into the room carrying an opened bottle and a couple of glasses and an expensive-looking envelope. 'The envelope is from Sir Pericles, my lord,' said Rhys. 'He says you are to read it first.'

'This recipe,' Powerscourt read it aloud, 'comes from no less a personage than Lord Pembroke, he of Wilton House near Salisbury and the Double Cube Room and all those glorious Van Dycks. The good Lord was in the habit of saying to his guests at dinner, "I cannot answer for my champagne and claret, as I only have the word of my wine merchant that it is good, but I can answer for my port wine. I made it myself." Here it is, from the Family Receipt Book of 1817:

'"Mix well together forty-eight gallons of turnip juice, or strong rough cyder; eight gallons of malt spirit or brandy; and eight gallons of real port wine; adding a sufficient quantity of elder berry juice to colour it; add some of the branches of the elder tree to give it a proper roughness. Keep it, in cask or bottle, about two years before drinking it. This is Lord Pembroke's recipe: which perhaps may be improved, with regard to roughness, by the juice or wine of sloes; and, in colour, make to any required tint, by cochineal, logwood, or Brazil wood. French brandy will certainly be better than malt spirit; and perhaps, either a good-bodied raisin wine, or even a raisin cyder, may sometimes, according as excellence or cheapness is the object, be advantageously adopted instead of rough cyder or the juice of turnips."'

Powerscourt and Lady Lucy laughed. She put her arm through his as Rhys carried on.

'This bottle is from Mr Nathaniel Colville, my lord, my lady.' There was a brief pause while Rhys remembered his lines. 'He says, you are to drink one glass of this wine before you go out, two if you like it. He says you are to note what it says on the bottle. He says, Mr Colville, that the label is the first of its kind to be printed in this country.'

Rhys slipped away. Looking at the label, Powerscourt saw that the spirit that had made Colvilles great was still there, that even in adversity a family could show its resilience and that a dynasty founded fifty years before, when Victoria was twenty years on the throne, still had sap in its bones and fire in its belly.

'Bâtard Montrachet 1904', the label said. And below that, 'Colvilles and Co., 1857–1907, Fifty Years of Excellence. Wine Merchants of distinction. London Edinburgh Bordeaux Burgundy.'

ACKNOWLEDGEMENTS

With thanks to Christopher Fielden, author of *Is This the Wine You Ordered, Sir?* from which many of the recipes within this book were taken.